SEVERED

THE LINKED TRILOGY
BOOK TWO

CASSIE SWINDON

ISBN: 978-1-7373469-3-7

Cover Design by: Christian Bentulan

Interior Formatting by Jennifer Laslie

SEVERED

Kyra Kozelski

I'm Linked with not one but two Mystier men: Jadox, my rock—and Isaac, the enemy who threatens my new Magik. I'd give up my left drumstick to sever this forced bond with Isaac. But the president's army ambushed us, creating chaos and forcing us into different plans. Since Isaac led them to us, I'll make him suffer more than he could possibly imagine.

Isaac Nilson

This Magikal Link will be the end of me. Kyra's power has me wrapped around her finger. Are these feelings real, or is the Link responsible for a phantom love? Since she wants me gone, I don't feel guilty for using her powers to save my son. Especially when all Kyra can focus on is my nemesis, Jadox Griffin.

ALSO BY CASSIE SWINDON

LINKED TRILOGY

Scorched

Severed

Shattered

GOLDEN CHAINS TRILOGY

Break the Stone

Hunt the Storm

Stop the Clock

Andalatiel

&

BeeBop

ACKNOWLEDGMENTS

Developmental editor: Kirsty McQuarrie at Let's Get Proofed

Copy Line editors: Kirsty McQuarrie at Let's Get Proofed and Kelly George at Polished Proofreading

Proofreading: Kelly George at Polished Proofreading

Trilogy Covers: Christian Bentulan at Covers by Christian

Interior Designing: Jennifer Leslie

Beta Readers: Aubree Anderson, Ana Maria Tufescu, Paula Llyod

Map Designer: Adriana Pausenwein

Character Illustration Artist: Claudia Hopkins

Short Story Covers: Anna Cackler

TRIGGER WARNINGS

Recommended for age 18+ due to profanity, violence, sexual content, and other sensitive topics that could potentially trigger the reader. Read at your discretion.

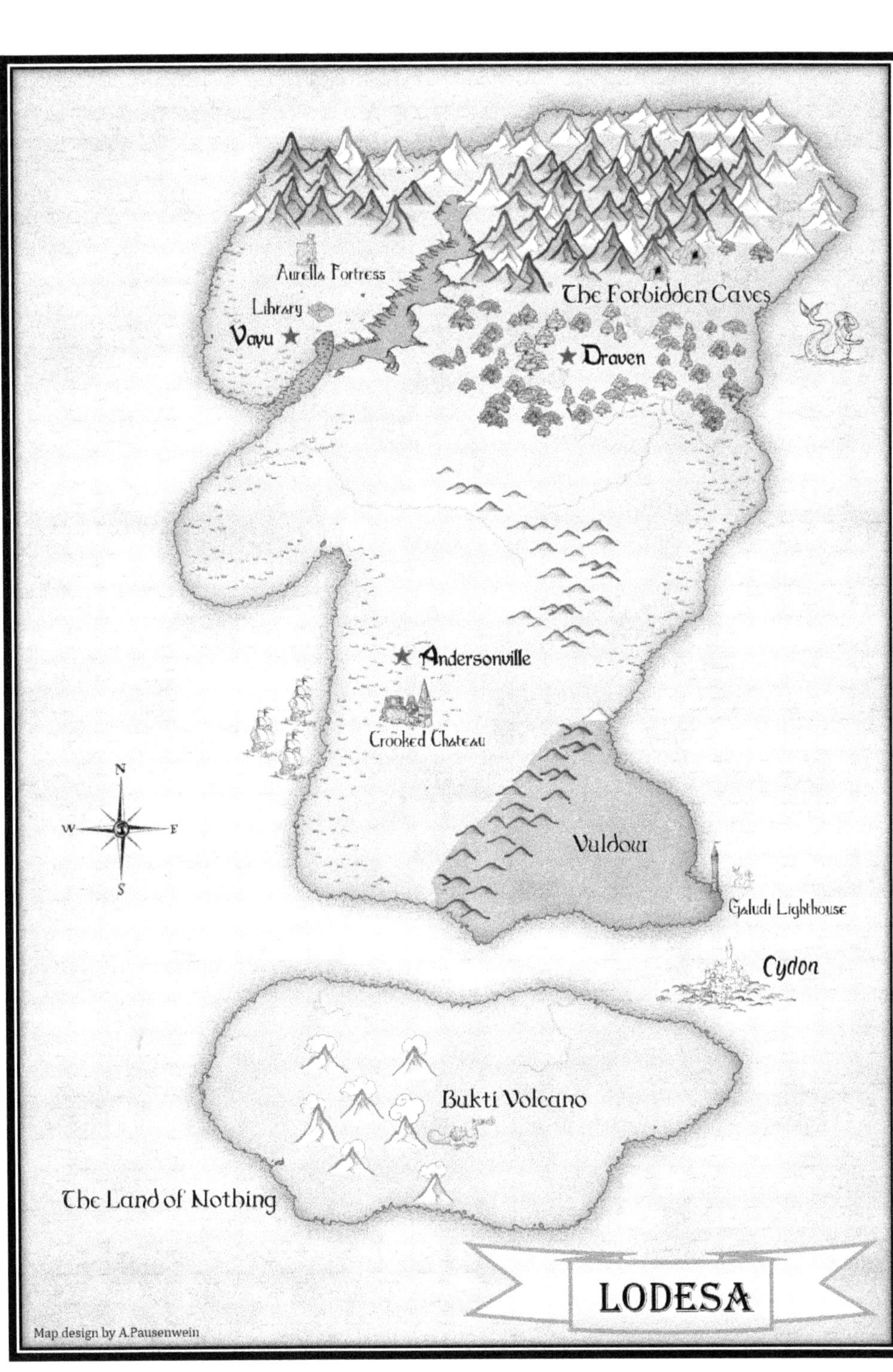
Aurella Fortress
Library
Vayu
The Forbidden Caves
Draven
Andersonville
Crooked Chateau
N
W
E
S
Vuldow
Galudi Lighthouse
Cydon
Bukti Volcano
The Land of Nothing
LODESA
Map design by A.Pausenwein

I

KYRA

The tattoo on my stomach swirled with heat, and Magik shot through my veins. I stood in the doorway of one of Draven's dens with both hands on my hips, glaring across the clearing at Jadox. Scrumptious, as always, he casually leaned against his door, bringing a steaming mug to his pillowy lips. With a little eyebrow raise, he clearly communicated his desire.

I nodded towards my den and its heap of blankets being slowly illuminated by the rising sun. Jadox winked, his thick, long lashes tormenting me. His inviting body, formed by constant training, was overflowing with masculine features that had never matched those eyelashes. Somehow, I was the lucky girl who got to kiss him every day and night.

Jadox turned and disappeared inside his hut, leaving the door wide open as was his routine invitation. Damn him and his ever-flamin' stubbornness. Not once in the last Lunar Cycle had he slept in my bed.

I stomped through the thin layer of snow, leaving a noticeable print of my boot, brown layered on glimmering white. My breath fogged the crisp, frigid air. Maybe I'd be smarter to train with Alaska again instead of succumbing to my never-ending thirst for Jay.

I marched straight through his door, ready to gobble him up for breakfast. In fact, I was always ready to devour him thirty hours a day, seven days a week. Yet, Chocolate blocked my attempt. She pounced happily, and both her paws landed on my stomach. The silly pup knocked me straight into the ivy-covered rock wall. Laughing, I stroked a hand through her mass of brown fur and kissed her forehead.

"Our dog obviously has a new favorite," I said, trying to keep a straight face.

"She has good taste." Jadox's devious look made the butterflies in my stomach erupt into dragons. "Now, take off your clothes, Kyra."

"No way, it's colder than a witch's tits in here."

"And when did you last feel a pair of witch's tits to know any better?" He pulled off his shirt. "Get naked. Now."

I strutted past the crackling fireplace and playfully shoved Jay onto his bed, pinning him between my legs. Jadox folded both hands behind his head and smirked, his dark eyes devouring my impatience. He belonged to me, and I belonged to… well, that was up for debate.

"What are you looking at me like that for?" he asked.

"I bet you three cookies you'll give in and kiss me first."

His gorgeous gaze narrowed playfully. "I bet you four that you're wrong."

We might be two bodies, but together, we were one soul. In a single sweep, he twisted my body, flipping me flat on my back against his sheets. One of his large, calloused hands cradled my neck as the other tickled a slow pattern around my Möbius Circle tattoo, strengthening the spark between us.

Somehow, I wanted him even more than yesterday. Impossible yet possible. I arched my back, moving towards him and latching my legs around his waist. Pulling him in, I smiled and licked my lips.

He growled and hovered his mouth just a bit above mine. "That's not fair, my wicked Petal; you're too damn beautiful for your own good."

Desire surged through my veins, and I used every ounce of

willpower not to kiss him first. "What's not fair is how much I care for you."

Jay groaned and planted his lips on mine. His tongue explored my mouth like it was our first, last, and only kiss. I'd never get enough of him. Our connection ran so deep that I'd suffocate without him near me.

"I told you…I'd…win," I stumbled out the words between kisses.

"Mmm…is it *my* turn to win now?" His hand pulled up my shirt, cupping my breast.

A sigh escaped my lips, and his expression confirmed what I already knew. He'd sacrifice his life for me. But I'd never let him because a day without Jadox was meaningless, inconceivable. I'd give up everything just to keep that hint of a smile on his face.

The last few weeks in this fantasy bliss had sped by too fast, and our time to solidify a plan was running out. Now, we had to accept the responsibilities that came with our choice to Link. Our joint power brought the burden of leadership. The Draven population trusted us to keep our barrier intact. Jadox and I could achieve it as a team as long as nothing or nobody separated us.

"Slow down your brain, Kyra. Just think of this, of us."

I could make a fortress out of just his kisses. My mind turned to mush again as I pressed against his firm chest. Behind us, Chocolate whined and put both front paws up on the den's windowsill, shifting the ivy-covered stone. I kissed Jay once more, then tried to wiggle out from under his strong hold.

"My dog needs me."

"You mean *our* dog." His lips grazed my neck, sending goosebumps down my spine. Needing more of him, all of him. "What's mine is yours. Forever and always," Jadox mumbled into my skin. "I'm not the one who wanted to live in separate dens."

"Landon needs me. I can't move him in with you just after his mom died." The sharp tone made me cringe at my voice.

Jadox nodded, pulling away. Lines were etched into his skin as he sent me a message through our bond.

That's not what I meant, Petal.

I know. I'm sorry. There's just a lot to deal with.

I'm here for you. We'll figure it out together.

Chocolate whined again and started pacing, then a deafening crash echoed from afar.

"What the Flames?" I pushed against Jadox and jumped out of his bed towards the door.

Outside, a fierce wind slapped my face. The bare trees swayed above as if a tornado was on the way, and a child screamed from somewhere further in the village. Doors swayed open and shut, smacking against all the stone dens. A pack of gorulas zoomed by, hollering and swinging from tree to tree away from the threat. Some days, I still missed Goldie, but nowhere near the ache that settled in my heart from the loss of Hallie.

"It's another avalanche," Jay said.

"Not again!"

Ever since I Linked with Isaac, the weather had behaved chaotically. I possessed part of his Vayu powers now without knowing how to control the Magik air vibrating within me.

I spun around to call Jadox, but he was already standing right behind me. His two tattoos blazed brightly through his shirt, the red Elidi mark contrasting with his camouflaged Draven Circle.

"We can protect Draven again, just like last week. This time, you take the east. I'll take the west."

I grabbed his hand. "No, we're stronger when we stay closer."

As we sprinted through the village, I yelled, "Go inside!" to any friends who bustled around their dens collecting items that were blowing away.

We tore through the forest, crunching over snow that grew deeper the further we raced. I panted as the hill sloped up toward the mountain peak. Snapping sounds grew louder like a thunderous beat from inside the earth itself and dug a hole of fear in my chest. Huffing and puffing, I prayed to the goddess above for a miracle. The rolling snow would destroy Draven's village if we didn't stop it.

Not another avalanche!

It's okay, Kyra. We can do this.

It's all my fault.

No, it's not. Focus. We can control it again.

Jadox sped ahead to the tallest, thickest pine. He kneeled, and I knew what was expected of me without it being said. Leaping on his leg, I shoved off Jay, launching myself to the first branch. I climbed. Fast and strong. Bark scratched through my sweater, and little pine needles pierced the fabric, poking my skin. I tried to forget my fear of heights.

Jay followed. The snowfall accelerated, and the temperature dropped. Wind flurried in a frenzy, and my foot slipped on a branch. I scrambled to grab ahold of it.

"Kyra! Focus!"

Finally, at the top of the tree, I braced my feet and gulped down any hesitancy. Success was the only option. If I failed, all the Mystiers I had grown to love in the last few weeks would be buried in snow. Landon had to survive. Even Alaska deserved to live another day, no matter how much she resented me for Linking with her brother.

"There it is. Half a mile away." Jadox pointed.

My tattoo scorched with raw power from three elements. Mine, and the two borrowed from the men Linked with my soul. Fire, earth, and air all cycloned into a mass of energy. But I didn't know what would happen this time. Even after weeks of training with Alaska, I still didn't fully understand this three-way Link. Apparently, no Mystier like me in history had been recorded, so I was on my own.

Wait, no, never alone. I always had Jay.

Next to me, he summoned all the fallen logs, twigs, and branches below and cast a high blockade between us and the massive wall of white. The snow rolled closer like a wave of death, swallowing anything in its path.

I released a blast of flames, but they faded before reaching the roaring snow. Waiting until it was close enough felt like torture. I drummed an insane rhythm on my thigh, then pointed both hands forward again, Magik at my fingertips. Glancing to my left, I watched Jadox's jaw clench tight. His nervousness flooded through our bond.

Focus, Kyra. It's almost here. Forget about me.

That's impossible, Jay.

All of a sudden, the tsunami of snow barreled into the tree line directly in front of us. The current of snow washed in closer like a fast-rising tide. The harsh sound of trees breaking were like bones splintering and cracking, paralyzing me with uncertainty. I had caused this.

Power zapped through my tattoos and whirled forward. A roar of flames blasted into the avalanche, colliding head-on with such force that the forest floor trembled. Gorulas screeched in the distance.

With one last push, my flames barely slowed the massive incoming drift. Jadox borrowed some of my fire and shot spurts of heat from his hands, melting some of the snow.

You have to tap into your Vayu powers!

No! It's too dangerous!

Atop the tree, I moved in front of Jadox in less than a wink, protecting him from any damage I might create. A spiral of intense heat rumbled through my core. It exploded from my hands, firing ahead. But the avalanche rolled stronger. Even combining forces with Jadox wouldn't defeat it this time.

Kyra, use Vayu Magik now, or it'll kill our people!

I can't risk letting Isaac into my mind.

I braced myself for impact and held my breath.

"Kyra! Do it. To save Draven!" Jadox screamed, shaking my elbow from behind.

Against all my better judgment, I lowered my mental wall against the new Vayuian powers within me...and against Isaac. A stream of energy knocked me breathless. Air. Wind. Knowledge. Books. Storms. Isaac's lips. Gray eyes. Clouds. Clarity. They all pounded straight into my chest. The added power welded to my personal enhancement, and ancient spells hummed a chant in my soul; I hoped one would work.

Tla hesdi prohib. Tla hesdi prohib. Tla hesdi prohib.

Immediately, the advancing snow stopped moments from smacking into our tree and fell to the ground in submission. I let out a huge sigh and met Jay's wide eyes.

"You did it." His teeth chattered, and his lips turned purple from the freezing temperatures.

"Jay!? You don't even have a shirt on."

Shaking, he leaned into my arms like my hug was as comfortable as a blanket near a fireplace. "Warm me up?"

My heartbeat returned to its natural tempo as I flared a fire bubble around us, not letting it touch the trees like last time. A forest fire would be too much to handle when we were this drained. My body relaxed into his, celebrating in the safety net of my one and only love. But a twitching sensation scratched against my senses.

You've been quiet for weeks, love. Have you missed me?

Isaac's voice hissed at me through the still trees for the first time since we fled the battle in Vayu. I wrenched away from Jadox's hold.

"Did you hear that?" My eyes darted in each direction, wondering how close he was. Had Isaac found Draven, even through the shield?

"Hear what?" Jay studied my face and tucked a strand of my golden hair behind my ear. "Let's go rest. I'll make pancakes, and you'll eat them…naked."

But adrenaline pumped in my veins. Without a doubt, I had accidentally connected with Isaac when I used my new Vayu power. Shit. That was exactly what I had feared. He better not find us.

"Rest? No way. Competing against an avalanche just amped me up. I've got an idea. Let's finally settle that argument from yesterday." I scrambled over a long branch that connected to a treehouse plank. Balancing across with both arms out like an old aero glider, I shimmied across the narrow bridge, high above the forest floor.

Don't roll your eyes at me, soldier.

You can't even see my face, Petal.

I know you.

Fine, but then we go back to bed and finish what I started.

All you think about is me naked.

We laughed together as he raced me—from limb to limb—soaring through the morning air, high on life, and smiles spread wide. Our joy quickly replaced our fear from only minutes before.

"Remember, if I win...." I struggled to project my words so he could hear them as I jumped. "We leave Draven. My wind power is only putting the others at risk. I need to learn how to control new Magik somewhere else."

"And if I win...." The smile in Jadox's voice was evident, but I had to focus on my footing. "We stay and build our home here and bunker down together. Forever."

"You can't keep me in a bubble, Jay." I leaped from branch to branch, closer to the finish line.

"And you can't impulsively run without a plan, Kyra."

He's right, love. I need you safe and whole. All of us need you.

When Isaac spoke, his voice sounded like an actual whisper in the wind, which was different than when Jadox sent messages mentally through our bond. I stopped mid-stride and stumbled into a treehouse. Terrified of the controlling pull Isaac claimed over me, I wrapped my arms around the trunk and sunk down, crouching on my heels. Unsure if communicating with him in return would make it worse, I squeezed my eyes shut and gritted my teeth. Tension thrummed through my thread with Isaac.

Go away, Isaac.

I could feel his dismissal through the bond. He'd never listen to me.

Not until you fulfill your promise. And I know you want to hear the rest of my secret.

The truth wrapped tight around my gut and strangled me. I'd been clinging to the secret he had told me weeks ago, repeating it in my mind over and over again. What would it mean if he was right?

Can Jadox hear you? We're all connected.

No, love. This is just you and me. Like it will be, eventually.

No matter how much I hated Isaac Nilson, curiosity about our three-way Link took hold.

Where are you, Isaac?

Planning our date, love.

Stop calling me that.

We belong together.

I belong to—

His chuckle rumbled through the winter breeze, making my skin crawl. I shouldn't be contacting him or encouraging this.

"Kyra? Are you okay?" Panting, Jadox's broad frame blocked out the morning sunlight for a moment as he stood in the doorway of the treehouse. "I looked back, and you had disappeared. Are you hurt?"

I stood, brushing off the dirt from my yoga pants. "No, I'm fine. Had to pee."

"You peed…out of a treehouse?"

"Are you judging me, macho man?" I pushed against his rock-hard pecs, not making any impact.

Jay pulled me closer. "You always know how to make me smile."

"Good because you always look like *this*." When I imitated his brooding expression, his frown only deepened.

"I do not."

Somewhere below, Chocolate barked, and the sound of children laughing was music to my ears. Landon called out for Gemm, asking about waffles. I sighed and wrapped my arms around Jadox's sturdy torso for a rare, soft moment of tranquility before everything changed again.

At least all the Mystiers still had both genders left; sons and daughters, nieces and nephews. But because of me, Landon was the only male Ordull alive on our planet.

For some reason, I believed deep in my gut that the answers to solving this crisis didn't only lie within me. There were missing pieces of the puzzle—Isaac.

Jadox only knew half of the reason I wanted to leave Draven.

President Stirk held a Cydian prisoner captive who knew information about my family. Maybe that Cydian guy knew who my real father was- my last living relative.

"Hungry?" Jadox took my hand in his and led me to the treehouse ladder.

"You know me. I could eat all of Gemm's eggs and bacon."

"What if I'm the one cooking?"

"Then you better be wearing an apron only, sir." I slapped his ass just before he turned to descend the ladder.

The cacophony of a joyous village below eased my tension. I breathed in the last few hours of this peace before I left and searched all of Lodesa if I had to. At twenty-five o'clock, I'd pack the rest of my stuff to find that prisoner, whether Jay agreed to come with me or not. Isaac's eerie whisper stabbed tiny prickles at the back of my neck again.

I'll be waiting for you, love.

2

JADOX

Before Kyra scaled down the treehouse ladder, I wrapped an arm around her waist and pulled her straight into my chest. Goddess above, she smelled so good—like hot cocoa and holly with a tinge of burning wood. Noticing the scratch along her neck, I hovered a hand over her injury and instantly healed her pain. The angry scratch mark was sealed shut in an instant.

"Thank you." Her eyes seemed distant, belonging to another place. "Did you get hurt too?"

"No, and I'm so glad Gemm figured out a way where every injury doesn't impact one another anymore."

"Yeah, you were a baby when I got my menstrual cramps." She clutched her stomach dramatically, dropping to her knees and faking death. "You were like this."

I smiled. "Yeah, just don't make me live through giving birth or anything."

Her eyebrows shot up.

"Anyways." I caressed her cheek. "I've never been more grateful for my gift of healing than after I met you. That's what I'm here for."

"You're passable for another thing or two." Her smile was my everything.

"Just passable? I may need to practice more. Come on, this is a perfect time."

Kyra wiggled playfully against me, squirming in feigned resistance, then looked up through those long lashes. She was simply exhilarating. Intoxicating.

"Madam, I am the guardian troll of this treehouse. You shall *not* pass without payment."

Kyra rose on her tiptoes and lifted her chin. "How much do I owe you, sir troll?"

My eyes dropped to her neck, where thick swoops of her golden hair spilled over her shoulders. "I'll accept a lifetime of… servitude."

Her amber eyes narrowed in amusement as her hands began exploring my chest. "Is that a proposal or a punishment, my valiant troll?"

This woman had no clue of the power she held over me. She used the word "proposal." I sucked in a breath, wondering if she had found the engagement ring I had tucked away. It didn't feel too early to ask her to be my forever since we were Linked. Our souls were already forever connected.

If I was being honest, I'd have no problem staying within the borders of Draven for eternity, forming a hermit life together in some tiny forest corner where we'd rarely be bothered by another soul. Except for Chocolate, of course.

We'd have safe, peaceful days of quiet, surrounded by nature without fighting, drama, arguments, or problems. We both made a vow to ask each other before lowering our mental walls completely, so I never knew for sure how much of her thoughts and feelings she shared with me.

But what if she only cared for me because of our Link? What if our connection was capable of change once Isaac found us? It was only a matter of time. I'd rather prevent any encounter with him.

The scent of warm biscuits rising from Gemm's den below snapped me into the present moment.

"You have your thinking face on, troll." Kyra kissed my bare shoulder blade, sending tingles to my toes and a zap through my tattoo.

My Magik longed for her, reaching out at every waking moment. Even when I trained her with fighting skills, my thoughts would rush me straight back to her in bed. Day after day. Minute after minute. I needed to be inside her. The all-consuming desire exhausted me into a coma each night, but I didn't regret a thing we had done together over the past few weeks.

"I want you, Kyra," I said while running a fingertip under her jawline to her neck, massaging her skin.

"You have me already," she whispered, almost as soft as the morning winter breeze blowing through the branches.

"I want more of you, all of you."

I shuddered when her mouth moved to my chest while her fingers traced loops over our Linked tattoo. We were bound until death by Magik, which felt stronger than any proposal or ring.

The floorboards of the treehouse creaked as I took her in my arms again, hugging her body to my flesh. "What would you say if I asked you to choose for eternity?"

She froze like a statue, for only a moment, before resting her head softly on my chest. The treehouse planks creaked as she shifted even closer, wrapping her arms around my waist.

"Jay, I…"

"Tell me what you want."

Suddenly, the freezing winter air warmed into a bubble of privacy, enveloping our bodies. Her golden tattoo glowed brightly through her sweater; I needed to see it immediately.

Her eyes turned wild as she tugged my workout pants to my ankles and dropped to her knees. Kyra slid her hands up my thigh so softly that it sent every nerve firing raging. Her mouth started on my inner thighs and slowly glided higher, higher. My breathing turned heavy in anticipation, and I memorized each of her movements. No one else would ever compare to her.

"Whatever you do, don't—" I started. "Oh, Divinity."

Kyra took me in her mouth. Wet. Warm. Fuck! Both my hands

cradled the back of her head, just how she liked it, and her soft moan vibrated on my cock. I felt drunk. High. Delirious. She lowered her mental wall a bit, sending me her genuine feelings in spurts of ecstasy. My legs trembled, and just as I was about to pull away, she grabbed my ass with both hands and sucked deeper.

"Shit, Kyra!" My heartbeat slammed faster.

She looked up at me, solidifying my endless devotion to her. Her tongue swirled, torturing me into a sensation so hypnotic it felt unreal. Slowing, she moved shallow, then deep. Up and down my cock. Driving me wild again and again. My muscles flared, and I was about to burst at any moment.

"Woah, Petal, slow down!"

The fire gleaming in her eyes showed me the intensity was the same for her. Giving or taking, we both devoured each other. Every time. Day after day. Night after night. Goddess, this woman was my everything.

A sweet smile tugged at her lips as she pulled away and swiped off her shirt, kneeling topless in the treehouse. The curves of her breasts were perky and delicious. As she looked up at me with such love, my only option was to trust that what we had was real. Linked or not—we were meant to be.

Lifting Kyra to her feet, I pressed our chests together, her hard nipples rubbing against my skin and her hands stroking me everywhere. Fast. Slow. Tight. My head spun with raw need. She tugged off her yoga pants. No underwear. Damn.

"Did you just growl at me?" Her devious smirk painted a picture of perfection on her face.

"What are you gonna do about it?" I dipped to the treehouse floor, slowly dropping Kyra's straddled legs on either side of my chest.

"Oh, you want me to do all the work, soldier?"

My cheeks hurt from the grin plastering my face from ear to ear. I nodded silently and watched her move exactly where I wanted her. The heat radiated from her skin like a drug, cocooning us in an invisible blanket. I chanted the Magikal spell we memorized for protection, reading her lips that made the same movements. Her smile unraveled my beast within.

And Kyra lowered herself onto my throbbing cock. Goddess above. She was home. She centered me.

"Ohh…" Kyra tilted, lowering herself until she accepted all of me. She moaned each time her hips thrust. "Jay…fuckin…flames," she jerked out her words with each plunge.

My hands wrapped around her small waist, empowering her movements, guiding her deeper, angling into her harder each time our bodies merged. Her neck craned back, hiding her face from view, but I knew her eyes were squeezed shut, and her mouth hung open in awe. When Kyra arched her back, taking me as deep as possible, I let out an uncontrolled howl. Her attention snapped onto my face as her adorable nose scrunched up in curiosity.

"You like that?" she asked.

No words. Talking was impossible. I licked my lips, needing more of her, all of her, all at once, every second. Just this. Just us. She picked up her tempo, hammering onto me harder, faster. The treehouse creaked and shook under us. Kyra gasped, and her hands smacked into my chest as she bent forward. I seized the opportunity, grabbed her ass, and slammed up into her over and over. Her whole body tensed and stilled. Her eyes were glued together, and her mouth was wide open. She was close.

Jay! How? How do you feel so good?

Only for you. My Goddess.

She moaned in ecstasy through our bond. I pumped up into her harder, gritting my teeth, using every bit of strength. Kyra's nails dug into my chest as she bit her lip, her eyebrows tight. Fuck, this was it. I felt her tighten around me.

Jay! Jay! Jay.

My Circle charged with power just as an animalistic sound I'd never heard before escaped her mouth as she came. Nothing beat this. Ever. Her body went limp over me, shaking and exhausted. I rolled her slowly to her side and pinned her hips with my hands, slowly sliding in and out. She felt so damn good. In and out. So wet. Sweat dripped from my temple. In and out. My biceps flared.

In and out.

Her sleepy eyes drifted open slowly and locked on mine. "You're mine, Jay. *Mine*."

And with that, she ended me. I ravaged her thoroughly until I saw stars and climaxed inside her, Magik coursing through my veins at the same intensity as my orgasm.

Kyra was perfect. I kissed a trail from her forehead to her breasts. She shivered and covered each nipple, shielding me from the sensitive skin. Easing down, I slid Kyra's back against my chest. Her body still trembled slightly. Our lungs rose and fell fast in unison.

I slowly sketched circles on her hip, wishing I could imprint my soul with hers, but I guess we already had with our Link. Some days, I wondered if the prophecy about her Link hadn't been referring to me. What if that was still true and we weren't supposed to be together? I shook the thought away and gulped down my fears. Kyra equated to air. No, she was something better than air. Kyra was the root anchoring me into the soil, the foundation of life.

"Nicely done. That was top five, mister troll." Kyra wiggled around to face me and kissed my ear, sending a spark of shivers up my spine.

"Top five? No way, that was the best one yet. And tomorrow will be even better."

"Actually, I need to talk to you about tomorrow." When Kyra curled into herself, her source of light tensed into a tight ball of cosmic energy. That strength reminded me of a meteor with the potential to tear apart planets.

"I know. We need to take Chocolate on another hike tomorrow. Which path should we take this time?"

"I'm leaving tomorrow," she stated confidently.

I quickly sat up, noticing the bubble of heat surrounding us had evaporated. The cold breeze reminded me of our sweaty, naked bodies, so I laid back down and held her close. I prayed she wasn't planning to fall into Syvonne Stirk's trap. The president would promise a Mystier their darkest desires for her scientists to be able to complete studies with our blood. "What do you mean you're leaving?"

"I can feel Isaac sometimes," she whispered.

That wasn't what I expected her to say. My breath hitched, and it felt like I was swallowing lava. "What do you mean?"

"He spoke to me in the forest earlier." Her amber eyes studied mine. "Jay, I need him to teach me how to control this weather Magik, or I'll hurt everyone I meet. Plus, I promised I'd try to bring his son back. I owe him that."

My fists clenched, but I counted to ten in my head before responding. She was an angel for thinking she should help that moron. "Owe him? Nilson *captured* us, *tortured* us, and he is to blame for your sister's death."

"No, Zeph shot Hallie. Isaac apologized for her actions."

Why was she defending Nilson? I pressed against her mental shield, desperate to see everything that words couldn't explain.

Kyra, open up. Let me in.

Instead of showing me all of her thoughts, she played a memory like a video flashback. My vision faded from the treehouse to a different time, to a scene at midnight. She showed me what happened during the battle in Vayu and what she experienced the night I'd almost died.

Among the battle's raging tumult throughout the city, a monstrous tree swallowed a body whole. Pain seized me as I experienced it all from Kyra's perspective. Sobs racked my chest in a ball of whimpers. The sensation was surreal, and raw pain shocked me to my core. I pounded my fists against the tree, then kicked it again and again.

"Let him go. Let my Jay go!" Nails clawed at the trunk. "I'm the monster. I caused all the pain. Let Jay live!"

The tree shifted, stepping back little by little until the roots cushioning her—well, me—unraveled my limp body. Somehow, I was watching myself die. As the roots were untangled, there wasn't a scratch anywhere on my body.

"I don't want you to go; I need you to stay here with me, Jay."

Agony ripped through my bones.

"Okay. If you have to go, Jay...if it hurts too much to stay...I'll forgive you for leaving. If you can't stay here...I'll try to understand. But you know my heart. I'm always selfish. Please come back."

"Shh, I'm here," Isaac whispered like a phantom, sounding genuine and concerned.

My heart broke at those last words—words I had never heard that day. From her point of view, I could feel the intense pull she had with Isaac at that moment. I needed out of her head; this was too much. Ghost tears pooled until the memory jolted to a stop.

Gasping, I stared at Kyra with my body shaking. "You never showed me that before."

"I needed you to see how much Isaac cares."

Of all things, that wasn't what I expected her to say. Slowly easing away, I threaded my legs into my pants and pulled my shirt on.

"I can't lie to you about this connection with Isaac. There's something between us, but I don't want it."

"I know how much you care about me. I can feel you here...." I pounded my chest a few times. Uncertainty and terror shook me as she dressed slowly.

"How am I supposed to kiss you every day knowing how you feel pulled to Nilson?" I asked. "Do you love me, Kyra?"

Her mouth opened, then closed, answering the question without a single word. What was I supposed to feel when she didn't answer?

Kyra sighed. "I don't want to have any connection with Isaac." After she pulled her long golden hair into a high ponytail, she sat behind me and began massaging my back.

"It's terrifying. What if you see him and change your mind about us?" I asked.

"That will *never* happen. I just need a little more time to say the thing you want me to say." Her fingers stopped kneading.

"Okay, I can give you eternity. We can stay here together. I'll help you control the weather."

"I know you hate that I'm putting the village at risk." Her thumbs dug into the sore spots again. "I won't let you choose between your tribe and me."

"You, I, and Chocolate will find a spot away from the others, maybe by the forbidden caves, and there, we can grow ancient together. We could become a legend, the two Linked Mystiers who vanished."

She actually laughed, fully snorted, at my wish. "Right, ha, that comes right after I make best friends with a sea siren and name an elf my uncle." She tapped my shoulder. "Jay, look at me."

Hesitantly, I looked into her eyes. I knew she needed me. I held both her hands and waited for what she really wanted to say.

"Tomorrow, I'm leaving to figure this all out. I can't stay here. It's too dangerous. Maybe I can find a way to sever the Link with Isaac without killing him."

I kissed her knuckles. "Then I'm coming with."

She reached behind her to the box we had stored the Draven and Elidi necklaces in weeks ago. After opening it, she rubbed a hand over the ruby. "I wish we understood more about these necklaces. They seem broken ever since the Vayuian battle." She groaned in frustration and tucked the necklaces away. "If you come with me, who will keep Landon safe?"

"Gemm and Alaska will watch over him. He likes them better anyways." I studied her face. "Do you *want* to be away from me?"

"No…I…I'm afraid, Jay. I'm afraid to share my whole plan."

"So, there's more." I tucked a golden strand behind her ear. "I'm listening. Always. We're on the same side, Kyra, and we can figure it out together."

"And if we disagree?"

"That's nothing new." I kissed her thick lips. "Besides, the only thing I'd veto is going to the president. No matter what, we can't submit to Stirk's bait. I know you won't go looking for Caspian."

She backed away, anger already written on her expression. "What did you just say?"

As I realized my mistake, my heart hammered a triple beat. *Shit.*

"Jay? Do you *know* that Cydian prisoner?"

Cringing, I nodded. "Yeah…Caspian is the leader of Cydon, but he probably doesn't know anything about your family. It's a trap."

"You should've told me this."

"I didn't think it mattered."

She marched across the treehouse and flung herself onto the first step of the tall ladder, practically falling down them in her haste to get away from me. Standing alone, I pulled at my hair, cursing silently. Secrets between us would be our demise. It felt like stones were lodged in my throat. I reached out to her through our thread, dropping my walls.

Kyra, I have one secret. I'll tell you everything. I'm sorry. Please come back up.

3
ISAAC

Vayu's silver skyscrapers towered to my right. Atop the library's roof–my sanctuary–I gazed out at this amazing city. Afternoon clouds camouflaged into the sheets flapping on a clothesline nearby. Together, their outline took the form of a sail. I couldn't tell where the sky ended and the sheet began. They reminded me of a simpler life when Wes was younger, a life I'd give anything to get back.

Now, I was alone. Except for Tawoli. My jaw clenched tight. Sensing my mood, my venti nudged her creamy, feathery cheek against my ear. Tawoli was taller than me, and when her wings were outstretched, their length was double my six-foot height. I scratched right under her beak, and her chin lifted to the clouds as she whinnied like a horse.

Birds chirped and flew around the feeders set up on lower rooftops. With everyone's curtains opened, as was the custom, I stared at the floating books inside people's apartments.

I sighed. No one in this city knew what I was going through. The only soul who understood an inkling was Kyra Kozelski, the woman Linked to me who had been hiding out of reach for weeks. The

Golden Girl had already gotten a sneak peek of my deepest thoughts, desires, and pains.

I sighed. Crouching down to stare into the ancient telescope, I slowly changed its angle to find the one place I shouldn't focus on: Rajitha's empty cottage. The scope's lens finally landed on the trail of flapping flags. They led to a view of where Wes last slept, but it was empty.

Rajitha never would've believed me if I had told her that a Magikal land of skyscrapers, protected by an invisible dome, stood a mile from her front door. At least she never learned that our ten-year-old son had powers too. It didn't matter anymore. Now, they were both gone.

And I was alone.

It was crazy to think back to high school graduation when Rajitha dropped the bomb that Wes was on the way.

"I'm pregnant, Isaac."

"What?"

Wind secretly roars from my fingertips, ripping our graduation banner in two. The script showing "Congratulations Class of 71T" tears in half and flutters to the ground. I suck in a breath to block the second burst of wind and hold it until I find the nearest exit. I know storming out on Rajitha is the stupidest choice of life, but my emotions can't contain the looming clouds rolling in.

Until the day our son was born, I slept on pins and needles, waiting to see if Wes would be Vayuian or not. I knew the second my gaze latched on to his large gray eyes. He was like me—blessed and cursed with Magik.

All the questions I had been researching for the past year were irrelevant now. It didn't matter whether other hybrid kids existed or not. Because all the males were stripped away in a single night. And the man I had originally blamed played no part in their disappearance as I had assumed. Unfortunately, Jadox Griffin was innocent in that respect, so pummeling him into the afterlife was out of the question. Because it was *her* who stole Wes from me. Kyra Kozelski—the bouncing ball of energy and a constant, unmovable thorn in my side.

Rocks lodged in my throat at the thought of Kyra, followed by an intense need to speak with her, to see her freckles in person, and learn her every quirk. As much as I wanted to hate her, I wanted to memorize her body posture, how she stirred her cocoa, and the way her smile curved when she petted an animal. They were ridiculous, stupid ideas.

My old Vayuian tattoo was now looped with the fresh red one on my stomach. They both burned in desire for her. Divinity, I hated what Kyra did to me. Forcing her to Link with me had changed everything. I needed to shake her from my consciousness before this obsession became a problem.

Through the telescope, my enhanced vision picked up the twitch of a beetle on the stone on Rajitha's patio, painted all shades of blue. I could even see individual paint streaks. My ex never knew that I was blessed with an extra layer of sight, gifted to me as a descendant from the strongest family in our village.

I'd trade my enhancement and all my Magik for a chance for Wes to return. Our son was only a wobbly toddler when we painted that porch, and he had knocked over a bucket of paint. I chuckled at the memory. His baby feet tracked little footprints all over the front patio, and we didn't have the heart to ever cover them. As I stared at the prints of his baby toes, faded by the sun, my hand shook from grief on the telescope.

"You have to let them go," a familiar voice scolded from behind me on the rooftop.

I turned to see Zeph. The morning sun reflected off her glasses, blinding me momentarily. When my pet venti, Tawoli, stepped forward, Zeph's features also came into view. With one hand on her hip, Zeph wore her full spandex uniform that blended into the environment, currently the cyan buildings of our city.

"You've been so tense, Isaac," Zeph said.

Zeph drifted over as if she was gliding on air and repositioned the telescope to point in the direction we knew Draven sat, miles and miles away. "Time is running out to find the girl."

"Zeph, we've been over this. I know where Kyra is."

"Then why aren't we there now?"

I had to lie again, so I ran a hand through my long hair and said, "Because I don't know where the *exact* entrance is." There was no way I would tell my ex that I was nervous about the all-consuming connection I felt with Kyra through our new Link.

Another gust blew through my shirt, the cotton shifting against my skin and exposing the Möbius tattoo claiming my hip. It was now looped with Elidi's red Circle. Through her glasses, Zeph's gaze absorbed the view of my abs as if she hadn't seen me sprawled on my bed just last night.

I shuddered at the memory of my mistake—sleeping with Zeph again only conjured up the past. It was stupid when I should've devoted all my time to finding Draven's entrance. The wind caressed my skin. Today would be another cold day, especially with Zeph's icy eyes taking me in.

"You're needed with the troops downstairs," I stated.

"Probably. But I never had the chance to tell you last night that I may volunteer to work undercover, to join one of President Stirk's teams and learn inside information."

"Wait, when did this get decided? I didn't authorize this, and I don't want you to get hurt."

"Since when do you care?" Zeph snapped.

The tightness in my chest eased away. "I've always cared, Zeph, just not as much as you want me to."

Her face blushed red as her lips formed a tight line.

I tapped my solar-powered watch, realizing it was the first day of a new month. The screen flashed the date, *Cold Moon 01-82T*. An old image of Wes laughing flashed on the front screen, twisting my gut into knots. His gray eyes were replicas of mine, just like his long hair pulled back in a high bun mirrored my style. That devious smile matched the one I wore, but his skin tone was darker, like Rajitha's. I missed him more than words could express.

Zeph peered through the lens, the frame of her glasses rattling against the metal. “Am I coming over again tonight?

“About that…we need to stop.”

“That’s what you said last week.” Her ringlets bounced in front of her face as she smiled.

“I’m serious. I’m not interested in this game anymore.”

Zeph snorted. “I bet you the Unetlo Book that you’ll come begging at my door.”

I shook my head. Grief sex was just a distraction from everything that mattered.

Suddenly, an image of Kyra invaded my mind, with those thick cranberry lips, high cheekbones, silky golden hair, and eyes made of pure honey. Her contagious spunk and dynamic spirit felt like Magik itself. My heartbeat quickened in hopes of seeing her again soon. When we had Linked, I witnessed all of Kyra’s essence, everything that made her tick, but for only a few seconds. I already knew her more than I ever had understood Rajitha or Zeph, which was just cruel. Maybe this Link was Ꮳsμwi, and we were already doomed without knowing it. That was probably the karma I deserved—a dark curse.

How would this three-way Link even work? None of my research over the years had shown a history of a Mystier surviving a Link with two others. Maybe I could find a way to get rid of Griffin for good. Yesterday, it was so comforting when Kyra finally responded telepathically.

No! What was wrong with me? I was grieving Rajitha, sleeping with Zeph, and craving Kyra at the same time. For fuck’s sake! I dug my nails into my palm, wanting to whisk these thoughts away with the wind. They weren’t welcome. Kyra had no place in my thoughts.

Zeph ran a fingertip down my forearm. “Maybe I’ll kill the Golden Girl myself to eliminate your stress.”

My insides burned into lethal torches, aflame with rage, but I inhaled deeply, knowing Zeph was no match for the woman I was Linked with. “Go ahead and try.”

"I know you, Isaac. You only want what you can't have. But don't consider going after this one."

"You don't know what you're talking about."

"Rajitha was an Ordull, so she was off-limits, yet you couldn't keep your mind off her."

My bones rattled together, but I focused on the calming source of power humming through my tattoos.

"Now Kyra is off-limits because that wild boy is banging her senseless, and you can't do anything about it. She chose the Dravian, not you."

I slammed my fists together, and a cyclone of wind tore a chunk of brick off the corner of the rooftop. A second later, a horrendous smash crashed below where it hit the pavement. Zeph's eyes widened through her glasses as she ran to the edge and checked the street.

"Isaac! Have you gone crazy?! It's noon. Anyone could've been walking down there."

"Don't. Talk. About. Kyra." I gritted out.

Her eyes narrowed, and when her hip popped out to the side, the blue jumpsuit wrapped around her curves, creating an hourglass figure. "You're different now. Your energy is all..." She twined her fingers into a jumbled knot. "...tangled up. You're a walking mess."

"I don't only want what I can't have," I mumbled, not meeting her eyes.

"Hm, that bothers you, huh?" Zeph reached to my cheek, but I turned away. "Maybe I'll start playing hard to get, and you'll be more interested again."

"We're over, Zee."

"Yet you still call me by the nickname you gave me."

Tawoli stretched her wings out wide and wrapped them around me in a protective blanket. For a moment, I eased into my pet's presence.

The breeze shifted, making the windchimes above the door strike a faster chord. "Please go downstairs. I'll search for the Draven entrance for another hour until our meeting."

"Fine. Message me if you find anything. Today is your last day before I fly over there and drag her out by her hair."

"We need to be peaceful and logical about this."

"Wrong. There's too much at stake. Stirk's army is looking for Kyra. Their actions are worsening across the country."

My only option for convincing Kyra to help return Wes would be to convince her to leave Draven. After getting a crash course on her past, I knew she'd need support and a kind ear to listen to her struggles and turmoil. And Griffin wasn't up for the job. Once Kyra and I were alone, I'd finally have the chance to develop our relationship from enemies to… something.

Zeph finally disappeared through the rooftop door, leaving me alone again. I gazed through the telescope lens. Hills. Slopes. Bare trees. Patches of snow. Gorulas climbing a cliff's edge. Suddenly, a small silhouette moved in the distance between evergreens. I gasped and moved the scope a bit. Squinting, I made out the brown and green camo outfit—definitely Dravian custom attire.

I twisted the knob on the telescope and zoomed in further. My heart slammed into my chest at the sight of a golden blur of hair cascading down over narrow shoulders. Damn, there she was. My Golden One. *Mine*. Kyra belonged to me. Fuck—no. What the Flames was wrong with me? Why would I think that? Warmth coiled tight in my stomach, and desperation exploded in my veins. I had to see her. Now.

"Tawoli, drop."

My venti immediately crouched, allowing me to jump on and wrap my arms around Tawolis' horse-like neck that I was so familiar with. I tapped my back pocket to confirm the electric grenade was still secure, then gently kicked her sides. "Up!"

We rose. Higher. Weightless. To our right, an eagle soared and dove fast. Clouds greeted us with a welcoming hand. As I patted Tawoli's feathers, I tapped my right heel on her side, swerving her left. I prayed to the goddess above that Kyra stayed outside the shield all afternoon because we'd need to fly at full speed for at least an hour to reach Draven.

Anticipation crawled up my skin, but I shut down the hope swelling within me. I didn't truly want to see Kyra—I was only seeking her out to save Wes. Kyra didn't possess anything of interest to me. My heart drummed faster, reminding me how she jittered a beat on her thigh whenever she was nervous. Was she doing it now? Could she feel me approaching? Naturally, I scraped a wordless plea against our Link's tether, but Kyra's mental walls were ironclad strong and solid.

"Kyra. Wait for me," I whispered in the wind.

Only Tawoli screeched in return.

I stroked her massive feathers again and leaned over her side, squinting into the distance. "Faster."

Far below, ladybugs fluttered, bees swarmed around a hive, and butterflies flapped poetically. But even with my enhanced vision, I couldn't see Draven anymore without that telescope. We had to fly faster.

Canyons and rivers stretched endlessly in an abstract painting of blues, whites, and rusty browns. A daydream sucked me into the past.

Little Wes hiking, leading me up a steep trail. Wes marking our route with flags along the bushes. Wes smiling as he dug for a snack in his tiny blue backpack, fingernails coated in dirt. Then...Kyra's smile.

Tawoli screeched. I glanced below, recognizing the area outside of Draven. How long had we been flying?

Suddenly, an arrow whizzed straight past my ear. An arrow? Seriously?

Tawoli dipped, and I almost fell off her back. She turned quickly and screeched her battle cry. I gripped onto her with my thighs and pointed my hands down, shooting a gust of strong wind with such force it'd uproot a tree. Another arrow zinged, swiping against my bicep. Blood dripped down my arm, streaking my Tawoli's feathers with crimson. She zig-zagged in the air, awaiting orders.

"Shit!" I flattened onto Tawoli's back. Retreat or land? Fight or flee? What if Kyra was in danger? "Down!" I yelled as soon as the last thought entered my mind.

Her squawk protested earnestly. My vision turned fuzzy. I glanced down at my arm again. The wound had been ripped open and was gushing blood.

"Down!"

Tawoli dove. Fast and hard. I clung to her neck tightly with one arm. Shaking, I reached back into my pocket and pulled the stun grenade out. The world turned to a haze of browns as the baren treetops grew larger. More arrows were shot from everywhere. No, not arrows. They were just sharp twigs turned into deadly weapons. Damn Dravians and their stupid trees.

Sweat pooled under my hoodie, and warmth enveloped me to an unbearable level.

Then, suddenly, I could hear her. Feel her. Kyra.

In the calamity of the dive, Kyra's lively voice rang clear. "Stop shooting!"

Tawoli landed on the ground with a thunk and galloped behind a line of trees. I rolled off her, collapsing into a pile of snow. I crawled behind a pile of logs, panting and trembling, staring at my wound. Weakness overpowered any possibility of using my Magik. When I glanced down at my arm, the veins all popped red. Ugh, poison! I'd probably lose the function of my damn arm in less than a minute, or the venom would travel to my heart.

"Kyra, I need you," I whispered weakly into the wind.

A twig cracked behind a tree to my right. Squinting, I only saw more browns smudged with white flakes, a blur of dirty winter. The world was a strange fog, too fuzzy to see.

"Isaac?" Kyra's voice, animated and full, calmed my racing nerves.

She was safe, right here. Before losing the nerve, I pulled on the grenade's pin with my teeth and chucked it with my good arm as far away from her as possible. A deafening explosion erupted where the bomb landed. One scream resounded throughout the forest.

A hand smacked my temple. "Why did you do that?"

"I...can't see...I can't breathe." Tightness clamped around my throat.

"Ugh, I hate you," Kyra snapped at me while ripping the sleeve off my shirt and tying it around my injury.

"My...arm," I stammered as I fell over to the side. "Poisoned."

"No shit, dumbass." Her voice sounded muffled and far away.

Her fingers traced a circle on my wrist, sparking a surge of power in my tattoo.

"Hm, it's not working this time, so I guess you're dying today. See ya."

My face lay in the dirt, and my mouth started foaming. Suffocated. I clutched at my throat.

"I'm gonna kill you for this." Kyra pressed her hands to my chest. Her words barely registered through the fog. Daylight turned dark, and everything stilled. Stars barricaded my senses, like a glittery wave of gold and red, rushing at me full speed as if it was in a time warp. Tiny dots glowed and grew quickly until fireworks burst into my vision. Then, Kyra's mental shield suddenly dropped, and we were one.

I basked in the relief and warmth of her spirit. Maybe we were already dead, but somewhere, she chanted a spell lullaby, *Terra angakok. Terra angakok.*

Memories full of Wes spun on a reel.

Wes, at three years old, with deep cheek dimples coated with dried macaroni and cheese. Wes, at six years old, with tears as he accidentally rode his bike over a lizard. Wes, at age nine, with a giant smile as he built a model aero glider by hand.

The unconditional love for him was woven deep within me and felt unbearable. Kyra somehow pulled the poison from my veins, and her face came into view. She gasped, and I knew she had seen the memories of Wes too.

"You stupid asshole. Why would you throw that electric grenade? They're all gonna come for you."

You saved me, love.

You're delirious.

My arm stopped bleeding, and the wound clotted closed. As quickly as Kyra had let me in, she forced her wall back up. I groaned from the whiplash. The forest became clearer, more vivid. Some of the mahogany shades I assumed were trees started moving. Dravian villagers circled me, all armed with sharp branches directed straight at my temple.

"Come on, let's get you out of here." Kyra brushed a finger over the newly sealed wound.

"Uh, Kyra? This asshole just fuckin' blew up our shield. We should restrain him." A slightly familiar woman with long raven hair, dressed all in brown, stepped forward.

"We're Linked." Kyra smacked my shoulder with boundless spirit. "He will listen to me and is no longer a threat."

I met Kyra's brutally gorgeous golden eyes, and a heat wave passed between us. The edges of her features were sharper than before, rough from her sister's death, unfortunately, at Zeph's hand. I should apologize again for the grief my ex had caused.

"Well, I'm gonna go warn our people." With that, the woman touched a tribe member's shoulder, and they both disappeared into thin air.

"Teleportation?" I asked, starting to remember how I knew that woman.

"That was Alaska." Kyra's frown covered her face. "You shouldn't have come here, Isaac."

"Well, I'm here."

"Why?"

I struggled to contain a moan from the last bit of my arm healing. "I never told you the other half of my secret, love."

4

KYRA

I shoved Isaac into a tree trunk. "You lied before. I already asked the Elders about this so-called *Blood Maiden* you told me about." I made air quotes with my fingers. "She's only a myth."

"The Blood Maiden's name is Moroka, and she is very real. She can answer any questions about your roots, your real father, or your golden tattoo."

My ears deceived me. If she was real, would this Moroka have answers about my family? Where was she?

"In fact, we've both met one of Moroka's sisters: the notorious Surh-Sig."

Intrigue washed over me. I sighed, unsure how to proceed, though every part of me wanted to slap his chiseled face—of that, I was sure.

If he was telling the truth, then I had two ways of learning more about my heritage and the meaning of my Golden tattoo— through the Cydian prisoner or the Blood Maiden. Which was safer? Syvonne's prisoners would have an army guarding the cells. Yet, Moroka would be a legit demon. And if she was anything like her sister....

I stared at Isaac with his deceptive dimples. There was no way he came to our borders alone.

"You shouldn't be here." I glanced over my shoulder.

His arms opened wide. "Well, here I am."

Divinity, his arrogance was annoying.

"So, where does this infamous Moroka live?"

"Galudi Cove."

Thinking back to the maps I had seen in tattered books, I tried to place how far away Galudi's Cove was, then turned to my lingering teammates who were eavesdropping, "Hey, I'll meet you all inside Draven."

"Are you sure?" Claire asked.

"Yes, thank you."

"You sound *special,* my lady." Isaac's treacherous lips formed a smile that shouldn't be legal.

"I'm not special."

"Of course, Your Majesty." Isaac bowed, showing me the tip of his blond bun. "It's not like they're looking to you for orders."

"You know the Griffin family is the strongest clan in their village."

He nodded, then brushed the dirt off his hoodie. "I know. Gemm has prophecies, Alaska can teleport, and your boy toy can—"

Rage barreled through me like a tsunami. I pulled a dagger from my belt loop. And thrust it against Isaac's throat.

"Don't call Jay that."

"Of course, love." He gently pushed his neck against the blade and hovered his lips over mine. "What does the Griffin family status have to do with *you*?"

"You're the smart one. You should know that Jay and I belong together."

"Do you?"

I used all my effort to keep my face neutral. Maybe I didn't know the answer to that yet. I sheathed my dagger and studied the man in front of me. Either Isaac had turned paler in the last few weeks, blending into the wintery snow, or I had grown accustomed to Jay's darker skin. Shadows under Isaac's eyes hinted that he hadn't slept a full night since the last time I saw him in Vayu. Each time a partial chuckle parted his lips, it felt forced. Even though I healed his physical injuries, it appeared that Isaac was still in pain. Could I help him? Why would I want to?

My emotions whirled, so I focused on the soothing sounds of the forest around me. A cardinal tweeted in the distance, and the river's ice layer crackled and broke apart. I tried Alaska's meditation training, but it still seemed useless. *Usganola tardu.* Focus. Think. I blew out another breath. *Usganola tardu.* Sometimes, when my centering practice gave me a twilight-zone sensation, the crackle of the sun's core sang a message to my soul.

"Tawoli?" Isaac's slippery voice snapped me back to reality. "Where'd you go, girl?" His gray eyes narrowed as he squinted into the forest. "Have you seen my venti?"

"Maybe you blew her up with your electric grenade." I thrust a careless wave to where our shield used to form a mirage of endless trees. Now, it only showed Draven in its entirety, vulnerable for any attacker to spot. I jogged towards home–away from this monster.

"Wait for me. Slow down," Isaac chuckled. "Just take a breath. You're such a typical Elidian."

I turned on my heels. "What's that supposed to mean?"

"Elidians don't think before they act."

"I may still be learning about Mystiers and Magik, but I still understand stereotypes and judgment when I hear them. How would you feel if I said all Vayuians were—"

"Ridiculously intelligent?" he interrupted.

"You act like a damn child."

"What's life without a bit of fun and games?"

"Isaac!" I put both hands on my hips.

"Kyra!" He imitated my movement.

I growled and turned, stomping towards Draven.

He followed, of course. "Seriously, Kyra, don't worry about that grenade. The electric current in that thing wasn't strong enough to deplete you. Your power will return in a few minutes."

"But what about all the others who don't have a damn Golden Circle or an enhancement...or a Link?"

"Hmm...um..." Marching next to me, Isaac scratched his

atrociously sexy stubble. "It may take a few hours for Dravians to feel back to normal."

"Goddess, you're such a selfish douchebag. How will my people defend themselves now?"

"First of all, Dravians are not *your* people. Secondly, just wish for no threats for a day or so. I heard you're great at making wishes come true." The sudden bitterness in his voice was layered thick.

Ahead, Draven's magnificent treehouses towered at dozens of various heights and rock dens camouflaged into the cliffs. Isaac whistled between two fingers until a monstrous, white-feathered beast swooped down, snowflakes coating her beak. He ran a large hand over her shoulder and stroked a spot on her forehead affectionately.

"Thank you, girl. Stay close." Isaac kissed her cheek before she launched from the ground, scattering snow under her hooves.

I scanned him properly for the first time. The giant hoodie was snug on his upper body.

"Kyra?"

"What?"

"My eyes are up here."

I snapped my gaze to his, diving into the depths of those grays. "You are the absolute worst." I stalked forward again and tried to punch his gut, but he bounced away playfully.

"You can't lie to me anymore, love. I've *already seen all of you,* and I know our attraction is mutual." Snowflakes stuck to his hair, giving him a falsely innocent expression.

"You wish you'd seen *all* of me."

"We could take care of that, you know...the rest that has gone *unseen.*"

I rolled my eyes. "Isaac, there is no way in our lifetimes that you'll ever see me naked."

"You're lying straight to my face, love. It's okay. This game makes it more fun."

"Let's get this over with." I stopped mid-stride. "Come here."

Isaac stepped forward fast, puckering up sarcastically. "Yes, ma'am."

"Not *that,* you idiot." I slapped his shoulder again. "Why are you really here? I know you don't care about some legend demon."

His expression turned stone cold in a heartbeat. "You owe me, my son."

"Right." I sobered quickly. "I know. Let's get this over with. Let's try to return Wes. Now."

His lips pressed together, matching the sudden seriousness of his eyes.

"When Landon returned, we...I used the spell, *Reditus atsutsa*."

Isaac took my hands in his, slowly rubbing his fingertips over mine. He took a long breath, looking nervous for the first time since we met. "I'm gonna close my eyes. Sometimes with my enhanced vision, you're...distracting." Isaac sealed his eyes shut. "This is your chance to kiss me if you want."

Chills spiked along my spine as I shook my head. "How can you joke right *now*?"

"Who said I was joking?"

The warmth of my tattoo trickled through my veins to his skin. I watched his face soften and took advantage of his eyes, finally not scrutinizing my every move. His pointed nose was pink from the chill, and each time he exhaled, his visible breath fogged the air for a moment. Tilting my head, I absorbed the slight wrinkles around his eyes, evidence of his malicious smile.

"How old are you?" I asked.

"Almost twenty-nine, love. My birthday is coming up. Are you gonna buy me a gift? I know just what I want."

"In your dreams."

"Your wall is still up, love." The corners of Isaac's lips curved up just a tad. "I'm waiting oh so patiently."

"Fine. But let's be quick. Jay is on the way."

"We'll be quicker than a venti."

I sucked in my courage and let my wall crumble for Isaac. Immediately, a charge bound us together in a violent compression.

Glued. Eternally Linked. Air pumped my lungs with life, and a breeze tickled me from the inside out. Gravity ceased to exist. My feet levitated off the ground, and I gasped.

Trust me, love.

Isaac sent reassurance through our bond and squeezed my hands. Seconds passed. A lifetime. It felt like I was flying, exploring the skies. Heat gurgled in my core, and burbling lava surfaced in my heart. Isaac's hope for Wes overfilled his heart and leaped straight into my own. We could do this. The love he held for Wes transferred to me, and tears stung behind my eyes. Longing. What Isaac needed, I did too. I needed Wes like I needed air. My heart pounded at an uneven tempo.

"Reditus atsutsa," we both hummed, and Isaac added "Wes" in a whisper.

An attack from within my body imploded from my center, rupturing my spirit. Power gushed through my blood in a heap, and a cry pierced my ears. A scream from nightmares. My eyes snapped open, meeting Isaac's. Our hands tore apart, and we both fell to the cold, hard ground from our floating positions.

"No!" Isaac screamed, falling to his knees with a cyclone beginning to swirl untampered around him. "We have to try again."

I sighed, rubbing my elbow where I landed. "Our powers need time to recharge."

"Aargh!" His scream made me flinch. "This was supposed to work!"

"We can try again later." I buried my head in my hands, wishing I didn't feel the same devastation that Isaac was suffering. Quickly, I blocked him out of my heart and mind once again. Forcing myself to hide away from someone I was Linked with felt so unnatural.

"Why could you and Griffin return that Landon kid?" he hollered.

"That *kid*? You mean my sweet nephew?" I snapped. "Probably because my connection with you isn't strong."

Isaac stilled, and he eyed me. Despite his failed attempts to scrape against my mental wall, which was already reconstructed, an arrogant look plastered over his face. "We can become closer, love. All you have to do is allow it."

"That'll never happen."

He stood quickly and leaned against the tree. "Then quit picturing what's in my pants."

"I wasn't." Glancing behind me, I checked for Jay. His energy grew stronger and closer. "You need to leave, Isaac."

"No, I *need* Wes back."

"We can't right now."

"In the last few weeks, have you tried to return Wes...." Isaac cleared his throat. "With...with Griffin?"

"Yeah, about a dozen times. I'm sorry."

"Sever the Link with Griffin." He jumped forward and took both my hands. "That's what's holding us back. I just know it, in my gut."

I twisted free in an instant. "If you knew me as you claim to, you would never ask that of me."

Isaac pushed a button on his s-watch, which projected an image of a broken-down lighthouse onto a tree trunk. "Okay, fine, we'll talk about it later. Look..." As if sensing that Jadox was closer, he rushed his words. "This is where Moroka was last seen. Legend states that she will answer one question for each visitor who sacrifices something to her."

"So, you think it's a smart idea to collaborate with a Blood Maiden after what happened with Surh-Sig?"

A thousand times, I'd contemplated where Surh-Sig had run off to after the battle, but I still had no clue. Where did she go?

Isaac stepped forward with dominance but gently held both of my elbows. "Kyra, we have to try. If you returned a boy once, you can do it again. Wes is my everything. Please understand."

I did. When enveloped in his memories, I experienced Isaac's love that ran eternally deep. Unfathomable love. I never loved Hallie, Mom, or even Landon in the capacity of what Isaac felt for his son. Maybe it was a parent-child relationship I was yet to experience.

Obviously, my heart belonged to Jadox, but it wasn't comparable to Isaac's devotion to Wes. This man would suffer through torture a thousand times over for his child. Regardless of how annoying, frustrating, devious, and manipulative Isaac was, I had to respect that type of deep devotion.

I chewed the inside of my lip and tapped a beat on my thigh. "The Blood Maiden is a bad idea. Alaska has a theory about using all four necklaces together. Maybe that will bring him back."

"Do you know where the Cydon necklace is?" He rubbed his blond stubble. "Or if it's even still out there somewhere?"

"No, have you found the Vayuian one?

"Not yet. I could use your help with that too."

"No. My place isn't with you, Isaac."

His eyes turned colder than the fresh icicles hanging from the branches. A gorula happened to be jumping from limb to limb and shook one loose. The icicle fell fast, the pointed end shooting straight toward Isaac. I pulled him to my chest, crashing our bodies together. The icicle missed him and lodged itself into the snow with a fierceness stronger than a knife slicing through stone.

"What's going on here?" Jadox's voice rang out.

I glanced down at Isaac's hands around my waist, and the neckline of his shirt wrinkled in my fist. Pushing away, I whirled around to see Jay's hardened face and rigid posture. His question also pushed against our bond, and I lowered my shield to show him my memories of the last few seconds—my innocence.

But Isaac's mischievous demeanor quickly masked the agony he had shared with me only moments before about Wes. He turned on his witty charm in a face-off against Jadox.

"My girl missed me," Isaac said calmly. "I came to fulfill her needs."

A low grumble erupted deep in Jay's chest as he shifted his stance. "Go home, Nilson."

"Not yet."

Jadox switched his stance, more limber on his toes. "I've been wondering, how did you get free that night in Vayu?"

Isaac met my eyes.

Have you told him?

No.

I shook my head slightly, begging Isaac not to rat me out that I freed him when Jay was unconscious.

"I'm Magikal, Griffin. It doesn't take a genius to figure it out."

"Leave." Jadox moved towards him, and I held my breath.

"Hold on. We have a problem." Isaac stopped Jadox's progression with one hand pressed against his chest. "I hear that my girl isn't quite *satisfied*. It's just outright beastly of you to keep her trapped without at least pleasuring her so she's not faking it every time."

Jadox swiped Isaac's hand off his chest and stared silently.

"Want to settle this now?" Isaac lowered his chin. "Duel. Winner gets the girl."

Jadox didn't move a muscle.

Their brainless male egos matched off like a pair of alpha wolves, claiming their turf. I rolled my eyes and crossed my arms but couldn't help comparing the two. The two men were sky and earth, light and dark. They were complete opposites. Isaac was taller than Jay, though, by only an inch, with much fairer skin, pinker lips, and a sharper nose.

In one corner of the impending battle, my boyfriend, ever the soldier, silently stretched his shoulders like he was prepping for a boxing match. My heart rammed faster just staring at Jay's juicy lips and brown eyes. Divinity above, I loved him no matter how stupid his current actions were. Why couldn't I tell him out loud that I loved him?

Then, in the rival corner of the clearing, Isaac casually rolled up his hoodie sleeves and ran a hand through his blonde hair up to the high bun. I barely knew him, yet I had already witnessed his ridiculous energy and charm.

They were both challenging, strong assholes—but they were *my* assholes. No, just Jay. Only Jay was mine. What was wrong with me?

"Okay, boys, you both have enough chest hair. Let's not be medieval and compare dagger sizes too."

Isaac smiled lethally, and Jadox's eyes flew to mine.

"I mean…not that I'm thinking about Isaac's…dagger," I groaned. "Come on, let's go inside Gemm's den and make a plan."

"Not with him." Jay curled his fist at Isaac's face. "Leave. We tried to bring your kid back already. It won't work. You're not welcome here."

"It's because you're terrified about my dagger size, isn't it? I can understand your concern, man, really. You should be worried."

Jay's growl vibrated silently along our thread.

I bit my lip, heart racing. "As entertaining as this is, I need to check on Landon."

Chocolate ran through the forest to Jay's heels and circled his leg, whining, but he ignored the pup.

"You're responsible for Hallie's death, Nilson." Jadox slammed a punch into Isaac's stomach. "You abducted Landon. You put Kyra in a cell; she almost died because of you!"

"Jay, stop!"

Isaac straightened from his folded position and raised both hands in mock surrender. "Did you write all that down to remember it all? It looks like one of your veins will pop from holding too much information in your tiny brain."

A jolt of power twisted in my stomach, swirling between the three tattoos looped together in an endless pattern. My fists melded into tight balls, and I cast my arms out wide. A blast of wind pinned Isaac to a tree while four giant logs corralled Jay to another. Goddess, they were both morons.

Isaac's eyes widened. "Good move, love."

"Get out!" Jadox's beastly voice bellowed so loud and deep that it felt like the forest floor shook. He broke through my log binding and charged Isaac.

Snow changed shape at my boots. Shit, the ground was actually moving.

"Um, Jay?" I whispered, but the look of rage on his face confirmed that he hadn't registered my words.

The heat of my Circle flamed almost unbearably until Jay roared wildly beside me. The ground cracked in front of us, forming a divide between Isaac and us.

Isaac was stronger than me and took command of my wind. "I've seen you make a trench already, Griffin." Isaac leaned in. "It looks like you are overcompensating."

I rolled my lips, trying not to be amused by Isaac's wit. But he met my eyes, and the playfulness sparked so brightly that my heart leaped.

Laying a hand on Jay's back, I turned him toward me. "Hey, he's not worth it. Let's go inside and figure out how to turn Draven's shield back on."

"We can't yet," his voice growled so low. "I already tried. This guy's grenade broke it. Everyone is exposed, and we have to evacuate."

Terror buzzed strongly through me, rattling my bones. I didn't dare curse out Isaac because the energy surging through my tattoo would explode him. He had singlehandedly destroyed all Dravians' chance of survival against President Stirk's forces. Now, we'd have to run and seek shelter. I glanced up at Jay's seething eyes as he continued to stare down Isaac.

Jay, where's Landon?

He's safe with Gemm.

A high-pitched whizz sound penetrated the air from far above in the sky. The noise made my skin crawl. All the hairs on my arm stood on end. The whirring chime grew closer, louder. Then a screech echoed so quietly that I may have imagined it. My heart rampaged against my chest. Jay lifted his nose and sniffed the air for only a moment.

"You filthy rat!" Jay hurled any rock nearby straight at Isaac, but he blocked them with a jet of wind. "Who did you lead here?"

"What are you talking about?" Isaac spat.

"Someone's coming." I pointed to the faint hissing sound from something above. Isaac squinted through the high trees, and dread covered his face.

"Shit! Griffin, we need to hide Kyra. Now!"

5
ISAAC

Two miles off, weaving between the clouds, I spotted Zeph's venti leading a troop of Ordull soldiers straight to us. That was the final straw. I silently vowed never to speak with Zeph again.

"We have to warn everyone!" Kyra sprang toward Draven's village.

I sprinted after her. Angry footsteps crunched the snow behind me—Griffin—of course.

In the village, I almost fell over some trees from shock. Trees grew parallel to the ground. I didn't have time to absorb the beauty of it all, but it was absolutely breathtaking. A sea of pines disguised a bunch of Dravians kneeling near a crate. One pulled out a bow and arrow. Tension bit the air as one villager held up the chorded shrapnel from my grenade. We had to hurry.

"Hey!" Kyra waved her arms, yelling as she slammed to a stop. The group all snapped their attention toward her.

Alaska jogged out from a den I had first assumed was a cliff wall. Her brown outfit stuck to her tall, slender form, making her blend into the tree trunks—and matching the rest of the tribe.

"What's wrong?" Alaska asked.

"Attackers. Two miles away, we only have a few minutes."

Alaska shoved me against a tree. "Because of *your* grenade, our people can't defend themselves."

Beside me, Griffin's fists balled tight and commanded me like a Sergeant. "Nilson, go fetch your venti and create a diversion."

"Fine." I whistled, but Tawoli didn't swoop down as expected. Only a chocolate lab scurried to my feet and circled my boots. "Uh, I can't. Tawoli flew off."

"Then go get her!" Griffin's voice could tear apart a mountain.

Kyra jumped in front of him, one hand on his chest, never thinking things through, and said, "Jay, this isn't the time. They're coming."

"What should we do? None of our Magik has fully returned." Alaska gestured to the crowd of Dravians holding spears, sickles, axes, and ninja stars. "There are children in each den."

Darkness dripped over Draven Valley as the snowfall accelerated. Kyra inhaled sharply, her eyes continually darting back to one den in particular. "We protect what is ours."

"Okay, follow me." Griffin pointed to the biggest men holding the largest weapons. "You five, stay up front."

"I'll be right beside you." Kyra joined Griffin at the hip.

"Wait, slow down, love." I stepped forward, but the pointed ends of a dozen javelins immediately blocked my access to her. "Calm down. I'll never hurt her."

Kyra tilted her head questionably, but all murderous glares stayed trained on me. "Listen, they're here to bring Kyra to the president. We only need to—"

"There is no *we*. There is no *us*." Kyra's words slapped me on the face as sharply as a palm.

"Please, hide. I can't lose you too," I rushed out my words and checked the skies again.

She checked with Griffin, who didn't move at all but said, "I won't order you around like *Nilson*, but I welcome you by my side if you want to fight."

"I know. I'll be with you," Kyra whispered nervously. "I can hear them one mile away. There's more than a dozen ventus."

Suddenly, a round older woman with long gray braids hobbled out of the den. "Once, there was a Magikal poison, just in case."

The old lady handed Griffin and Kyra a small vial of shimmering black liquid, then limped over to me, supported by her cane. She took my hand and placed a matching tiny bottle in it. "Once, there was a reason to drink to take away all pain."

"What is this riddle?" I shook my head and glanced at Kyra.

Griffin spoke instead, "Gemm, is this cyanide?"

"She's crazy." But I pocketed the lethal drug and marched to Griffin. "Come on, we can still create a distraction without my venti."

Griffin looked at Kyra for a beat, and she nodded. Both knew I was right. Griffin stooped down, planting an unnecessary kiss on Kyra's forehead, then raced into the trees. The other men trailed in a single-file line with Griffin as their obvious commanding officer. Kyra tried to lunge after him, but I grabbed her wrist.

"Please, please." I met her vicious eyes and lowered my wall, letting her feel how desperate my plea was to keep her alive.

Shock and disbelief strained between her eyebrows. "That pull you feel toward me isn't real," her voice shook in confusion, "it's just the Link."

I threw a gust of guilt at her, showing what I experienced when Wes disappeared. I hadn't kept him safe. My entire purpose in life revolved around my son, and I had failed. With his big blue eyes, I shoved an image of Landon at her, and she finally nodded in understanding.

Only then did I rush off after Griffin, praying to the goddess above that Kyra knew of some underground tunnel. I needed her alive, not just to bring Wes back. Her safety felt as necessary as the blood in my veins.

I ran. Sprinting toward the unknown, frigid wind whipped my face, and snow fell harder, faster. The Dravians ahead were slowing their pace and hiding behind trees, pointing their weapons at the sky. They could turn on me at a moment's notice in revenge for destroying their barrier.

Panting, I stopped a few feet behind Griffin and whispered, "Hey, can Kyra still feel our pain if we're injured?"

"Shhh!" His venomous eyes remained trained on the sky, his nostrils flared wide and alert.

If any injury Griffin sustained in this battle would threaten Kyra, I'd have to keep him out of harm's way. "Give me a weapon."

Griffin's gaze darted to mine for a moment, then he whipped a dagger from his belt loop and laid it in my hand. The forest held its breath.

Then, it started. Giant chunks of white shot like cannons as if the clouds were chucking snowballs. *Smack!* A huge sphere of white knocked into one Dravian man so hard that he stumbled from behind a tree. Scrambling, the man righted himself, crouching behind the trunk. That wasn't natural snowfall.

Smack!

A massive globe of snow blasted onto Griffin's back. He tripped forward, and just as I tried to catch him, a chord wrapped around my wrist like a snake tongue and lurched me forward. I dug my heels into the snow, and snow caked my face.

Behind me, more thundering *smack* sounds were followed by even louder grunts. Screams filled the air. One by one, Dravians fell. *Thump, thump.*

My heart beat a million beats a second as I reached for the tree's root and held on tight. The yank of the chord on my wrist popped out my entire shoulder. I screamed out in pain. It dragged me, ripping out my joint from the socket. Terrified that my pain mirrored our Link, I sent her a message.

Kyra, can you feel that?

Silence.

I struggled to free myself. Snow piled down the back of my sweater, and cold leaked into my boots. Dravians writhed by me, struggling in the snow, all entangled in electrical cords on any exposed body part: their ankles, knees, wrists, or necks.

Finally, I managed to grab my dagger and slash the electrical rope. The coils snapped off. Free!

"Griffin?" I hollered among the chaos of bodies being hoisted away.

A tingle of Magik twisted in my Circle—not enough. I needed my power to return and fast.

My chest burned, and each breath came heavily, so I crouched behind a tree. Ventus creatures blended into the blizzard, forming a line in front of their riders. All the female Ordulls had a strange contraption on their chests, like a vest with a long rope that extended out from the center. Each was wheeling in a Dravian villager like a fish on a hook.

In the distance, Zeph seemed to lead their charge. My temples throbbed, and cuss words scratched at my throat to holler at her. Traitorous bitch. I squinted. Her mouth moved fast, but I couldn't read her lips from this distance.

Some Ordull women wore rare guns, but their orders were probably to bring Mystiers back alive. Zeph pushed up her glasses, then pointed to the treetops where contraptions were launching ginormous snowballs. The soldiers launched more cords. At least ten shot out. More Dravians collapsed and screamed as they were lugged across the white terrain.

Long lines marred the snow where their bodies were dragged. Some managed to free themselves. The second they did, a zap shocked them into paralysis. They lay flat on the ground, chests still moving but with glassy eyes fixated on the sky.

"Griffin?" I whispered through the chaos.

"Shh!" A strong hand pulled me up.

I whirled around. Angry scratches marked Griffin's face, one dripping blood down his neck. Snow and twigs were all stuck deep in his hair, and half his shirt was torn off, exposing his chest. A shiver rocked my spine, observing how cold he'd be.

"We have to retreat." I scanned the trees behind him, searching for the safest route to Kyra.

"I can't leave my people," he said with certainty. There was no room for persuasion.

"So, you'd abandon her?"

Griffin grabbed my collar and shoved me against the tree. The bark skidded against my back as the murderous spark in his eye dared me to bite back.

My fist was still clutched around the dagger. I raised it slowly and angled the blade right to his neck. Griffin didn't flinch, though I could slit his throat in one movement. His jaw clenched so tight I could hear his teeth cracking. We were so close I could see every brown speckle and fleck on his irises, his pupils growing larger by the moment.

"I'll go to her alone, then," I said, "It'll give me some time to show her my dagger."

Griffin growled like a fuckin' bear.

"Seriously, man? Get your hands off me."

Another soft flick of energy spiked my tattoo, and I focused on it, hoping to draw more strength. His eyes widened again, showing he felt it too. If I distracted him for a bit more time to keep him away from the fight, it might give our Magik enough time to charge back up.

"I'm not leaving my men behind this time." Griffin's voice was spiked with venom.

"This time? Interesting…" I whispered. "That sounds like a story I could pull out of Kyra's memories some night in the future when we're looking for a quick laugh."

Griffin's spiteful eyes burst with fury.

"I know you won't hurt me…just in case it hurts her too," I said.

"You're the one hurting her by showing up here." Griffin spun away, darting toward his friends. Right before I was about to run back to the village, a piercing ringing sound screwed its way into my brain. I dropped to my knees. My hands clamped over my ears.

The ringing stabbed me so hard that I cringed and rolled over, looking for its source. If Griffin just died, maybe his end was the agony I felt through the joined Link. Doubtful. I'd never get so lucky.

I finally spotted him through the chaos. A little bit away, Griffin's eyes churned with panic. His fingers mirrored mine, blocking his earlobes from the sound.

Kyra.

We shared a knowing, terrified look—one moment of union. Kyra needed us. We both jumped to our feet. Griffin was faster. Stronger like a damned action hero on steroids. I sped after him. The terrible sound died to a constant high-pitch hum; either that or my ears were permanently broken.

Griffin bounded over the snow like a leopard, dodging the sporadic wires shooting from the Ordulls' vests.

I flew over the snow, barely registering a terrible scream. Sweat pooled on my neck. Frantic breathing and fear overtook any other sensation.

Kyra? Kyra!

Silence on her end still, but my tattoo started to sing with a steady beat of power. *A thump, thump* of Magik. Then absence. *Thump, thump* of Magik. Absence.

"Kyra..." I spoke into the wind. "I'm coming."

Silence. What if that intense scream I felt was her final moment?

Griffin sprinted faster, harder, leaving me behind. I followed his tracks as the forest turned into a maze. Trunks whizzed by in brown blurs. I knew Griffin wouldn't see the entire clearing yet like I could, but he must smell the copper blood.

Far ahead, crazed ventus creatures swooped low, ripping the roofs off Draven treehouses, breaking the wooden flooring to bits, and clawing at the doors of dens.

Not all Dravians had gone into hiding. A few remained outside with spears pointed at the majestic white beasts, aiming for their riders. A weapon soared up, spearing an enemy making her fall from her venti, her chest impaled straight through with blood pooling under her body. The Dravians weren't surrendering, but their Magik still hadn't returned. They were losing.

A venti dove. Wires shot out from an Ordull vest and wrapped around another Dravian. It yanked the poor soul into the air. The Dravians lost yet another fighter. The gap in their formation showed golden hair sprawled over the snow. At the center of the huddle, a figure lay flat, motionless. My heart hammered. I already knew who it was.

I gasped.

"Griffin!" I pointed Kyra out, redirecting his focus to where boots were protectively rounding her body.

We sped forward, but before we reached Kyra's side, she staggered to her hands and knees in the snow, then rose. Determined. Relentless. I had to keep her safe. Power charged in my Circle. Her hands outstretched to the attackers. Flames spurted out pathetically, then flickered to the snow.

Wait! The closer my body was to hers, the stronger my power sang, ready to cyclone into a mass. I ran violently. Forcefully. Arms pumping and legs throbbing. Another venti plunged straight for her.

"Kyra!"

The venti screeched again, its rider egging it on.

Kyra raised both hands, hot red sparks teasing from them, but it was pointless. Our Magik wasn't fully recovered. She didn't have enough. None of us did. My stupid-ass grenade ruined it all. I pushed my legs, upping my speed. An electric cord whipped free and zoomed straight toward Kyra.

In slow motion, it shot like an arrow toward her. At the last second, Griffin shoved Kyra aside. She fell into the snow. The coil wrangled Griffin's neck, then his torso. Kyra screamed.

The cord wrapped Griffin tightly, head to toe. Kyra crawled frantically but not fast enough.

The cord lifted Griffin airborne and tossed him onto the venti, strapping him down. The venti flew higher. Higher. Faster. Kyra's panic seared through our Link.

Griffin disappeared into the blizzard.

Then our Magik zapped on with full force. Without wasting a moment, Kyra's hands lit the damned air on fire. Power whooshed so rapidly through me that I stumbled back into a den's wall. My tattoo scorched, and my wind Magik joined hers. Together, we shot balls of fire into the sky. All the remaining ventus cried and retreated.

Draven was safe. But Griffin was gone.

And Kyra screamed. And screamed. And screamed. She dropped to her knees, tears flowing down her cheeks. Her agony ripped me to pieces, and I knew there was no turning back from here. I'd do anything to make her smile again.

6

KYRA

My throat was raw from screaming. Panic consumed me. I lowered what little remained of my mental wall to speak to Jadox and reassure him that I'd follow him.

Jay, are you okay?

Silence.

Jay, answer me.

Nothing.

Jay! Fight them. Get free!

Silence.

Come back to me!

Someone was shaking my shoulders with two hands. I snapped my eyes open to Isaac's sweaty, dirt-smeared face.

"Kyra, we need to hide. They'll come back for you," he said, terror in his voice.

"No, we're going after Jay!" My eyes lingered on the remaining Dravians, all panting with lowered weapons. They all backed away, shaking their heads.

Claire spoke softly, "Griffin gave us orders not to follow if something like this happened."

"What? I don't care. Let's go get him!" Every muscle in my body tensed.

"We made a vow," Claudia added.

Throbbing pulsed in my temples, and the world spun until Isaac snuck his fingers through mine. The warmth of his skin shocked me compared to the freezing temperature surrounding us. Snowflakes fell on his long eyelashes as his concerned gray eyes narrowed.

"We'll make a plan after we get you safe," he promised.

"I don't matter! Jay matters." I pulled away and jogged through the crimson-stained snow where an Ordull woman lay dead.

Isaac trailed after me, step for step, regardless of my increasing speed. Different scenarios gutted my mind.

Jay falling off the back of the venti to his death. Jay laying on a cold, metal table, screaming out as President Syvonne Stirk sticks needles into him. Jay locked in a cell, cold and alone. Jay strapped to an electric chair. His brown eyes glistening with unshed tears.

My heart rammed so hard that my chest physically hurt. I stopped and doubled over, vomiting all over Gemm's garden. Placing a hand to my stomach, with the other braced on the stone den wall, I sucked in a deep breath. One. Two. Three. Then another. Every inch of me trembled.

"Kyra, you need to sit down." Isaac's hands gently wrapped around my waist and guided me inside Gemm's den as the room swayed.

Her apothecary bottles, shelves of spell books, and pots stacked high all zoomed in and out of focus like a dream. Without realizing it, I was sitting on a wooden bench, folded in half, my head between my legs. A strong hand rubbed slow circles on my back as a wet nose nudged my forehead. Chocolate licked my ear. Tears pooled, and I strained not to cry. My hands found her brown fur, and I stroked her soft head lovingly. The way she stared at me broke my heart in two.

"It's okay. I'll bring him back, girl." I held back my sob.

I'm sorry, Jay.

The absence of the tug of his thoughts and feelings felt surreal like I had never lived a day in my past without being attached to my Jadox.

Isaac cleared his throat next to me, then a glass of water appeared as he held out his hand. "Please drink, love."

I raised the glass to my lips, not taking my gaze off him because each time our eyes met, a tingle of power scorched my Circle, growing stronger each time. I needed that fuel to recharge. I'd have to use my Link with Isaac to free Jay. Alone, I wasn't strong enough to face Stirk's army, but we could accomplish more together. I simply needed to convince my "enemy" to help me.

I gulped down the rest of the water, and as I set it down, the glass toppled over the table. It shattered to pieces, raining tiny crystals into my shin. I didn't even have to close my eyes or wave over the injury—just staring at Isaac healed the scrapes it caused. At least I knew I could still borrow powers from Jay, so he was alive somewhere.

With each passing moment, my Link with Isaac felt stronger. But that didn't matter because I chose Jay. I loved Jay. I wanted Jay.

My dizziness decreased when I locked onto Isaac's eyes, and raw energy surged into my core. The sensation was so intense that I froze. "Has our Link felt this strong for you before?"

His warm breath tickled my neck. "No, love," he purred. "Something is changing. I feel it too."

"Do you think Jay is…."

Isaac shook his head. "Griffin will be fine. We'll save that soldier, one way or another." Isaac's smile was evident in his words. "But on our adventure, tell me when you're ready to kiss me." His voice was as smooth as silk, almost calming my fury with his words.

A strange rush flooded my ears when his voice claimed my mind like a Magikal siren. Isaac had said, "we." Was he really going to risk his safety to help me find Jadox? I didn't even have to convince or trick him.

His fingertips played piano keys on the front of my neck.

While swallowing hard, his fingers rose and fell as my throat bobbed. I moved my hand atop his, unwilling to break eye contact, and shifted his hand away. "You'll help me free Jay?"

"Yes, my love, because you are mine. And what you want, I will support."

Isaac was right. His gray eyes solidified what I already knew. I belonged to him in some strange way, and he belonged to me. I'd never admit it aloud because even if we were meant to be, I loved Jay and only Jay.

I shoved a finger into his solid chest. "I am using you for your Magik, and after Jay is free, I'll try to bring back Wes once more. Then I never want to see you again."

His devilish smile boiled my blood hotter than imaginable. "If you say so."

Before I set off on this rescue mission, there were a few things I needed to take care of. First: Landon. I stood, and my hair whirled from the wind blowing through the den's window. I walked towards the trap door where Landon was supposed to be hiding. Gritting my teeth, I crouched and pulled on the lever of the trapdoor by my foot. Darkness led to a pair of little eyes, another, and a third.

"Auntie?" Landon's sweet voice called from the bunker.

"Yes, it's me. Come out, little guy."

Landon, Alaska, and Gemm all climbed out into the room.

Alaska disappeared into thin air like a lightning bolt while I checked Landon's body for any marks. Not a scratch. Gemm stooped to clean up the glass I'd dropped earlier. "Once, there was a brokenness that couldn't be healed."

Who was broken? Who couldn't be healed? My hand tapped my pocket where the bottle of cyanide was tucked safely. Had Jay kept his suicide poison? Would the president find it? How much torture would Jay endure before he considered using it?

"We need to know what's going on in the media." Isaac tapped his s-watch and projected a live news stream on the den wall.

"...Despite the death of two soldiers, President Stirk is claiming this as a victory against the witches. Our army captured ten from a northern village called Draven, believed to be the last known location of Kyra Kozelski—felon, mass murderer, terrorist, and dangerous witch. Do not engage with this criminal; she is lethal and unstable. A specialist team has been ordered to obtain this so-called Cursed One. This specific witch, as you know, will be the answer to our problems. When found, she will return all of our males. Remember, electricity is your greatest line of defense against these creatures to incapacitate them. Stay in well-populated cities."

He sighed and turned off his watch. "We won't be able to go to The Crooked Chateau to free Griffin if that's even where they're taking him. It'll be too heavily guarded," Isaac said. "We need a plan, then a backup plan."

"Why is *that* place her headquarters? It doesn't make sense to use an old gallery for a government security hold," I whispered.

"So many other places were bombed. Because it's in the middle of the capital in Andersonville, it gives the president a large, central residence in Lodesa."

Alaska popped back into the room, yanking Zeph along with her. "This is the only surviving Mystier I found. There are no more living threats in the village or the woods."

I used all restraint not to rush the murderer and choke the bitch to death. Zeph. The woman who had killed Hallie was now responsible for Jadox's capture. I marched to her, nose to nose. "Is this what you wanted? You betrayed your fellow Mystiers for what? What purpose?"

Zeph glanced at Isaac, her long ringlets blocking her bruised face.

"Look. At. Me."

She did, then said calmly, "I came to warn you. Those weren't my people. They were chasing me."

"I don't believe you."

"You're not special, Kyra," Zeph snarled. "Just because some call you the 'Golden One' doesn't mean anything."

Isaac's energy curled into a ball of anger next to me, but he didn't move a muscle.

I turned to Alaska, wishing we were better friends at that moment. "Are you willing to teleport Landon to a safer place?"

Alaska hesitated, and I waited for her rebuttal and request to fight for her brother by my side.

"Please. You're the only one who I can trust with Landon."

She sucked in a breath and nodded. "I can't transport them at the same time without the Draven Emerald working. Stay here, so I can move Gemm first, then Landon."

We both ignored Zeph's whining under Isaac's relentless grip as Alaska started collecting food into a backpack from the corner of the den.

"But, if we are to be hiding for goddess knows how long, I don't want to deal with *that* one's attitude." Alaska gestured to Zeph. "So, take the prisoner with you and use her as leverage, bait, or kill her, I don't care, but I'm not babysitting her." Alaska laid a hand on Gemm's shoulder. "Are you ready?"

Before they disappeared, Gemm's wrinkles formed along her frown as she said, "There once was a boy, and not all was as it seemed."

I held her hand. "Gemm, I don't know what that warning means. Can you just tell me?"

She smiled faintly and ran a hand down the side of my face. "The Gold fire runs in your heart from another."

"Another? Who?" I asked.

Alaska huffed loudly, and they both disappeared. Chocolate barked, reminding me that we didn't have much time. Syvonne's army could return at any moment with reinforcements, but what about the rest of Draven? How would the rest of the people escape?

I kneeled in front of Landon. Even though he rarely made eye contact, his bright blues seemed to absorb my feelings without a word. While staring out of the den's window, Landon pulled the keychain of pictures from his back pocket. He pointed to the image of Jay we had recently added to his options.

I fought back the tears. "He went away to take care of something, but I'll bring him back."

Landon pointed to the image of me, then a heart symbol.

My chest clamped tight. "I love you too, buddy." I knew better than to try and touch or hug him, so instead, I bit my lip to keep from crying. "Listen to Alaska and Gemm and be good. I'll be back soon."

Alaska whizzed back into the room alone. "You never bought a new s-watch, Kyra. How am I supposed to communicate with you?"

"Send any messages through Isaac."

"I don't trust him," Alaska said.

He shifted on his feet. "I can hear you."

"And clearly, he's a certified genius," Alaska growled.

"For now, it's Isaac or nothing, but stay off comms unless it's an emergency," I said, "We don't know what's being intercepted."

Alaska eyed Isaac. "Kyra, be careful with that one. He's not right for you."

"You don't think Jay is right for me, either." Despite the seriousness of the situation, a smile crept across my face. "Alaska, you *hate* me."

She quickly tucked a paper from her pocket and shoved it into my hand. "No, you're as close to a sister as I'll ever have."

An image of Hallie flooded my mind. I was losing everyone I loved. Quickly, Alaska pushed her watch against Isaac's to obtain his number, then disappeared with Landon, pulling my heartstrings along with them.

"And then there were three," said Zeph.

Chocolate shoved against my knee. "Four. I'm not leaving her behind."

"That'll be a sight to see... you trying to get past armed guards with a dumb dog by your side." Zeph laughed.

"Shut up. And tell me what you know about the attack." I grabbed a fistful of her curly hair.

"Ouch! Quit it," Zeph said. "I don't know anything. I just came to get you to sever the bond with Isaac."

"No." He stepped between us. "That's not an option."

"Why isn't it an option?" she asked.

"The only known way to sever a Link is for one of us to kill the other."

"No way. There must be some other answer," Zeph said nervously. "Maybe it's written in the Unetlo Book."

"Do you happen to have that huge book in your bra?" I asked.

"Ha-fuckin-ha-ha," Zeph snapped. "No, *Golden* Girl. Surh-Sig stole it during the last battle."

Shit, that didn't help our situation. Luckily, I had many of the Unetlo Book's spells stored in my mind like a glossary, even if I didn't know what half of them were for. I started packing, choosing which items would keep me alive the longest.

"I've read all of the Unetlo Book except for three ancient scripts that didn't have a translation." Isaac rubbed the short beard on his stupidly handsome face—a beard I despised.

"Maybe I can interpret the last three," I mumbled while grabbing soup. "My enhancement is a connection to ancient spells."

"Maybe, but we don't know where Surh-Sig is. However, we *do* know where Moroka is. And she will be able to answer one question for each of us. Pick what you want to know the most and be clear with your wording."

"I'm gonna go change," I said, contemplating our options. "Keep Zeph inside the den."

"We need to work on your please and thank you's, love."

I slipped into the small adjacent room with Chocolate at my heels and clicked the door shut behind me. My knees wobbled, and I sank to the ground, my back scraping against the wall. I clenched my teeth and screamed into my sleeve, blocking any sound from escaping.

Jay, where are you?

Silence.

Please answer me so I can find you.

Our connection felt empty. Destroyed. Sliced. But I knew it wasn't possible because if Jadox had died, there was no way I could still be breathing, thinking, and moving. I'd definitely know. Though, his essence had already faded away to less than a drop. A faint ghost. I kicked my boot heel against a bedframe post. *Damn it. Damn it.*

"What should I do? Where should I go?"

Chocolate responded by laying her head on my lap.

"He shouldn't have sacrificed himself for me." I ruffled her ears. "What will they do to him, girl?"

I still had choices: go to The Crooked Chateau or Moroka, the Blood Maiden. The worst option would be sitting stagnant.

"Okay, okay, I got this." I pushed off the floor and tore off my clothes, letting them fall into a puddle on the floor.

A winter breeze blew through the window, making my naked skin shiver as I walked to the closet.

A knock rapped on the bedroom door. "Kyra?"

"Hold on a sec."

"Kyra, we can't stay here any longer." Isaac's voice was syrupy-thick through the barrier. "Please hurry, love."

Since I wasn't in my den, I pulled on one of Alaska's brown shirts and black yoga pants. She was taller than me, but our hips were about the same size. One of Jay's sweatshirts was draped over the back of the bed frame. I grabbed it and shoved it to my nose, inhaling his woody scent.

"I'll find you, Jay," I whispered to myself.

Fully dressed again, with three of Alaska's daggers hanging from my hip, I crossed the bedroom, unsure where we'd head next. My boot slipped, and I skidded into Chocolate. She jumped up with her tail wagging, thinking I had begun a wrestling match.

A folded piece of paper fluttered on the floor. "Alaska's note!"

Except when I unrolled it, the handwriting wasn't Alaska's. The top half was ripped off, and the bottom read:

Alaska,

Caspian made a negotiation with President Stirk. So now he is free. Avoid Caspian at all costs. He is headed straight for Kyra. Stay far away from the Cursed One at all costs.

I'm hoping more memories will return in bits and pieces eventually. It's very confusing, but I'll find you.

Love always,

(Except when I couldn't remember you. I know you laughed at that)
Paola

I balled the note into a wad and shoved it in my pocket as questions swirled in my mind. Who was Paola? Was Caspian the same guy that was on TV? What negotiation did he make with the President? Why would he chase after me?

My tattoo burned with a warning, and the forest outside the window was filled with an eerie calm. After putting the backpack on, it weighed me down, hindering any fast movements. We needed a way to travel fast. The whole point of going to the Chateau was to ask the prisoner what he knew about my family. But he's no longer there, and our enemy could've taken Jay anywhere. It'd be a waste of time to hunt aimlessly through the hundreds of prisoners; Stirk might detain Jay. Moroka was the surest bet.

"There's no going back now, Chocolate."

She sneezed, making me smile. I hovered my hand over the bedroom door handle, swallowing any fear.

I swung the door open to see Isaac stuffing a bag with supplies. When I met his eyes, the fact that I had more of an ally than just Chocolate hit me hard. He was on my team–for now.

"I'll go with you to Moroka since she will tell us how to free Jay, but I won't stop at saving only him. I'm going to free *all* the Mystiers that the president has captured."

Isaac nodded and walked to me with such confidence my breath hitched. "There's one more reason I want to go see Moroka."

7

ISAAC

The snowfall finally stopped.

"There's more to my secret, love. I didn't tell you everything before."

Kyra stared at me, questions soaring in her eyes.

"Your real father, Brent, is still alive. He's President Stirk's prisoner."

"How do you know this?" Her voice was soft, delicate.

"I'm Vayuian's badass librarian. It's my job to know things."

She tilted her head, eyes narrowing. "You mean you have spies."

Shrugging, I leaned in close. "Kyra, I know this is a big deal for you. We don't have to be sarcastic around the clock. I know I should've told you right when I found out, but—"

She turned on her heels and marched outside into the clearing.

I chased after her, crunching through the snow. "Kyra, you must have a thousand questions."

"No. My mom must've had a good reason for not telling me about him. Brent never tried to contact me, so I don't care."

"What if he also has a Golden tattoo?"

Her gait altered, but only someone who had memorized her

movements would've noticed. "Jay is my priority over a father who abandoned me and over you too. Don't expect otherwise."

I cleared my throat and whistled. This time, Tawoli finally appeared high above, swooping down to us. She landed gracefully in the packed snow. Desperately, Zeph hopped on her back and nudged Tawoli forward in a lousy attempt at escape, but my venti wouldn't follow our prisoner's orders.

"I'm going to find Jay," Kyra said after rolling her eyes at Zeph's failed attempt. "Are you coming or not?"

A flash of something I couldn't pinpoint rushed through her eyes. If only she'd let down her wall again, we'd be unstoppable. Until then, I'd have to keep guessing her thoughts.

"Come, Chocolate." Kyra tightened the straps on her backpack as she walked toward Tawoli.

"The dog stays."

"What? No, she's the last piece I have left of Jay."

Her gaze met mine, and I wanted to erase the hesitancy living in the creases of her face. "Believe me, the dog is safer here. Moroka will probably demand her as some sort of sacrifice."

"If Chocolate dies while we're gone, I'll kill you." Kyra jumped on Tawoli, sitting in the front, deliberately separating herself enough from Zeph that it was implied I'd have to sit between them for the ride. "Can we leave this traitor here too? Maybe Chocolate will get hungry enough and eat Zeph. She hasn't even fought back. It seems like she wants to come with us. So, we should probably do the opposite."

"I'd rather keep her where I can track her," Isaac said. "Plus, she might have insider info that'll be helpful later—"

Zeph cut in, "Don't believe him, girl. Isaac fucked me a few nights ago and wants me around for more."

Heat rushed to my face as Kyra stiffened. Inhaling on a prayer to Divinity above, I slid between them, straddling Tawoli. As I scooted closer to Kyra, my inner thighs cradled her ass in the worst and best possible way. My cock briefly tightened, and a shudder ran through my body. Of course, Zeph latched her arms around my waist and snuggled her chest to my back. We should've tied her up.

The tension between the two women could crack an iceberg in half. Zeph had killed Kyra's sister, and there was no way Kyra would ever forgive her. I dug my heels in Tawoli's side and steered her south to Galudi Cove.

The dog barked until we were finally out of earshot. Only then did Kyra's body relax into mine. Soon, the treetops sped below as we soared through muggy clouds. The wind blew on my face, but my body stayed warm from being sandwiched between the two women. I should've offered to ride in front of Kyra to block the stinging wind. Her eyes were probably tearing up.

"Are you okay?" I asked.

I don't like heights, she admitted hesitantly. *Please distract me.*

Surprised by her admission, I gave her waist a little squeeze. Her fingers tapped a little beat on my thumb, almost stealing my breath. Was she starting to trust me?

"I fly daily," I said, hoping she could hear me over the wind. "I'll never get bored of it. I used to take Wes once a week. We stayed low, though, just in case he fell."

Show me how Wes responded when he got his tattoo.

Kyra let go of Tawoli's feathers and leaned into my chest. I was surprised she remembered that Wes had received his tattoo early. Somewhere deep down, the woman cared about me. I inhaled the citrusy scent that laced her golden hair. Her encouragement was all I needed. Focusing on the past, I fixated on one memory from over a year ago.

My sneakers skid over loose pebbles as I run to Vayu's dome barrier in search of my son. My calves burn, and my feet thump on the gravel, more like flying instead of running. A pair of Wes's little blue sneakers lay beside a tree trunk outside the barrier.

The thrum of my power slices through me. Widening my stance, I inhale a deep breath and raise my arms straight to the sky, desperate for help, but notice a flapping piece of paper. Wes's sloppy handwriting covers the note.

> Went to see Mom. Don't be too mad. I'll do extra laundry tomorrow to make up for it.
>
> P.S. You didn't tell me the tattoo would burn me. You Liar!

The memory disappeared as quickly as Wes had vanished from his bed that fateful night.

You must hate me for making him disappear.

I sighed at Kyra's thoughts, then whispered in her ear, "Some days I wish I did, but I've seen your past and can no longer fault you. I often wonder if I had met you before you made that wish if..."

Don't say it.

Another layer of her mental wall dropped. Kyra's essence swarmed with heat, raw authenticity, and passion. If only Zeph weren't here. I needed to change the subject because otherwise, nothing good would come from this conversation.

When we Linked, you gave me some of your weather powers, but I can't control them yet. If we have time...will you teach me?

The vulnerability in her question sent a tingle to my tattoo. All I wanted was to wrap my arms around her tighter.

"Of course, love. What else do you want?"

When Tawoli swerved to the left, Kyra drummed a beat on my hand, *tap tap tap.*

I need to free all the prisoners. Can you promise to help me after we save Jay?

The mention of Griffin made my muscles tighten. "I'm always here."

Why did I ever hate you before?

I laughed. "Good question."

Oh, I remember. Because you're an ass. And because the girl you're fucking, killed Hallie.

Her silent bitterness ran deep through our bond, and I couldn't tell if it was jealousy or grief. Was she just pretending to be sweet to manipulate me?

"I'm sorry for what happened to your sister. I should've been able to prevent that. I leaned my chin on her shoulder, ignoring Zeph's pulls for attention behind me.

If I hadn't been so reckless and selfish....

I moved my hand to the front of her neck and slowly tilted it to the side. "Don't ever speak badly about yourself in front of me."

Or what? You'll punish me?

I wished I could see her face. I pictured her one eyebrow rising and her lips hovering a few inches from mine, taunting me with their fullness. I wanted to give myself to her, drown in her. But it was an impossible desire.

I released the pressure of my hand and spoke into the wind that pierced my cheeks. "Kyra, know your strength. You're so powerful that you could do anything you set your mind to."

A few minutes of silence passed. Below were miles of Ordull cities, vast farmland, then another cluster of buildings. At least the temperature grew warmer as we flew south to Galudi Cove.

How much further?

"If Tawoli keeps up this speed, we will be at the cliffside in an hour. You'll probably see the lighthouse first; it's seven stories."

What lighthouse?"

"On the beach at the edge of Vuldow."

Vuldow? Her body went rigid. *Are you crazy? We can't fly through a nuclear wasteland.*

"It's not nuclear?" I asked, "What do you mean?"

Her shoulders sloped, and I could almost see her wheels turning as her position shifted in front of me.

"Isaac." Zeph poked my back. "Isaac, what are you whispering in her ear?"

I didn't want to talk to Zeph.

"How can you just forget everything we had and flirt with her?" Zeph snapped.

"How could you betray our kind?" You put us all at risk by leading the army to Draven." I had to turn my head because of the wind.

"I thought you wanted—" Her lips were so close to my ear.

"Don't act like you know me, Zee."

"That Cursed girl will destroy—" Her words were thankfully chopped by the wind gusting by.

Ahead, a shadow cast a gloomy darkness, spreading as far as the horizon.

"Moroka was last seen on the cliffside near the lighthouse." I pointed in front of us.

But...Vuldow has been abandoned since The Fall. If no one lives out there, who saw her?

The few remaining Elidi often roamed Vuldow and used the run-down area as a haven. They'd sometimes report suspicious activity to the leaders in each village as a trade for supplies. I smiled at Kyra's never-ending curiosity and wondered if she'd figure out the rest for herself.

The steady wind blew her golden hair in my face, and I couldn't help but savor her scent. Divinities, above. I was a fool for pining. She didn't want me.

"Have you thought about the question you'll ask Moroka?" I asked Kyra.

I've...narrowed it down.

My chest tightened, feeling her hesitancy. "You'll need to be very specific when you ask."

I know. I'm...thinking.

I could ask Moroka if Gemm's prophecy to Kyra meant me instead of Griffin. Or how to keep all Vayuians safe from President Stirk. Or where the crystal necklace was hidden. But none of those compared to my need to know for certain how to bring Wes back to me. I had to save him, and I'd never give up.

The air itself shifted in a thick, sickening wave, and my Circle sparked to life in a warning. Now that Kyra possessed some of my weather powers, I'd have to be prepared for any type of accidental storm until she mastered her new Magik. In the fog, lightning shocked the sky and set a building far below on fire.

"Shit!" Kyra pointed her hands toward the expanding flames but quickly withered in on herself in frustration. "I'm sorry. I must be nervous. Isaac, can you get rid of it?"

"You can do it. Focus."

More heavy fog rolled in with purpose. She growled, giving up. "I can't see anything."

Tawoli dipped lower through another mass of clouds, and mist still packed the air when we emerged on the other side. The density suffocated every breath. Even my enhanced eyesight was partially blocked by the heavy haze.

"This weather is…weird," Zeph mumbled. "It's so dark, but the sun hasn't set."

"I don't know how to control the weather," she grunted. "Or how to fix this."

"Maybe it's not you, Kyra. This land is haunted. There have been multiple claims of mystical events happening around here."

After a few minutes of silent riding, the scent of salt water tickled my nostrils. We were close.

"I can hear the ocean waves far off." Kyra angled her head back toward me as she spoke.

Tawoli dove lower still, making us all lean forward, clutching a fistful of feathers. Lower. Lower. My pet stayed quiet as if knowing the possible dangers of our arrival. At first, I half-expected to be shot out of the sky by a gun, cannon, or electrical weapon, but no living threat moved between the skeleton buildings. Squinting, I knew neither woman could yet see the ghost city's shadowy remains. They'd share my reaction soon, all the hairs rising on my arms from the horrific view.

Destruction layered every surface, buildings burnt to a crisp muddled with piles of bones laying in the streets, and old gas-fueled vehicles abandoned in alleys. Charred tree trunks scattered the ground of a deserted park. As if we were characters in a thriller movie, a sinister swing teetered back and forth in the nonexistent breeze on a playground. This was an entire civilization forsaken because Elana Elidi had Linked with a man from Cydon long ago, exposing our kind to the Ordulls. No one deserved this fate—Mystier or Ordull.

A loud, high-pitched scream pierced the smog. Quickly, Tawoli reared in the air.

Isaac...um, exactly what kind of demon is Moroka?

"It's okay, love. I'm here. We're stronger together."

So, you don't know? I thought the epic librarian master knew everything.

"If I knew everything, I'd know how to get you to kiss me." I rubbed a single fingertip over the back of Kyra's neck.

You're trying to distract me from our impending doom.

"Is it working?"

Tawoli slowed and landed on a dead branch. It snapped under her weight, and she flapped her massive wings until we landed safely on the ground.

Zeph slid off Tawoli fast and bolted ahead, almost disappearing into the thick fog. Still, I kept an eye on her shadow as she ran through the deserted streets.

"She won't get far," I said.

Kyra shrugged. "It's better to let her get eaten first by whatever is out there. I'll be able to hear her screams, so we know which direction *not* to walk."

Chuckling, I slid off Tawoli's feathery back and stretched my legs in a quick squat, thighs burning from the long ride. When I held out a hand to help Kyra down, she actually accepted it.

"Wow, Prince Evil has manners?"

"Until I'm in the bedroom." I winked, and she nudged me playfully.

Raw desire zapped through my tattoo, and I needed to inhale deeply to center myself.

"That's never gonna happen, Isaac."

"A man can dream."

"It's just the Link." Kyra laid one hand on her chest and one on mine. "This feeling isn't real."

"So, you admit it, then. You feel *something*?"

Her amber eyes flickered with bustling energy. "That's not what I meant. You don't even know me."

"Let's change that."

A battering sound in the mist ahead was followed by Zeph's yell. I raced forward, passing by neglected buses and storefronts with broken windows. Almost tripping on a cracked hoverboard on the sidewalk, I tugged Kyra's wrist to ensure she didn't fall. My boots skidded on the pavement underfoot as if the entire city had been coated with sand and dust.

"Help!" Zeph howled.

A flurry of crows darted over Zeph's balled position against a brick building. They attacked from all angles, pecking and stabbing her back with their beaks.

"Isaac!" she hollered in a desperate plea.

Before my Magik strengthened in my Circle, a burst of fire ignited next to me and exploded from Kyra's fingers.

"Roll away!" Kyra commanded.

The fire engulfed the murderous crows. Some collapsed to the pavement, others flew straight up, but the few remaining stared at me through the fog. I was a Mystier of the sky and air; birds and I were always one and the same, but these were no ordinary crows. Their ebony eyes locked on mine and a death-toned caw pierced the thick air. The first thing I thought of was ₾sµwi Magik.

Both my hands stretched toward the assault as I shielded Kyra. The wind rushed from my fingertips. Moist air sucked it right up, stealing my powers. A sharp beak pecked my shoulder. Another stabbed my cheek. Crows charged forward in an ambush of black wings flying in each direction.

"Ow! Fuck!"

Flusters of black chaos slapped against my cheeks. I blocked my face while my heart raced.

"Move!" Kyra lunged forward.

A giant wall of fire hurled toward the beasts, and all at once, they dropped down dead. Singed feathers, broken bodies, and snapped crow necks all lay scattered on the road. I shuddered at the sight.

"Are you okay?" I placed both hands on Kyra's shoulders and scanned her body for scrapes and blood. "That was unnatural. I swear, birds love me."

"Of course. Why wouldn't they? Everyone lov...likes you." Her smile stretched wider than I'd seen it for a while. "I'm okay. But your face is bleeding, here, let me—"

Before I could respond, her soft touch grazed my temple. Her honey eyes sparkled at me with the intensity of embers as she stared up. I didn't dare move, didn't dare breathe. Studying her features, I memorized the few freckles on her tanned cheeks.

"Thank you, love." I brushed my lips to her forehead. "I never had the chance to ask if you still feel my pain. When those birds jabbed me, did they hurt you?"

"No." She shook her head gently. "A few weeks ago, a handy spell came to me and took care of that problem."

"Do you think that spell will fade over time?"

"How about we never find out? Let's just stay unharmed."

"Wanna heal me too, Golden Girl?" Zeph slowly pushed herself up from the ground, scratches dug into her face like deep trenches. Little drops of blood streaked down her neck.

"Nah, I'm good."

Zeph's eyes widened through her thick lenses, and I shrugged as we walked past her. "Come on, Zeph, you better stick with us in case Kyra needs to save your life again."

She huffed and stomped behind us like a dramatic teenager.

In silence, Kyra and I trekked next to each other toward the edge of the city. Hopefully, the lighthouse was still standing. We passed crosswalks painted in bird shit, overturned trash cans, ivy-covered buildings, overgrown bushes, and cracked pavement every other step. It was a miracle none of us had twisted an ankle.

"I'm exhausted. Can't we ride Tawoli again?" Zeph eventually broke the silence as the muggy sky shifted to a bloody maroon sunset.

"No." I didn't elaborate.

"Well, then, how much longer?" Zeph twirled her ringlets around a finger. "I'm hungry."

"Eat your hand," Kyra yelled over her shoulder.

I pointed to something I knew they couldn't see yet. "The lighthouse is straight ahead."

"How far?" Zeph's cranky drone was like nails on a chalkboard.

"Thirty more minutes." I stooped down in front of Kyra. "Hop on."

"Are you kidding me? I'm not riding you, Isaac. Not in this way or…any other."

I tapped her nose gently. "I bet you'll change your mind one day."

Instead, she whistled for Tawoli and jumped on her back. I sighed at her stubbornness as they galloped ahead, leaving Zeph and me to walk in awkward silence the rest of the way.

As the minutes ticked on, I stared at my s-watch, a thousand questions running through my head. How long would it take to return Wes? Where did the army take Griffin? What color were Kyra's panties? How much food had she packed? Why was I ever stupid enough to sleep with Zeph? Why didn't Kyra have a stronger reaction when I told her that her father was still alive? What flavor ChapStick did she wear?

Finally, we stood by Kyra near the crumbling lighthouse. Behind it, the cliff's edge dropped into the sea. The light at the top probably hadn't been functioning for years, but a large owl perched at the top, hooting into the smeared, foggy sky.

Kyra scooted closer to my side and whispered, "I can hear something moving around in there."

I jumped a bit when Zeph whispered on my other side, "Maybe it's another crow?"

The door at the base of the lighthouse clunked open. Zeph hid behind me as Kyra stepped forward. My heart pounded against my ribs, and adrenaline spiked my tattoo.

Instead of the Blood Maiden, a tall man in a tunic stepped out of the lighthouse door and waved. I recognized him immediately. His smile changed the shape of the scar lining the side of his jaw, completely appropriate in the ominous surrounding.

"That doesn't look like a demon." Kyra gripped my hand and tugged me forward, stride for stride.

"That's because he's not," I whispered.

"Who is he?" Kyra gasped and squeezed my hand. "Wait, that's President Stirk's prisoner…the one that was on the news."

A burst of energy yanked my Circle to life, and power thrummed in my core. "Yes, love, that is Caspian Arno of Cydon."

"What is he doing here?"

My skin crawled as I studied the long scar stretching from his temple, across his cheek, down to his chin. I met Caspian's deep blue eyes— eyes that held a thousand lies. "Let's go find out."

8

KYRA

Caspian's messy hair dripped onto his tunic as he strode toward us. Built like a swimmer, his shoulders were twice the size of his waist, and his hands looked like paddles. I wondered how he had gotten that jagged scar across his face.

The scent of saltwater wafted through the evening breeze, reminding me of Jay's enhancement. What other smells would Jadox experience if he was here? And why couldn't I feel him through our Link? I tried to send him a message again, but the only response was high-pitched sonic dolphin calls echoing from the waters on the other side of the cliff.

Isaac whispered, "We may be powerful together, but Caspian controls the sea. Don't use Magik here unless it's a matter of life or death. We won't win."

"Right on time, mate," said Caspian, his island accent even thicker than his brown hair. "Thanks for bringing the Golden One to me. Your reward is inside the lighthouse." He gestured to the old, cracked tower leaning over the cliffside.

Um, this guy had better be joking. As I gritted my teeth, I didn't dare take my eyes off Caspian's wretched grin. "Uh, excuse me?" The crashing of the waves must have clogged my acute hearing.

"Don't believe him. I didn't lead you into a trap." Isaac stepped closer; the power surging through our Link intensified. "He's a liar."

"Yet, you called yourself an expert liar once," I lowered my voice, though it probably didn't matter with how fast Caspian was approaching us.

"Isaac still is a liar, Ky. Can I call you Ky?" Caspian stuck out his web-like hand, and I only stared at it. "Well, I'll call you Ky, so hopefully, you don't mind. Welcome to Vuldow." His aqua-colored eyes shone with mischief, and the white flecks mirroring sand grains held secrets of buried treasure underneath. "Of course, it's not as extravagant since The Fall. I could use your help in reconstructing it... after we assassinate President Stirk."

"Wow, you get right to the point." I tapped a beat with my thumb, *ba-bum ba-bum*. The tempo quickened as Caspian turned his attention to Isaac. "But you can go retrieve your prize and head home to Vayu. But watch your back because I'll be campaigning for a new leader to replace your position."

"Stop threatening my...my...Isaac." I stomped forward, flailing both arms.

Since I didn't know what Isaac was to me, the command sounded weak. We hadn't spent much time together, but I already understood much more about him than I should have. Regardless of his arrogant mask, Isaac had a heart of gold. For now, we'd have to be a team against this new guy.

Lowering my walls, I connected with Isaac through the bond and sent him silent reassurance. We were Linked—teammates—like it or not.

"Where is the Blood Maiden?" I asked.

Caspian's collected features faltered briefly until a fresh smile replaced them—just as untrustworthy as the last. "So, you're here to see Moroka?" And you brought the mandatory sacrifice...good." His gaze flickered to Zeph hiding, unsuccessfully, apparently.

No matter how much I had come to trust Jay...each man still needed to redeem himself one at a time. Caspian was no different, and I wouldn't let him hurt any woman under my watch. When

Caspian moved toward Zeph, I shielded her, placing myself between them.

"Back off," I hissed.

Caspian peered at me so intently that I swear he grabbed the depths of my essence and yanked it out through my throat. "Would you rather Isaac be the sacrifice, then?" he asked.

"Leave them alone."

"Interesting…you like him," said Caspian as he cracked his knuckles. "Tell me, does it bother you that Isaac betrayed you for a jewel?"

"What jewel?" Isaac demanded.

"Don't play the good guy, man. It's too late. Go grab your crystal and get out of here."

Uncertainty zapped through my Circle. Next to me, Isaac brushed his hand against mine, shaking me from some hypnotic trance. "It's okay, love."

Caspian tilted his head to the side, changing the shape of his long scar. "Love? That's an interesting nickname for you, Ky."

My fingers singed with heat. "You haven't earned the right to give me a nickname. You don't know me." Flames flickered from my skin and sparked in the air as a warning.

"I know you better than you think," Caspian said. "Isn't that why you came here? To ask the Blood Maiden about your family, your roots?"

I paused…a moment too long. "No, move out of our way so I can find Moroka."

"She won't come until summoned." Caspian gazed at the setting sun through the fog, scarlets swirling with poisonous oranges above, an omen of what was to come.

He's lying. No one controls Moroka. We can't trust a word he says.

Take Zeph and Tawoli out of here. I'll talk to him. He doesn't like you, Isaac.

No one likes me.

That's not true.

Now isn't the time to flirt, love.

Oh, shut up.

A stream of Isaac's affection flowed straight to my core, calming and supporting me. Maybe he wasn't all that terrible. But Jay would never agree with that sentiment. Jay—I had to save Jay. It was time to focus.

"Why would Moroka come to *you?*" I asked.

"That's a story for another time." Caspian strolled to the edge of the cliff. "This could be entertaining. I wouldn't mind hearing Moroka's answers."

Caspian curled his long finger. Like a puppet, I followed his command and started walking straight toward him.

"Wait," Isaac said behind me.

"Stay where you are, mate," Caspian raised his voice for the first time, punctuated with a thick accent. "Don't make another move. I'm tired of you already. You betrayed one of your own for a jewel. You're disgusting."

"You've been given the wrong information."

"Do *not* test me."

Alone, I joined Caspian near the cliffside and gazed over at the foaming sea. White splashed and crashed into the stone cliff walls about ten feet below, showering my ankles with cool spray.

"What do you want?" I asked.

"You, Ky." One of Caspian's thick brown eyebrows arched like a dolphin's fin when he looked amused. "You're the only one powerful enough to kill Syvonne Stirk. We have to end this war, quickly, before more Mystiers suffer."

"I'm not killing anyone, especially a woman."

His blue-green eyes dug deep within me again. He absently rubbed his long scar while studying my every breath. I concentrated on my breathing and the meditation skills Alaska had taught me. I sucked in pleasant memories as a child with Hallie on each inhale.

. . .

Riding bikes. Setting up forts. Painting alleyways with graffiti. Jumping in pools. Pools. Water. Ocean. Waves. My brother being ripped away by the waves. He disappeared. Gone. Oblivion. Panic.

"Kyra!" Isaac yelled from a world away. "Focus."

Panting, I snapped my eyes open, unsure when they had closed. Caspian's strong hands steadied me as my knees were wobbling underneath. What was going on?

"Kyra, let's go. This isn't worth it. We can find another way." Isaac still sounded distant as I studied Caspian's blue eyes. They shifted to turtle green, then back to azure again with a mind of their own.

I pushed away from Caspian's grip. "How can I summon Moroka?"

"You can't." His irritating smirk taunted me. "Only I can."

I huffed, pretending my nerves weren't on edge. "Then do it."

"For a price."

On the horizon, dark indigos blended in with the deep navy, merging into one being, one unit. It reminded me that my two Links weren't the only forms of entwined force.

"What's your price?" I asked.

"A party." He circled me. "I need you to accompany me to President Stirk's grand ball honoring the Lieutenants." Caspian's tone reminded me of eerie tentacles, changing directions frequently.

"Why would the president hold a party in the middle of a war?"

"I'm not going to pretend I understand her lunatic ways. I just need you to kill Syvonne."

I craned my neck to the faint stars. Billions of sparkling diamonds stretched on for eternity. I wished I could pull fire from the constellations at that very moment.

"When is this party?" I asked.

"In one week."

I paused, considering my options. "If I agree, Isaac comes too."

"Why? He gave you up for this." Caspian pulled a sparkly crystal necklace from his tunic pocket.

My fingers were drawn to the sharp edges of the jewel. "You said that was in the lighthouse."

Caspian paused while watching me. "It's time to summon Moroka," he said, shoving the necklace back into his pocket.

"We haven't agreed on a plan. I need Isaac to help me with—"

"With finding Jadox Griffin. Yes, I know where the soldier is."

"What?" Flames exploded from my fingers and burst forward toward Caspian's chest. "Then tell me where he is. No more games!" Before I could blink or breathe, a wall of water blocked my fire. They clashed together with such force that I fell flat on my ass.

Isaac sped toward me.

Wait, I can do this.

"Kick his ass, love."

Isaac stopped, but his rapid breathing competed with Caspian's. In a triangle, we stood in a face-off, but I'd be the first to attack. Borrowing energy from Isaac, I let his power swirl in my core, tingle through my veins, and rise to my hands. There was no way I'd allow this corrupt, despicable man to direct our every move with secrets and deceit.

Strong, boiling heat was ready to explode from my fingertips. It whooshed from my body into Isaac's hands, and he hurled a bluster of wind at Caspian. I swore under my breath. Anyone else would've flown off the cliffside, but Caspian stood his ground and attacked back. Waves climbed the cliffside and towered behind him like a monstrous army.

I had already lost Jay; I couldn't lose Isaac too. He was mine to protect now—*mine*.

I raised a hand to Caspian. "Fine, I'll go to the party with you, but Isaac comes too, and you have to swear not to hurt him."

"As you wish." With the flick of a wrist, the massive water wall hovering in the air lowered and washed back into the sea as he turned to face the cliffside.

Caspian's toes stuck out over the edge as both long arms extended forward. There was only the sound of waves lapping below. No sacred spell or chant parted from his lips, yet, in only seconds from the darkness, a soft melody hummed from the waters below. With each passing moment, the song grew louder.

Each man longs to bury you alive,
You've let their darkness swallow your soul.
Forget what you know and take the dive,
The true answers lie in the murky depths below.

"Did you hear that?" I looked up at Isaac, whose jaw had dropped.

"Yeah, but how does the Blood Maiden know Wes's name?"

"She didn't talk about Wes. She...oh..." Realization struck of this uncanny sort of Magik, singing a unique poisonous lullaby to each of us separately.

Isaac radiated anxiety in his energy. "Love, can you give us some light, please?"

I ignited my fingers like a torch and cast it out over the cliffside.

Below, a haunted hand emerged from the waves, pale-skinned and almost translucent with black veins. Lanky arms followed, tangled with sea algae. The Blood Maiden's head jutted out from the waves. Moroka's hair was spindly like a spider's legs. I gasped when I met her sharp red eyes. They leaked rouge, running down her already soaked ghostly face. Each time one of the blood tears met her vermillion lips, she licked it, capturing them in her mouth.

She crawled out of the water, her hideous torso flopping like a fish behind her. No legs. Moroka's immortal body was sliced in half, oozing a path of unending blood behind her. A shiver ripped my spine. I held my breath as she crept up the side of the cliff to us, dragging herself up the wall like a snake. She sang slowly again, in a deep pitch, captivating my fears with each note.

Your family hunts you to stay alive,
Let down your guard, or they'll devour your soul.
Forget the Link— a true Elidi will thrive,
Without a man to make her whole.

When Moroka pulled herself to Caspian's feet, she hissed, "Caspian, you brought me dinner?"

Every muscle clenched, but Isaac pulled me closer to his side.

Moroka's red eyes cried continuously. Her entire body wreaked of decayed fish, and she licked a blood tear from her lips, cocking her head at the sight of me.

Yanking free from Isaac's hold, I kneeled so Moroka and I were eye to eye. "I was told you would truthfully answer any question I have for you."

"Yes, only one question. Do you wish to ask where the Draven soldier is being tortured?"

I stiffened, dread erasing any confidence. I couldn't endure the thought of Jay being tortured. Choking on my words, I glanced at Isaac.

"I'll go first," Isaac said. "Moroka, how can we free Jadox Griffin from captivity?"

My hands clutched my chest. Isaac had sacrificed his one and the only question for me.

But Moroka only laughed, spurting out blood that trailed down her neck. "You could've phrased that better, Isaac Nilson of Vayu." She wiggled closer to his shoes and clawed at his pants. "Are you sure, puppet? The Dravian you seek owns the Cursed One's heart."

"Tell me the answer," Isaac growled.

"The most successful way to free Griffin is to attend the President's Ball."

Isaac kicked her off his legs. "What else? Be more specific."

"That's my answer. Do better next time," she snarled and licked another crimson tear streaking her cheeks.

Caspian traced his long scar and cleared his throat. "How can we successfully kill President Stirk next week?"

Moroka's gaze snapped over to him. "Ah, you choose to play this time, my wicked puppet?" The Blood Maiden smiled, but no teeth glimmered, only one long tongue coated with a layer of blood. "President Stirk will die when the Golden One reveals her true identity."

Caspian grunted in frustration and turned away, running a hand through his wet hair. "You play tricks, Moroka."

"I learned that from my sister." She writhed at my feet. "And what is *your* one question, girl? What do you seek to know more than anything?"

There were too many options. I could ask how to keep Landon safe forever. Or how to fix the broken Elidi necklace. Or ask for clarification on exactly how to save Jay. I could ask if the love I felt for Jay is real or only reliant on our Link. And most importantly, there was still the question of how to return all males. Instead, my heart pounded with raw need.

"Why is my tattoo gold?" I rushed out the words.

Moroka nodded, then made a gurgling sound like she was choking on her tears. "Your tattoo is gold because Brent Elidi's tattoo is gold. Your father is alive but is being used by a deranged Mystier. Golden for Golden."

Moroka slithered over the rocks toward where Tawoli and Zeph were hiding.

"Wait." I jogged after Moroka. "What does all that mean? How can I save my father? How can I avoid being captured if I don't know who the threat is?"

Moroka spun and hissed, blood sputtering at my feet. "Too many questions. It's time for payment." She snaked away fast into the fog wall, leaving a blood trail. In the darkness, a cry of pain shrieked like a nightmare.

"Zeph!" Isaac darted past my shocked, frozen body into the mist. I hadn't thought Caspian was genuine with his sacrifice comment.

Unable to see anything, I blocked out the chomping, slurping, and fighting sounds, hoping it wasn't already too late.

"You're different than I assumed," Caspian spoke softly, ignoring the gruesome sounds from the shadows.

"Why aren't you helping them?" I lunged forward, but Caspian held me back.

"A sacrifice is part of the deal. I won't let it be you."

I shoved his chest. "You could have sent your insane water to attack Moroka or summoned her back into the water."

"Moroka demands payment for her answers. Why don't you cast a fireball into that chaos?"

Chest heaving, I hugged myself tighter. "I could hurt Isaac."

"You *do* care about him?" Caspian asked.

"I…I don't know."

"He betrayed you."

"No, he didn't."

Moroka's revolting sucking and chewing sounds in the gloomy darkness made me gag. My stomach turned on itself, and bile rose, but I swallowed it. Silence.

"Isaac?" I whimpered into the fog.

I need you.

I rushed into the unknown, lighting a spark to see. Alone, Isaac lay on some bloodied white feathers. No, no, no. His pants were torn to pieces, and blood poured from his thigh.

"Isaac!" I hovered a hand over his wounds and chanted *Terra angakok. Terra angakok.* Quickly, the gaping hole was sealed shut.

"Thank you." Isaac brushed a finger over my jaw.

I glanced next to him at the trail of blood leading to the cliffside. Tawoli and Zeph were gone.

"Moroka took them," Caspian stated without a hint of emotion.

"We have to go after them," Isaac croaked out, tripping forward, but I held him upright.

Caspian's scarred face emerged from the darkness. "No, Moroka probably dragged the girl underwater. She's gone. We need to get to the capital for the President's Ball."

"No matter how much I hate her." Tightness formed in my chest. "We have to try to save Zeph."

"One life doesn't matter when we're trying to save thousands. Look at the bigger picture." Caspian picked up our forgotten packs from the dirt and marched toward the cliffside. "Let's go."

I despised Caspian. Mystier men didn't seem much better than Ordulls. Instead of saving women from evil, they kept dying.

My mother.

Rajitha.

Fiozee.

Hallie.

Zeph. She didn't deserve to be eaten by a monster.

Women were still hurting and dying. I scanned the lighthouse and the eternal ocean beyond. "My venti was murdered. How will we get to the capital?"

"Trust me." Caspian held out a hand, waiting for me to take it.

9
ISAAC

Kyra grabbed Caspian's hand before I could stop him, pulling her off the cliffside edge into the sea below. I yelled after them like a madman. When I peered down, a soft splash crashed into the sea, but no heads bobbed in the water.

"Kyra!" Alone, I screamed her name into the darkness.

The door of the lighthouse behind me creaked open and shut on rusty hinges, the only sound other than the ocean waves.

"Kyra!"

I clumsily scaled down the rocky slope. At the bottom, water sopped my shoes, making them full and heavy. I limped toward the waves that had devoured Caspian and Kyra. Despite her healing efforts, my leg still burned from where Moroka had chomped into it. Kyra's healing powers hadn't yet reached the efficiency of Griffin's. At least we knew he was still alive somewhere if she could borrow parts of his Magik.

Scanning the sea, I half-expected the ghastly Moroka to return and slaughter me. I shuddered at the memory of the Blood Maiden hauling Zeph away, faint echoes of the siren song still whispering in my ear:

Your little boy is barely alive,
Hanging by a thread left of his soul.
Forget the Cursed One and take the dive,
To find little Wes in our depths below.

Did the demon truly know about my Wes, or was it a trap? My chest ached at the possibility. If she offered me a deal to switch my life for his, I'd take it right now, here on this abysmal, goddess-forsaken beach.

For miles and miles, devilish water stretched until it met the cruel stars above without a sight of the Blood Maiden or her crimson teardrops. Usually, the stars felt like where I belonged, but since our Link had formed, my home resided in a five-foot-five woman with golden hair and more fire than a celestial being.

Kyra's energy finally tugged on our thread.

Isaac?!

Thank goddess, are you okay?

She faded quickly, most likely distance decreasing the pull of our Link as our spark grew faint.

"Kyra!"

"Why are you screaming?" Caspian's hoarse voice made my head whip to the left, where a silhouette emerged dripping from the waves.

"Bring her back to me!" I stormed to Caspian and slammed my fist straight into his nose.

He stumbled back, staggering into the water. "Fuck! Good one, mate. Got that out of your system?"

"No! Where's Kyra? Tell me where she is."

"You don't listen, huh?" He pointed both hands to the water, and a bubble of giant water encircled his whole body as a forcefield. "Fine, we can do this the hard way."

No matter how many gusts of wind I cast at him, they only ricocheted back at me. Each time, it made me rear back and scrape against the cliff wall.

"Calm down, mate. I took her to get ready for the President's Ball." Caspian's gravelly voice was muffled by his heavy accent.

"Where *exactly* is she?"

"Ky was right about you. You're kind of narrow-minded, huh?"

"Shut up!"

"Yup, you fixate on one thing and fail to see all the options available." His serpent smile slithered higher on his cheeks.

"Where is she?"

"She's safe, miles underwater." Caspian gestured to my tattoo, most likely glowing brightly through my shirt by now like a lighthouse beacon. "But we need to chat."

My fists clenched tighter.

"I have what you need." Caspian pulled out the crystal necklace again, his tone spiked with venom.

Moonbeams shone through the gem, reflecting on the waves.

"I don't need that," I said.

"Don't be arrogant. None of us know the necklaces' true potential. Well, except for Surh-Sig, Moroka, and their other sister, what's her name again? I forget."

"What's your point?"

When the crystal dangled on the chain, it cast another glaring light from the moon to the sea as if the sky and ocean were communicating.

"What if all four necklaces could bring back your Wes?" Caspian finally lowered his water shield and repocketed the Vayuian necklace. "What if Ky could return all the hybrid boys if she had all four necklaces at the same time?"

What if my Link with Kyra felt all-consuming sometimes, yet my true commitment was to Wes, not a woman I barely knew. I couldn't believe I was about to betray her.

"I know where two necklaces are," I whispered Kyra's secret.

"Which two?" Caspian's eyebrows rose to his hairline.

"Give me that one first. It's not meant for Cydian hands."

"No, call it collateral. I'll give it to you once Ky assassinates the president."

"Why does Stirk have to die?"

"Not all secrets are meant to be told under the stars." Caspian stared at me, holding a deeper truth in his eyes.

"Just kill the president yourself."

"I've already tried and failed." Caspian rubbed his brown stubble. "Ky's Golden tattoo makes her more powerful."

"She wants to free Griffin, not go on some assassination mission."

Caspian ran his hand through his wet hair and grinned. "That must be frustrating for you."

My teeth ground together, sharp and fast. For now, Caspian needed to believe I was on board with his deranged plan.

"How do you expect her to cooperate with your plan?" I asked.

"I'll give Ky what she wants," he said simply.

"So, that means you know where Griffin is."

Caspian nodded. "You take this crystal and go on your merry way. I'll take Kyra to the ball, and you won't have to be burdened by her anymore."

"It's obvious that you don't want me near Kyra," I asked. "Why?"

"Because you weren't supposed to Link with her." An edge flared in Caspian's eyes, either possessiveness or protectiveness.

My temples throbbed, but I maintained all composure, faking comfort.

"The prophecy was about me. Both you and Griffin got it all wrong."

I dropped my head in my hands and spoke to myself, "Divinity above, seriously? Now I have two guys to compete with?"

"Wrong again, Nilson." His accent was heavier when he chuckled. "I have no interest in Ky the way you want her."

I rolled my eyes. "I assumed the same thing until we Linked. The connection isn't something you're able to control."

"I'm telling you now, I'm one hundred percent certain my mind will never change. I don't want her like that. Trust me, I'm married."

"Marriage doesn't mean anything compared to the force of this Link. It feels...divine."

He sighed. "You still don't understand what I'm saying."

"Then help me see more clearly." I tapped my s-watch. "Are you married to a guy?"

"No."

"Then you'd still be affected by the Link."

"I'll never see Kyra in the same light you do."

"It sounds like you hate Kyra. What'd she do to you?" I asked.

Caspian growled. "Just stop thinking about this so hard, mate. Once you two go your separate ways, I'll get what I want when the president's dead. She will get what she wants from Griffin…in and out of bed."

I'd had enough of his bullshit. I bolted forward and rammed my head into Caspian's stomach. He punched my temple. My stomach. We both slammed into the shallow waters, soaked and wrestling as waves crashed onto my back.

We rolled over the surface. Gasping. I pinned him. My muscles pulsed as water knocked into me, but I gripped his throat with my bare hands. His face turned purple until I shoved his whole head underwater. Through the clear sloshes, Caspian smiled underwater and sucked in a gulp of water. I froze. At that moment, he flipped me over and wrestled us into a new position. Caspian ended up on top, straddling my body. My clothes were soaked, and rocks dug into my back in the shallow water.

"Take a look around, mate." Caspian grinned. "You're on my turf."

From underneath him, I spat out water. "What is it that you really want?"

"I already told you. I need Kyra to kill the president. That's it."

"You're avoiding the truth. Why do you want the president dead? Why would you go through all this effort to kill the most powerful Ordull?"

He leaned closer, those blue-green eyes promising danger, and whispered in my ear, "Who says Syvonne is the most powerful Ordull?"

Before I could respond, Caspian pushed me underwater, holding me there. I kicked. Squirmed. He pushed me deeper, weighing my body down with his. Then he dragged me where it became deeper.

Lower into the abyss. Deeper. The moon disappeared. Caspian breathed in the water again, taunting me in my last moments.

Calm down, Isaac.

Kyra?

My chest was about to explode. Air. I needed air. My lungs burned, and my arms flailed.

I said calm down. Breathe.

The pain became so great that I opened my mouth and inhaled a lungful of water. At least the last words I heard would be hers. Hopefully, she'd survive, and our severed Link wouldn't damage her power after I drowned.

Except—I was safe and breathing.

Breathe, Isaac.

Body shaking, I responded with the only amount of sanity remaining.

I am. I did. I'm breathing...underwater. How?

Come to me, Isaac.

Kyra's voice sounded like a siren the lower we sank. Caspian swam into the depths and pulled me by some invisible leash. How was this possible? No resource book in Vayu's library ever detailed a Mystier who could hold his breath for such a long time or harness the ability to share that power with another. Was this an enhancement? Was Caspian the descendant of the strongest Cydian line?

The temperature dropped, and our speed accelerated. Every time Caspian stroked his long arms and kicked his feet, it propelled us like a sea animal with fins, streamlining through the water with immeasurable precision.

After growing accustomed to the pressure in my chest, I focused on our surroundings as Caspian dragged me effortlessly. A school of tuna diverted to our right. Coral reefs swayed and bobbed below, and I wished the sun would rise sooner to shine a light on the colors. Further underwater, a long pipeline flickered with an aqua-marine glow, textured like scales. Caspian swam straight for it. The further we dove, the larger the pipe appeared. I squinted as water continued to rush by my cheeks.

My eyes deceived me. It wasn't a pipe but a series of underwater houses, complete with doors and windows combined with steel tunnels. Each house was mushroom-shaped with a long stem connecting it to the wreckage of ships below. Most exteriors of the mushroom shapes were covered in blue, green, and silver barnacles. Marine gardens surrounded the little village with sponges and sea thickets.

I can feel you.

Where are you, love?

In some underwater palace.

I'm not near a palace. He must have separated us.

But just then, Caspian swam around a curve of the mushroom house, zig-zagging between the swaying plant life. The raw power emitting from the central location of the village was mindboggling. In the middle of the community floated a colossal, spherical palace. The outside of the orb looked as if it was painted in watercolors with a faded navy that transitioned to sage green and washed-out whites. It wasn't even possible to estimate the height of its magnificent size. It mirrored a perfect sphere, or bubble, majestically centered in the underwater community.

A thousand questions lingered on my tongue, impatient to be asked. How many Cydians lived here? How had the rest of the Mystiers not known about this kingdom? Was there air or water inside the structure? My librarian mind longed for answers, knowledge, and research.

Caspian pointed to a side door. Unable to resist, my body followed his instruction, floating through the water. The village still slept, and only turtles passed us for the last few yards to the entrance. Yet, I felt threatening eyes on me from the shadows, evaluating my every move. Caspian pushed a hidden lever, and the door swung open. My body tensed, awaiting what was on the other side.

IO

KYRA

I pressed both hands against the thick aquarium glass serving as a window. My hands tapped a quick drum beat. *Tap, tap, tap*. That son-of-a-bitch Caspian hadn't even offered me a choice when he seized my wrist on Vuldow's cliffside. My freedom was obliterated the moment he dragged me into the ocean's depths. I was completely at his mercy, locked in this spare room without knowing Jay's whereabouts. At least I had oxygen in this underwater castle and didn't have to grow gills.

Dawn's light from the surface slowly shone on the purple and green reefs shifting outside. Sunlight glistened on silver scales, glittering above as minnows swam under sea turtles. Two sharks glided between the swaying underwater houses. I wished I could have captured the image for Jay.

Where is he? Is he safe?

From afar, sirens wailed as if afraid of what would happen when the sun rose and stole away their beloved darkness. Their taunting cries warned me to escape, so I did the only thing I could think of and plugged my ears. The voices still echoed with whispers spiraling into shrills of tormenting song.

Resting my forehead against the cool glass, I stared out at the swimming sharks and tried to communicate with Jadox for the thousandth time. Life felt miserable without his stern eyes, terrible jokes, quiet steadiness, and protective nature.

Jay, this isn't funny. Please answer me.

Silence.

A group of Cydians, each swimming with their own bubble of oxygen, gathered in a circle. The morning rays reflected off their wetsuits, creating a mermaidesque shimmer. Their arms swayed overhead like they were exercising. Underwater yoga? Seriously?

Long streams of liquid ink jetted between them like a game, a slit of purple bouncing from each Cydian as they waved their arms. The artistic flow of the colors was entrancing enough to be a performance.

I sighed. I wanted to travel Lodesa with Jay and experience new cultures like this without our lives being at stake. I'd show him how the Cydians created art with their Magik one day.

"He's still alive somewhere, love. We'll find Griffin."

I whirled around, knocking a stack of old books over. Isaac leaned against the bookshelf, a puddle pooling on the hardwood underneath his feet. Between us, a dozen bubbles floated in the air, each full of different ocean colors. Instead of showing Isaac how happy I was that he was here and alive, I reprimanded him.

"Hey! You'll wreck those books with that water. Move." I jogged through the floating bubbles, popping them as I went. Right when I pulled Isaac's shoulder away from the book, a charge zapped my tattoo, reminding me of all my choices—good and bad. I was still undecided on whether pairing up with Isaac would be my biggest regret.

"No regrets, love. I'll prove you wrong."

Shit, he was in my head. In a heartbeat, I secured my mental wall against him, yet his little smirk that always partially undid me rose on his cheeks.

I tried to wipe the book dry with one hand. "Wait, it's already dry."

"We're in a Magikal palace." He shrugged. "I've seen crazier things in the last few hours."

"How are you so calm? You're supposed to care about…." I wanted to say me, but finished, "...About books. Why aren't you freaking out that this book was almost destroyed?"

Isaac smiled and tucked a strand of my hair behind my ear. "What I care about is answers. Such as, does this book *want* me to read it? Does this book *want* to be in my hands?" He gave me a knowing look and continued, "Is this book full of possible romance and happily ever after or not? If it's a fantasy world full of heroes and damsels, then maybe it's a waste of time if it can never be real."

I snatched the book from him and slammed it shut hard, making him blink.

I wanted to be angry at his insinuations, but I couldn't hold it. "If you could write your own story, what would it be?"

He prowled forward with such force and dominance I took a step back, my heels banging into the bedpost. Isaac's minty breath caressed my lips only an inch from my face. "You want to know my story?"

I scanned his wet shirt that clung to sculpted muscles underneath. Reading my mind, he tore off his sopping shirt and tossed it to the floor with a *thwop*. For some reason, my walls against him shattered and my heart felt completely exposed, open, raw, and...full of Isaac.

He placed his hand on the small of my back and whispered, "Once upon a time, life was perfect. Then, a man's entire world was swept out from under his feet in a single night."

I swallowed, wondering why he stood so close when blaming me again for Wes's disappearance. Yet, there was no hostility in his tone this time, and, for some reason, I wanted him even closer.

The heat of Isaac's breath on my neck sent goosebumps all over my skin as he continued. "That man thought revenge was the only option. But he found joy in the most unlikely time. When he met the one."

"The one?" I whispered, my gaze locked on his face.

The devil danced in his eyes. "The one who would teach him how to live in the moment. The one who would show him determination and perseverance. The one who taught him how to let his guard down again."

A rock must have lodged itself in my airway because Isaac ran his calloused fingers over the front of my throat. I hated it, and I loved it. And I despised that he knew it.

"It's time to stop pretending, love, and embrace us." His hand caressed my spine, and I involuntarily arched into him.

"Embrace what, Isaac? I'm with Jay, and you know that."

"What if you had never met Griffin?"

Instead of digging deeper, avoidance sounded best. "Let's get out of here so we won't be trapped together anymore."

His eyes flickered with rage. "Trapped? Did Caspian *lock* you in here?"

"Yes. No. Well, yes, he did. But that's not what I meant."

Isaac glanced around at all four walls towering with piles of dusty books. When his focus wasn't directed at me, I studied his features, seeing through his assured stance and taking note of the lines etched into his forehead. Maybe he was also grieving for Zeph now. My throat tightened, and I shuddered at the thought of the suffering his ex must have endured being chewed to death by Moroka.

I hesitantly pulled away, questioning why my body wanted to be wrapped in Isaac's strong arms. If I could just stab him through the heart right now, it'd solve all this confusion. If he were dead, then all my problems would be gone. Our Link would be severed, and it would erase the passionate pull toward this man.

I wasn't supposed to like Isaac. But I could never hurt him. I recalled his cry through the fog when we were on the cliffside. His pain had stomped a heavy beat on my soul. It was all too much. My emotions were seesawing too rapidly.

"There's got to be a secret exit." He started pawing at the walls.

"Wait, we can't try to escape yet. I have to go to the President's Ball. Moroka said it's the only way to free Jay."

He closed the gap between us again, and I held my ground as my breathing accelerated. His mouth parted. Our lips were so close that I couldn't even inhale because I'd be breathing him in.

"Kyra, love. What if it were just us? Do you think you'd ever want that?"

I gently pushed his chest with both hands. "You said you'd help me find Jay."

"I will as long as he is who you truly want, but I can feel a shift in you."

"You're wrong. And I won't change my mind."

"You can't know the future."

"I can." I stormed away from him and crossed my arms, staring out the window.

Silverfish flickered by, reminding me how dangerous our situation was, being caged so far underwater. Isaac's warmth still lingered behind me. I fought against everything in my body that was begging me to lean against him.

"I'm gonna hug you now, don't hit me again, deal?"

Isaac's chest pressed against my back and both arms looped in front of my stomach, hugging me from behind with ease as if we had been together for years. His chin rested atop my head gently like two puzzle pieces that fit together. An involuntary purr escaped my throat. Unable to help myself, I leaned my head back against his bare shoulder, feeling his muscles flex briefly, then soften. Immediately, my Circle flared hot like lava.

"I don't know anything anymore." My voice shook with fear from what the admission meant. "But Jay is *mine,* and I am his. I'm not trying to hurt you intentionally, I swear."

"Spending time with you isn't painful, love." When he spoke, his voice rumbled into my back; the soft vibration felt divine.

With one swift motion, he swiveled me around. I fought the urge to run my hand up his bare chest as my gaze met his. His rapid heartbeat pounded hard, and the desire in his eyes was clearer than the necklace Caspian had teased us with on the cliffside.

"Wait, what happened to the crystal?"

"He still has it." Isaac tilted my chin up again, and the sea's fury lived in his eyes. "But I needed to apologize for what happened on the cliffside, love? That man should *not* have grabbed you." I could've sworn a minute tornado formed around him, sucking in the air in his wrath as he said, "I'm sorry I wasn't fast enough."

Isaac froze. His rage singed my tattoo from the inside out, automatically igniting the fire at my fingertips. The flame bounced to his hand, then back to mine, then back to his again. We watched in amazement as our Magik worked together.

"Wait, let me try something." He extended both hands and commanded the flames to swirl in his mini-cyclone. My fire spun, mixing with his air, burning and growing in strength. Power consumed my core, and my body tensed so tightly that I felt like I could burst. Books fell from shelves. Suddenly, the immediate need to kiss Isaac consumed every thought, need, and desire–my lips on his meant life or death.

Amid the chaos in our room, I grabbed his neck, wide-eyed and gasping. The world was made of only us. Isaac's sharp jaw twitched as we stared at one another silently. I wanted to kiss him. I couldn't kiss him. Terrified of our connection, I lowered my walls and purposefully showed Isaac my happy memories with Jay to end this terrible attraction once and for all.

After only a few moments, he raised both hands, backing away. "Okay, okay, that's enough. Don't ever show me memories of Griffin doing that to you again."

I scanned him up and down, still panting from the spark between us. "We need boundaries, something to stop this thing between us."

"Okay." He licked his lips. "But when you ask me to break your rules, don't expect me to fight you on it."

"I won't ask that. And no kissing. Ever."

"Worried you won't have any self-control?"

"No. I just...wanted to be clear." My chest rose and fell rapidly as my cheeks warmed.

"What else?" Playfulness danced on his face.

"No massages, no hand holding, no touching my hair, no showering together, no changing in front of each other, no dancing, no cuddling, no—"

"Those are all physical rules." Isaac picked up his wet shirt from the floor and walked through the Magikally floating bubbles into the connected bathroom.

"Come back and finish this conversation," he said.

He was the epitome of carnal masculinity, with his shoulders held high and his chest puffed out. Isaac ran a hand through his wet hair.

"What about rules involving promises?" he asked. "What about deep conversations? What about talking each other's ear off until two in the morning? What about saving each other's lives? What about sharing our deepest secrets and biggest fears?"

I was pretty sure my jaw hit the floor. "Uh, you *want* those things?"

"Yes, love. I'm greedy. I want everything." He rubbed his blonde scruff. "Are there rules against those?"

"Um, no, friends can do those things. We can be friends."

He cast me a look that erupted my insides. "Until you change your mind."

"I won't."

He paused, studying me intensely. "Kyra…." Hesitancy crawled over his face. "What will you do if Griffin doesn't respond to your messages?"

"He…Well. That's already happened."

"Is he ignoring you on purpose? Hm, maybe he has a good reason," he said softly, trying to lighten the blow.

"Isaac, stop trying to piss me off!" Power streamed through my tattoo, and I had half a mind to light the entire bookshelf on fire just to get it out of my system and thoroughly enrage him simultaneously. But I couldn't do that to books.

"If I wanted to get you riled up, all I'd need to do is straddle you on our bed," he said.

Glancing at the one and only bed in the room, covered in poofy cotton blankets, I pushed away the dirty thoughts from my mind and blamed them on the damn Link. "I'm gonna nap, so please stop all this." I waved my hands, encompassing his body so he could catch my drift.

When I moved to the bed, he mirrored my every step on the other side.

"What do you think you're doing?" I asked.

The devil lived in his smile. "What? You never stated a rule where we couldn't sleep in the same bed together."

I palmed my forehead, slipped into bed, and snuggled against the marshmallow fluff. As his knee nudged me, I blew out a secretive relieved sigh that he was there. That I wasn't alone. Even if caged and captured underwater, I had someone who cared about me.

Staring out the window again, I spotted three dolphins swimming through the sunbeams, bubbles forming around one. Their sonic communication pierced my ears.

"Hey, Isaac?"

"Yes, love." His deep voice soothed my racing nerves.

"Do you think Landon is okay?"

His long arm draped over my side and wrapped around my stomach. "Of course. Alaska is protecting him. Don't worry."

I flopped his arm off of me. "You forgot, no cuddling."

"Right." He grunted. "It's my turn to ask a question."

I closed my eyes, allowing the heavy drowsiness to overtake my senses.

"Kyra?"

"Mmm?" I groaned half-heartedly.

"Maybe you only cared for Griffin because of the Link."

"That wasn't a question. But I refuse to believe that." My head sunk further into the pillow. "Plus, if that were true, wouldn't you be upset that this *thing* between us is also fake?"

"So, you admit there's a *thing*." The arrogance in his tone almost made me turn around and slap him.

"Nope. Go to sleep." The faint sea siren songs helped me slip into a meditative trance.

"And Kyra?"

"Yes, Isaac?"

"Do you believe your father is alive?"

"I've been trying not to think about it." I resituated my hair on the pillow. "I don't care about Brent—he abandoned me."

"We probably need to come up with a plan, then a backup plan," he whispered into my hair.

A shiver cascaded over my body. "I'm more of a spur-of-the-moment kind of girl."

"I know, love. That's why we're perfect together. We balance each other out."

No, Jay balanced me. "Goodnight, Isaac."

"And Kyra?"

"Yes, Isaac."

"I'll keep you safe."

I sighed. "I know."

He mumbled something under his breath. It was tougher to despise this man since he'd promised to help me save Jay at his expense. Isaac was dragged underwater as a prisoner, just like me, yet hadn't shown one ounce of resentment for me putting him in this poor position. But I never wanted to Link with Isaac. I only did it to save Jay.

I needed to save Jay.

I'm coming, Jay. Don't give up.

Then Isaac's snoring started as his chest curled around my back. Somehow, I belonged with Isaac too. A single slow tear slanted sideways down my cheek. The answer simmered just below my skin, teasing me with a life long forgotten, far away yet as true as my heartbeat.

From afar, the soft siren pleas melted into cries of warning. We couldn't stay in Cydon long.

11

JADOX

Old vomit and blood still coated my dingy fatigues, but the wretched smell was nothing compared to The Cavity. I hated the president for mandating this task on me. If given a chance, I'd rip Crimble's heart out through his throat. But the electrical collar wrapped around my neck controlled me and prevented any use of my Magik without supervision.

As I walked through the basement doors, the smell of death hit me first, then shit mixed with rotten and decaying flesh. I staggered into the shadowy tunnel underneath the president's headquarters, in The Crooked Chateau's basement, wishing there were windows to at least see the moonlight occasionally.

The president had ordered me to try and heal another prisoner. I don't even remember how, when, or why I was transferred to this project. Until a few days ago, the last thing I recalled was being overseas when the bomb detonated. I watched my entire platoon go up in flames just before passing out. Now, I was back in Lodesa, and things weren't adding up. Something was off, but my duty was to follow orders, even though I was a prisoner.

Soldiers weren't supposed to be leashed like this.

My mind was blank. Even the memory of my family seemed faded.

I knew Alaska's face was carved from sharp features, yet memories with her felt like a dream or a nightmare haunting me each night. Gemm's long gray braids mingled in my mind like abstract art, swirling with long vines. Nothing was clear anymore. Where were they now? Were they safe? Most days, it felt like someone had taken a pair of scissors to my brain and cut slivers of my life away, leaving bits and pieces layered nonsensically in a scrap pile.

"Griffin, the next one is up. You ready?" Lieutenant Perez said.

She didn't even have to tug on the electrical cord wrapped around my neck this time. In Topell, Paola and I could've been problem-solving teammates on the battlefield. Instead, she treated me like vermin because I was Magikal and she wasn't. But what complicated things was that Perez was Alaska's secret girlfriend. Maybe I could find a way to separate them.

All my memories were blurry images with dreary spaces in between. "Did you find the answers to what we talked about yesterday?" I asked Perez. "Did any of my teammates survive the bomb? How did I arrive at this facility?"

"Don't start asking your thousands of questions again, Griffin." Her round face held layers of secrets that I wasn't sure if I needed to unwind.

My stomach rumbled with hunger. She pulled me into the basement's main room, where horrifying cries came from the people caged in electrical boxes. Aisles of prisoners lined The Cavity walls. At the center of the dark room sat four lab tables and one electrocution chair. I despised it here. It was absolute torture.

"Okay, Griffin. Here's our next subject." Perez reluctantly unlocked a cage from the top tier and pulled out a teenage girl.

My heart sank, already mourning the life this girl could've had. Her ratty clothes, which might have been white or beige once, were now painted brown with her feces. The distant look in her ebony eyes mirrored my own. She knew it was useless to fight back at this point. Lieutenant Perez rolled down the waistline of the girl's pants just a bit to show a turquoise Möbius Circle tattoo, then wrote *Cydian* on her paper.

Perez glanced at me, then whispered into her s-watch, "The date is 04—check log for the year, on Crust Moon...."

Despite my exhaustion, my attention snapped to Perez. "Wait, why aren't you saying the year? You did that yesterday too."

"Don't worry about it, Griffin. Just follow orders." Perez continued, "Patient number 202. Cydian. Thirteen years. Female. Diagnosis: cerebral palsy. Symptoms: tremors, asymmetrical features, and poor muscle tone. Onset: birth." She turned to me and paused before saying, "Private Griffin reporting for healing."

My heart rate tripled as Perez lifted the weak girl into my arms. The little girl's arm flopped, dangling from her body as I held her. I stood there like a frozen statue, staring at the hundreds of cages before me, all filled with deprived patients the president wanted me to heal, Ordulls and Mystiers alike.

Why did it feel like I had missed years of intel from one head trauma? How was it possible that I lacked awareness of this facility? How long had Ordulls and Mystiers been working together here?

"Alright, Griffin. You're up. Make your Magik work this time. We can't keep failing." Perez pushed a button on her remote, and the electrical current coursing through my muscles disappeared. My tattoo fizzled with weak energy, begging for release, a savior, or death — anything to relieve me of this tortured agony.

"I've told you before, Perez. The electricity in the collar sucks my energy dry. You need to take it off or give me more time."

"You know Stirk won't allow that."

I paused. "Who's Stirk?"

She froze, and her eyes widened. "I meant President Crimble."

"That's not what you said." I swallowed, wishing my throat wasn't so dry. "Who is Stirk?"

"Never mind, I misspoke. Do your job, soldier."

"What Crimble's asking is impossible. Doesn't he know Mystiers need rest?"

"Heal her, so we can both finally sleep," Perez begged.

I focused on my Magik, squeezing my eyes shut to try and heal this girl.

Please, please. Please work. Please fix her. Please heal her. Please.

Desperate tears pooled behind my eyes that I wouldn't allow to fall.

Jay? Jay! Is that you? Jay!

The strange voice in my mind distracted me. I shook my head, ridding myself of the hallucination, and bore down with all my muscles, cementing myself to the ground.

"Lieutenant Perez, I need soil, dirt, trees, rocks, anything. Then maybe my power would grow."

The girl's floppy body turned heavier. I glanced down at her depressing face. She was so weak and thin that she had fallen asleep in my arms.

"Whatever President Crimble expects me to do, I can't. Tell him it's useless. I can't heal people born with a disability."

Perez formed a steeple with her hands. "Please try again, Griffin. I don't want to...I can't endure another...." Tears glistened in her eyes this time.

With a tight chest, I set the girl down on the cold floor and knelt over her form. She shivered and curled into a ball. Hovering one hand over her temple, I sucked in a deep breath and dug down deep, summoning Magik to my fingertips. For some reason, the spell I needed was buried deep in my mind, lost. No spark jolted my tattoo. No energy rattled in my bones. My head dropped, and dread ripped apart my flesh.

"I can't do it."

"Maybe we can hide this one." Perez knelt by my side. "Maybe we can sneak her out the back."

Bricks stacked on my shoulders in horror and dread. "How far will she make it without food? How far could she run on shaky legs? Who will take care of her?"

"He's right, Lieutenant," an unfamiliar female voice colder than ice gripped my soul from the shadows.

All the whimpers from the cages silenced as a woman sitting on a hoverchair floated through The Cavity. She parked her chair under the spotlight near the science tables and nodded to the electrocution chair.

I noticed the presidential symbol on her suit, but it didn't make sense. Why would she be wearing Crimble's clothes?

"You failed again," the lady said. "Just like yesterday and the day before, you know what comes next."

"Do you work for President Crimble?" I asked. "Please tell him we're wasting our time down here. What he's asking me to do is—"

"Silence!"

I swallowed my tormented thoughts and masked them with the face of a soldier, ever-obedient. Yet, the room spun as I stared at the straps on the electrocution chair, then glanced down at the girl splayed out in front of me. Maybe her fate was merciful compared to being trapped as a prisoner. Maybe...

"You're doing her a favor." The woman tore the Velcro from one strap. "Carry her over."

Murder. This was murder. I was the monster haunting all soul's nightmares.

On unsteady legs, I picked up the girl again and lumbered to this stranger. The girl's eyes opened, and she locked her gaze onto mine in a silent plea. My chest rose and fell fast. This wasn't supposed to be my job. The army wasn't supposed to be like this. How did I end up here?

"I'm sorry. I'm so sorry," I whispered as I set the girl in the repulsive chair.

Her lip quivered as her weak head lolled to the side from hunger, exhaustion, or cerebral palsy. I'd never know. Because these were her last moments alive.

"No, please, no," a small, weak voice gasped from a cage in the darkness. "My sissy, please, no."

And my heart severed to pieces. Unable to breathe, I stepped back as the woman tightened the deadly straps around the girl's torso. The smell of fresh urine wafted to my nose as the girl's clothes darkened further.

"Wait! She's only a child. You can't do this."

"I can," the woman in the hoverchair's emotionless voice answered.

"What right do you have to end a life?"

"I have every right." The woman lifted her chin. "I'm Syvonne Stirk, the President of Lodesa."

That was the vice president's name. But in all her elected time, she never wanted to be shown in the media due to her amputations. I shook my head in confusion. "The President of Lodesa is a man."

She laughed. "I'm gonna have a lot of fun with you, Griffin." Stirk lowered her chin, her silky white hair shifting over her flawless face. "But maybe you're right. I won't do this to the girl."

My shoulders relaxed, and Perez let out a relieved sigh behind me.

Stirk rolled her chair around me, grabbed the execution switch, and shoved it in my palm. "I won't kill this girl because you're going to. You failed your duty by not healing her. You aren't trying hard enough to access your power. This is *your* fault."

My knees buckled. They were asking an impossible task of me. The little girl kept her eyes on me.

"Come on, Griffin, I don't have all day." My Commander-In-Chief tapped her long fingernails on her hoverchair's armrest.

"I'll take the patient's place." I handed the switch back to the president. "Take her to a doctor, then kill me instead."

Stirk pinched the bridge of your nose. "You're not so smart." Her heavy sigh struck deep within my heart as she rammed the electrocution switch back into my hands. "Sacrificing yourself would be pointless. You are a healer. You need to heal me so I can walk again. Killing you would be a waste of this project." She gestured to all the cages. "You want the Ordull deaths from yesterday to have no purpose?"

My heart raced, ready to explode from my chest. I needed help. I needed someone more powerful.

Please, if anyone's out there, any goddess, please help me. Save the girl. I can't keep going like this. Please. Please. Please.

Stirk snapped in front of my face. "Soldier, if you don't do it, I'll have you sit here and watch as I execute the entire top row of cages. We can always find more cripples, freaks, and invalids to practice on."

I stared, dumbfounded and completely lost.

"Don't look at me like that. None of this is my fault," Stirk said.

"Then whose is it?"

"Kyra Kozelski is the one responsible. If you want to blame anyone for this project's purpose, it's her," Stirk hissed.

I had never heard of that name—Kyra Ko-something. Maybe if I played my cards right, I'd be able to persuade the president to change her plan. Maybe there was something else Stirk cared about more than healing her legs.

"Let me go serve justice," I offered.

Stirk batted her eyes. "I'll tell you what…if you can heal the next child, we will put this project on hold. She has a partial amputation. If you succeed, I'll let you hunt for Kyra Kozelski and bring her to me alive."

"But who is Kyra Kozelski?"

A wicked grin smothered Stirk's face. "Do we have a deal, soldier?"

"Yes, ma'am." I nodded, despite the feeling of utter uselessness consuming me.

Stirk's jaw clenched tight. "Now, watch carefully so you understand the consequence if you fail again."

"No, please don't!" I pleaded.

"Quiet!"

Please. Please help. Please save us. I can't keep going. Please. Please. Please.

I'm coming, Jay. Hold on.

What was that voice in my head? Who did it belong to?

Syvonne Stirk flipped the switch on the electric chair. The little girl writhed violently for a moment, then her eyes rolled to the back of her head. Dead. Screams from the cages sliced a hole in my heart.

I gritted my teeth and averted my eyes but stayed cemented to the spot. It felt like an aero glider had crashed into my chest.

"Now, you understand. Her little sister is next in line if you don't succeed." Stirk turned her hoverchair and glided out of The Cavity. After the furthest door creaked shut, I dropped to my knees again and buried my head in my hands.

"Griffin, listen to me," Perez said quietly. "This won't make any sense, but I've been lying to you. Stirk is too. But I can't stand by anymore and watch this happen. This is getting out of hand."

I could barely focus on her. "What are you talking about?"

Through blurry tears, Perez met my eyes. She pulled me to my feet and unstrapped the dead girl, who collapsed to her side. Heaviness suffocated me at the sight of her ghostly face. If only I could bury it deep and forget the anguish.

"Carry her to the crematorium quickly, then I'll explain."

Perez's combat boots clomped down the aisle of prisoners. I held my breath against the decrepit stench as I sloshed through filthy puddles. Desperate hands poked out from the bars paired with crying voices, begging to be freed. Some pleas belonged to the youth, some to men, some women, some Ordulls, some Mystiers. Silently, I cradled the lifeless body in my arms, refusing to look away from her glazed eyes. How did Stirk capture them all? How could she be selfish enough to initiate Project Cavity to heal her disability? Why weren't my healing powers working?

In a trance, I lay the girl down on a steel table—her last resting place. I brushed a finger along her dirty jawline.

"I'm sorry. I'll keep your little sister alive. I'll free her," I promised.

Perez filled out a form and ripped off the paper, handing it to the mortician. "Come on, soldier."

Like a zombie, I plodded behind her into a small office. Immediately, she locked the door and turned off the security camera in the corner, even though she knew that extra unit of electricity protected her from my Magik.

I shot her a look, the fast movement making my head spin. I could barely form thoughts at the sound of the cremator machine rumbling to life. Goosebumps rose from the thought of crushed bones, open flames, and melted flesh.

"Okay, now, listen up. We have to move fast." She unhooked the metal collar from my neck. "I should've told you earlier," Perez said. "Stirk erased a few years from your memory."

"What?" Confusion coiled so tightly in my body that a flicker of fire shot from my fingertips. I jumped back. "What the fuck? I shouldn't have fire Magik!"

Perez sighed. "Griffin. She. Stole. Your. Memory. Things have happened in the last few years that you don't remember anymore."

I backed up. "No, no, that's not true."

Perez's eyes landed on my stomach, right where my two tattoos were hidden under my fatigues. Although I never recalled receiving the second tattoo and didn't know what it was for. Maybe she was right.

Jay! Jay? Can you hear me? Please answer.

I jumped out of my skin.

"What is it?" Perez asked.

I massaged my temples. "Nothing. I need sleep and food. ASAP."

Perez's watch dinged with a call from the president. She cringed, then said, "We need to leave. Meet me here in an hour. Pack your things, and don't let anyone see you."

She walked out, leaving me behind. Completely alone. No Alaska. No Gemm. And despite not knowing who, my Magik longed for someone else stolen from me, where now only a void remained. Who was I missing?

Was Perez telling the truth? What would she gain by lying? She was right about one thing. Staying here wasn't an option, but when I stepped toward the exit, the cameras in the corner followed my movements. I tugged my shirt up, trying to hide where my collar would normally be.

How was I going to escape?

12

KYRA

Five days. I was trapped in the underwater room with Isaac for five days, tortured by Isaac's adorable smirk and nonstop attempts to get me to smile. I tried to ignore him as long as possible since I continually felt Jadox's faded plea from somewhere. Waiting until Caspian freed us was no longer an option. We had to escape. He was probably lying about the president's party anyway.

"Yup, another happily fuckin ever after." Isaac snapped shut the fourth book resting on his legs, then looked up. "What's wrong, love?"

"Jay needs me. I can feel him." Out the sole window, the ocean caging us in its depths laughed in victory.

"I can feel him a bit too." Isaac stood from his spot by the bookshelf and crossed the room, popping the randomly floating bubbles along the way. "I know a way to make you forget about him."

Ignoring his flirtation, I said, "We have to leave today."

"You know there's no way out. We've tried."

"We have to *keep* trying." I ran my hand over the slick, cold walls.

Isaac trailed me around the room and followed my lead, brushing his large hands on every seam and corner of the walls. "We've searched everywhere since thirteen o'clock yesterday. There's no way out."

"I'll never give up. I can't wait days for this ball anymore. Jay needs me."

"But we still have no idea where he is."

Hot tears pooled, and I wasn't sure if it was because of how badly I missed Jay or how sincere Isaac was in his intentions to help me.

Isaac caressed the crevices of the room's baseboard on his knees, yet again searching for a hidden lever. "I have a better idea of what to do with my hands than *this*."

Instead of giving in to his attempts, I tried to get Isaac to be serious for once. "Tell me about Wes's mother."

Isaac's gray eyes flickered to mine for a moment. "Her name was Rajitha." His voice quieted, holding layers of memories.

"Did you love her?"

"I'm not sure if I know the meaning of that word romantically, only how I feel for Wes." He sighed. "Rajitha and I were high-school sweethearts. But every day, week, and lunar cycle with her was a lie. She never knew of my Magik or who I truly was. That part was torture. Those secrets were why I could never propose, why we could never live together. Every minute, I was strangled by not being allowed to tell her the truth."

"So you wanted to give her everything but couldn't?"

"Exactly."

"That's how I feel right now. I want to give Jay comfort and release, reassurance, strength, and freedom, but it's impossible. I'm stuck and forced into a position that wasn't my doing. I didn't decide for Jay to be captured. I didn't choose to be dragged underwater by rotten Caspian. I didn't ask to be separated from Jay, so now, I'll do anything to fix it. I'll save him in any way possible."

"Just like I'd do anything to return, Wes."

I stopped groping the walls for a secret lever and stared at Isaac's earth-shattering gaze. "Yeah, we both care, but it's not for the same reason, so fall into the idea that you and I are meant for each other. The only real thing in our Link is that we have to work together to get what we want. That's it."

"It sounds like you're trying to convince yourself," Isaac smirked. "I didn't even bring *us* up."

Heat flushed my cheeks. "If we're going to work as a team, we need to start trusting each other."

"I already trust you, love."

"Fine, then I need to figure out how to trust *you*. No more secrets."

"Deal." He spread his arms open wide. "Where should I start? I'm the Mystier's highest librarian. My brain is an encyclopedia. Ask me anything, and I'll do my best."

Isaac's s-watch pinged with a new message. I was surprised it hadn't been confiscated or that it still had any battery. After Isaac hit the button and projected the image, Alaska's face covered the entire wall.

"Are you safe, Kyra?" she asked.

"Don't worry about me. How's Landon?"

"Your nephew is fine." Alaska altered the viewpoint and showed Landon sprawled on a white rug, playing with a tablet device in front of a fireplace. She angled the camera back to her, showing her raven hair in a knotted mess. "Gemm wants me to ask you if you still have the potion she made…just in case."

I tapped my pocket where the tiny vial lay and glanced at Isaac. His hand swiped his hip, then he nodded. "Yeah, we do. But we won't have to drink it."

"Have you had any communication with Jadox?" Alaska's eyebrows knitted together.

Terror sliced a hole in my heart. "No, but he's going to be just fine. I agreed with Caspian to attend the President's Ball in exchange for your brother's location."

"No! Kyra! Didn't you read the note I gave you?"

"Yeah, but who is Paola Perez? Can we trust her?"

"My ex. She's the Ordull who Jadox caught me kissing years ago. Jadox erased Paola's memory with a spell so we couldn't be together."

"Wow, so how does Paola remember you to send you a warning letter?"

"It sounds like her memories are returning. Maybe the spell fades over time." Alaska moved, showing Gemm sitting on a rocking chair in the background. "But, Kyra, where are you?"

Isaac shook his head and raised one finger to his lips.

Secrets were over between Isaac and me, but secrets might keep others I cared about safe. My heart raced. "Um, Alaska, you swear Landon is still safe?"

"Yes, I promise. Now, answer my question."

I cringed. "I can't."

"You can't, or you won't?"

"You wouldn't believe me if I did." I huffed, glancing at the floating bubbles by the bookshelf. "It's better this way."

"Paola messaged me that Caspian and President Stirk formed an alliance. With his help, she found the last Cydian hideout. There's no more left. They're all captured."

But she was misinformed. Out the window, dozens of Cydians weaved through the water in their personal pocket spheres, moving between the mushroom houses, waving to one another and smiling. It wasn't true. Alaska didn't have the whole story.

The reception crackled and fuzzed. "Ky...we...dark."

"What?"

The call dropped.

I sighed, dropped onto the bed's mattress, then flopped back, making the blankets poof under me. Above me, Isaac hovered by my knees. I no longer cared that he always closed the distance between us. For the last day, trapped in this room, my tattoo spiked with euphoric energy every time he neared. Instead of fighting it, I just accepted the inevitable. We were Linked—until I found a way to sever it. For now, I'd embrace the hypnotic tug Isaac claimed over my soul. Temporarily.

"If you're not gonna sleep with me...." He pulled his blond hair into that high bun and wiggled his eyebrows playfully. "Then, you're right. We need to find a way out of here." He grabbed my hand and eased me to my feet.

"Seriously? Why is sex the only thing you ever think about?" I smacked his chest but breathed in his fresh scent, frowning when I realized I couldn't remember what Jay smelled like anymore. "No spell I've tried has worked to escape this room. Let's try to join our powers again."

"Are you sure, love? I don't want to hurt you again like this morning."

"You won't."

Isaac frowned.

"If that happens, I'll just heal myself. Come on, we're wasting time." I hooked a finger through Isaac's belt loop and jerked him toward the door.

His savage smirk stirred a fire in my core, daring me. "Move your hand a little lower if you wish."

I rolled my eyes and hid a smile. Right by the sealed door, I stared at the handle, calling my fire alive. Flickers lit all ten fingers in a rush, and a tiny tornado whirled around Isaac's left boot, raising to his hand. When he gazed into my eyes, a rumble deep within flared with an immediate need to touch Isaac, anywhere, everywhere, all at once and forever. Our power merged fiercely. Goddess, I desperately needed to kiss this man.

My fire roared larger, spinning within his cyclone of wind. Heat warmed my knees, stomach, then face— a twisting death trap. All at once, Isaac directed it towards the door, but just as it touched the sleek surface, it simmered to embers and disappeared.

"Damn it!" I stomped.

Isaac slid his hand over the sleek door for the hundredth time. As he studied it, he rolled up his sleeves to his elbows. I absorbed every feature of the cut muscles of his forearms. A new tingle zapped my tattoo.

His eyes whipped to mine, reading my mind, burning in immediate desire. "What are you thinking?"

I gulped and walked closer, making the decision as I placed my fingers on the veins running along his wrist, following them up to his elbow. "I think our Link thrives on physical contact…for our Link to work stronger…we might need to be closer, just this once."

"So, what got you to change your mind? My smile or my wit?"

"Your body." I made a fake gagging sound.

"He stepped closer and ran a thumb over my top lip. "Whether you believe me or not, I feel how much you care for Griffin. It's real. I know I joke around, but I can't be the one to create pain and conflict for you. You've already been through enough."

"If merging our powers is a sacrifice needed to save Jay, then I'll do it."

Sadness swept over his face. "I don't want you to sacrifice anything for me, but I think you might be right. What if this Link isn't like any other relationship?" He stepped toward me. "What if the only way to save Jay is to...."

"Kiss."

"Well, you don't have to steal my words, love. It's a little arrogant." He licked his lips while danger, adventure, and deviousness flashed in his features all at once.

I wanted him so badly and was tired of fighting the desire for these past few days. Isaac's face softened into relief as he studied me. I became pinned to the door. Captivated by his riveting eyes, I let myself sink into his gaze.

Isaac's mouth hovered over mine. A whisper of promise filled the sliver of air between us. We both waited, holding our breath in checkmate. Who would make the first move? My heart drummed fiercely, and his slammed even harder, faster, as his gaze drank me in. The man was fuckin' thirsty. My tattoo begged for me to crash my mouth into his.

"You have no idea how badly I want you," Isaac whispered.

My chest was about to explode with raw need. Isaac's hands were suddenly on my back, pulling me up to him. His restraint was hotter than the sun. Strong. Patient. He was waiting for me to close the distance, to be sure this was what I wanted. But it wasn't possible. I stepped back. Pain cast deep canyons on his face for a beat until he covered it with a forced smile.

"It was worth a shot," he said softly.

In a heartbeat, he hijacked my Magik while jumping toward the door. With the vigor of a god, he propelled the flurried mix of wind and fire through the barrier. It cracked down the middle. Then bent in half, erupting into pieces. Shattered completely.

"How did you do that?" I asked, shocked.

"I tried a different emotion."

Wide-eyed and panting, I hopped through the hole and ran out of our room. Isaac matched me stride for stride through the hallway. His gaze bore into my flushed cheeks, but I kept my sights on the far end of the hall. We sprinted down a corridor lined with small circular windows. Groupers, trappers, and trout circled on the other side of the vast sea, reminding me that we still had no plan to access the surface.

Between each window, framed pictures decorated the walls. Cydians of all ages, colors and genders wrapped their arms around the shoulder of Caspian, the leader of the sea. They all seemed to trust him. What was his end game?

Isaac's footsteps were almost silent, as though he flew. He effortlessly glided through the tunnel like a bird. He was a creature with wings trapped without a sky. And I was a dragon caged against my greatest enemy. Water always extinguished fire. I couldn't win in this land. The tunnel led to a fork.

Which way? Right or left?

I turned the corner and ran straight into a stone statue, falling to my ass. Upon looking up, Caspian's marine eyes flashed with pride and rage at the sight of me sprawled at his feet. Great, not a statue—just my warden.

"It took you long enough to escape." Caspian rubbed his long scar, then reached down to help, but I lunged up on my own. I slammed my foot atop his, but the man didn't flinch.

"Cute. What'd you convince her to do to make it work, Nilson?"

Isaac's fists balled tight, but I jumped between the two before they initiated a macho battle of male egos.

Frustration lit flickers at my fingertips. "Why am I here?"

"I told you already..." Caspian said, "...to kill the president."

"What are you hiding?"

"Nothing."

"You've probably never had one truth leave your lips. You're probably just delivering me on a platter to the president."

"I'm not."

"Can you say anything that would make me believe you?"

He paused and snapped his fingers which popped each floating bubble in the hallway. Water burst from each one as drops splattered over the floor. The water ran towards us and circled our ankles without Caspian taking his eyes off mine.

"No, you have no reason to trust me," he said, "I have nothing to say that you'd believe, but my wife might convince you of a thing or two. You can join us for dinner."

"Now?"

"I assume you're hungry since we haven't given you a meal today."

I glanced down at my clothes which were unfit for a palace dinner. My leggings and an oversized red t-shirt that drooped loosely over one shoulder looked more like a casual outfit I would've worn on stage to a gig. My life as a drummer felt like an eternity ago. I tapped a fast rhythm on my thigh while taking in Isaac's attire. He looked like a meal no matter what he wore, and I'd rather ravish him than whatever octopus or squid they'd serve me at dinner.

"No, thanks." I sidestepped Caspian and finally dodged around his quick feet. "We're going to the surface. Maybe there will be some fast food up there."

He laughed, the hoarse quality evident in each sound. "How will you hold your breath for five minutes? I don't suppose you know a thing or two about the pressure this far underwater either?"

"I'll take her," a female spoke behind us.

Isaac turned first, squinting, no doubt using his laser eyes to spot any threat. My ears perked up.

"This is my wife, Narelle."

"Evening, Cas. You didn't tell me we had *visitors*." Her silver-slit eyes scanned me up and down, ignoring Isaac completely.

"We aren't visitors. Your lovely husband captured us days ago."

"Is that so?" Her eyes narrowed at her husband.

"And I'd love to take you up on your offer to take us to the surface."

I pushed out a sweet demeanor. "Can you hold your breath for a mile too?"

"No, we have transportation. Do you really think all Cydians are trapped down here until my husband takes each of us to the surface?" Narelle said.

She was a boss lady embodied in a tunic. When she walked toward me, the seaweed strands hanging off her shoulders looked like the train of a dress.

"Is your transportation those strange bubbles I saw out my window?"

"No." Narelle's chin lowered. "But you better follow my directions at the stables if you want to keep both legs."

Isaac rubbed a soft circle along my waist, calming my racing heart. When Caspian's glare settled on Isaac's grip, his eyes narrowed to the smallest cracks.

"Actually, before you go to the stables, there's something I need to tell you," Caspian said.

13

ISAAC

Kyra's golden hair shimmered like treasure when the rare sunray sparkled through the windows. I wished she didn't take up residence in every corner of my mind. Ahead, Narelle and Caspian guided us through the long tunnel.

I felt Kyra's impatience slither through our bond and wanted to reach forward to grab her hand, but she was speed-walking behind them. She always did everything fast, jumping into situations without thinking everything through first. One of these days, I'd convince her to sit still for more than thirty seconds.

Over his shoulder, Caspian chuckled. "You picked wrong, Ky. Twice. You weren't supposed to Link with that Dravian soldier or Nilson. You're meant to Link with me."

She snorted. "Very funny."

I didn't have to see her face to know she had rolled her eyes too. At least Caspian kept his story the same for both of us, no matter how idiotic it was.

Their pace quickened as we walked down the eerie tunnel. She and I would drown if there was a single crack in the windows. That thought wasn't exactly soothing. A shadow passed over one window. I slowed, peeking into the abyss. Time stood still as a far-off voice sang a mysterious song in another language. Hopefully, the perilous sirens couldn't reach us.

Far ahead, at the very end of the corridor, there was a dead end with a glass door leading to the sea. In the water, plants swayed over the fungiform buildings. But outside the structures, revolting sea creatures were tied to posts with long seaweed ropes as reins. Their green scales and long snouts resembled crocodiles, but the curled shape of their tail reminded me of a seahorse.

I gasped, making Kyra whirl around fast in the tunnel to look at me wide-eyed. "What is it?"

"It's a trap. They're leading us to monsters."

She stayed by my side, squinting. "I can't see anything."

"They're still too far away for you to see."

Caspian turned around nonchalantly. "Hydracos aren't monsters. They pull our chariots to the surface. Come on, let's get you back to your room. There's an incoming storm, and it's not safe to travel...."

Kyra marched to Caspian, pointing her sharp fingernail like a dagger in his face. "I'm not being dragged along blindly anymore. I don't care if we're on your turf." She shoved him hard into the tunnel wall. "I don't care if you think I was supposed to Link with you. Listen to me because I'll only say this once. I only care about getting Isaac and me to the surface safely."

Shock erupted within me. Before, she would've said the only thing she cared about was freeing Griffin. Something in her tone had switched.

Caspian smirked under her fierce hold. "That's the *only* thing you care about?"

"Yes!"

"Funny, you didn't mention Griffin once this time. Has your allegiance changed? And so quickly."

Her jaw dropped, and I felt Kyra's confusion wash through her. "I...We need to get to the surface...to save Jay."

Caspian wiggled a mocking finger in her face. "That's not what you said. You only mentioned Isaac."

Kyra slapped his face, and Narelle jumped in the background, covering her mouth with one hand. "Oh, I like her, Cas."

Caspian barely flinched, despite his cheek turning pink.

"Tell me where Jay is being kept prisoner," Kyra huffed. "On the beach, you said you knew."

"Griffin will be present at the ball."

My heart plummeted from her renewed hope. Our Link would never be stronger than whatever connection she had with Griffin. I couldn't force her to love—I mean— to care about me.

"You promise?" She glared at Caspian.

He smiled a menacing grin. "Would you trust my promise?"

She lit her fingertips on fire and slowly moved the flame closer to his face. "Take us to the surface."

Caspian slowly moved out of her hold and moved down the tunnel. "Fine, I bet you'll like our hydracos, Ky. They share your fiery spirit. The alpha is mine, Brynn. She'll lead three others during our trip. Follow my rules if you want to keep your legs; they like to bite."

Kyra's gorgeous amber eyes pulsed with vivacity.

Isaac, should we trust him?

I moved towards her, brought her hand to my lips, kissed her sweet knuckles, then sent a silent response.

We'll find Griffin. Trust me. I promise.

You promise?

I promise. You'll live happily ever after. You'll do what you came for, save all the prisoners, take care of Landon, and everything will be okay.

She smiled, brightening my day, then nodded. We formed a single-file line again, walking down the tunnel until the stables were within view for her too.

Kyra rushed to the door and pressed both hands against the barrier. Her breath fogged the glass. Genuine awe rushed through our bond at the sight. Four green creatures architected from mythical storybooks hovered in the water. I was right. Up close, they were an inexplicable mix of crocodiles and seahorses. With each breath, bubbles rose from their giant snouts.

An eerie presence loomed as a hydraco's all-white eyes met mine.

It had no pupils, but I felt its stare. Were they blind? No, I was sure it saw me, even with its unearthly features.

Over ten feet long and probably weighing over two-thousand pounds, the one in front of the pack was connected to long reins that looped around its wide neck and fit around the curved tail that spiraled around itself in a loop. It held so much history in its wicked gaze.

"I want to touch one." Kyra's voice suddenly had an edge.

"What?" I asked, seemingly the only one to hear her. "Caspian said they bite."

A warning rampaged through my veins, and burning sensations jolted my tattoo.

Caspian's hand hovered over the latch on the door. "So, when this unlocks, we have ten seconds until the chamber space fills with water. Take a giant gulp of air before it does, then we swim straight to the chariot. Use that time to fill your lungs completely; I can help you to the chariots if needed, but dragging two of you is more challenging. Whatever you do, don't approach the hydraco's faces. They're very possessive creatures, especially of their personal space."

I have to touch it, Isaac.

Kyra's frantic urge put all my senses on overdrive.

What? No, Kyra, didn't you hear what he just said?

My tattoo pulsed with need, but it wasn't mine. Kyra's inexplicable frenzy shot desperately straight at me.

Kyra! Take a deep breath.

She slammed both fists against the glass as if she was possessed.

"Hey! What are you doing?" Narelle lunged toward her, holding both her arms down. "Stop it."

Kyra didn't even register her touch, escaping from Narelle's grip quickly and continuing to scream, "I have to touch it!"

"What the goddess is wrong with her? Calm her down!" Caspian shouted, covering both ears.

Utterly astonished, I shoved myself between the glass door and Kyra and sandwiched her cheeks with both hands. "Kyra, look at me. Focus on my voice."

"Isaac? She's calling to me." Her breath sped so fast it looked like her chest would explode. "I need to go!" Kyra's eyes were locked on the hydraco, stuck in a trance.

"Kyra!" I snapped in front of her entranced face. *"Kyra!"*

"We can't wait any longer if you want to make it to the surface," Caspian said. "The storm is coming."

Even though Caspian waited to push the button that would open the door, with worry in his eyes, Narelle smacked it herself, initiating the countdown.

"Ten," an automated robotic voice echoed in our little area, and the glass door slid open.

Freezing water gushed in, drenching my shoes.

"Nine."

Kyra started thrashing and kicking, struggling against the water pouring in and trying to leave the space too early.

"Restrain her!" Narelle yelled.

"I'm trying!"

"Eight."

"I have to touch them!" Kyra yelled.

"Seven."

Kyra turned even wilder and more erratic, possessed even. I fought to contain her with my muscles clenched around her in an iron grip. She was too strong. Fear choked me as Kyra's frenzy turned violent.

"Six."

Water soaked my stomach.

Kyra broke free and dove into the cascading waters prematurely. She disappeared into the water.

"Kyra!" My heart pounded.

"Five...four..." the automated voice continued, and I focused on sucking in a breath.

"When I go after her, I won't be able to help you," Caspian warned.

"Just go. Keep her safe!" I yelled.

Caspian vanished into the waters, leaving Narelle and me in a stare-down for the last few seconds of oxygen.

"Three."

I gulped in the air as water reached my neck.

"Two."

"Follow me to the chariot," Narelle ordered.

"One."

Our tiny area was brimming with water. I dipped lower and dove after Narelle. Fish darted away with each movement. My shoes weighed me down. Fear corkscrewed in my Circle at how unprepared we were for this and how little Caspian had informed us. It was a trap. He'd meant to kill us both.

The chariot grew closer, and I tried to zero in on Narelle's form, but my gaze defied my command and searched for Kyra. Horror struck a chord deep within. Where the Flames was she? Caspian was nowhere in sight either.

My chest burned. Bubbles oozed from my nose. I swam harder. Faster. Almost to the chariot's door. As I was about to suck in water, a hand latched onto my wrist and pulled me inside. It sealed shut Magikally, defying physics. I sucked in the air, panting and dripping.

Gasping, I bolted from the sopping floor and pressed my nose against the window. "What the goddess is going on? Why did Kyra freak out?" I pounded my fist on the window.

"Calm down. I thought you'd try to use your air Magik to fill your lungs and stay under longer."

Shit, that would've been smart.

"Where's Kyra?" I demanded.

Narelle's soft hand landed on my shoulder. "Look, she's right there. See them?"

Out the window, Kyra was riding atop the alpha hydraco, steering it up to the surface. Caspian straddled the monster behind her, one hand around her waist. Kyra was alive—*and* leaving me behind.

I swiveled around and glared at Narelle. "What did you two do to her? She's gone crazy."

Narelle shrugged. "I've never seen that happen before."

As she walked through the interior of the sea chariot, we passed by an extravagant liquor shelf.

"Want a drink?" She poured tequila into a glass and reached into the large fridge.

"No, I don't want a drink. I want answers."

Pulling out the juice, she mixed it in the cup and swirled around the contents with a metal straw.

"We have to go around the entire southern coast of Lodesa. This will be a day's journey or longer if the tropical storm is as bad as Caspian predicted. You can sleep in the back room. Food will be brought for dinner, breakfast, and lunch. We have suitcases packed for you with gowns and tuxes for the ball."

"Her gown? I don't care about our clothes right now. Why are you so calm?"

"Caspian is keeping your girlfriend alive."

"But there's a storm. She has no protection."

"Do not doubt my husband," she growled.

"I want to know what happened to her." I hammered the top of the bar. "Why did she say someone was calling to her?"

Narelle sighed. "Probably something to do with her Golden Circle. You're a smart guy. Think about it. Why would it be gold? Why is Kyra the only one to Link twice without catastrophic repercussions? She's different. Maybe she has some connection to dark Magik. Maybe Moroka called to her. It's probably because part of Kyra belongs to the sea too." Narelle scrunched her nose. "You seriously hadn't considered this already?"

"I…I don't know." My heart rate tripled.

"Well, if she matters this much to you, you'll want to help us convince her to Link with Caspian." Narelle gulped down the rest of her drink and filled it again.

I leaned against the barstool, completely baffled. "So, you know your husband wants to Link with her, and you're fine with that?"

She shook her head. "He doesn't want to. He *has* to. There's a difference."

"Why does he have to?"

"Because of Elana Elidi."

"Are you saying Caspian received some divine wisdom from the underworld?" I rubbed my temples, hoping this was all a nightmare. "This makes no sense. Why would you be okay with Caspian starting a relationship with another woman?"

Narelle laughed. "Excuse me?"

"The Link will make him feel romantically connected to her. Caspian will be able to communicate with Kyra telepathically. Their Magik will be stronger. He won't want you anymore."

Narelle laughed again, the sound resembling the dangerous sirens swimming around the sea. "Oh, dear boy. You are very wrong. The Link doesn't force anyone to fall in love."

My jaw clenched. "Have you Linked with someone before?"

"Of course not."

"Then you don't know what it's like." My tattoo hummed with the desire to whip a tornado of wind at Narelle's face.

"Maybe you just really like her." She waved one finger. "Caspian will *never* want Kyra romantically. I can assure you of that."

"Nothing in life is certain."

Her sly smirk crept up. "Are you *certain* about that?"

I gawked, unable to help myself from staring at Narelle. "If you want to keep your husband, ask him not to go through with Linking with her."

Kyra would be too dangerous to be connected to all three of us. I'd rather sever my Link with her than put her in harm's way. How could her soul be split three ways?

Narelle shook her head. "I swear, Isaac, you have it all wrong. The Link doesn't force love."

"If you're right, then just tell me why he's doing this. Why does Caspian want President Stirk dead?"

"Follow me to the cockpit. I'll show you." She sighed while walking away.

A whisper, quieter than the ocean floor, scraped the vowels of my name in a hiss.

Iiiiiisaaaaac.

Iiiiiisaaaaac.

It grew closer, louder, clearer.

Iiiiisaaaac, you're so alone.

I whirled around, but Narelle had vanished down a hallway. The chariot echoed with the silence of an empty midnight.

Iiiiisaaaac, I know what you fear.

"Isaac."

Just outside the chariot window, Moroka's half-gnarled body floated and swayed with the current. I jumped out of my skin at the voice speaking in such proximity. Power hummed to life.

My fists curled tight, though what chance could I possibly have against a demon? Her claws scratched against the glass.

"You fear being alone, Iiiiisaaaac. Come with me, and you'll never be alone again."

"Shut up. Go away."

"Time is *ticking*." The demon couldn't smile even if she had the right anatomy, but a smirk crept up in her expression regardless. "Tick tock, tick tock. Hurry, little puppet."

"For what?" My skin crawled with unease.

"You have one lunar cycle."

"Until what?"

"The ₾sμwi comes," Moroka hissed and slid into the murky depths.

I shook my head and rushed down the chariot's hall, hoping to erase the last few moments from existence. After taking a seat in the cockpit, Narelle pushed a button that whipped the remaining hydracos into action. They pulled away from the stables and swam up. Up. Up to the surface, hopefully following the direction of wherever Kyra had disappeared to. The water's current strengthened, and we bobbed about, making my stomach curl on itself.

Gritting my teeth, I focused on calming myself and faced Narelle as she piloted the swift vehicle. We zoomed by whales and coral, and the water turned a lighter shade of blue with each passing minute. Energy in my Circle spun to life and surged with Kyra's flames. She was nearby and safe. My heartbeat settled just a little.

"So, why does Caspian want the president dead?" I asked.

"Because she's the one who has Brent Elidi under her control."

"Kyra's biological father?" I rubbed my temple, processing the new information. "Why would Kyra's father be with the president? I thought he was imprisoned by some psychotic Mystier."

Narelle's knuckles turned white on the steering contraption. "President Syvonne Stirk is no mere Ordull. She is the strongest Mystier alive."

Panic and fear twisted together within me in a chaotic knot, blocking any rational thought from existence.

Kyra, come back, love. You're in danger.

14

KYRA

As we breached the surface, I wrapped my arms around Brynn's rough neck. Her scales scraped my forearms through my shirt. Rain poured and streamed down my face. The harsh wind slapped my hair, but it only seduced me further because new raw power mixed in my Circle—taunting me. Fire ignited and swirled with the air I sucked in. But now, a hint of water Magik pulled at my core too, teasing and dancing just out of reach.

I wasn't Linked with anyone from Cydon, so why was this happening? Who was I? Where did I belong? Why did the ocean suddenly affect me so strongly? Frustration clamped my muscles tightly.

Since I hadn't been raised around Mystiers, I had limited information about Elidians, but this didn't seem normal for someone with fire Magik. Did it have to do with my Golden tattoo? Confusion coiled in my stomach. It wasn't fair. Who was I?

"Who?" I yelled into the storm.

"What?" Caspian asked from behind me.

"Nothing."

While riding Brynn, the ocean felt more natural than Draven or Vayu. The waves thrashed into my hydraco's sturdy frame, trying to buck me off her back. Angry clouds shook their giant fists and cracked with thunder again and again as if in a warning. But I didn't care because strength rushed through me. The sea called, and I finally understood the meaning behind the sirens' songs that had etched themselves into my mind.

Lightning split the sky in two, flashing so bright that I spotted a beach to the north.

Kyra, wait for me, please. You're in danger.

Isaac's message seared strong, snapping me back to reality. Then the soft hand around my waist twitched. I gasped, forgetting Caspian was behind me.

"Lead Brynn to land!" he roared in my ear, competing with the crashing waves enveloping us.

"Will Isaac be okay?" I screamed over my shoulder.

Only the water responded. White foam collided with my knees as Brynn wiggled toward the beach on short crocodile legs. I shivered and leaned closer to her strong, thick neck, but my beast was cold-blooded, unable to share her warmth.

Caspian's tense energy behind me kept me alert. The man had a trick up his sleeve. I could feel it. If only I had more clues to determine what he was hiding. I tried to squint through the monsoon, but so much water blocked my vision that I could only squeeze my eyes shut and concentrate on the sounds.

Pat pat of my heartbeat.

A *boom* of thunder

The *swoosh* of waves.

A familiar sensation tugged at my memories but was hazy and hesitant.

The *thump thump* of Caspian's heart—something vaguely familiar.

Tension seeped out of me as I grasped for Isaac's Magik. A ping spiked at my tattoo. By using his weather power, I commanded the storm to calm.

Whock whock whock of rain finally slowed, so I could hear their individual drops, thousands of beads merging into the sea.

Finally, the strong current subsided to an easy sway until Brynn's movements shifted underneath my thighs. All splashing stopped, and a rough sandpaper sound made my spine arch.

"Kyra. Open your damn eyes." Caspian's voice was ahead of me instead of behind me.

I snapped them open and met his aqua-marine eyes studying me. Hurricanes churned in Caspian's eyes as he traced his long scar, apparently a habit of his. Caspian stood on the sandy beach, ringing out the bottom corner of his shirt despite little raindrops falling on his shoulders. His brown hair dripped, forming tiny holes in the sand at his bare feet. In the distance, seagulls circled over beach houses on stilts, each one with wooden planks boarding their windows.

"Explain what happened to me down at the stables," I demanded.

"You'll figure it out soon enough."

Jumping off Brynn's back, I stumbled to the sand, the grains coating my wet hands. The hydraco lowered her head and licked my whole face with a bumpy tongue.

"That's…interesting. She doesn't like anyone but me." Caspian cocked his head to the side, then rubbed his dark stubble. "So, would you rather wait for Isaac to arrive or head to the safehouse now?" He turned and marched off. The rain lessened with each step I trailed after him until it was a mere drizzle.

"Something happened to me under the water. Tell me why."

"You aren't ready."

I grabbed his wrist. When Caspian turned, he crouched like an animal ready to pounce, back curved and shoulders hunched.

I stopped in my tracks. His movements reminded me of something—someone. A dream. Or a nightmare. Brynn nudged my side affectionately, and I ran a hand over her scales.

"The ball is tonight." Caspian exhaled, then stood again while tracing his long scar once again. "If you still want to save Griffin, we must get ready. Follow me."

Guilt rammed into my chest. I had forgotten. My heart hammered a fierce rhythm. How could I have forgotten Jay? He was fading from me. Panic gripped my soul and wrenched it tight.

"Tonight? But you said it was tomorrow."

"We traveled underwater for hours around the entire western coast. You slipped into an unconscious trance."

For the first time, I registered the temperature. It wasn't Draven's snowy winter and definitely not humid like Galudi's Cove by the lighthouse, but somewhere in between.

"So, where are we now?"

"Close to the president's headquarters."

"Andersonville? This is where I'm from. But I thought the capital was bombed."

"It was. The ball is at The Crooked Chateau in the middle of downtown, one of the buildings still standing." He pointed ahead. "And through that alley is a safe house where Isaac and Narelle will meet us."

"I know this area. I can lead you. What's the address?"

Caspian pressed his knuckles against his temple. "Aren't you like twenty-five now? Yet you never learned how to slow down."

"Excuse me?"

"You're not what I imagined, Ky."

"Stop calling me that."

"Why?" There was a honed challenge in his eyes.

Only one person had ever called me that, and I'd never share that part of my life with this jerk. "Forget it."

"Follow me." Caspian's speed quickened as he darted behind a building. Rain guzzled down a gutter and sprinkled a small leak through the siding of one house. An unsettling feeling of being stalked crept up my spine. When I almost stepped around the corner, Caspian stiff-armed me, blocking my movements.

"Shh!" He pushed me behind him against the siding of the beach house. "There have been revolts around here led by the Aurum Orbis Society. Not every Ordull agrees with Stirk's policies to imprison Mystiers for testing. Bombs and shootings are common, even in the middle of the afternoon."

I glanced through the fog towards the beach where Brynn peeked above the sea grass, munching on lunch. "And what if an Ordull sees a half-crocodile-half-seahorse wandering the beach?"

He shrugged. "Gorulas and ventus have already been spotted since Mystier barriers have been shattered. Ordulls need to get used to a different life now."

A loud crash echoed down the block.

"Come on, we can't stay out here. The safe house is down the street."

We tiptoed around the puddles, and I jumped out of my skin when an explosion erupted from several streets down. A scream pierced the air, then silence. Holding my breath, I trailed after Caspian, wishing I had a weapon at my disposal. My Magik felt faded the further I moved from the sea. Or maybe I felt weaker the further I moved from Isaac.

Isaac? Are you there? I'm sorry.

Where are you?

With Caspian, headed to a safe house.

It's a trap.

Caspian halted in front of a door with chipped paint. I smacked straight into his back and almost tumbled to my ass, but he caught me with one hand.

"You're a walking disaster."

"Don't make me kick your ass."

"Water outranks fire, genius."

The way his smirk curved up sent a shock of nostalgia through my veins. Why? Who did he remind me of?

Caspian twisted the doorknob. It was jammed. Water ran out of the crevice under the warped wood.

He sighed and mumbled, "another flood," then shoved his shoulder against the barrier. It was completely stuck. I rammed my shoulder against the door too. Nothing. With a quick flick of my wrist, fire shot out, burning a perfectly circular hole through the center.

"There's your proof that fire outranks water, turd," I said.

Caspian rolled his eyes and gestured for me to enter into the unknown. Despite the heavy clouds, more shadows lurked and crept with every passing second as the afternoon drifted by, giving the safehouse an eerie vibration.

"You want me to go in there first? No way, after you, Your Royal Highness," I layered on the sarcasm.

"Fine." He stepped through the hole. "I was just trying to be polite to my *elder*."

"Did your mermaid momma teach you manners at underwater tea parties?"

Caspian pivoted so fast that I feared his hip would bust out of the socket. Like a ruthless villain on steroids, his gaze pinned me against the wall, and his blue tattoo glowed under his wet shirt, thrumming with evident rage.

"Don't you *ever* speak of my parents. You know nothing."

"Calm down, dolphin boy. I'm sorry." Gulping, I raised both hands and nodded to the staircase marked in graffiti. "I don't think this safehouse is as *safe* as you expected."

His finger traced the phrase *"death to all witches"* on the wall. "Come on. There's a way to communicate with Narelle upstairs."

"You don't have a fancy s-watch?"

"They're no longer safe. Most are under surveillance from Stirk's people."

Stepping over a rotting, three-legged coffee table, I followed him, managing my chorus of creaks and groans with every step up. Caspian knocked against a spot on the wall, and a lever fell out. He pulled it, and a small section of wallpaper peeled away, revealing three s-watches, snacks, water, and a gun. Caspian handed the weapon to me.

"I don't know how to attach this," I said.

"You don't need to put it on yet since we still need to change. Just hold it and keep watch out the window for a minute."

"Can I have an s-watch?"

"Sure, but it's pointless, and be careful. They might tap into your streams."

He tossed one over and fumbled with his buttons. I racked my brain for Alaska's number, unable to recall it offhand. The only contact I had memorized was Jay's. With a heavy heart, I pushed against the steel wall that gated Jay's mind. He was still not letting me in, or he was unable to. I shuddered at the thought of what torture he had endured. Instead, I typed in a message and sent it to his number.

Safe

Chateau - Twenty-five o'clock

My watch ticked on, seconds slicing through time, but no response was returned. Narelle's voice came from Caspian's watch, "You may not have many more chances to tell her."

"What's that mean?" I asked. "Tell me what?"

Caspian's eye twitched, but he recovered fast, then clicked off his watch. "Mind your business."

"You're hiding something."

He threw me a protein bar from the stash and ripped one open, chomping on the corner. "Technically, I'm hiding everything from you."

My fists clenched, and I almost chucked the snack straight at his long nose, but the rumbling in my stomach won out this time. I bit into the crunchy granola and let the smooth chocolate melt over my tongue.

"You're a terrible lookout." He nodded out the window to two fast-approaching figures as I nearly choked on the granola.

Upon immediately recognizing Isaac's quiet huffs and puffs, I relaxed.

"Don't worry, it's just your wife, keeper of all holy secrets and betrayals."

In a matter of moments, thuds clomped on the lower level, then up the stairs. Isaac's wet blond bun appeared first, followed by his gray eyes swirling with concern and then those pretty lips. Before I knew it, my body lunged across the rickety floor and into his arms. I buried my head in his chest, heaving with a rapid heartbeat.

"I'm sorry," I whispered into his solid frame. "I didn't mean to leave you. I swear, I didn't mean to. I couldn't help it."

Isaac kissed my forehead. Holding both my hands in his, he kissed my knuckles and gazed down at me. "Don't *ever* scare me like that again."

I nodded, holding back tears. Why was I so emotional? Why was my chest so tight? His smoky gaze calmed my racing heart in an instant when he slipped one finger under my chin. He looked like he cared, but I needed to tell him he was wrong, that he didn't care, he couldn't care.

Isaac continued, "Promise that you'll never scare me like that again."

An impossible ask. So, instead, I followed my heart and rose on my tiptoes. I was tempted to lick the sea salt from his lips. He would probably taste of treasure and rain and hope. A sudden jerk zapped my tattoo, and Isaac leaned into my shoulder, groaning into my skin. The *'almost'* sensation was driving me insane.

Caspian cleared his throat. "Stop it. We need to dress for the ball."

When Isaac hesitantly pulled away, his face twisted with layered questions, but I still held him in a hug.

Ignoring Caspian, I whispered to Isaac, "I don't know what this thing is between us, and I don't want to lie to you."

"Then tell me the truth." Isaac smiled, melting my insides into gooey marshmallows.

"I still care about Jay, too."

He tucked a strand of my crazed hair behind my ear. "And me?"

"Maybe a little."

"That's all I needed to know." He nodded, wrinkles forming on his forehead. "I can deal with that."

Pressure clamped on my chest. "What if I can't deal with caring for two men?"

"Then we figure it out—after we save him."

"By *him*, do you mean Jay or Wes?"

His lips found my forehead. "Both, love. We will both get what we need."

"What if what we want is different than what we need?" I whispered into his neck.

"What do you want, love?"

I stepped back, sharpness digging at my Möbius Circle, communicating something I didn't want to hear. Desperate for a distraction, I zeroed in on a suitcase sitting by Narelle's feet. She was watching us like a soap-opera fan.

She clapped slowly. "You two are something else, but we have no time for dramatics. You boys, go change downstairs." She clicked her tongue and pushed Caspian and Isaac out the door.

I leaned against the wall and watched Isaac leave, memorizing his every movement until he disappeared around the corner. The obvious sound of his clothes dropping to the floor flooded my brain. I used every ounce of energy not to picture Isaac in his boxer briefs. Not to imagine pinning him to the wall and climbing him like a tree. To not visualize his broad hands gripping my waist and hoisting me on the banister.

"Kyra?"

"Huh?"

Narelle shook her head. "Dear, you have it bad."

"I don't know what you're talking about."

"Hurry, change into your gown for the ball," Narelle said in lieu of disagreeing with me.

"Um, I can't go to a ball. I smell like decaying fish, and my hair is a ball of knots."

"I can fix that with an easy spell." She smiled, delicious deviousness written in her expression. "Honestly, if you perfected this spell, you'd never have to shower again and still be perfectly clean."

"Tempting. But I happen to enjoy scalding showers."

Narelle said a spell under her breath like a fairy godmother with a gleam of a demon in her eyes.

"What are you doing?"

"Giving you a makeover. Any Mystier can learn a spell with lots of practice. But it takes energy and years of studying. Most of us can master three or four complex spells within our lifetime, but I've heard you have a convenient enhancement."

She pulled out a dress. My hair dried and whirled with a mind of its own, curling and shaping into an elegant updo. A faint layer painted my face with the swish of her wrist, and I knew without a mirror that she'd feathered makeup on my cheeks and eyes.

"I'm coming back in on the count of three," Isaac's sexy voice sailed through the hall. "One…" He jumped through the threshold. "Aw man, you're not naked."

"Very funny."

"I'll let you two chat." Narelle passed by Isaac on her way out.

When I met his gray eyes, my breath hitched. In his tux, Isaac looked like a godly king. The tux was miraculously snug in all the right places, outlining his muscles and wide shoulders; he stood as a masterpiece. Maybe Narelle's makeover spells tailored it to him specifically. I might have drooled. In fact, I probably did.

"Your face looks like the sunrise in spring," he said.

I laughed. "What exactly does that look like?"

"Like life." The growl in his voice made my spine prickle. When Isaac held up the silky, black cocktail dress, he commanded, "Now, strip." One eyebrow rose, daring me to defy him.

Deciding to surprise him by not fighting back for once, I peeled off my wet clothes and let them drop to the floor with a heavy *shlop*.

His eyes turned hooded as his hungry gaze swept over me, lingering on my breasts, then my three Linked tattoos. I stretched the side of my underwear away from my hip with one finger. He helped me slip on my dress with such tenderness that tiny gasps escaped my lips when his fingers slid over my skin.

"You're so beautiful, love."

He stole my breath by not even trying to make a move on me. The black dress draped off both shoulders, and the bodice with a corset-style boning lodged into my ribs, stealing my breath as he tightened it. Smooth silk fell to my knee, and along my thigh, a slit flashed.

Narelle entered again, and we jumped apart.

She smirked and glanced between us. "Well, you two couldn't be blushing more." She smiled wider. "Wow, Kyra, the way it gathers at your waist really flatters your curves." She tilted her head and scrunched her nose. "But you're missing something."

"Uh, shoes?"

"No. Hey, Cas, come here."

He trudged from the hallway with a severe scowl as the only accessory to his tux.

"Give me the Vayu Crystal." Narelle snapped her fingers in the air.

He stepped back. "No."

She gave him a stern glare. "It doesn't belong to Cydians."

"But it doesn't belong to Elidians either." Caspian pouted like a twelve-year-old boy being scolded.

"Well, it's a good thing that I'm Vayuian." Isaac held out his hand.

Reaching under his shirt, Caspian pulled out the chain and palmed the crystal. With narrowed eyes, he shot a death glower at Isaac and handed it over.

"Let me do the honors," Isaac said.

Surprised that Isaac would hand it over to me so willingly, I let him drape it over my neck. His wind power mirrored the energy exuding from the necklace. The crystal fell between my cleavage, on full display.

I cleared my throat. "Um, won't this stand out too much?"

"Exactly, the president's staff will recognize her and shoot on sight," Caspian agreed.

"Not with a disguise spell," Narelle mumbled again, and a strange sensation trickled through my bones.

"Woah, your hair is brown again." Caspian circled me.

"Again? You never met me when I had brown hair."

"And your eyes, they're dark brown too," Isaac said, his eyes widened to the size of saucers. "You're…you're not you." His hand traced my jawline. "How long will this last?"

"Until the clock strikes twenty-seven o'clock." Narelle picked a hair from the back of my dress.

Isaac frowned. "So by the time we arrive, we'll have three hours of disguise."

"Estimated."

"You need shoes."

Narelle pointed to her suitcase. "There's boots in there."

"I can't really bend over in this."

"Let me help." Isaac stooped in his tux and placed my foot on his knee. "Hold onto my shoulder."

Heat radiated between my legs, and I had to pinch myself awake from this fantasy.

He laced the high boots one string at a time. Each time he tightened it, I gripped his shoulder harder, feeling his muscles flex under my grasp.

From his knee, Isaac locked his gaze onto mine. "I like how you look as you truly are, amber eyes buzzing with life, no makeup."

"Stop fishing for compliments." I gently slapped his pecs. "I'm not saying how handsome you look in or out of a tux."

"You want me out of a tux? Done!" His grin could light up a demon's cave. "Well, nothing can go wrong with you dressed like this."

Caspian grunted and hid the gun under his tux. "We'll be lucky if we all come back alive. Let's leave before the revolutionaries attack again."

15
ISAAC

If we walked straight through the front entrance of the chateau, it'd be suicide. Who else already knew that President Stirk was actually a Mystier other than Narelle and me? What if Narelle had lied about that as a distraction? I shook my head. What purpose would she have to lie? All I knew was that until it was proven, I wouldn't worry Kyra with gossip.

As we walked under the sunset, painted in violet threats, I lasered my sights around Andersonville. For the next five blocks, armed guards stood at posts on each building's corner. A tiny red dot flashed on their s-watches, catching my attention. They were all in sync, probably relaying some message or command. Except, at one corner, the guard's watch didn't flicker. Squinting, I checked her watch's time. It still showed yesterday's date. Broken.

"This way," I whispered to Kyra and Caspian.

At least Kyra wore boots, making for quick movements in the shadows. Yet, the fancy shoes Caspian had lent me slipped uncomfortably on the pebbles. If anyone was to slow us down, it'd be me. The scrape of gravel skidded lightly underfoot as we hopped from shadow to shadow.

When we rounded the corner, a huge net of electric wires enclosed the chateau like a circus tent. When I stopped, Kyra ran straight into my back.

"Ooof, sorry. What do you see?" she asked.

"We can't go in there. Too much electricity. Our Magik will be stripped, and we'd be defenseless."

I didn't have to use any heightened senses to feel Kyra's mixed feelings. She glanced between Caspian and me, then her hands rested on her black dress, hovering over her tattoos.

"We planned for this," Caspian said, "It's okay. Narelle will turn off all the electricity once we're inside."

Kyra's eyebrows knit tight. "There's no turning back if we go inside."

"Stick to the plan." Caspian leaned in. "Remember, Isaac, go to the spiral staircase in the lobby. A trap door leads to the tunnel where they're keeping prisoners. Griffin should be down there."

My heart slammed in protest. None of this would work.

"Ky, I'll introduce you to the President," Caspian whispered. "Then you'll shoot her with this." He flashed the gun at his hip. "Narelle will turn off the power. We'll use our Magik to flee. Tada! Everything is fine." He stared at the crystal necklace draped over Kyra's front.

He's hiding something, love.

I know. Let's just do this quickly.

Are you genuinely going to kill the president?

Of course not. But Caspian needs to believe he's in charge. Just find Jay. Please.

I will.

"Act as though you belong." Caspian straightened his shoulders into rigid corners and strutted ahead.

My gaze climbed the flame-like building, wide at the base with a slick, curved exterior that seemed to reach the moon with its pointed tip. The sleek red metal of the chateau reminded me of the flames Kyra controlled at her fingertips. I linked my hand through hers and lifted my chin while ignoring the guard. The closer we marched to the electrical tent, the more our connection faded.

Kyra squeezed my hand three times, reminding me how she tapped a beat on her thighs whenever she was nervous.

This guard's watch is broken. She can't send a message to her team.

Silence. Maybe she couldn't feel my thoughts anymore. I was never sure when she had her mental wall up against me. Her mind seemed like an iron tank at times.

"It's okay. We'll be in and out," I breathed.

Kyra nodded and pulled me toward the side entrance.

"Name?" The guard swooped a finger over her tablet's screen.

"Caspian Arno of Cydon, this is Sir William Beckett the third and Lady Ava Terrington." He grabbed the tablet from the guard's hands. "Syvonne is expecting us. Don't keep her waiting."

The guard's jaw clenched tight as she yanked the tablet back from Caspian's grip. "I'll need some identification."

In a flurry of irritation, Caspian tugged out the shirt from his dress pants and flashed his blue tattoo for the woman to see.

Her eyes widened, and she glanced at another soldier who wasn't giving us the time of day.

"Okay, fine. You go in, but not these two."

My fingers wrapped around Kyra's waist, and I pulled her to my side, unwilling to risk a scratch.

"They're my personal guests," Caspian spoke with assertion. "The president requested their presence. Soldiers like you are not qualified to question me. Move aside."

I glanced at the badge on her uniform. It only showed a number.

I sidestepped the guard, but my chest rammed into a metal rod in her hand. Lights flashed and flickered along the pole.

"Step back, witch."

"Or what? You're going to beat me with that?" I nudged Kyra towards Caspian, hoping they'd sneak in with the group passing us.

The guard flipped a switch, and electricity sparked from the rod. "Or you get a fun, little zap."

My fist bunched the guard's collar into a tight ball, and I growled in her ear, "Don't become my problem."

Thankfully, Kyra squeezed into the knot of women herded up the front staircase. When she turned around, searching for me, I pretended not to notice, hoping she'd continue.

"Release me," the guard muttered.

"It's too bad you can't call for backup. And if you yell out for reinforcements, you'll cause a scene. Syvonne doesn't want an issue now, does she?"

Ahead, Caspian and Kyra were atop the chateau's staircase. But, in the blink of an eye, Kyra's fake brunette hair switched back to gold. Fuck! She might not even realize her disguise had faded. Caspian slipped a hand on the small of her back, guiding her.

Suddenly, a shock jolted my shoulder, and I collapsed onto the pavement. Electricity surged through my veins. The guard kicked my stomach. Pain rammed into my gut. I gagged, choking on nothing. The rod collided with my back, and I fell to the ground. Rocks scratched my palms and cheeks. The guard knocked the rod straight into my cheek.

Stars flooded my vision. A crack popped in my mouth then I swallowed something small and hard. My tongue found an empty spot where my molar should've been, and the taste of copper flooded my mouth.

Guests in long dresses stopped and stared or peeked over one another's shoulders. A flare flickered, then another violent electric shock jostled me. My muscles stung and cramped. My limbs twitched and writhed. I shook with the fierceness of a severe seizure. Breathless, it finally ended. The guard acted like I was a rock on the street and addressed the wide-eyed guests next in line.

"Get out of my sight in ten seconds, or I'll put you in cuffs!"

All energy had been sucked from my body. My arms shook as I crawled away, coughing and spitting blood. Rounding the side of the building, I grasped the metal gate and pulled myself up. Both legs trembled, weaker than a newborn fawn.

Kyra, I didn't get in.

Silence.

Kyra?

"Damn it!" I yelled.

"Hello?" a familiar female voice whispered from behind a parked hovercar.

I spun. "Hello?"

"Isaac?" Is that you?"

"Zeph?"

Zeph's eyes poked out and grew to the size of saucers. "I thought you were dead!" When she lifted the rest of her head, ropy scars covered her face as if a wild animal had clawed her to shreds.

I limped over to her, checking over my shoulder for any guards. "I thought Moroka had eaten you!"

Zeph waved my comment away like it was old news. At the sight of her, relief swelled in my chest. I had spent years with Zeph by my side, helping me take care of Wes on the weekends. Even if she did betray us by leading the Ordull soldiers to Draven, she'd always hold a part of my past.

"Are you okay?" She stared at the blood on my shirt.

"I'm fine." I leaned against the tree for the needed support. "You?"

Her fingers hovered over her scars. "A woman doesn't have to have a perfect complexion to be beautiful."

"I know that." Guilt wrecked me. "Do you…are you in pain?"

"Not anymore, but what are you doing here?"

"I have to get into the chateau."

"Me too." She pointed at a grate below a hoverboard.

The guards in the front of the building were oblivious to us, allowing each guest to enter after scrolling through their tablet.

"Are you with the Golden Girl still?" Zeph asked.

Warnings bombed my chest, exploding with such intensity that I knew I should walk away. "Um…Kyra was captured days ago. I'm here to free Griffin so he can help me find her."

"Okay, then." Zeph studied me, then pulled out a screwdriver. "Stay quiet and be my lookout. I heard Stirk is a Mystier."

Did Zeph hear the rumors too? If it was true, it didn't make any sense. Why would Stirk disguise herself for so long? Why would she lead Lodesa, a predominantly Ordull country? Why had she wanted to collect and test all Mystier males? Why did she command her army to attack Vayu if she was one of us? It was too much, and my mind spun wildly. It had to be false.

An owl hooted from afar, and the stars watched in curiosity as Zeph twisted the tool and tried to heave the heavy metal from its position.

"Help me open it," I said.

I helped Zeph haul the metal and winced when it clinked loudly against the frame. Without hesitation, Zeph lowered herself down a ladder into the darkness. The smell of chemicals and poison met my nostrils, reminding me of the suicide vial Gemm had given us. I tapped my pocket, feeling the vial safely tucked and wrapped in soft tissue.

"Come on!" Zeph said.

I lowered down. The icy metal of the ladder rungs under my fingers screamed for me to leave before it was too late.

"You go first." She pushed my back. "I'd rather you fall into a pit before me."

"Gee, thanks."

I ran. Sprinted. It was easy to see through the darkness of the tunnel.

"I can't access my Magik down here," Zeph said.

"You won't be able to until Narelle turns off the power."

"Who?" She panted behind me, occasionally splashing in the little puddles I had already seen and avoided.

Sweat dripped down my temple. As Zeph caught up to me, a sliver of light reflected off her glasses and caught my attention. Despite shaky legs, exhausted muscles, and a pounding head, I forced my legs to move faster. The light came from a slit in a vent that showed a clear view of the ball.

Zeph's heavy breathing pulsed in my ear, reminding me of all the times she panted like that with me for other reasons. I shook my head, washing away the memories. We stopped at a dead end where the light poured through the vent from my eye level. Zeph rose on her tiptoes.

"Wow, that's a lot of fancy shoes." Her fingertips gripped the vent, and she scrunched up her nose.

Red heels and black stilettos all blended in a sea of endless feet.

"What kind of shoes do you think President Stirk wears?"

"She doesn't have feet. Stirk will be in her hoverchair." I didn't even have to look at Zeph to know she was scheming. But the question was if her plan would work for or against ours.

"The decorations are gorgeous in there," Zeph's voice sounded fairytale whimsical.

Swaying dresses blocked most of my view of the chateau's ballroom, which seemed to serve a double purpose as an art museum. Blasts of scorching red and orange paintings hung each at a crooked angle. I tilted my head, interpreting the shape of one as fireworks exploding. After I blinked, its shape shifted into a tree trunk with jutting branches.

Zeph gasped and covered her mouth with one hand. She pointed to the corner of the ballroom.

"I can't see from this angle. Scoot over." I bumped her hip and craned my neck.

A dozen cages held shirtless male Mystiers. They each stood with their arms spread wide out like a cross. Electrical cords bound their wrists and ankles that were stretched and tied tightly to the corner of the cages. The men ranged in age from about twenty to forty, all extremely fit. Their tattoos were on display and ranged from Draven green to Vayuian blue swirls and, finally, Cydian aqua—but no Elidians. Most men had their heads hung, drooping near their chests. The women danced as if they were completely unaware of the cages. What the Abyss was going on?

A thunderbolt of fury attacked my chest. If I had control over the skies, I'd free them all instantly. My jaw gritted so hard that I might lose another tooth by the end of the night. I squinted, and my heart rate tripled at the sight. A sign marked each cage with a list of facts. The first read:

IQ of 115

Witch power - air, wind manipulation (strength 6/10)
No surviving relatives
No prior significant medical history, hospitalizations, or relevant diagnosis
Height- 6'0"
Genitalia- 8.4"

"What the fuck?" I shook my head and reread it. "Why does it have their dick size?"

Zeph glared ahead. "This ball is an auction. It's a way for the president to invite the most prestigious, influential, and rich women left in our country to claim the rare treasure."

"Uh, no, no, just tell me about the dick info, now."

"Stirk is keeping prisoners and electrocuting those who are handicapped and can't be healed. Others have been subjected to DNA testing."

My breathing turned rapid. "Tell me why the sign has their *dick* size?"

"Isaac! It's obvious. There are barely any males left. If Ordulls want humanity to continue, they have to make a plan. You've heard about the required applications for women to be selected to carry a child from the sperm bank...."

"Yes, but...but their dick size." I wasn't sure if my thoughts had turned into words.

"Stirk is trying to control the genes of what babies are born in the next generation."

"What about sperm banks?"

"Didn't you hear? The banks were ambushed, and most of the specimens were destroyed. What's left will run out quickly."

"Why would someone do that?"

"It was religious groups who believe this is the end of humanity and want us to follow our fate."

"Okay, okay." Panic was creeping up faster as I crazily waved at the sign. "But what about the *dick size,* Zee?"

"From what I've figured out, the male Mystiers that she thinks will make her the most money are sold to the highest bidder. I'll let you guess why these women care about their length, though, if you ask me, it's all about the girth." Her eyes lowered. "You know what I like."

Automatically, my hand covered my crotch.

"The men out there are still alive for the sake of reproduction. The Ordull women are here for an auction to win their prize. See the scars on the side of their necks?"

"Yeah...." My heart was spasming.

"Part of the payment is for a device that controls surgically implanted electrical nodes. These men will be toys."

My forehead dropped into one hand. "This is not what I fuckin' expected to walk into today."

"Have you heard of the Aurum Orbis Society?" Zeph paused and pointed to someone outside one of the cages in a guard's uniform colors but with shoulders much too wide to be female like the rest. "Wait, look. Isn't that Kyra's...."

"It's Griffin!" My body froze. "What is he doing as a *guard?*"

Griffin's sharp eyes scanned the ballroom. Like the ever-soldier, he noticed each subtle movement from the chatting women. He paced in front of the cages, serving as a buffer between the males on display and the women in power. Why wasn't he on display too?

"Crap! I need to get up there."

Zeph pulled something metal out and stuck it in the screws of the vent door, twisting it around and around. The feet parted to create an aisle among the mingling shoes, and the room quieted to a hush.

"Hurry up! Stirk is coming." I tapped the grate.

The aisle led straight to the cages, and Stirk swept straight to Griffin.

"Hurry, Zee," I whispered.

The vent finally busted loose, and I lifted myself, shimmying my hips through the small hole. Zeph pushed my ass and legs from below as I grunted. Behind the crowd, I bolted to my feet. The last voice I wanted to hear right now echoed throughout the ballroom.

"Jay!" Kyra's voice rang clear, and all heads turned toward the double doors where my love stood without any disguise. "Jay! I'm here."

A gunshot pierced the air.

16

KYRA

A scream attacked my ears. An Ordull woman slumped onto my ankle in a heap of tulle, blood leaking from under her hand that gripped her stomach, staining her pink dress. More screams.

"Guards! To me," President Stirk commanded from her hoverchair.

My heart punched my ribs as I pushed through the mass of people toward Jay. Where was the attacker? I glanced at the exits. Double doors behind me. High windows I couldn't reach. A low rectangular hole near the floor where a metal vent dangled from one corner.

I shoved each woman aside. One tripped on her dress and flattened to the floor.

"Jay!" I met his perfect brown eyes, relief flooding through me.

He was alive. The moment I saw him again, clarity rang true. He was my everything, my future. I belonged to him, and he to me. Without him in my life, nothing made sense or mattered. No one compared to my Jadox, my anchor, my roots.

"Jay!" I yelled while being knocked around by the mass.

A look of rage covered his face when he met my eyes. Confusion barreled through me.

"Jay?" I reached up as the mosh pit pushed against me.

His eyebrows straightened into a single threatening line. Realization struck. He must not recognize me in the disguise Narelle had cast.

"Jay! It's me."

"Hold your position!" Jay told the other guards as he aimed a gun straight at me.

The sea of screaming women parted. I froze, panting, and rose both hands. "Jadox," I whispered among the chatter of women encircling us. "It's me."

His finger hovered over the trigger. "I know who you are. You just made my job much easier."

"What?"

Out of nowhere, a woman with long ringlets bounced close by and aimed a weapon straight at Jay. I leaped mid-air and launched myself between them. An electric jolt rushed through me. My back slammed into the hard floor, knocking the breath from my lungs. I gasped. Paralyzed. An electric current ripped through my veins, tearing my body in two. My ears rang from the toxic electricity robbing me of strength.

A flurry of sounds blitzed my senses. Screams. Doors slamming. Commands shouting. Footsteps thumping. Voices fighting.

Strong arms lifted me, drooping me over a broad shoulder and carrying me to the corner. He set me down, sandwiched between the wall and his back. A blond bun poked my nose. Isaac.

"Isaac?"

"I'm here, love. Take a breath."

"What's happening?" I wheezed out the words. "I don't understand. Jay, he—"

"Shh," Isaac said over his shoulder, still crouched low, shielding me.

The woman with ringlets squatted next to him, an electric rod poised at the center of the ballroom. "Sorry, Kyra. I didn't mean to taser you."

"Awful shot, Zeph," Isaac snarled.

"Zeph?" I peeked over his shoulder. "Isn't she dead?"

A woman with glasses wrapped in duct tape winked with the one eye that wasn't stitched shut. The rest of her skin was gnarled with jagged scars. How had she survived Moroka's wrath?

"You're alive?"

"For now. Stay down."

The dozen women remaining in the ballroom plastered themselves to the far wall. For the first time, I noticed a line of cages, each with a man stripped and tied inside. My skin crawled. What the Flames was happening?

"Cuff them!" President Stirk shouted. "Take this Golden One to my office. Bring the blond male downstairs. Do what you want with the other girl." She rapidly floated from the ballroom with five guards trailing. The ballroom's double doors shut behind them with a finality ringing through the room.

Jay marched forward and leveled his gun straight at Isaac's temple.

"Move out of my way. I killed that Ordull. I'll kill this felon, too," Jay growled without a flicker of emotion on his face.

"Jay, it's us. It's me," I whispered and grabbed a loose strand of my hair, "They disguised me. Look, my hair is only brown—"

"Stop babbling, girl. Your hair is gold, and I know exactly who you are—a wanted criminal. Now, stand up."

I glanced down at my obvious golden hair. The room froze in time as I met Jay's guarded eyes again. A flurry of muddled questions bombarded my skull. I desperately tugged on our thread.

What are you doing?

Agonizing silence.

Jay, answer me!

He stared at me with such hatred that I forgot how to breathe. This wasn't possible. Jay must be pretending. He must have some plan against President Stirk. I'd have to play along.

"Come with me," Jay commanded with a voice as sharp as the knife sheathed against my thigh. He pushed the barrel so hard against Isaac's temple that his body weight pressed against my chest.

Isaac reached behind him, curled his hand into mine, then

whispered, "There's a hole behind you. Slip into it, and I'll fight Griffin off."

"No, it's okay. I think he has a plan. I'll go with him."

"Kyra, no." Isaac tightened his grip. "Something's not right. He's not himself."

And before either of us could convince the other, Jay pointed his gun straight at Zeph. Screams stabbed the ballroom again. My heart struck fiercely, unable to process the last few minutes.

Suddenly, the lights all flipped off.

Darkness cocooned us like a coffin. Shrieks and wails rippled from each corner, and a strong hand pushed me backward. I squirmed and squeezed through a hole. My side whacked against the cold ground. More gunshots were fired. Then the sound of liquid splashing grew louder and stronger, turning into the roar of a waterfall. Another body slumped through the hole, and the stench of blood followed.

"Isaac!" I scrambled to the vent and reached my arm up. "Jay!"

Grabbing someone's heel, I yanked as hard as possible. It was Isaac. Just as he was midway through, his body doubled in weight. Groaning, I heaved him down. He landed in a *thunk* with another person strung along.

Glancing between my two men, intense feelings stole my breath. They were both here. Isaac and Jay. Alive. In front of me. Severe confusion catapulted at me from all directions. My undeniable love for Jay felt bewildered by this jarring hostility from him. Confidence and protectiveness streamed from Isaac. My appreciation and respect for Isaac and confusion at Jay's venom warred emotions within me. It was all too much, too strong, too entwined.

Isaac put Jay under a wind restraint.

"Let him go," I pleaded and knelt by Jay's tormented, thrashing body.

"No, he's under some spell, love. He doesn't recognize you."

My veins flushed with a vicious force. Every inch of my body ignited with heat, and flames hovered over my black silk dress.

"Calm down. You're going to hurt yourself," Isaac said, sounding panicked.

Water started dripping through the vent hole from the ballroom floor, then it rushed down. Gushing. Pouring. Water spilled down ferociously. Screams still speared the darkness above. At least we had Magik while the electricity was turned off, but I could only use my fire as a torch to see.

Isaac's eyes widened. "This is Caspian's doing. He used us. We need to run."

Ordull women above in the ballroom were drowning, and those men were trapped in locked cages.

I bolted up through the vent into the lake of the ballroom. Darkness and screams whirled insanely. But I didn't need light to understand my surroundings anymore because the sounds created a map for me. Water spurted from each high window in the pitch blackness, splashing into the quickly flooding room. It rose higher by the second to my knees. The windows shattered. Glass exploded across the room.

Women in dresses sloshed through the mess. Barstools floated on the surface. The harmony of erratic heartbeats pulsed together into a symphony. Metal creaked from the cages as male Mystiers stepped out. Free. With the electricity out, they'd use their power and possibly create more problems.

I stood motionless for a second as I reconsidered that. I had seen the sign displaying the men's bodies in a sterile, cold manner. These women weren't innocent. They were obviously planning to purchase one of the caged males. My wish for males to disappear had destroyed society in more ways than I had possibly imagined.

Amid the chaos, something sharp sliced into the back of my leg. I winced from the searing pain, but I fixed the scrape immediately with the healing powers I stole from Jay. As long as the power was out in the building, my Magik would stay strong. For once, I felt invincible.

"Ky! I need you," Caspian's voice pleaded from across the room.

Something in his voice resonated deep within my bones. A memory I couldn't ignore. My body moved toward him before I could even register why.

"Ky! It all went wrong," Caspian gasped. "I need your help."

Rapids formed in the room and doused the walls. They sucked women toward the edges and trapped them under the current. Screams dwindled to only the sound of roaring water. Despite the water engulfing me, I kept my hands above water and squeezed every muscle until flames sparked at my fingertips. A bright light shone ahead of me. Flashes of my fire shot in every direction against the raging water. Bodies floated face down, and the water rose higher. Higher. Shit! My dress turned heavier.

In the corner, Caspian was pinned under something metal. He pushed with all his might. "Ky! I can't stop the water."

"You'll be able to breathe underwater."

"Not if the electricity turns back on!" he yelled desperately.

"You're the one who started this flood, so stop it yourself! You deserve to be stuck. You set me up and brought me to this castle as a pawn to hand over to the president!"

"What? No, that's not true," Caspian said. The water rose to his neck, and his eyes turned frantic. "Did you kill her? Is she dead?"

"No. I couldn't. I'm not a murderer."

"Syvonne isn't who she says she is. Just go kill her! It can only be you!"

I was already moving toward him. "I won't leave you."

"Yes, you will, just like you did when we were kids. It's okay, Ky, go. It's all up to you. It always has been." Exhaustion was clear in his eyes as he tried to heave the metal again.

My heart stopped, and the entire world around us ceased to exist as I stared at him. When I looked into Caspian's blue eyes, there were no Mystiers or Magik. There were no Dravens or Vayuians, or Cydians. There was only my brother, pleading with me. Only Caldo had ever called me Ky.

My brother. *Brother*. Caldo. Caspian. Were they the same? Our childhood flashed in his eyes.

. . .

Games on hoverboards. Playing tag between alleyways. Finding an old warehouse where we hid a box of our most prized treasures. High-fives. Smiles. Hide-n-seek. Macaroni and cheese.

Now, water covered Caspian's forehead. He'd disappeared. Again. For the second time in my life. I was letting him drown, sinking lower and lower and lower. The electricity flickered back on, a few ceiling lights at a time. My power immediately faded. Fuck, Caspian wouldn't be able to hold his breath without Magik.

I dove until I gripped the metal pole caging him. Hauling it little by little drained me of all oxygen. Underneath, Caspian's brown hair swayed in the water, and his eyes closed. Bubbles rose from his open mouth. I'd save him this time. I wouldn't lose him again. Never again.

I gulped air, swam back down, and yanked the metal pole. I shoved it and heaved it. Useless. It was too heavy. Terror wrecked my soul until another pair of hands settled next to mine. Isaac. Pushing it together, harder and stronger, we finally dragged the pole off my little brother.

I grabbed him and lugged his heavy body up through the water. My muscles burned. Heaviness buried me in a grave until we reached the surface. I gasped for air. Caspian wasn't breathing. No pulse.

"Please, Isaac, do something." Isaac immediately laid a hand over Caspian's chest. "He needs air."

"I don't have access to my power, love." Isaac's eyes bulged. "I can't help."

"We have to do something!" I sobbed.

The water lowered fast, but we were still trying to keep Caspian's body afloat. Isaac started punching Caspian hard in the chest. Pound. Pound. Pound. I winced each time Isaac's fist slammed, imagining cracked ribs. Finally, Caspian lurched forward and gasped.

Alive. Thank the goddess. My brother was alive. The leader of Cydon. My brother.

"Thank you, love." I wrapped my arms around Isaac's neck.

"Love?" His voice was so delicate.

I couldn't respond or acknowledge what I had just said. The water lowered to shoulder height, then waist, and eventually calmed to an eerie stillness. Clutching his ribs, Caspian kneeled in the water and gaped at all the dead bodies floating around us—Ordull women and some of the male Mystier prisoners. As we treaded in place, the rest of the water drained from the room. Down. Down.

My younger brother looked ashen. Brother. Nothing made sense. All I could think about was where the water had suddenly drained away to. Within a few seconds, only a few puddles remained among the debris and bodies on the ballroom floor.

"Wait, where's Jay?" My sopping dress dripped over bodies as I jumped over the dead towards the vent. "Jay?"

Footsteps thundered from the chateau's lobby hallway.

"Jay!" I wiggled into the hole, followed by Isaac and Caspian. The four of us stood there for a beat, all panting, soaked and wondering who would speak first.

"Where's Zeph?" Isaac glanced around.

"If you mean the blonde, she ran down the tunnel that way." Jay pointed.

"This way." Isaac stepped in the lead. "I know a way out."

"Who are you?" Jay's stern face broke my heart when he looked at Isaac like a complete stranger. He wasn't faking it.

"We're besties, Griffin. But Kyra is injured." Isaac crouched, his finger sliding down my bloodied leg. "Heal her. At least that way, you'd be good for something."

Jay shook his head. "I can't. I haven't been able to since…wait, how do you know I can heal? I've never met you."

My ears started ringing. Shit. This couldn't be real. How did he not know us? But as Jay's fingers slid over my large scrape, the pain subsided slowly. The sharpness turned to a mild dull, and when I angled my calf to the side, my skin was healed.

Jay's eyes snapped up to mine, and he stood again. "Well…I don't know how…I haven't been able to do that…how did that work?"

"I'll explain later. Please come with us," I begged but didn't dare touch him.

Jay met Caspian's eyes, who nodded encouragingly, then glanced over to Isaac, who casually acted as if he had something stuck between his teeth.

"Fine." He wouldn't take his eyes off my healed calf. "I'll come, but I'm *not* your ally."

"Just besties for life, man." Isaac snorted. "Don't worry, I've always hated you. Now, come on."

Without Magik, Jadox, Isaac, Caspian, and I jogged through the puddles in the tunnel until we reached an opening outside. Skyscrapers soon towered behind us, and in front, a lush forest beckoned us in. Where would we go? Who was on my side?

"Follow me, boys," I said, pushing away my complete confusion.

"No, you seem like a terrible leader. You don't think before acting," Jadox sneered. "You don't know how to work with a team."

Devastation hit me like a truck. What was I supposed to do if he didn't know me? If our story was erased, he wouldn't know how we met or what my hand felt like in his. Our inside jokes would be wiped clean and forgotten. Did he even know his memory had been taken? I'd have to find a way to fix this. We couldn't have a future if he didn't know our past.

"*You* are my team!" I pointed in Jay's face. "You're my *whole* team."

Beside me, I felt Isaac's misery through the Link at my last words.

Jadox backed up and said, "If we were a team, you wouldn't have let *this* guy restrain me."

I reached out both hands, and hot tears stung my eyes. "A part of you knows something is wrong, or you wouldn't have followed us, Jay."

"No one has ever called me Jay."

Isaac let his wet hair fall loose from his bun. "We're following Kyra wherever she wants to go."

"No." Jay lifted both fists and glared at Isaac. "Let's settle this now in a fight. If I win. I get to decide where we're going."

Isaac took off his tux jacket and rolled up his wet sleeves. “And if I win?”

Jadox straightened. “What is it that you want?”

Isaac glanced at me, and for the first time, I wasn’t confident he’d say Wes.

17

KYRA

I grabbed Isaac's wrist and lugged him down the street, away from The Crooked Chateau. "You two aren't fighting," I said over my shoulder. "Let's go."

"We can fight later. It's not like the time will make a difference to the outcome," Jadox snarled like he was a totally different person.

I'd trade my soul for just another minute of how we used to be, of Jay remembering me. Was this his personality before we had met?

Merging with the shadows of the skyscrapers, we stuck close to the alley walls. The crescent moon stalked us, as well as the soft steps of Jay and Caspian. If I kept walking, at least Isaac would follow—maybe I'd create enough space between me and all my problems. I needed to think and give myself distance from the electric fence.

My brother was alive. Alive. I choked on a stifled sob. My chest squeezed tight.

Jay doesn't remember me. My brother is alive.

I'm here for you, love.

"It's not possible." Ignoring Isaac, I kept whispering it over and over. "Not possible" until warmth from where Isaac touched my side spread everywhere.

His hand brushed against mine with each step through the sleeping city. I could lace my fingers with his, but then I'd be letting Jay go. The thought crushed me like a pile of boulders laying on my temple. I had two options. Lie down and accept this, or fight for what belonged to me. Because Jay was *mine* and always would be. Hopefully. Maybe.

Goddess, I don't know anymore.

We weaved down alleys, around dumpsters, and from corner to corner in the darkness. It felt like my spirit left my body like I was a demon myself. Moroka's song returned to me.

Each man longs to bury you alive,
You've let their darkness swallow your soul.
Forget what you know and take the dive,
The true answers lie in murky depths below.

The Blood Maiden must not have meant the murky depths of underwater Cydon because I found no answers there. But at least I knew now that all men weren't pure evil. Isaac had stood next to me, time after time, making sacrifices for me. Maybe he was the smarter choice. Plus, Isaac wasn't full of darkness. Even though I stole Wes from him, he had forgiven me and didn't hold any resentment. Yet, hatred oozed off of Jadox's aura. It was hard to process my relationship with all three of these men at once.

Glancing over my shoulder, I caught Caspian's blue-green eyes. Why had it taken my brother twenty years to find me? A million more questions tumbled through my head about his powers and how he had survived. It was all too much.

Suddenly, I couldn't handle it anymore. I needed a moment alone just to think. I quickened my pace, but all three men chased me with only a soft tapping on the pavement. Ahead stood the disgusting bar where I used to play gigs while a member of a band. It felt like a lifetime ago. Maybe it was good that Caspian never saw me play there. He also knew nothing about my drumming, my love for pasta, or my hatred for the color purple.

On the left, the playground I had climbed with Landon held a lonely swing. It creaked back and forth in the slight breeze. Caspian might not even know about Landon. How many memories did he even have of our sister, Hallie? I rushed to the stoop of the vintage coffee shop where Hallie used to meet me on Thursdays. Caspian didn't know I'd dump four packets of sugar in mine every time.

"Kyra, slow down!"

But I didn't care. Tension whirled and coiled in my stomach so tightly. I slipped behind a building and placed one shaky hand on the brick wall. The bricks shifted into the Blood Maiden's face and a little mouth formed, dripping blood.

Each man longs to bury you alive,
You've let their darkness swallow your soul.

I clutched my chest and swayed like a drunken sailor.

"You okay?" asked Isaac.

My chest heaved up and down. "Please give me some space. This is all too much."

Not only did I gain a brother, but I had lost a boyfriend.

"Okay, love, just breathe."

Isaac brought out my softer side and made me come alive again after so many disasters. With Jadox, I thought I finally had someone to trust and rely on. He challenged me, pushing me forward always. He was my rock, or maybe they both were, but for different reasons.

"Jadox Griffin!" I yelled, faking confidence.

He wiped sweat from his brow.

"You *have* to remember me."

"Stop."

We danced the tango, all wrong. Every time I stepped toward him, he'd retreat.

"Think, Jay. You saved my life when we first met right over there, at that bar. You have to remember that."

Jadox patted his pockets, probably checking for a weapon. "I can't keep track of every damsel I rescue."

"You insufferable pig-headed ass! I'm not a damsel. I saved your ass in the forbidden caves."

"I'd never be stupid enough to set foot in there."

"You did. You went in for *me*. Remember. Please, remember."

Uncertainty flickered in his eyes. "I've been in the army for years, ma'am."

"Wrong. A gorula cursed us, so we were connected by the wrist not long ago." My voice turned ragged, stretched out, and thin.

"You have a very vivid imagination," Jay scoffed.

"*You* are the reason I wished away all males."

His eyebrow rose. "So you plead guilty to the charges? I'll need that repeated into my watch."

I moved closer, wanting to punch sense into him. "You were there when I received my tattoo." Tears fell, blinding me, and Jadox's heartbeat still thudded like the bass beat to my existence. "You first kissed me in your treehouse." I slid one hand up his arm. "Jay, I know why Draven shunned you from their tribe. I know the guilt you carry from what happened to your parents. I know about your foster families, about how you tried to find Draven."

He stepped away, obviously shaken. "That's enough!"

The air turned sharp like a whip, blowing my hair around like a whirlpool. When Jadox turned with a frown, Isaac filled the empty space. Turmoil played tug of war in my tattoo, and my arms felt stretched between the two like elastic, ready to snap.

"He's the worst, huh?" Isaac smiled and tried to lighten the mood with his tone. "I can just knock him out if that makes it easier for you."

Isaac was being too nice, and Jay was a certified ass now. They had switched places, and nothing made sense. My mood felt like a pendulum swinging from one extreme to the other. I knew the best way to deal with this was to take a step back and meditate, but the fire inside my tattoo flared wildly. I squatted, holding my stomach with both hands.

"Let's get you some water." Isaac rested his hand on my back.

"Don't touch me!"

"Kyra—" Isaac started.

"No! I can't do this. All of you are liars!" Hot tears threatened to fall. "Caspian, or Caldo, or whoever the Flames you are, you had *so* many opportunities to tell me you're my brother, but you chose not to."

"I—" Caspian started, but I stomped and cut him off.

"No! It's my fuckin turn. You, Isaac, you need to stop acting like you'll stay with me when Wes returns."

His jaw dropped in silence. I probably wasn't being fair, but I couldn't hold back any longer. If I were a stronger person, I'd be showing gratitude for this support. But life, and this entire mess, was rapidly suffocating me.

When I met Jadox's eyes, the tears pooling in mine streamed down my cheek. "And *you*. You're the worst of them all."

Choking on my sobs, I pointed at his rotten face. The eyes I had fallen in love with narrowed. They were an enemy's eyes.

"If you can't remember me, then your feelings were never real. *We* were never real. You should know me!" Unable to contain myself, I slammed my fists against his chest. "You should've come home to me. You should've kept your memories. You shouldn't have left me!"

He stared down the alleyway silently.

"Don't ignore me," I cried. "I've been parading all over Lodesa to free you."

"I didn't need to be freed," Jay said. "I'm a soldier."

"How dare you forget me! How dare you forget us! I wish I'd never met—"

Isaac grabbed my waist and twisted me away from Jadox. "Don't say something you'll regret, love."

I buried my face in his shirt as Isaac wrapped me in an embrace. "I'm here. And at least we have some good news," he whispered.

Through bleary tears, I looked up. "And what could that possibly be?"

Isaac tucked a strand of hair behind my ear. "We know the Link doesn't only force a romantic connection. You're still Linked with Griffin, and he...well...he feels differently now. The Magik is not forcing him to care for you."

I swallowed my words, but a thousand stones scraped against my throat and settled in my gut like hardening cement. "Gee, thanks for rubbing it in."

Isaac's lips brushed my forehead, and he breathed out a huge sigh. "It means what I feel for you is real."

My heart rate doubled. I couldn't imagine being separated from either Jadox or Isaac. I wiped my cheeks and turned. Wait, Isaac was right that Jay and I were still Linked. I could try the Link.

Jay, can you hear my voice?

Staring straight at him, I sent the message through our thread. I felt the steel barrier in his mind, but a slight flicker of his eyes told me all I needed to know.

You can hear me still, Jay.

Jadox shifted on his feet and looked at anything but me.

I'll bring you back to me. I promise.

His throat bobbed as he crossed his strong arms.

"Okay, I'm in charge, boys." I wiped my face, feigning confidence. "First thing, I need to get Jay's memory back. Maybe this Vayu Crystal could help." I tugged the necklace off and handed it over to Isaac.

"We know less about these necklaces now than ever. I don't want you to get hurt by accident." He tucked it into his pocket. "We can't use it yet."

I began pacing in the shadows. "If there's a spell that could help, it isn't revealing itself to me."

"The Unetlo Book will have a memory spell. But we don't have a venti to fly."

"We need to contact Alaska and have her teleport us to the Unetlo Book."

Jadox cleared his throat. "No, I already formed a plan during your ridiculous outburst. The chateau is currently weakened. Many guards drowned, so the president will be disorganized. I must free the prisoners in the basement before the president takes her anger out on them."

"Ky, that's actually a solid plan," Caspian said. "Instead of the ball serving as a distraction, we can use the flood to our advantage. We'll sneak in, and you can still kill her."

"Goddess! I'm not going back in there. It's suicide. We don't have any Magik while the power is on. We can't risk it. I'm always the one to jump into action, and for once, I'm the only one thinking rationally."

"Sis—"

"Don't you dare call me that!" I lunged forward. "I might not even be your sister."

"You are."

"How do you know?"

"Narelle stole your hair from your pillow when you stayed in our guest suite. Our lab confirmed it."

"You could be lying."

Even though twenty years had passed, his eyes were the same as his younger self. No matter how much I tried to deny it, I knew for a fact that he was my blood, as true as the Golden tattoo scorched onto my skin. But he'd have to work to earn any loyalty back.

"What is the name your mother gave you? Tell me your real name, and then I'll believe you." I pressed him against the wall.

"Caldo," he whispered.

I stumbled back, one trembling hand covering my mouth.

"Believe me now?" He resituated the collar of his wet shirt.

"When was your birthday? What city were you born in?"

He ran a hand through his chestnut hair. "I was born here in Andersonville in year 59P of the Blue Moon, making me twenty-three years old."

It was him.

"Hallie's dead," I whispered and stared at our reflection in a shop's window.

He pushed both hands into his pockets and dropped his eyes. "I know."

I wished I knew if these movements were a trademark when he was nervous. What was Caldo—Caspian—like as a teenager? Who had raised him? Did he ever miss me? Did he ever come looking for me? When did he learn he possessed Magik?

"What are you trying to achieve, Caspian? Tell me what you're up to." I cleared my throat as fresh tears stung my eyes at the thought of missing his entire life.

"I'll do anything to free the Cydian prisoners. One life doesn't matter compared to an entire village, but we need to kill the president to save them."

Jadox interrupted, "We could use *her* as bait to free the prisoners." He rolled up his sleeves.

"No, we're not handing Kyra over to anyone." Isaac jumped between us.

I drew circles with my fingertip on Isaac's inner wrist. His shoulders loosened, but not for long.

A sudden burst exploded in the inky black night, the corner of a building crumbling into a pile on the street. Isaac yanked me behind a dumpster. Five hoverboards erupted into pieces and scattered in the alleyway. The fire sizzled the small bushes framing the sidewalk. Flames grew higher, and screams and cries shrieked from homes, filling the air.

"It's the A.O.S.," Caspian yelled through the smoke. "They're attacking the president's headquarters."

Isaac shielded me and coughed from the debris. "We're stuck right in the middle."

Gunshots blasted to the right. Left. Above. Shutters slapped open and long barrels poked from dark windows. Isaac shoved me into the street. My silky dress split, tearing high, and pebbles scraped my thighs.

"Stay low." Isaac pushed me to the ground.

A shot vibrated in my ears. Above, blood rained from a window. We needed to move further from the electricity and fast.

"There!" Jadox pointed, and I tracked his finger.

Shadows clawed at me in the alleyway, which was covered in rotting trash. Another loud snap echoed in the alley. A crack. A ping. Shot after shot. One ricocheted off the cobblestone by Isaac's loafers.

My heart spasmed, and I stumbled forward. The noise was unbearable. My ears picked up every sound.

"We have to get out of here!" someone yelled.

"What?"

Caspian peeked around the corner and tapped his s-watch. The sound was muffled, but I thought he said, "Ten seconds, then follow me."

"What?" I covered my ears. The fire crackled and popped.

"Eight seconds, and we sprint across."

"No way! We won't all make it."

Isaac shielded my head with his arm, curling me into his chest. "Stay by me."

Jadox's gaze darted in all directions, checking every possible option.

"Look!" I gasped and spotted Zeph pushing a metal grate from a hole at the base of an apartment complex. "Come on, this way."

We rushed forward. Underfoot, the cobblestone shifted. Soldiers yelled angry commands. Isaac magnetized to my side, blocking their access to me.

"Dive for the tunnel!" Isaac yelled.

Bracing myself for the painful scratches, I dropped and skidded on my side. Razor-sharp stones cut into my hip, slicing open my skin. I bit my lip and dipped into the hole.

Despite being twice my size, all three men crammed through the opening and dropped into a pile of muscles.

Grunts and a round of *"get off of me"* were followed by a triangle standoff between the three, with me stuck in the middle—again.

As Zeph rambled something to Isaac about being involved in the secret society, she put both hands on her hips. I tried to wrangle in the chaotic thoughts flapping around like an injured bird inside my brain. This must be what it felt like to go into shock. Jay didn't know me. My brother was alive. I called Isaac, *love*. And the sounds of war surrounded us, deafening me.

"Kyra," two male voices harmonized. "Focus."

"You weren't listening, were you?" Zeph pushed her glasses further up her nose.

I ground my teeth and nodded to Zeph. "Take us to the society's leader."

"Why?"

"You cared about Isaac once. I'll never be able to return Wes if I get blown up."

"Fine."

Isaac slowly moved his lips to my ear. "Listen, love, before we go. There's something you need to know about the president." Isaac rubbed his hand slowly on my back, and when I met his gaze, those gray eyes held only complications and obstacles.

18

ISAAC

Experiencing Kyra's emotional turmoil through our Link was like being conscious while a meat cleaver shredded every organ in my body. How could Griffin act like he didn't feel her agony? His expressionless face might have been architected from stone once upon a time, but even I detected the flicker in his eyes. He was holding something back. That asshole had better start treating her with respect after all she had sacrificed for him.

"What do I need to know, Isaac?" Kyra asked again.

I walked as a buffer between the two women as Zeph guided us through the dark tunnel. I felt Kyra's eyes on me and her guesses at what I was about to tell her. I doubted her guess would be about Moroka's ominous threat she had revealed to me during my chariot voyage. What exactly had the Blood Maiden meant when she said that ₾sμwi would soon come?

A tickle nudged at my tattoo. With each step further from The Crooked Chateau, my power gradually sparked alive again. A little flame ignited from Kyra's fingertips, and she breathed a sigh of relief. Her light glowed on the path ahead, showing me that the tunnel eventually came to a dead end far ahead, something the others wouldn't see yet.

"If this is a trap—"

"It's not," Zeph spoke to me over her shoulder, her ringlets bouncing. "I just wanna get you in the dark again, Isaac."

Kyra's jealousy rushed through our bond. She rose her fiery hand to the back of Zeph's head, ready to light those curls aflame. I stopped Kyra, gently lowering her hand before she lit my ex on fire.

Kyra didn't even glance at me as she said, "I think now is a good time to spill all our secrets in case we get...separated."

"I won't leave you, love."

Kyra tapped her fingers on her thigh. I watched the steady beat increase in speed. Why wouldn't she look me in the eye? Hmm, maybe she planned to leave *me*. Kyra's gaze flitted over to Griffin as if unable to contain herself.

"Hold up, everyone. Take a pause. A time out." I jogged in front and held out my arm to block them. "Kyra's right. We need to get everything out in the open. Now."

Kyra seemed like she was shrinking in on herself from fatigue. Maybe she didn't need to know about Moroka's warning yet. For now, she had enough on her plate. But I still needed to be upfront about one secret eventually.

Instead, I said, "Well, Narelle warned me that Caspian wants to find Kyra's father—I mean, his father—both of your father." I stared at Kyra until she finally looked at me. "Brent is trapped in one of President Stirk's quarters."

Exhaustion buried the light in her gaze, and she simply leaned against the tunnel wall. I wanted to hold her, comfort her, and make promises never meant to be said.

I moved over and let Kyra rest against my chest. "Before we make any decisions...you need to know...President Stirk is no simple Ordull. She is the strongest Mystier in history."

Kyra groaned into my chest, and her body seemed to melt into mine in defeat. "I can't do all of this. I can't bring back Wes, save the prisoners, fix Jadox's memory, free my father, *and* stop the president from dominating Lodesa."

"No one is asking you to, love. Let's do one thing at a time."

"It's all too much. We're hiding underground in this rotten, dark tunnel. Enemies surround us. Even our possible allies in the society out there were shooting at us by accident. There are too many things to fix."

"We always have hope if we have an Elidian on our side." I lifted her chin and forced myself to ignore Griffin's penetrating stare next to us. I brought her hand to my lips. "You are the light in my darkness, love. As long as I have you, your flame will guide me through any unknown."

Kyra sighed, long and slow, then pushed away reluctantly and faced her brother. "I'm guessing you know more about our biological father?"

"Possibly." He folded his arms, and his jaw twitched. "We need to keep moving before the guards find us." Caspian marched ahead.

Everyone whispered and picked up the pace. Mice scurried by our feet and ran up the wall, and spiders crept along webs on the moldy ceiling, spinning intricate webs. The sticky string glued to my forehead.

"I don't suppose one of you'd carry me?" Kyra bumped against my side. "I'm exhausted."

I crouched low. "Hop on, shortcake."

A drowsy smile made it halfway to her eyes. "A new nickname?"

"Don't like it?" I rose with her draped across my back like a little monkey and followed Griffin's steps.

"I like what you've always called me," Kyra whispered and lay her head on my shoulder.

"I thought you hated me calling you love, love." The warm skin of her thighs in my palms fueled a desire so strong that I wished I could tear the rest of the silky dress straight off her body for a moment.

"Mmm, love, love, love." She sounded tipsy on budding dreams of unicorns and fairies. "Did you hear me call you that before? It was an accident."

I gulped. "Would you ever use it on purpose?"

"What would I get out of it?" Her grip around my neck weakened, so I held her tighter and shifted her higher.

"Presents. I'll buy you a kitten, then a drum set, of course, all the chocolate and coffee on this side of Lodesa. What else do you want?"

"Goddess, I'm so tired. I want a bed," she purred. "The biggest bed possible with the softest sheets known to all of Lodesa with the fluffiest pillows and extra blankets. Oh, did I say soft pillows? I need about eleven."

Another smile plastered my face. "Consider it done, love."

"Mmm, thank you, lovely love, lover." Her finger traced lazy circles on the back of my neck. "I used to hate you."

"You're delirious. Go to sleep." I laughed at her sudden drunken-like state. "You're cute when you're sleep-deprived."

"You're always cute. It's not fair." Her voice turned throaty and husky.

"Oh really? Tell me what else isn't fair."

"That hearts can be split in two, like this, *crack...*" Kyra made a soft cracking sound deep in her throat, "Love c-cracks hearts in half. Kkk is a strange sound. Love k-kicks me defenseless. Say that sound. It's so weird. Kk for kill. Kk for kiss. Kill or kiss? Kiss or kill?"

"K for Kyra. Go to sleep."

I'd rather fall asleep next to you.

A soft snore had already sounded in my ear.

Surprise gripped me that she was still willing to open up to me, touch me, and use our Link, especially with Griffin nearby. At least now, we knew the Link didn't force these feelings on us. It was real. Otherwise, Griffin would still be infatuated with her. Why wasn't he trying harder to detain us, though?

"Stop!" Griffin jumped to my side and stiff-armed me.

"Divinity above, be careful. I'm carrying her."

Kyra jerked on top of my back and slurred, "Wh-what happened?"

Jadox sniffed the air. "Do you smell that?"

"No." I squinted through the darkness. Down the tunnel, a strange mist hunted us. Thick fog climbed the tunnel walls and flowed like a thundercloud. Now that Kyra's flames were extinguished, only darkness plagued us with threats of the unknown.

"Caspian?... Zeph? Where are you?" I called out.

"Poison!" Zeph coughed violently ahead. "It's a poisonous gas."

"Run!" Griffin turned toward where we came from, taking point.

An itch scratched my throat as I coughed. Strong fumes enveloped us. The tunnel zoomed in and out like an adjusting telescope. Dizzy. So dizzy.

"Kyra! I have to lower you."

I slid her off my back, grabbed her hand, and pulled her along. We wobbled and teetered forward, or maybe sideways. No wonder she was talking nonsense earlier. My loafers slapped in the shallow puddles. She stumbled through puddles and staggered back and forth. My shoulder rammed into the tunnel wall. I coughed so hard that acid rose in my throat and mashed into nasty bile in my mouth. I swallowed it back down and tripped to the side.

"My head is throbbing." Her voice sounded too weak, too far away, even though I still clutched her hand.

I felt like I was choking on fumes. We both toppled to the side, landing with a hard thump. Dazed, I pushed off the concrete, but every muscle turned to jelly. A loud crash exploded. From where? Only darkness cloaked us in a never-ending pit of horror.

"Get down!" Griffin commanded.

We flattened to the tunnel floor. An entire tree flew passed, creating a barrier between us and the incoming toxic gas. Then another tree. And another. They soared by and created a wall against the impending danger.

I glanced back. "It's not working."

Kyra braced to shoot fire from her hand.

"No!" I yelled, "If it's flammable, the fire might make it worse."

"Come on!" Griffin yanked Kyra's elbow, pulling her away from me.

There was no way I'd be separated from her. Maybe this was all planned as Griffin's way to distract the others and divide us. My Circle pulsed with energy.

"I can't...breathe." Kyra sputtered the words, further from me now.

I covered my mouth with one hand, coughing again and again

while blundering blindly. My brain turned to mush, and I had to force my feet forward.

Gas was simply molecules and atoms. I focused on the chemicals in the vapor. I had always created or manipulated air but never changed the individual particles.

"I need more energy," I willed the words from my lips. "I need more...."

Griffin touched my shoulder. Power from the Link surged to me from both of them.

Their raw Magik consumed me from head to toe. I breathed strength in and out. Un-fuckin-stoppable. Turning fast, I held out both hands to the storm of gas. Needles prickled my skin, and a ball of heat seized in my core.

An ancient spell ran from Kyra's mind to mine. "Tohiyus elawe! Tohiyus elawe!"

Wind shot straight from my hands and pressed the gas back from where it came. Pushed. I dug my heels in as it fought back. Every muscle tightened.

"Tohiyus elawe! Tohiyus elawe!"

Poison grappled against my spell, oozing forward and shredding my sanity. A part of me wanted to slip into a deep sleep and ease into the hollow oath of Lady Darkness. What harm would it do to rest for a minute? Or eternity?

Kyra coughed again, then a thud sounded through the fog.

"She's unconscious!" Griffin yelled within the mist. "Hurry up."

"Get her out of here." I wrestled against the toxins. Haggard and worn, my biceps pinched. My calves stiffened, and my abs coiled.

A hiss from the whirl of poison whispered, "Iiiiiisaaac, when your love is taken, you'll be alone. Alone. No one. No one. Alone, Isaaaaac."

"Nooooo!" A deep bellow roared from all angles until I realized it was my voice.

"Use her fire, Nilson," Griffin yelled. "Use it!"

It was dangerous, but it was our last resort. Every hair stood on its end. I summoned Kyra's fire, and heat spouted from my hands.

The steamy smog dissipated, then vanished completely. I was in shock that it had worked. That shouldn't have worked.

I doubled over, coughing and panting. "Is…she…okay?"

"She's…breathing." Griffin held a hand over her chest. "But she's unconscious."

Dizzy, I staggered to her side and dropped to my knees. "Heal her."

"I…I can't anymore." For the first time, terror gripped Griffin's face.

"Yes, you can. You did it earlier."

"That was a fluke…." Griffin's hands shook. "I…the president…the prisoners…" His eyes widened, and he turned to the wall.

"Fine, I'll do it." My body trembled too, as I touched Griffin's shoulder for borrowed energy.

A new sensation pelted me like hail. One of his memories joined with the impact of power borrowed from Griffin. I saw Griffin's life from his eyes.

Wading in a river with Alaska as a child.

Riding a gorula's back for the first time as it swung through the treetops.

Parents collapsing in an alleyway. Blood.

Children's exclusion from games at recess.

Receiving a Draven tattoo, scorched into skin.

Slipping out of foster homes at midnight.

Staring up at the waxing moon.

Torturing prisoners in a dark basement.

Meeting Kyra's terrified eyes on a rooftop in the pouring rain.

I gasped and snapped out of the trance. "You remember her."

"I don't," Griffin snapped.

"I saw it. I saw your memory of Kyra."

"You're wrong."

Kyra groaned and rolled to her side, mumbling, "A pillow. Need a pillow."

I followed her voice, but only blackness was in front of me. Squeezing my eyes shut, I rubbed my lids, then opened them again. Only black.

Endless black. I blinked. Again. Nothing.

Darkness. Fuck. What happened?

"Isaac?" Kyra sounded close, but I couldn't see her.

My heart slammed against my ribs. I rubbed my eyes. Again.

"I can't see, love."

"What do you mean?"

I held both hands out in front and felt her face. A loose strand of hair swayed in front of her pointy nose. I tucked it behind her ear, brushing my fingers along her cheekbone on the way.

"You can't see this?" she said.

I felt air swoosh in front of my lips. "No."

"Okay, it's okay. Jay can heal you."

"No, I don't heal anymore," Griffin said.

"Jadox! Get your ass over here and help him! We can't escape this tunnel if he can't see."

"You do it," Griffin mumbled. "He brought you to consciousness by stealing my powers. You should be able to do the same."

Her hand lay on my chest while I focused on my breathing, using all effort not to royally flip out in panic.

Blind, I was blind.

"*Terra angakok. Terra angakok,*" Kyra whispered, her hand pressing harder against my pecs.

Terra angakok. Terra angakok. Say it with me, Isaac.

Terra angakok. Terra angakok.

No power spun in my Circle. We were both spent and empty.

"It's not working. We can try later when we have more energy."

Until then, I needed a plan for us to escape Griffin. First, I'd have to convince Kyra he was no longer on our side. Griffin was lying to us both. He remembered Kyra and decided not to tell us.

"I'll be your eyes for now. It's okay," Kyra said sleepily. "Don't let go of me."

"I don't ever plan to." I moved closer. "Be my torch, love."

Footsteps thudded softly but from the wrong direction. Crap, I should've been looking out. I whirled my head, forgetting that I couldn't see.

Suddenly, a delicious smell wafted closer, and I sucked in a deep breath. A thick sweet taste coated my tongue.

"Ooh, you're *pretty*." Kyra's words slurred.

"Aw, you're sweet, but you're prettier." A ridiculous sensation of giddiness overrode everything else.

Laughter. "Not you, Isaac." Kyra couldn't stop giggling. "A girl in a lovely purple jumpsuit. Did I ever tell you I hate purple?"

"Noted." I laughed, and my head swam with strange jokes. "Got it, no purple kittens."

"Or purple drums." Kyra giggled, sounding high as a kite.

Disoriented, I laughed with her, unable to stop. Our laughter filled the tunnel, sending me spiraling into ecstasy.

A metal rod poked my chest, followed by a female's voice. "Follow me."

"Are you Lady Darkness?" I sputtered on my hilarious joke. I could star in a comedy show—an invincible comic.

"Lady Darkness, that's a good superhero name." Kyra chuckled and snorted. "Purple tights, hahahahaha."

Her laughter made me want to lick ice cream under a rainbow. Or create a fort out of pillows. Apparently, my girl needed eleven of them.

"Eleven pillows." I laughed aloud again with an unquenchable thirst to hear Kyra's giggle again.

"Eleven, beleven, televen," Kyra sang.

"Let's go," said Lady Darkness.

"Paola, is that you?" Griffin's voice finally appeared in my blind hallucination–because there was no way any of this was real.

But the rod shoved into my chest harder. "Stop laughing. You two will come with us."

"Us?" I shifted my head towards Griffin, acting like I knew where he stood. "Lovely."

"Lovely love." Kyra giggled. "Wake me up later, then surround me with pillows. A pillow castle."

Morning warmth hit my cheeks as we trudged out of the tunnel and into the fresh air. But everything stayed dark.

Maybe things weren't so funny after all.

19

KYRA

Blindfolded and tied to Isaac, I stumbled over something and ran into a wall. No, not a wall—Jadox—the heartbreaker who severed me into bits of nothing. He shoved Isaac and me into a room. On the other side of the door, Jadox whispered with that Paola chick, the one who had sent Alaska a warning letter to stay away from Caspian. But she wasn't to be trusted. Paola must've drugged us in the tunnel. Somehow, Jadox seemed immune to whatever toxic gas exploded in the tunnel, so it must be his team who had launched the attack—or maybe he initiated it himself.

And Caspian was nowhere to be found, probably dead in that tunnel from toxic suffocation. I had to shove the image out of my head and calm my racing heart rate.

Jadox and Paola's voices grew snappier. I leaned toward the door, but my enhanced hearing had vanished since the poison took hold. I never realized how much I relied on the rhythm of another's heartbeat to gauge the danger of a situation. At least I could still hear. It wasn't fair that Isaac's vision was gone.

Warm sunlight spilled upon my cheeks as I tried to wiggle out of the wrist restraints.

"You okay?" Isaac rubbed against me, trying to push the electric wires off.

"It's not fun being blindfolded."

"Try being blind." He laughed. "Sorry, that's not funny. I don't think these drugs have fully worn off yet."

He was right. My temples still throbbed.

"Can you bite this blindfold off of me?" I asked.

"You're into biting? Maybe when I wiggle free, I can try to find some chocolate syrup and candles to set the mood."

I couldn't help the smile as I nudged his shoulder. "Come on. One of us needs to see."

His body moved against mine. Rubbing. Shifting. Repositioning like a pretzel. The electrical cords tightened on my wrists, and I winced as Isaac managed to move to his knees.

"Just don't leave a mark," I said.

"No promises."

I groaned. "I'm a certified contortionist now. Hurry up."

"You and the constant rushing. Take a breath, love." Isaac's lips melted against my forehead.

A shiver shook my entire body.

"Oh, you like that?"

I growled at him.

"Feisty." His laughter filled me with everything I didn't know I needed. "Relax, I've got you."

In a quick motion, he bit the blindfold off. Morning sunlight flooded the room, but I could only stare at Isaac's broad chest as he towered over me.

"Your turn to help," he said.

"They were stupid to blindfold you if you can't even see." I bit the fabric and pulled, shaking my head back and forth so it would loosen. It fell over his shirt.

"Can you see me?" I asked.

"No, love. Tell me where we are." Sadness flooded his face.

I scanned the room for the first time. "I can see…a hammock bed hooked to the ceiling. Oh, my goddess, there are more than seven pillows, but that's about it."

"No, Kyra, I've always relied on my sight. I need more details."

"Okay, well, the walls are a blueish cream. It's like doves painted the walls blue." I tilted my head to another angle. "There are scratches and dents on a table holding a full red wine bottle and an old backpack. Um...."

"Good, tell me more."

I scanned his form, momentarily wondering how I'd explain his features to someone. "Stand up."

We shuffled together like penguins, passing a little bathroom to the right of a barred window. "Okay, we're really high in one of the skyscrapers in Andersonville. The ocean is about a mile to the west. Below are a few buildings on fire, and smoke is rising. People are running like bugs." I turned and met the grief covering his features. "I'm sorry this happened, Isaac."

"Don't apologize, love." He forced a smile. "I just need you to be my eyes."

"We'll both need to be more aware because I think I lost my enhanced hearing too."

The door creaked open, and Jadox walked in—stoic as ever as he threw a lump of clothes on the table. "Eat, drink, change, sleep. Don't fall out of that swinging bed. It'll leave a mark. In the morning, we'll leave, and I'll accept a thank you at any time."

I wouldn't let my devastation take over. "Tomorrow, we will find a way to get your memory back."

"No." Jadox glared. "I don't want it back."

"What?"

"If I ever knew you, you must have had me under some spell. You're a terrible influence. Miss Kozelski, you led your team into danger. You don't think things through. You're irresponsible. You're generally selfish, impulsive, and—"

"But I—"

He raised a hand, clutching a knife.

I backed up further, shielding Isaac.

"Kyra, what is it?" His breath hit my ear.

"Brace yourself," I whispered.

As Jadox approached, I leaned back against Isaac and pushed off. My legs flailed in crazy kicks straight at Jadox's hand.

"What the Flames? Calm down, woman. I was just going to cut off your cuffs." He shook his head. "See, I told you...impulsive...you two are equally dense. You belong together."

He slashed our cuffs in half and stomped out the door. I stared at the place he used to stand. There was emptiness. Hatred. Love. Confusion. Since the cuffs no longer bound me, I summoned fire and was ready to shoot it at the wooden door. But nothing came. We must still be surrounded by electrodes.

Talk to me, my love.

I can't. I'll cry.

It's okay to cry.

With a sigh, I melted into Isaac's hug.

He wrapped his arms around me. "I bet this hurts. You cared for him."

"I still do."

"The same as before?"

"I don't know. Have you ever lo—liked two women at once?" I shivered from head to toe.

"Yes, years ago. Zeph and Rajitha."

"How did you choose?"

"It wasn't really an option. Rajitha was an Ordull. In order to keep her safe from our world, I had to lie to protect her. Zeph was a friend who helped me with Wes when I struggled."

"Did you lo—like them both?"

"In different ways, yes."

I paused and stared at the bed. "Did you like one more than the other?"

Isaac tucked a piece of my hair behind my ear again. The gesture never came across as condescending or possessive, just sweet. For some reason, I adored it when he did that.

"It doesn't have to be a competition, Kyra. You can have feelings for me without guilt. Griffin doesn't know you anymore," Isaac said softly.

"Does that matter? What if it's a sickness? Should I just abandon him? It's not his fault."

"Only you can make this decision." His lips pressed against my temple. "But know that I want you, Linked or not." He sighed. "There's something between us, like we...."

"Belong," I finished.

Isaac slowly massaged my tense shoulders as we stood there, silent, holding one another in the middle of the enemy's lair. First, we were caged by my brother under the ocean. Now we were caged by my ex-boyfriend. Wait, ex? Was Jadox truly my past? No, I couldn't accept that.

"I'm gonna wash up and rest," I said. "Whatever is leftover of the poison is still making my head pound."

Isaac nodded. "We can plan after a few hours of sleep. It's not like we can fly out that window without our Magik. Plus, the streets aren't safe right now."

I stared at his blond bun, its wispy pieces falling out, and his devious lips and straight nose. Now that Isaac was blind, I didn't have to worry about him catching me studying his features. For the first time, I absorbed every intricacy. He had a tiny scar below his left nostril. And three eyebrow hairs that needed plucking, which stuck out of place.

"Quit staring at me," he said playfully.

I jumped.

"We're Linked, my love. I can sense your thoughts." His smirk was brighter than the sunbeams reflecting off the table.

"You can't read my mind."

"Wanna bet?"

"What am I gonna do next? Maybe I'll strip right here," I teased.

Isaac's fists clenched, and his jaw twitched. "You wouldn't."

"Oh, I so would. Payback for when you were super evil to me."

"Fine. I dare you."

"Well, actually, I need help out of this corset. It's tied so tightly in the back that I haven't taken a full breath in hours."

The floorboards creaked as he closed the gap between us. "Turn around." His voice turned husky.

"It starts at the top. You need to loosen one at a time."

His finger caressed my neck. "Like this?"

Soft lips brushed against my upper back and the dress loosened with a tug. His fingers worked magic so quickly that before I knew it, my dress was a puddle of black at my feet.

I exhaled, releasing all the tension from my body. Unwilling to stay close to Isaac without my clothes on, I swiped the bread from the table, then rushed to the bathroom. After clicking the door shut between us, I double-bolted the lock, just in case.

"I'm not that scary." His laughter sent another jolt through my Circle. "Alright, I'll scope out the place while you're in there. Get it? Because I can't see."

"You're right. It's definitely not funny." I twisted the shower knob, and water gushed out of the faucet. It was music to my no-longer-sensitive ears. However, it sounded muffled compared to before, like the harmonies and melodies I'd grown so accustomed to had been stolen from me. That must be how Isaac felt about his sight.

"We'll fix your vision," I said through the door.

"Maybe I don't need to be fixed! Maybe I want to explore you with my hands instead of my eyes."

"You're so wicked." My voice echoed within the small bathroom.

Hot drops cascaded over my shoulders. The shower wiped away the fears that Jadox didn't remember me. Water cleaned off the shock that Caspian was my brother. Soap scrubbed my hesitancies over what to do next. Shampoo erased the filth that existed in President Stirk. Lastly, the conditioner enhanced the hope that my feelings for Isaac were okay.

After the bathroom was full of steam, I dried off and drew a smiley face on the foggy mirror, adding a set of devil horns. Leaving my undergarments on the floor, I swished open the door. Mist followed me out, merging with the air. I swear I could see where the molecules combined.

"Better?" Isaac asked.

"As better as I can be for now. I'm exhausted."

He nodded to the bed. "Go lay down."

"Are you sure you can't see? You just pointed straight to the bed."

"Eyes aren't the only way to take in the world, love. Now, go make your seven-pillow fortress. I'll wake you if there's another Armageddon, don't worry." He walked over. Our bodies were so close, and he didn't know I was still naked with little droplets of water streaming over my breasts. If only....

Clean, fed, and safe for the moment, I climbed a ladder on the wall that led to the suspended mattress that swung like a hammock and hung from the corners of the room by a thick rope. The bed required more core strength to balance on than I had anticipated. I wiggled and swerved, making the corners slam into the wall again and again. I nearly toppled off the side.

"What the?" Isaac's face pinched together below. "What's happening?"

"I'm..." *Bang*! "I'm fine...Woah..." *Bang*! "Hold on...Jeez!"

The bed rammed into the wall and created large dents in the paint.

"Woah, Isaac!"

"Kyra? You got it?"

"Stop moving." I laughed. "*Isaac*!"

Gripping the ropes, I finally wrangled the platform relatively still and sucked in a deep breath. Giggles threatened to burst when I caught his hilarious expression.

"Sorry, this thing is not suitable for...well, anyone. I'm not sure how I'm gonna sleep up here without falling off."

"Is that an invitation for me to keep you safe?" One of his eyebrows rose, and I smiled since he couldn't see my face. I loved that look he gave me.

"Actually, it may not be the worst idea since two bodies up here might balance it out more?"

"Done." He nodded and tore off his shirt.

"Isaac!" I glanced at the closed door. "Don't even think about it."

"Too late, my love. I always think about us."

I stifled a laugh and peeled my eyes away from his chest.

I snuggled into my pillow castle and shut off my mind. No thoughts of Isaac shirtless. Only cotton. No worries about Jadox. Only softness. No concerns about brothers returning. Only peace. No murderous Blood Maidens. Only warmth. No hidden secrets or unknowns. Only belonging. I belonged to this pillow. This pillow belonged to me, and together, we would live happily ever after. Everything would be fine, eventually.

Lips trailed over my neck. I took his hand and slowly guided him to my breast. His eyes turned ravenous and dark. He explored every slope and curve until my nipples pointed so straight that he couldn't help but pinch and twist. I gasped and arched. Then he reached up and hovered over my other breast. My heart cartwheeled with anticipation. I watched his fingertips twitch just above my skin. He licked his delicious lips. His hand cupped my other breast. Each stroke and caress sang a song to my senses. I let out a long breath, but that did no wonder in slowing down my pounding heart. I wished I could hear his again too. I laid a hand on his chest and felt the fast thumping behind his ribs.

He kissed my jawline down to my chin. His lips brushed my neck—a torturous game. Suddenly, I wasn't sure who was touching me. I glanced up, but his face was a blur, fogged over in a dreamy state. Who did I want to be touching me? Jadox or Isaac? Brown hands traveled over my stomach and traced near my three tattoos. Jadox—of course, it was him—I loved him. But then his hands lost some of their tanned hues. Isaac's mouth hovered over my belly button, and fire surged through my veins. He slid his hand lower between my legs.

My breathing turned ragged. And it felt so real, but nothing else made sense. There were no walls, no bed, no draft from the air conditioner's vent, no sounds from outside the window, just him.

Isaac's hands skimmed my inner upper thigh, where I was extra sensitive.

I trembled with every tiny pressure. I arched into him again, and a soft puff escaped his lips like he was using all his effort to contain himself.

"Kiss me, Isaac." Had I said it out loud? No sounds came from my mouth.

His lips grazed mine with such tenderness my chest coiled tight with need. Our chests met. Skin on skin. So right.

"It's okay, love. Fantasies are okay."

With every muscle on alert and every part of me crawling closer to him, ready to meld together, I dipped my hand under the sheet at his waist. Longing swelled in my tattoo as I felt down his hip and gripped his cock. He was huge. Long, thick, and hard.

I pulled away from his lips and searched his smug face. Pausing, I rolled the sheet all the way to his ankles.

"You're beautiful."

We smiled through our kisses, and I began stroking him up and down. When Isaac's fingers found my clit, sparks tingled through my veins. My neck craned, and I clenched my eyes shut. He kissed me as if it were our last night alive. Our last hour. Last minute. I couldn't help but gasp into his mouth as his fingers pulsed and circled low, sending me into a frenzy. Maybe this was real; maybe it was a different type of magic. Because if this was only a dream, I never wanted to wake up.

Isaac moaned into my mouth. Then he pushed a finger into me. I gently rocked against his touch. Another finger was added. He swirled his fingers. My legs shook, and I pushed my hands against his abs, unable to take the pleasure. Isaac flattened me, controlled me, weighing me down. Goddess above—he felt so good.

Isaac's third finger entered, and my body crumpled into a heap of bliss.

"I can't wait. I need to be inside you," he growled between his kisses.

Isaac spread my legs wide and mounted over me. His log of a cock pointed straight, the tip rubbing between my legs. Was this real? He licked his lips again. The end barely pushed inside. Then eased out. I held my breath, soaking in his body. He pushed in just a little. I bit my lip. My hands clutched a fist of blankets. I was floating, soaring, flying.

Out.

In.

I bucked against him, trying to push him deep. "You're gonna make me beg, aren't you?"

Out. His smile destroyed me.

In.

Out.

In.

"Isaac. Please, *all the way."*

"Like this?" He shoved in, and I let out a euphoric scream, clawing at his back. Isaac drove inside me—all the fuckin' way—filling me up with his girth and stretching me.

"Uuuuh, sweet goddess above, my love." His forehead rested on mine as he thrust. "Every day. I need you every day." His hips undulated, pressing in and out in such a perfect rhythm.

"Every day," I whispered.

"Mmm. Hold onto me."

I gripped his neck.

He whispered something I couldn't hear, and we both levitated in the air. Now, I was certain this was only a dream. Our bodies floated, combined. There was nothing below me. The only thing I could feel was Isaac's body. The only thing touching me was him. For a few minutes in ecstasy, we existed, just us two.

When he lowered me back down and picked up his tempo, my pleasured screams filled my head with each thrust. He plunged in and out. Again and again. I couldn't breathe. Couldn't move. I was so close. Every muscle clenched around him.

"Come for me, my love." His voice in my head was like smooth candy melting me to nothing.

The tension grew. He moved faster. Relentless. Deeper. Harder.

"That's right. Feel me."

"Fuck, Isaac...fuck! Isaac! Isaac!"

I erupted in a wave of paradise. And he followed, jerking atop me. Beautiful. Raw. And mine.

. . .

"Kyra, wake up." Calloused hands shook me. "Love, it's just a nightmare."

"Wh-what happened?" I sat upright in bed, rubbing my eyes.

"You were screaming my name." Isaac lay on his side, shirtless, head propped up on his palm as he drew an invisible line back and forth on my collarbone. The giant hammock bed swayed a little. I wondered what clothes remained on his lower half but didn't dare move the sheet to investigate. Breathing suddenly became difficult. That dream was too intense, too real. Too amazing.

"Um, how…how long did I sleep for?" I asked, glad he couldn't see how red my face was.

"Probably eight hours…." Isaac smiled, loosened his watch, and wrapped it around my wrist. He pushed several buttons by memory, and a message popped up. "Can you read this?"

"Yeah, Alaska is on her way. That's not good, right? It's dangerous." I read further. "She asked about Paola…Why? Oh, right, they were a couple."

"Some people simply belong together," Isaac said.

"Mmm, belong together." I scanned Isaac's chest, dipping like a washboard stomach in all the right places. I could never tell him about my dream and how real it felt…how much I wanted him.

When Isaac shifted, his muscles flexed, and I gulped. No man could possibly meet the same level of sex-god status as my dream, but I couldn't stop staring at his hands. He puffed a pillow and collapsed into it, flat on his back, leaving a wet mark from where his damp hair soaked the fabric. He must've showered while I was asleep.

"Do you want to talk about your nightmare?"

"No."

"I bet it includes a trapeze bar. Oh, I know, it must have been about kittens, cupcakes, and pillow fights."

"You don't know me." I tried to keep humor in my voice and stay off the topic of my crazy sex dream with him. I shook my head, trying to forget the images. Did he look like that in real life? Would he be that good at it?

"Of course, I know you...because of this Link," Isaac said. "But I also know you without it."

"Prove it." I nudged him playfully.

"Your lips scrunch to the left when you're about to do something brave. You twist your earring when you're overwhelmed. You drum your fingertips on your thigh when you're nervous. And when you smile, it lights up the entire room."

I sighed, terrified for him that his sight was still gone. "You can't see any of that anymore."

"I don't have to. I know you rely on a mental shield to block yourself off from me. But it won't work, love. I'll keep trying to learn more about you. No matter how patient I have to be. Even when you're scared to let your wall down, I'll be waiting."

I didn't deserve him after all the disasters I'd caused. But I swallowed my fears, my uncertainties, and my sanity.

A starved look claimed his eyes. "I wish I knew how you are looking at me right now."

"Isaac?"

"Yes, my love?" He leaned closer.

"Kiss me."

"You're sure?"

"Yes."

"Goddess, above, Kyra, you have no idea how badly I've wanted to."

He tugged my neck forward and locked our lips. His hands worked within my hair with expert charm and his devilish tongue feathered against mine just before he bit my lower lip. His tongue swirled with promises of passion. He tasted of rain and mist and thick fog.

With my heart pounding, I moaned, unable to hold back. Why hadn't we been doing this all along?

Isaac's groan into my mouth unraveled me completely, and I kissed him faster like my life depended on it. Lightning cracked inside my chest as his body pressed against mine. Hard. In control. Fuck, he knew what he was doing.

A power stronger than a volcano ravaged my insides, counting down the seconds until eruption. Strength coiled into a tight ball, ready to burst. Breathless, I grabbed the back of his neck and pulled him tighter. He devoured me, making me lose all sense of time and focus, clinging to me like our spirits were intertwined. Because they were. Feeling how much he wanted this only tripled my desire. Through our Link, Isaac beckoned me to trust in us. To believe.

Our tongues twisted. I bit his lip, wanting him more, but a sudden jerk to my tattoo made me pull away. The spot where my Draven tattoo was seared into my skin turned hot to the touch.

"Wait, Isaac, I was wrong. I can't do this."

His Adam's apple bobbed, and he slowly backed away. "Okay, right. That's fine."

20

ISAAC

One arm hung limply off the side of the hammock bed while Kyra's head rested on my chest. I wished my eyesight would return, for at least a minute, to witness her in a peaceful moment. But, fuckin goddess, she needed to put a shirt on soon and put me out of my misery. Kyra wasn't ready for us, but she unknowingly held my whole heart in her hand, whether she wanted it or not. That kiss solidified what I'd already known. We were meant to be together.

We both understood now that the Link wasn't solely responsible for our feelings. Our path forward snaked into a thousand forks, leading to the unknown. Eventually, she'd have to make a choice: me or Griffin.

Outside, thunder cracked the sky, and raindrops beat against the window. Strong energy pierced my tattoo, and power sprung back into my Circle stronger than before. The door below flew open and slammed against the wall. Kyra jerked in my arms, and all her muscles curled into me.

"Wh-what are you..." Her voice turned edgy in a moment. "Wh-what are *you* doing in here? Get out!"

I felt the blankets shift up, covering our chests. My heart rate tripled. If I couldn't see my opponent, how was I to fight?

"Who's there?" I asked.

"You two cracked a hole through the wall last night." Griffin's voice.

Shit.

"No, we didn't—" Kyra's emotions swirled into a frantic mess through our thread. Devastation swallowed me whole at her severe response.

Shit, shit, shit. He's here, Isaac. It's Jay. He saw me. I'm naked.

It's okay, love.

No, it's not okay.

Why? We only kissed.

"I said get out!" she yelled at Griffin. The pillow under my elbow tore away, and a breeze swiped my face.

"How mature, a pillow as a weapon," Griffin grumbled. "Listen, the building's electricity is out from this storm, so we need to leave while our Magik is strong."

"This isn't what it looks like, Jay." Kyra's voice rose an octave. "I…we…."

I swallowed the hurt from her words. "Come on, let's get dressed."

"Can you, can you close your eyes?" Kyra sounded years younger, broken, and wrecked.

"Who? Me?" I couldn't believe she had forgotten so easily. "Uh, I'm still blind."

"Oh, my goddess, I'm sorry. Right, okay."

She scaled down the ladder without another word, without an ounce of reassurance to me. My heart cleaved in two. The energy turned so thick I could feel Griffin's eyes on her curves—even when blind. My tattoo scorched with envy. Fuck this. *Fuck. This.*

"We need to bring Wes back." I wrapped the sheet around my waist and followed her down, tapping the rungs with my toes to determine when I hit the floor.

"Right now?" she rushed out the words as if out of breath. The soft sound of fabric sliding over her hair met my ears.

"Yes." I held my hands out in front of me, hoping I wouldn't run into the table. "We can use Griffin's power before he turns us in."

"We're not turning you in. Paola and I brought you here to help you hide." Griffin snorted.

"I don't trust you." I threaded my arms through the spare clothes.

"Right, and I'm supposed to trust either of you?" Griffin chuckled. "Yesterday, *this* girl begged me to remember that we were a couple, but last night, you pounded her against the wall while she was screaming your name. You're supposed to expect me to believe anything either of you says?"

"No, no, no, wait a second." Kyra's voice was smaller than a mouse, more delicate than a rose, tearing me in half. "We didn't...."

She was vanishing under guilt, slicing my insides to shreds. I leaned against the table, needing support so my knees didn't buckle.

Kyra, talk to me.

Silence. Her turmoil radiated through our Link. I couldn't tolerate the anguish, so I also hardened a mental wall against her.

"We have no time for games. Let's go," Griffin commanded, his voice rougher than sandpaper.

"I'm not leaving until we try to return Wes. All three of us are here."

Thunder crashed, and wind thrashed against the window.

"Okay, we owe you that," Kyra whispered.

The way she said *we* was like she and Griffin were still a team. Goddess, that burned.

"Please, Jay, let's help him."

"We have three minutes," he groaned.

"Okay, touch each other's shoulder." Kyra's voice trembled as she laid a hesitant hand on me. "Then chant, *Reditus atsutsa*."

Griffin's heavy hand pressed against my other shoulder, and I reluctantly placed mine on both of them. The connection between the three of us was the last thing I wanted to think about.

Kyra and Griffin's Link with one another couldn't be as strong as ours. She'd eventually understand we were meant to be together, even if the journey to that conclusion was heart-wrenchingly difficult.

"On the count of three." I focused on how much I wanted to hear Wes' laugh and feel his hug. "One." I concentrated on how much he loved movies. "Two." Squeezing my eyes shut, I centered everything on the memory of his brown hair, gray eyes, and his momma's cheekbones. "Three." My tattoo pinched with desperation.

"Reditus atsutsa. Reditus atsutsa. Reditus atsutsa," we all chanted.

Thunder exploded outside the window.

"What are you three doing?"

Maybe Paola's voice?

"Ignore her. Try again!" I gripped their shoulders tighter.

"Reditus atsutsa."

Please, Wes, come back.

"Reditus atsutsa."

I need you.

"Reditus atsutsa."

Kyra dropped her hand. "I don't think it's going to work, Isaac."

"No! It has to work!" My thumbs shoved against my temples. "Are you trying with everything you have? I'm blind, and I can still see you withdrawing. Your entire spirit is disappearing."

"I'm not...."

Pretend to hate me all you want for that kiss, but I know you care for me. Now, act like it. Don't run from your feelings.

A zap rammed into my tattoo. Good. She was letting herself feel again—even if it was anger.

I'm not running!

Prove it. Kiss me again!

Now?

Right now, our Magik is stronger with our physical connection.

I grabbed her waist and pulled her to me, hovering over her lips.

I love you, Kyra. I will always love you.

Instead of what I wanted, she brushed her mouth over my cheek, soft, sweet, and meaningful. But I couldn't linger in the moment because it felt like a goodbye. The thought crushed me flat. I needed hope right now, not heartbreak.

"Reditus atsutsa," Jadox chanted.

Reditus atsutsa. Reditus atsutsa.

Kyra joined me again, silently through our bond, as we pulled apart.

Reditus atsutsa. Reditus atsutsa.

Thunder boomed across the entire universe. Kyra lurched further away, the kiss already haunting me.

"Oh, my Divinity!" she gasped.

"What is it?" My heart flipped a mile a minute.

"He's here, Isaac. Wes is right here."

All air was stolen from my lungs. I dropped to my knees and held out my hands. Quick creaks of the hardwood sounded closer with each one until a small body collided with my chest. Wes.

"Dad!"

He sounded like Wes, smelled like Wes, and hugged like Wes. I brought him closer, never willing to let go again, and ran a hand through his thick, wavy hair. Tears rushed down my cheeks. But I couldn't see him. Was he real?

"Dad!"

"I'm here, bud." My body grew wings and fluttered like a venti. "I'm here."

While clutching him even tighter, I murmured, "Thank you, thank you, thank you, goddess."

"Dad, what's wrong with your eyes? They're all hazy."

"I can't see right now, Wes, but we'll fix that later. You'll be my eyes for me? I need someone I can count on."

Beside me, I felt Kyra's energy stiffen.

"Of course, Dad. But where are we, and who are these people?"

I sighed and tried to wipe away my tears as I stood, but they kept pouring, matching the rain outside. "I'll explain later, bud."

"We need to leave. Now." Griffin confidently nudged my back, guiding me to the door. "Someone has found our location."

Kyra's s-watch beeped. "Um, Jay, what floor are we on?"

"Thirty-three, why?"

"Your sister just arrived downstairs."

I cradled Wes to my side, moving him away from them and lifting my son onto the table while they argued. The passion in their words couldn't be ignored. Even if Griffin didn't remember Kyra, his body obviously had a visceral reaction to her.

"Are you hurt, bud?" I patted over his face, down his puffy sweater, grazing every inch of him down to his holey sneakers.

"I'm fine, Dad, but where's Mom?"

My gut clenched. How could I tell him about Rajitha's death? "What's the last thing you remember?"

"Playing on a giant playground with dozens of other kids." His hands explored my face, as I was doing to his, like my mini mirror. "Except it was like a dream because outside the playground was only white light. No buildings or trees, just nothing."

The door whizzed open again, and another voice added to the mix. "Jadox! You're here. We need to go. The building is on fire." Was it Alaska's voice? "I'll teleport you."

"You can't. There are too many of us," Jadox said. "And I won't risk you coming back here. Take the boy somewhere safe. I'll manage the rest of them."

"No!" I shielded Wes with my body. "I'm staying with my son."

"I can take two at a time now," Alaska said. "Gemm fixed the Draven Emerald. And here, Kyra, this is yours. She fixed the Elidi Ruby too."

My hand automatically dropped to my pocket, housing the Vayu Crystal and the poisonous suicide vial.

"Okay, take Nilson and his son to the safe house." Griffin's commands sounded like a drill sergeant's. "I'll free the prisoners during this black-out while we have a chance."

"I'll go with you," Kyra spoke to Griffin.

Of course. I admitted my love and…and she…she had never said it back. She didn't return the sentiment. A wave of nausea hit me straight on.

"We need a way to contact Caspian in case he survived the tunnel," Kyra said. "Um, Isaac, can I keep your s-watch?"

"I don't care. Do whatever you want."

"Isaac—"

"Goodbye, Kyra." While holding Wes close, I reached for Alaska's hand. "I'm ready."

"Wait! Isaac—" Kyra pleaded.

"No, Kyra," I whispered. "You've made your choice clear."

"What are you two talking about?" Alaska huffed. "Of course, Kyra and my brother are together. I found the engagement ring while I was looking for the Elidian necklace. Here, Kyra, you probably thought you'd lost it."

Thunder split the sky, and its energy divided the room.

My brain detonated. "Engaged?"

"No, we...." Kyra's energy dwindled to a faint dim. "Isaac, listen—"

"Paola, I'll be right back. Wait for me." Alaska's hope was evident in her words.

"Of course, my little hummingbird."

At least one couple here was still going strong. When a whiplike sensation lifted us from the ground, our bodies spun through the air. I clung to Wes tighter. The smell of rain showered around us in a haze, but Magikally, we stayed dry. Time stood still and fast-forwarded at the same time. Seconds passed, or possibly minutes.

Gulping for air, I landed with a hard smack onto something soft, maybe a mattress, and rolled off onto a floor. Dirt coated my fingertips.

"Wes?"

"I'm here, Dad."

I held out a hand, and he took it, his small fingers completing me.

"Alright, you two, I need to check on Gemm quickly and let her know the plan. I'll be back in a minute. You're safe here." Alaska tapped my back. "We're up north by Draven now, so if you're cold, blankets are stacked to your right on those crates. Feel free to grab some food in the kitchen."

I gripped Wes's hand tighter when he tried to pull away. "Thank you, Alaska."

"Hey, Isaac?"

"Yeah?"

"What did you mean by Kyra chose my brother? What was that all about?"

I tapped Wes's back. "Hey, bud, go grab us a snack and stay close."

He scampered away, taking my heart with him.

"Explain," Alaska demanded.

"Kyra and I...kissed."

She gasped. "She cheated on my brother? I'll kill her."

"No." I reached out. "It wasn't like that. Your brother lost his memory when captive. He doesn't know Kyra."

A pause. "But that's impossible. Jadox knew me."

"He lost the last few years. I'm not sure how long, but he has no recollection of being with Kyra. Griffin thinks he's a loyal soldier for the president."

"What? That's crazy. He'd never switch teams."

"I don't think he's aware of what's really going on in Lodesa right now."

"Wait, wait a minute. So you took advantage of Kyra during this chaos?"

I groped the air behind me, found the bed, and fell back to sit. "No, we're Linked, and I love her. I know it's not ideal, but–"

"You need to talk to her to straighten everything out," Alaska said.

"I can't leave Wes. I just got him back."

"Dad, I just met another boy, Landon," Wes yelled from around the corner. "He's your girlfriend's nephew. He points to pictures to talk to me. It's so cool!"

"That's great, bud." I forced a smile, wishing I could see his again.

"Girlfriend?" Alaska jabbed my chest. "You need to clear everything up, Nilson."

"There's nothing to fix. They're engaged. I need to stay with Wes. We returned my son. Kyra will figure out how to get what she wants. She always does. Go. Paola is waiting, and they need your help. Just make sure Kyra stays safe. I need you to promise me that you'll transport her somewhere else if there's any danger."

"I can't make that promise. She's the Golden One for a reason. We have to stand up against President Stirk. Running isn't an option for someone as strong as her. I'm fighting for what's right, which means freeing the Mystier prisoners. And I bet Kyra will agree."

"Please, please don't let her get hurt."

Alaska sighed and said slowly, "From the look on her face back there, her heart is already destroyed. I don't think I can prevent her any further pain," Alaska huffed. "I'll be right back."

I reached forward in the never-ending darkness, but there was only air. At least my tattoo still sang with power, even if our Link was mangled, chewed, and spit out like old, stale meat.

"Dad, this is Landon."

I jumped. "Oh, hi, Landon." After sticking out my hand for a shake, Wes replied, "No, Dad, he doesn't like being touched. Hold on."

Little nail scratches on plastic met my ears.

"Landon is pointing to a smiley face and a dog," Wes said.

"That's great, bud. Hey, I need a layout of this room."

A beat of silence. "Uh, there were two rusty chairs by the food cabinet around the corner. In here, there are seven mattresses on the dirt floor, flashlights, crates of books, boxes of clothes, and a bowl of water on the floor."

"A bowl of water?"

A rough tongue licked my fingertips. "What the?"

"That's Chocolate, Dad. She's a lab and Landon's best friend."

I kneeled on the mattress and eased myself down, exhaustion taking over. "Are there any exits nearby?"

More silence passed. "I think we're underground, Dad."

"Okay, that's okay. Come here. We need to talk, bud."

I'd have to tell him about his mom, but maybe not right away.

"Okay, Dad, but eat this first. Maybe it'll fix your frown."

I couldn't help a small smile at that. An apple plopped in my palm, and I crunched through it, the refreshing juice spraying into my mouth. Somehow, my heart skipped with joy at the reality of Wes living and breathing next to me, yet it also plunged into a hollow cavity at the thought of losing Kyra. How was I going to tell my son I might not stay here with him? How could I possibly bring him into this chaotic world just before war was about to break out and then abandon him for a woman?

Unthinkable.

I'd stay. He needed me. Plus, Kyra chose Griffin. There was nothing to fight for anymore. I had my son again and didn't need to be greedy for someone who clearly wasn't mine.

"Dad, I made a funny face at you, and you didn't laugh. You really can't see me, can you?"

"No, bud, but I'll fix it. I'll get my eyesight back."

"Can I help?"

A fresh idea sparked fiercely in my mind.

"No, bud. It's not safe, but I think I know a way to see again."

"How?"

21

KYRA

I was the worst kind of person— eviler than a demon. What the Flames was wrong with me? In a single minute, I managed to hurt both of the men I loved. My heart stampeded against my ribs.

Loved? Both? No, this couldn't be happening. I'd never be able to choose between them. Not to mention, neither wanted anything to do with me.

"You and I are engaged?" Jadox spat out without looking at me. "I proposed? To *you*?"

"No, I didn't know you had that ring."

"Good, I'd never propose. But I do need answers. I've changed my mind and need my memory back."

Paola cleared her throat. "Um, you erased my memory a few years ago with a spell. I have gotten most of my memories back from Brent Elidi," Paola said. She must have seen the shock on my face because she continued quickly, "I met him as President Stirk's prisoner. He has a golden tattoo and a special mind-control gift. He put my missing memory pieces back together, and now I remember it all."

"So my *father* could return Jay's memory?" I asked.

"I don't need your help, Kozelski. Let me figure this out on my own," Jadox said.

I gulped at his harsh tone. There was zero chance of fixing my relationship with either man. Any life attached to me would sentence them to suffer. Now that Wes had returned, I'd probably never see Isaac again. The thought crushed me like all the walls were closing in on my body, threatening to squeeze the life out of me. How could I be so stupid?

My s-watch pinged with a message, snapping me back to the moment.

> CASPIAN
>
> Meet me on the beach three blocks west of the old capital building in fifteen minutes. I have reinforcements and a plan to free the prisoners.

I glanced out the window, where smoke still climbed from below. Thunderclouds rolled in, even more menacing and darker than the earlier storm. Squinting in the distance, I narrowed in on the crumbled capital building, then scanned a few streets over. On the sand, three tiny figures moved about a large, blue blob. Was it Caspian? Who was with him? Maybe he knew where our father was. That might be the only way to return Jay's memory.

"We need to get to the beach." I pointed outside.

Both Jay and Paola appeared by my side. "Why? We need to take advantage of this blackout."

An eerie feeling of being watched hovered in the air. I couldn't help but look around, checking every nook of the room.

"Caspian can help, and he's there."

"The smoke is rising to our floor." Paola coughed again. "We need to get out of here."

I took Jay's hand, and a spark ignited at the touch of his skin.

"What I'm about to do might suck out all my energy," he said. "If I pass out, leave me."

"What? No, Jay, what's your plan?"

Before I could pull away, a sharp zap bolted through my tattoo.

"Dehano huc," Jadox commanded.

Strength poured through my veins while distant cracks and booms resounded from outside. Jay's hand shook in mine. Below, hundreds of branches cracked and flew to the base of our building, quickly roping together to form a ladder. Jay's eyes were squeezed shut when I looked over, and sweat beads trickled down his temple.

"Dehano huc," he forced out through gritted teeth, his biceps flaring.

The sound grew louder as branches and limbs thrashed against the side of the building, scaling higher and higher.

"Dehano huc," he roared and then glanced to the window.

Paola looked out the window, saying in an awe-struck voice, "There's...a tall stalk-ladder made of branches outside."

"Open the damn window!"

Fierce wind attacked us, knocking over the plate from the table. The smell of smoke grew stronger.

"We have to get down!" Paola shouted over the roaring wind, her hair whipping across her face.

A crack snapped to my left, and I jumped in surprise.

Suddenly, Alaska and Isaac reappeared in the middle of the room.

"Thank, goddess! You came back." I ran to Isaac, but he reared back when I touched him, then shook his head.

My heart dropped into a fiery pit of death, but I hid my trembling hands behind my back. By breaking his heart, I had ruined any future with him. My selfishness destroyed everyone I touched. Why did I ever think either could be mine?

Paola sprang to Alaska and their lips crushed into one another's as their arms entwined around their bodies like vines.

Alaska finally backed away and smiled. "We need to leave now; teleport all of us."

"There's too many people!" I screamed over the crackle of the flames growing higher.

"We have no choice."

Paola touched Alaska's shoulder, then Isaac's.

Terrified that we wouldn't survive, I reluctantly reached out to Isaac, then paused. "Wait, you have to take us to the beach by the capital building."

Alaska's eyebrows shot up. "What? I thought we were going to the chateau?"

"I don't have time to explain. Just do it." I gritted my teeth. "Please."

Alaska glanced at Paola, who nodded. I laid a hand on Isaac and Alaska at the same time. We spiraled through the air, turning heavy and light at the same time. At least we wouldn't have to scale down Jay's makeshift ladder on the side of a skyscraper.

White light flashed before my eyes.

I was flat on the sand, my eyes opening to wet drops whirling onto my cheeks. Waves lashed with foam rolling higher and higher. Darkness spread over the vast ocean, completely masking the horizon.

"Finally, you're awake. Welcome to the party." The snarl of a male's voice crept through my blood. "Which will make this so much more entertaining."

From my hands and knees, I raised my chin and locked onto my brother's eyes, which were poisonous with intimidating wrath.

"Caspian? What's going on?" I asked.

Behind him, both Jadox and Alaska lay unconscious in the sand. Shit, she couldn't handle teleporting all of us.

No, no, no. Jay, wake up.

By the flapping seagrass, Caspian was binding the group, including Isaac, with electrical wires wrapped around their bodies and gagging them with fabric stuck between their lips. How long had I been laying unconscious here? Paola and Zeph exchanged terrified glances. How had Zeph even gotten there? What had happened to her when we split up in the tunnel?

"Get up, sister, oh precious Golden One," Caspian barked.

I was more like the Cursed One. I pushed off the sand, noting how much my legs shook with fatigue.

"What's wrong with you?" I yelled at my brother. "Let them go!"

Caspian's head tilted like a possessed demon ready to attack its prey. I had never seen him look like this, and that scar enhanced the devilish energy radiating from him. The term ₵sμwi flashed through my mind. Something was very wrong.

A cackle erupted from Caspian's throat and quieted the roaring waves. The ocean settled like a lake—eerie and still. Impossible.

I called fire to my fingertips, but exhaustion had taken its toll. I needed the energy from the Links. I needed Jay and Isaac.

"Why are they tied up?" I asked Caspian.

"I should have been the Golden One!" he screamed, rage wheeling in his ghastly eyes. "Water is more powerful than fire! I deserve the title after you left me to drown in the waves as a child."

A truth deep in my gut warned me his words were bound by the unnatural. Something seemed to possess him. But a strong sensation nudged me closer, urging me to gently take my brother's hand and snap him out of his frenzy. This darkness cloaking him was a lie.

"Caspian." I stepped forward, tentatively, "I can help you."

"No, you lost your chance. Now, we will never be a team, and all five of your friends will beg me to kill them."

I counted them on my fingers like a child scanning the beach. Jadox. Isaac. Alaska. Paola. Zeph. Five.

"This isn't who you are!" I moved faster. "What do you want?"

"To fulfill the prophecy. We were supposed to Link, brother, and sister. Yet, you chose poorly. You chose these weak men."

Whatever spirit resided inside my brother's soul brought the waves back to life, now doubled in chaos. A bell buoy rang in the distance, unnervingly fast.

Seizing the moment, I processed what he was saying. He wanted me to sever the Links. I wanted the same thing, to free both men from my wretched choices, to free Jay and Isaac from the pain I'd no doubt always cause them.

I nodded to my brother because he didn't need to know the limitations of my knowledge of Mystiers and how all this worked. "I'll only sever the Link if they both live."

Caspian's smirk climbed high, full of peril. "That can be done. They will live."

"How do you know?"

He pointed to his skull. "A little voice told me so."

Heaviness clamped on my chest. "Who is doing this to you?"

He snapped his fingers, and water soared to us, splashing Jay and Alaska's bodies and drenching them head to toe. Finally awake, Alaska crawled away on bound hands and scrambled to her feet, but a solid wall of water crushed her to the side of the chariot. Her eyes widened, and she tried to speak but was silenced by the cage of liquid encasing her.

"Let them all go!"

Jay groaned and slowly awoke, rolling over and gripping his side with one hand. "Where..." he mumbled. "Where are we?"

When Jay fully absorbed the scene, he jerked back. With a flick of Caspian's wrist, water pushed Jay to his knees, formed a rope, and tied his hands behind his back.

His toes lapped in the waves as both long arms extended forward. Lightning cracked the sky again, and darkness smiled above. From the water, a frightening melody sang from the depths. With each passing moment, the familiar lyrics grew louder.

Your family hunts you to stay alive,
Let down your guard, or they'll devour your soul.
Forget the Link— a true Elidi will thrive,
Without a man to make her whole.

"The Blood Maiden," I whispered, then darted my eyes to Caspian. "Don't bring her here."

I struggled against the wall of water, suddenly caging me. "Let them all go!"

A hand emerged from the waves, the skin translucent and covered with jet-black veins. Gangly arms followed, covered with seaweed. The Blood Maiden's head stuck out from the waves, and she slinked passed the grand chariot. Moroka's hair stuck to her pale face. I gasped when I met her sharp red eyes. Like before, they cried ruby tears, and each time one met her red lips, she licked it, coating her razor-sharp fangs with blood. She dragged herself out of the water with her shredded torso flopping behind, oozing a path of unending blood.

I held my breath as she crept up the sand and settled in front of Jay, licking his face three times.

"Get off of him!" I writhed against the power controlling my every movement.

"Ask me one question, Draven puppet." Moroka's claws dug into his thigh, and he sucked in a breath.

"Don't answer her!" I yelled.

"What is the spell to return my memory?" Jay asked.

My head pounded with terror. I met Jay's eyes, and he nodded. Glancing at Isaac, I wondered if he could hear from over there. He must be terrified, being blind in this mess.

Moroka growled, "Such an easy one. The spell is *Memi anvadis*."

"*Memi anvadis. Memi anvadis*," Jay chanted quickly.

Immediately, the wind changed direction and punished us from the east.

"I remember," Jadox said simply, deadpan.

Moments passed as all the blanks filled in the holes in his mind. Jay's eyes shut, and he dropped his shoulders. Painfully, agonizingly slow, Jay lifted his head. His eyes glistened with a thousand unshed tears. My hand clamped to my chest as I backed up. Step by step, moving away. I caused this.

"Kyra, I remember"—his chest heaved in and out fast— "I remember…you …. and Nilson."

The storm sucked away my breath. "Jay, I—"

"It's okay, Petal, you chose him. I understand."

"No…" Pain gripped my soul. Or relief. I didn't know. Fuck the entire world.

Suddenly, Caspian pushed his hands against his temples, bellowing, "What do you want to know, Golden One? This is your chance to get what you want by asking Moroka a single question."

Stepping away from Caspian and the beast-like power radiating from his body, I glanced at my row of friends on their knees. They struggled to stay upright against the slashing wind.

What did I want? I wanted to free my friends and the Cydians. But how long would they stay safe? My fingers drummed a rapid beat on my thigh. I wanted to keep Landon safe. To meet my father. To know who my soul truly belonged to in this life. Guilt coiled tightly in my stomach.

"Hurry up, girl!" The creature inside Caspian rumbled louder than the thunder claiming the sky.

"I want to belong to someone." My entire body shook as unsettling tears fell. "I want to know who is meant to be mine."

Caspian's deadly eyes never blinked as he floated toward me like a ghost. "Ask Moroka a question," he whispered in my ear.

"No."

Caspian dangled the golden chain necklace, swinging the pearl like a pendulum back and forth in a hypnotic fashion. "You deserve this." He walked to Jay with an insane grin plastered over his cheeks and dragged him next to Isaac. Side by side. My two loves.

A dark force beyond my control pushed me toward them. I dug my feet in the sand, but the strong force guided me straight to where they lay.

"Dearest sister, pick which will suffer the consequences—Griffin or Nilson."

"No."

Anger fumed on his possessed face. "Pick!"

"No."

"Fine! Then you've cursed them both, and they will both suffer. With your fire, you will brand what belongs to you." Caspian threw both hands in the air, and waves wrecked the nearest beach house, knocking it down to a pile of scraps.

"Caspian, fight against whatever is controlling you," I struggled to make my words come out.

Fire lit from my fingers and danced on the tips while the force pushed me towards Jay.

"You'll have the honor of branding them yourself." Caspian laughed, raking my spine with dread.

The puppet master was in control of us both, moving my hand to Jay's chest.

"Light him up," Caspian whispered. "Go ahead."

I gritted my teeth, tensing my muscles against the power. I tried to turn away. Unable to stop, my flame seared a red-hot line through Jay's shirt and into his chest, just below his collarbone.

Jay cried out. His body tensed, but he was stuck against the electrical cords binding him. His agony swept through our Link, and I felt a hint of phantom pain. Next to him, Isaac winced. I knew we both experienced only a small fraction compared to Jay's suffering.

"I'm sorry." Salty tears spilled, mixing with the rainfall soaking my face. "I'm sorry."

No longer in control of my body, I drew another deep gash in his chest. And another, impossibly trying to ignore Jay's turmoil. The lines connected as blood spilled from his wound. It formed an M-shape.

"Keep going. Claim what is yours." Caspian chewed on his nail excitedly.

A long score of my fire ripped another line, forming an "I" after the "M."

Jay's face was bright red, and his breathing turned ragged. Sobs racked my body, but I couldn't even double over or close my eyes. Whatever force controlled me wanted me to witness every second of agony.

"Stop! Please stop. I don't want this," I screamed.

My hand thrust forward, searing and full of power. Three more destructive lines seethed a furious "N" in Jay's chest.

He grunted and met my gaze, his eyes leaking tears now too. His defeated look shattered my heart.

Caspian kept rubbing monstrous circles with his thumb on his wretched necklace. "Keep going, dearest sister," he hissed.

"I'm sorry, I'm sorry." I sliced open Jay's chest with four more haggard cuts, finishing the word with an "E."

The word "MINE" scorched Jay's chest so deeply that blood trickled down his skin.

Panting, Jay gulped and swayed to the side, but the electrical cords kept him upright.

I wanted to drop to the ground, bury myself in the sand, and hide for eternity.

Moroka slid closer. "The price is blood."

"No, Moroka, stop!" I kicked and wrestled against the veiled hold that trapped me. "I didn't ask you a question!"

Moroka snaked in the sand, leaving blood in her trail. She hissed and sputtered red from her lips. The Blood Maiden stopped in front of Isaac and eyed him hungrily.

"No! No!" My throat turned raw, and tears streamed.

"Very well." The Blood Maiden slithered to Zeph. "We've met before, darling. I remember how sweet you tasted the first time."

Zeph spat in her face.

"I'll save you for later," Moroka sneered and moved in front of Paola, who looked like she was about to faint.

By the chariot, Alaska slammed her fists against the curtain of water restraining her, unable to break through.

No, I had to stop this, no matter what it cost me.

I summoned fire and launched an attack. "*Digati impetu*!"

Power grew in my tattoo, and fire spurted out, but not from my hands, from Isaac's. He jerked back in surprise. His fire hit the sand next to Moroka. The demon shrieked and lurched forward, chomping a bite into Paola's thigh. Paola screamed in pain, and the wind carried her agony into the mad winds.

"Damn it!" My throat scratched raw.

Moroka dodged all my attacks. "Say goodbye to the girl." She wrapped her mouth around Paola's throat as Paolo's gaze latched on Alaska's.

My breathing hitched. Lightning exploded above.

Wind thrashed.

Moroka chomped into Paola's neck with daggered teeth. Her head separated and rolled along the beach, blood coating the sand. Alaska's tears covered her face as she sank to the ground in shock.

Zeph gagged against the cloth in her mouth, and tears poured down her cheeks. Moroka sucked what must have been all of the blood from every last bit of Paola's body, leaving her empty. I couldn't move.

The air stilled. Fear consumed me, yet I was helpless, trapped, and imprisoned.

Moroka licked her blood-covered face and slithered in front of Isaac with a deadly smile.

22
ISAAC

I didn't have to see anything to understand the brutality. In this forever darkness, the gurgling sounds played on repeat in my mind, along with the savage slashing of flesh and meat. Moroka drank Paola dry. Dead. My heart spasmed dangerously with adrenaline. They better not lay a finger on my love. I needed Kyra to run far away and never look back.

Zeph whimpered next to me through something gagging her, probably a cloth like mine. I tugged against the ruthless cord to reach her hand and comfort the woman who had been there for me in the past when everything had fallen apart, but the barbaric restraints were too tight.

Kyra's energy felt as defeated and weak as mine, and Griffin's felt nonexistent. Was he still alive? Did it matter anymore? Kyra's silence and sorrow staggered through our bond. She needed my power, and I'd lend it to her, forever and always—even if that made me a fool. Maybe with my last bit of strength, she'd have a fighting chance.

The roar of the sadistic waves crashed against the shore as Caspian's voice boomed louder than the harsh thunder. My wet hair slapped and flailed against my cheeks. The only thing that could explain his behavior was ₾sµwi Magik.

"Moroka asked you a question," Caspian hissed. "Answer her."

I shook my head, unable to produce words through my gag.

A feral hand ripped it from my mouth. "Speak," Caspian ordered.

"I don't have a question. Free us now. You've done enough damage."

"No, Kyra has to choose between you. She will Link with me, so I will replace one of you."

"Please, we can find another solution." Kyra's voice was barely a whisper. "Stop making me hurt them."

"This was *your* choice. One can live while the other dies, or they will both suffer until we Link."

No one spoke for a long minute. The only sound was Alaska's heartbreaking whimpering.

Kyra kneeled in front of me and whispered, "Forgive me, Isaac. I'm not in control, I swear."

Lethal heat flared near my chest, and realization struck of what she was about to do. Griffin's pain was barely tolerable, and I only received a fraction of his warped anguish.

"I'm sorry, I'm sorry." Her voice was layered with scarred tears.

Without further warning, the sharpest, hottest flame pierced into my skin and slashed a line deep through my muscle. I cried out and arched away. Hot tears pooled behind my useless eyes.

"Please, Caspian. Stop!" Kyra whimpered, cries coating every word.

The pain stopped for a moment. Her shaking hand lay on my chest.

"It's the pearl. The Blood Maiden is wearing Caspian's pearl," Kyra whispered, but then she screamed out in pain, and the weight of her hand disappeared.

"What did you do to her?" I struggled against the restraints. "Kyra? Are you okay?"

"Moroka! Release Caspian from your control," she groaned. "Why are you both doing this?"

Moroka hissed, reminding me of the sound of leeches and maggots made underfoot. “Ahhhh! A question, at last, Cursed One, it shall be answered.”

“No, no, never mind, I didn’t mean to ask.” Kyra’s voice shook.

As malicious wind rammed against the shutters of the still-standing beach house behind us, I dropped my head in pain, sucking in air through clenched teeth. Every breath, in and out, was layered in agony from the fire still burning my chest. I squeezed my eyes shut and let the trickling tears fall onto the sand below. That was only one line. How could I survive more?

“Listen to my story,” Moroka began. “For a thousand years, my sisters, Surh-Sig, Oniskel, and I had free reign of the world. We were once nymphs with the gift to bless children with enhancements to their Magik, giving them a leadership role in their community. Mystiers worshipped us and were grateful for the blessings we bestowed.

One day, a greedy Mystier ruined us all. Elana Elidi was born with a wretched heart and sought destruction and power, even from a young age. When her tattoo was formed, she was the only one in her direct family that we did not bless with an enhancement.

Elana vowed then and there to seek revenge. As she aged, she translated an ancient spell in the Unetlo Book that morphed my sisters and me into these despicable forms. Because of these abominable necklaces, we were trapped. For decades, I’ve been cursed with an appetite for only blood. Come here, and I will avenge my sisters by devouring Elana’s heir.”

Horror seized my heart at her threat. I had to help my Kyra escape. But I couldn’t talk or move. Scalding pain tore open my insides where the branded line singed deep.

“No, Blood Maiden.” Caspian’s voice was strained like he was fighting against the darkness. “Take the other girl, the one with the glasses.”

Moroka hissed, “You no longer control me. I’ll take the meal that is due to me.”

Zeph sobbed next to me. I heard her crawling on the sand in an attempt to escape, but she wouldn’t get far in these cords.

"Take me instead," I stuttered through the lingering pain, unable to lift my head.

"No, no, no." Kyra's voice was muffled as if a barrier stood between us or she was being hauled away.

"Free my hands so I can feel my Magik once more, then I'll give myself to you," I forced out my plea quietly. "Spare the women and take me instead."

"Very well. The Cursed One already branded the Dravian, so you'll die soon anyway," said Caspian, his voice possessed once again.

A tug jerked my wrists, and the cord fell from my arms. I reached in my pocket for the Vayu Crystal as fast as possible, hoping it'd harness some miracle. My fingertips rubbed against the poisonous vial on the way out.

Kyra! I need a spell to save us.

But I wouldn't survive much longer. My breathing turned labored.

Ayasdi sospit, Isaac, Ayasdi sospit. Use that.

"*Ayasdi sospit*!" I rubbed my hand on the crystal and yelled again, "Ayasdi sospit!"

Zeph's squirming sounds stopped. Maybe the spell transferred her somewhere safe. Or maybe Alaska had teleported her away. Relief flooded me for a single moment. I wished my eyesight would return.

"Stop with this nonsense." Moroka's claws swiped the crystal necklace from my grasp.

"Give it back."

"It won't serve you when you're in the afterlife. Quiet now. I'm still hungry."

"Isaac!" Kyra's scream was muffled as she pounded on something that sounded like a glass window.

Where was she?

"Isaac, fight back!" Kyra slammed her fists over and over against a barrier.

Moroka's cold, coppery breath blew straight in my face. "You smell delicious. And there's so much of you, I won't have to eat for a month."

My heart rammed in my chest even faster—on overdrive. These were my last few moments. Acceptance.

My love, run away from here.

Isaac! No! Fight back!

The image of beautiful Vayu flickered in my mind for the last time. I wished I could see Wes's face once more. At least he was safe and had found a new friend in the safe house. Gemm would take care of him. Kyra had given me the greatest gift of all in returning my son. Even if our time together was short, even if she loved Griffin instead of me, she kept her promise by giving me Wes. I couldn't fault her for that.

Moroka's disgusting breath moved closer, crowding my space.

Kyra bawled through our thread, gasping and screaming. I didn't even have enough energy to block her out of my mind. She'd have to experience my death with me. At least I wouldn't have to die alone. Kyra and our Link meant I'd never truly be alone.

"Say goodbye, puppet," Moroka hissed.

Dread slithered up my spine. I didn't want to feel the pain. I didn't want to suffer in my last moments. No one should have to be murdered by sharp fangs. No one should have to be eaten alive.

"Nilson, the poison," Griffin's broken voice murmured from somewhere close.

My hand flew into my pocket, and I grabbed the vial. When the top screwed off, the smell of sweet vanilla wafted to my nose. I had no time. Raising it to my lips, I smiled across the sand, hoping Kyra would see that I wouldn't suffer.

"Isaac! Wait, Isaac!" She banged and slammed.

I gulped the suicide potion down, swallowing the sweet candy. The world stole all my breath as I fell to the side. A dreamy orb glowed brightly in my mind, and ghostly silhouettes waved me closer. All the sounds of the waves disappeared. Thunder seized to exist. My body drifted and floated. There was only light. If Moroka bit into me, I wouldn't feel a thing because everything turned numb.

"Spit it out," Kyra cried, quieter this time, exhausted. "Save him, Jay! I can't get out of this box. Heal him, please."

Rajitha's calm voice soothed me from somewhere so close and far away, letting me know I shouldn't worry about them. Kyra would eventually be okay. She'd move on and be happy. Kyra and Griffin would work it out and find their happily ever after without me. Rajitha called me home.

"No!" Kyra's voice blended into the howl of the storm.

"Don't be sad. Take care of Wes for me," I whispered to the wind, unsure if I had even spoken aloud. The wind would be with me no matter where I went in the next life.

A slimy tongue licked my neck, but then it stopped. "What did you do?" Moroka hissed. "I don't want your blood to taste like poison. I'll take the girl instead."

A heavy weight rolled on top of me. Zeph. Any attempt to help her was futile. I was already halfway gone—partially to the next world. This poison was the most intoxicating drug, rushing through my veins with such ease and warmth. But in my trance, I still felt Zeph writhing.

Light surrounded me, and my vision returned slightly spotty. But on top of my worthless body, the sounds of Moroka hacking through Zeph like a rabid dog kept me in this reality. I heard a spine crack. A lifeless blob rolled over my back. Slick liquid dripped down the front of my cheek. I licked it. Blood. Fuck! The smell of death fumed the air. Organs. Bile. Zeph was dead because of me. So many brutal deaths.

No, Moroka was supposed to kill me. My head drooped heavily. I wanted to block out the horror and slip into unconsciousness. But Kyra screamed and screamed and screamed. Her muffled voice was a chainsaw to my soul, gnawing away at the roots of my essence. I should've fought harder. I should've stayed. I should've....

I was paralyzed by the poison. Dying. Peace and torment together. Wes's eyes were the last thing I saw before a torched brightness swallowed me whole.

23

JADOX

Broken. Numb.

I remembered everything, and now the man Kyra loved was dead. Gone. Nilson lay on the beach, the empty cyanide bottle a few inches from his limp hand. Zeph's hacked body was draped on top of him, and Moroka continued to suck at her blood. The stench was unbearable.

Trapped in a glass cage, Kyra slammed against its thick walls again and again. Nilson's death was completely ripping her apart.

"Get up." Caspian's voice barely registered as a gush of his waterpower pushed me toward a second cage.

Pain scalded my chest where Kyra had branded me with fire, and I knew my body couldn't tolerate much more torture. Panic seized me, but Kyra's amber eyes were a point of light in my infinite black, and I clutched on for dear life.

24

KYRA

The unnatural storm tore a hole in the fabric of the sky and cried onto the crimson sand. Grief racked my body in shuddering waves. Isaac was dead. Emptiness sliced through me, and I sucked in broken gulps of air. Tears probably soaked my cheeks, but I was too exhausted to wipe them away.

"I'm sorry." On my knees in this glass box, I finally dropped my bloodied knuckles from the wall. "I'm sorry, Isaac."

Kyra, look at me.

My eyes snapped to Jay's concerned face on the other side of the glass barrier. Now he was trapped in a second cage adjacent to mine.

"I'm sorry, Jay. I'm sorry I hurt you." I stared at the angry welts on his chest that spelled *MINE* in uneven, crooked gashes.

Jay rested a hand on the glass, waiting for me to reach out. Instead, I sagged further onto the floor. There was nothing to say. I had ruined everything and was responsible for three more deaths.

Zeph—dead.

Paola—dead.

Isaac—d....

I choked on the thought and curled onto my side. One of Caspian's chariots dragged our cages into the water by some invisible leash.

Look at me. It wasn't your fault, Petal.

Jay was wrong, but I was too tired to respond.

Alaska survived. She'll take care of Landon and Wes until we escape.

More guilt scaled up my spine. I should have asked about her, but a heaviness crowded my head. Unable to think, unable to move, I simply stared at the current as we were lugged into the sea. The menacing clouds disappeared, and soon, gloomy navy liquid surrounded us. A school of fish swarmed by, and I wished my brain could be as small as theirs so I didn't have to deal with all this mess. We dropped deeper and deeper into the darkness. It wasn't fair.

From the corner of my eye, Jay moved even closer in his glass box, but I couldn't look at him. I had tortured him—a man I loved. My selfishness to feel like I belonged caused Jay's pain and Isaac's death. My desperation to have someone to call my own led to this utter disaster.

There was no point in continuing to fight. My decisions drove the ones I loved to suffering and pain. If only I had slowed down and formed a better plan, maybe things would have turned out differently.

Look at me. Please.

Jay pleaded through our bond as we sank. Sank. Sank. In the distance, the outskirts of Cydon's underwater village came into view. But I couldn't erase other haunting images flickering in my mind. Isaac's perfect lips on mine, those same lips closing around the top of the poisonous vial and the black liquid draining from the bottle into his mouth.

In his last moments, Isaac had smiled. That realization tore a hole through my heart, severing my soul. I gave away a part of myself to him, a part I could never get back. He couldn't be gone. It wasn't possible. Why? Why did he have to leave me? It wasn't fair! Now, I belonged to no one because even Jay hated me for my choices.

It's okay, Kyra. I'm not mad.

I finally raised my chin and locked onto his gaze.

You should be mad. I had given up on you, on us. I wouldn't forgive me, if I was in your shoes.

The current swooshed our cage violently as we trailed after the chariot.

We have to form a plan to escape.

No, Jay, it's over.

You have to fight back. Please.

That got my attention. Through heavy eyelids, I lifted my gaze again, surprised when love still shone from his eyes.

You're supposed to hate me, Jay.

I can never hate you, Petal.

I shook my head at the absurdity of how he was processing this so quickly. Why would he give me a second chance? Was it because Isaac was no longer competition? No, thinking about it like that was cruel. Pinning the two against one another was never the plan.

The beach is in the past. How will we move forward?

I punched the glass wall. "Move forward?"

He jerked back, his eyes on my mouth, reading my lips.

Yes! Move forward, Kyra. We need a plan to escape.

The feeling of bricks stacking on my chest stole all my energy again.

You don't understand. I was Linked with Isaac. And he's just gone. GONE! He took a part of me with him. How can I move forward? I'm not fully here. I can't breathe.

Jay leaned back against the wall and ran a hand over his face.

I'm trying to understand. I can feel part of your pain right now. I need to help to make it better.

I can't be fixed, Jay. You can't fix me!

You're not broken.

He sighed and placed a hand on his chest as if my feelings were actually crushing his heart. This time, he was wrong. His intense stare fizzled into softness, and, for a moment, I wished I could shatter the glass barrier and hide in his arms. But he deserved better. I shouldn't dump all my grief on him.

What do you want, Kyra?

As our cage drifted closer to the mighty Cydian castle, I fought through the agony and tried to process his question, knowing we didn't have much time left. Nothing about what Caspian was doing made any sense. I wanted him to return to his prior self so I could trust my brother again. And I wanted to see Isaac's smile again. But now, above all else, I wanted Jay to stay safe. I'd do anything to keep him alive.

I'd lost both Isaac and Caspian to some dark Magik. There was no chance I'd let it take Jay too. I gulped down those fears as the cage hooked on the side of the building.

Four silhouettes emerged from a side entrance and the Cydians, enveloped in their personal oxygen bubble, swam to Jay's side of the cage. When the glass door opened, water rushed inside. With spear-like weapons in hand, they grabbed him from all sides. Jay tried to wrestle, but the strength of the water filling his chamber thrashed him against the walls. The guards wrapped a rope around him and yanked him through the water.

"No!" I slammed my hands against the glass, making no impact. "No."

Helpless, I smacked my fists over and over on the glass until he disappeared into the castle. Through blurry tears, I craned my neck up and fixated on the swaying coral through the glass ceiling. Sobs erupted from my chest as I slouched into the shape of an empty shell once again.

"Please, if there's an ocean goddess or mermaid queen or anything divine down here, please help me. I can't lose him too. Please."

Time marched on, and the surface felt further away. The underwater houses all looked empty, as well as the abandoned marine gardens surrounding the little village with sponges and sea thickets. I stared up at the colossal palace, painted in shades of aqua-blue and green. It was in the shape of a perfect sphere, majestically centered in the underwater community. What was happening to Jay in there?

Suddenly, a strange force pressed against my remaining Link, an energy that didn't belong. I scrambled to my knees. Could it be Isaac relaying a message from the other side? Did spirits and ghosts exist? My heart slammed against my chest as I focused on the invisible power knocking at my shield.

My little firecracker, you've made a mess of things.

The deep male voice was hoarse but calm—not Isaac's or Jay's.

"Who are you?"

I squinted into the dark water, unable to spot a living soul.

I am a part of you, and you will always belong to me.

The choice of words he used basically stopped my heart.

"How are you in my head?"

I've always been in your head and your heart, little firecracker. I belong to you too, but you close yourself off.

Unease should've shaken my bones from the intrusion. Instead, an inexplicable peace washed over me.

"Tell me your name."

First, make me a promise.

Despite being silent, his voice boomed in my head, repeating the word promise over and over.

"Promises are worth more than a name," I said.

Smart girl.

"Where are you?"

Always close. You only needed to search to find me. Now, dig deep and discover your full power, Kyra. You've only skimmed the surface.

"Tell me your name." I swallowed hard.

Make me a promise.

I peered behind the lumps of coral above. No shadows lurked. "What promise?" Maybe if I convinced him to keep talking, I'd spot his face.

Link with your brother. He was always the one in your prophecy. It's the only way.

"That'll never happen. That monster just led Isaac to his death."

A pause. *My son is not a monster.*

The ocean faded away into oblivion as my hand clutched my chest. "Your son."

Silence.

"So, you're Caspian's father?"

Silence.

"You're Brent Elidi?" A disbelieving chuckle escaped my lips.

That's right, and I'm–

I stole a moment to suck in a breath. "You're my father."

Yes, Kyra. Forgive me, there's—

My fists curled into balls. "Forgive? Why should I be so kind? Who the Flames are you to randomly show up in my life and ask for a favor? This must be some joke, or I must be hallucinating."

We don't have much time.

Confusion warped all logic as I buried my head in my hands, whimpering, "Where have you been all this time?"

A prisoner. They're on their way. We don't have time to—

"How are you in my head?"

My gift involves telepathy. I can control consciousness and communicate, but my powers have been weakened under her control.

"President Stirk's?"

I'll explain later, but you must Link with your brother. It wasn't Caspian on that beach. It was Moroka. She used dark Magik with the pearl to make him say and do those things.

"Zeph is dead, and Paola is dead." Tears fell. "And Isaac...Isaac is—"

Slow down, firecracker—

"Stop calling me that! You don't know me."

I've watched you grow up and turn into the woman I am proud to call my daughter. There's no more time. I must go. Trust Narelle. When you escape, use the third door, not the first or second. The third door only. The Dravian boy will have until midnight before it's too late.

"Sure, will do." I sarcastically saluted the air. "Thanks, Pops. I owe you one."

Silence.

"Wait, are you there?"

Nothing.

Groaning with exhaustion, I shook my head to loosen the knot of thoughts that scrambled in my mind. Each time I paced from one corner of the cage to the other, the floor shifted slightly, up and down like a soft wave.

My heart fluttered at the words Brent had used: *I am a part of you, and you will always belong to me.*

Irritation gripped my throat solidly. If that was Brent, and he had watched me grow up, why didn't he do anything to prevent my pain? Why hadn't he warned me about the violent man who raised Hallie and me?

I belong to you too, but you close yourself off.

Did Brent try to reach out when I was younger, but I didn't listen? I yanked my wet hair from the ponytail and began twisting a braid to distract my jittery fingers. I didn't belong to anyone anymore. Not Brent or Isaac, or Jay. Especially not Jay when I'd only cause him pain. Relying on other people to define me was a waste of time.

"I belong to myself, and that's okay," I said aloud.

A spark zapped my tattoo for the first time since the beach disaster.

"I belong to Magik," I spoke to the walls of the sealed cage.

"I belong to fire!" A single ounce of tension in my chest evaporated. Even though it wasn't enough to feel fully free, the release provided renewed strength.

If I belonged to fire, there was no way out of this box. Water outranked fire. My fingers traced the corners, grazing for any tiny crack or latch. I swiveled fast, my blood pumping rapidly. A shadow lingered over me.

Inside a personal bubble of air, Narelle hovered from the other side of the glass. She put one finger to her lips and scanned behind her, up to the towering windows of the castle.

I nodded.

She tapped her finger over a small section of the glass, and the door slid open. Water cascaded in, drenching my shoes and ankles.

Narelle held one hand up as a *stop* signal, then mimed sucking in a breath. I gulped in the air, waited, and when the water almost filled my cage, I squeezed through the opening. She grabbed my wrist and pulled me toward a door. The first door. Brent said the third. Should I trust him? Was he even real?

My lungs started to burn. Narelle hovered her hand over the knob of the first door, but I yanked her back. Her eyebrows furrowed together. I shook my head and pointed to the third door. Narelle's head tilted to the side. I swam forward, pulling her along. As we floated in front of the third door, I strained against the immediate need to suck in a breath. My hand hovered over the knob, and I summoned the power to my Circle.

I belonged to fire, and I'd still save Jay.

25

KYRA

Narelle tapped in a code, and the castle's door slid open. We slipped inside the tiny compartment. My lungs were about to burst, but the door slammed shut, and water drained away steadily. My forehead felt the air first, then my nose, my lips. As the water reached my chin, I sucked in oxygen.

My head bobbed above the surface, and the saltwater lowered until we stood in a sopping mess. A hollow sensation echoed in my circle. I tried to ignore the heaviness of Isaac's loss. For now, I had to focus on helping Jay escape.

Narelle's fingers punched in a sequence on another small pad, and the interior door swiped open. "Why did you want to come to *this* door?"

"Because I'm stupidly listening to a voice in my head." I stepped through the threshold to the strong smell of gutted fish.

Twenty magnificent hydracos lifted their heads from barrels and glared with their all-white eyes. After deciding I wasn't a threat, they focused back on their meals. Inside this room, they seemed larger than when I swam with them in the vast ocean. At ten feet tall and probably weighing over two thousand pounds, their green scales shone in the florescent lights that hung like jellyfish.

"This is the indoor stables." Narelle petted the nearest hydraco calf as it pushed its snout against her shoulder. "We need to go down that tunnel where Caspian and Jadox are locked up."

"Why is Caspian locked up?" I snarled. "He's the one who dragged us down here."

Narelle sighed, and, for the first time, I noticed the dark circles under her eyes. "That wasn't his doing, Kyra. Don't you have any faith in your brother?"

Maybe the mysterious Brent voice was telling the truth.

I shuffled my feet. "No, not really. I don't know what kind of person Caspian has become after all these years."

"President Stirk has him in the dome, and she's controlling all of them."

"She's here?" I shook my head. "How? The president relies on a hoverchair."

"She stole a chariot." Narelle hustled across the puddled floor straight to a stall laced with a plaque adorned with fake pearls that read *Brynn*.

The hydraco turned in her stall and huffed happily at the sight of me. I rubbed the creature's forehead while sorting through my confusion. "So, do you ever…um…hear voices underwater? Maybe, like sirens—"

"No."

"Oh."

Narelle rushed around, gathering materials. "You have a golden tattoo. *Golden*. You probably have all the elements in your blood. Maybe that's why you can do things we can't."

"Like hear voices underwater?"

"Exactly. Caspian has Cydon Magik, and you two are blood-related. Maybe you have a connection to the water too."

I tugged at the contents: a sandwich, water, and a new outfit.

"Change," she commanded. "Otherwise, you'll leave a water trail for someone to track us in the tunnels. Quickly, while I gather our team."

"Who?"

Narelle disappeared around the corner, ignoring my question. Without wasting time, I stripped in front of the rows of hydracos and let the soaked clothes pile on the floor. Ringing out my hair, I donned the fire-red shirt and skintight black pants, my curves stretching Narelle's fabric.

In one of the aquarium-style windows, my reflection stared back at me. My posture looked unfamiliar, hunched, and drooped. I squared my shoulders and lifted my pointy chin, giving myself a mental pep talk. I could do this. I had to succeed–for Jay's sake. He might hate me until his dying day for kissing Isaac, but I'd still try to protect him as long as possible. As I reached through our Link, my hand found the Elidi Ruby draped under my shirt.

Jay? Are you close?

Nothing.

Only an uneasy feeling of being watched settled deep in my bones as I scanned the tall ceilings. High up, the walls held holes that seemed to part into tunnels, leading to other parts of the magnificent underwater castle.

"Okay, you ready?" Narelle strutted back from around the corner.

"Yeah, what's the plan?"

"Mount a ride. I assume you want Brynn?"

I nodded.

"If we get split up, ride to the central dome."

I jumped on Brynn's back and steadied her. "And then we free Caspian and Jadox. Right...simple enough. Nothing can go wrong." I glanced behind Narelle. "And where's our backup? Did you recruit Cydian villagers?"

"No, I evacuated them. I'm their leader; my job is to keep the people safe."

"So, what did you mean by 'team'?"

Narelle scrunched up her nose and didn't meet my eye. "Well, the help I asked for might meet us in the dome, but it's risky." She mounted a green hydraco and patted its back. "Kyra, be warned, they may choose the other side."

"Who are *they*?"

"It's safer if I don't tell you yet, they can smell fear."

"Great." My heart rate quickened, and I glided a hand down Brynn's curved tail that spiraled around itself in a loop for comfort. "I love surprises."

"If they come, you might need to convince them to fight for us. Keep your eyes open. Don't drain your energy until we have an escape route. I'm unsure how mobile the men will be on their own—they might need our help. Brynn can carry you and Jadox to a chariot I have waiting outside."

This was the perfect time to tell Narelle that my Magik had felt incredibly weak since Isaac died. But I couldn't risk prolonging the rescue mission. Fear rippled closer, and a shiver swept through me from head to toe.

"Why do I have to convince your *team* to help?" I directed Brynn to follow Narelle's hydraco to another door leading out of the stables.

"Because they know that you stole the emerald from the lagoon in the forbidden caves."

Memories whirled back. The only possibility I could fathom was the despicable sirens who had tried to drown me.

"Sirens? Wait! This isn't a good idea."

But the door slid open, and Narelle's hydraco crawled forward on stubby crocodile legs. Brynn followed silently. Apparently, it was still daylight because, impossibly, Magikal sunbeams sliced light through the water and into the tunnel windows. The light felt strange when everything inside me felt inky black.

The soft sound of water dripping one drop at a time rippled goosebumps over my entire body, ready to explode like a landmine.

A scampering sound came behind me, and I spun Brynn around, darting my attention toward the empty tunnel. "Come on," Narelle whispered. "It's probably just sea rats."

I gulped and tried to push away the ominous warnings flooding my tattoo, screaming at me to turn back.

"How far do we go through this tunnel?" I hissed at her.

Narelle only turned and raised one finger to her lips. A skittering tickled the ceiling, like tiny claws tapping along the surface. Ahead, she halted and craned her head to the right and left. Shivers erupted along my arms in warning.

Suddenly, a giant tentacle reached down from the high tunnel and grabbed Narelle straight off the hydraco's back. Her scream echoed through the tunnel as she disappeared.

Then, silence. It'd all happened so fast. Narelle was gone, and I was alone.

My heart thundered wildly, and I kicked both heels hard into Brynn's side.

"Go, go, go!"

Right as we lunged, another tentacle swiped down. I gasped and leaned forward, hugging Brynn's chest.

"Go, Brynn!"

Squeezing her scales with my thighs as tight as possible, I flattened down to stay out of the monster's reach. Brynn zigged and zagged, darting away from the titanic tentacle. Another swooped down, and another. We swerved. Darted. Four frenzied limbs. Five. All trying to scoop us up into oblivion. Ahead, the tunnel finally ended at a door.

"C'mon!" I dug my heels into her side again. "Hurry."

Brynn's stubby legs crawled as fast as possible, but this creature was meant for swimming, not running. I strained forward, reaching my hand out at the door. Groping it, I cursed under my breath. No handle—only a keypad with numbers to punch in an unknown code. I pounded a fist against the door. There was no time.

"Hello!" I screamed. "Open up."

A massive tentacle slammed into the wall next to us, creating a dent in the metal.

"Help!" My fists turned bloodied from knocking and all the pounding they'd done today.

Brynn shoved her long snout against the door, trying to push forward. I slid off her back and fumbled with the keypad. What would be the code? I punched in random numbers, but it flashed red. Fuck! Slats on the floor opened, and water poured in.

No.

My boots turned heavy in the water as I sloshed around. The

frantic whipping of the tentacles above thrashed against the walls. If it burst open a window, I'd drown before reaching Jay.

My blood pumped harder, making my head spin.

I stabbed in another code. It flashed red lights. Then the water cascaded in faster. Higher. A tentacle gripped Brynn's leg, yanking her away into the tunnel above.

No, *now* I was truly alone.

Terror zapped through my Link. The water rose. I stayed afloat at the top, but my boots weighed me down. It lifted me higher and higher to the tunnels near the ceiling, and I kicked to keep afloat. Four paths. One held the monstrous octopus or octopuses—who knew how many there were. I swam as far from it as possible, stroking toward the corner. My muscles burned.

Ten feet away.

I swam faster. Harder.

Eight feet away.

A tentacle latched onto my ankle and pulled me backward. It dragged me underwater with such force that I couldn't catch my breath. Kicking. Writhing.

I fought back. I was out of breath, out of time.

I grasped at nothing as liquid slid through the cracks between my fingers.

Jay, help!

Nothing.

Caspian!

Nothing.

Use a spell, firecracker. A spell!

Brent's unique voice barreled through my mind.

What spell?

Frantically, I twisted against the octopus' grasp, running out of oxygen.

"Vand zalit." Bubbles came out of my mouth. *"Vand zalit."*

Immediately, the grip slackened, and I stroked up with all my remaining energy. I gasped at the surface and swam straight to the far tunnel. The water didn't fully meet the level of the tunnel. I slipped against the metal over and over until my heel finally hooked onto the tunnel floor.

I pulled myself up with shaking arms and crawled on all fours into the darkness. This tunnel, unlike the others, showed no windows or let in any light. Panting and uncertain about what monsters lay in this tunnel, I crawled forward, longing to reach Jay's side.

My knees turned raw from skidding against the metal ground. I finally stood on trembling legs, skimming my hand against the cold wall to guide me, unwilling to use my power to form a torch.

"Get up. You're the fuckin' Golden One. Act like it," I said to myself.

Marching on, I finally caught a glimpse of light ahead. Tiptoeing in squishy shoes, I peeked out of the tunnel hole and sucked in a gasp. The tunnel led out to the top of the ceiling dome. I was way too high. Fish swam on the other side of the glass, and the light flickered off their scales. I gathered all the courage I had left and peeked far below. There was a huge circular platform surrounded by water.

In the very center of the platform were three men. In front of them, President Stirk's hoverchair glided back and forth.

The first Jay.

The second Caspian.

And a middle-aged man with brown hair.

They were all strapped vertically to science-lab tables. A fin glittered from the waters, and then a flash of cyan hair streamed by. A siren.

"They came," I whispered to myself. "But will they choose our side?"

I scanned the three-story wall covered in coral from the base to my tunnel. When I slowly inched my foot over the side, I hoped they'd hold my weight. I blew out a steady breath and dropped my legs further, sliding my hips over the edge. The distance of the drop felt like it doubled in height.

I carefully moved down, pretending it was only a rock-climbing wall. My fingertips gripped the coral like my life depended on it. If the president turned and spotted me, I was doomed. If I made one wrong move and slipped, I'd fall to my death. Or if any of the three men spotted me and reacted, it was over.

Each agonizing movement lower helped me hear President Stirk's voice better. She spoke to them like a mother disciplining her children, clearly in the middle of a monologue.

"...Pointless to steal a Cydian chariot if she doesn't show up! Pointless to put on this elaborate show if she doesn't care enough to rescue you."

Only when I lowered further did I notice the electric rod she continually stabbed Jay's torso with. My heart ransacked in my body, and a surge of power flowed through me.

She better not hurt him!

In my distraction, my foot slipped, and I bit my lip to hold in a scream as I dangled by only my fingertips. Flailing in the air with straining arms, I resituated my feet on the thick coral, breathed out a sigh of relief, and zoned back in on the president's speech.

"...Pointless that I captured you to heal me when your powers are worthless," Syvonne Stirk's voice scratched.

"Can't use you for Golden offspring if you're this..." She paused. "What was that sound?"

I froze and crunched my forehead against my pale knuckles, waiting for something to rip me off the wall. I held my breath. Nothing happened.

No attack. No threat.

Risking everything, I peeked over my shoulder and squinted. President Stirk pointed from her hoverchair to the adjacent wall where a tunnel hole led to dark unknowns. Maybe the octopus had found a way to the dome too. I used the distraction and scurried down more corals. I was almost at the bottom. Something sharp scraped my wrist.

"Ouch!" I hissed.

"Guards," Stirk spoke into her s-watch, "Check the dome's north tunnel. Now."

Only eight feet from the bottom, I scanned my options. The wall dropped straight into the dark waters where the sirens circled. If I lowered into it softly, I could wade over to the platform, hopefully, without them noticing me. But then what? Shove Stirk into the water and watch her sink? Could I do that to someone without legs?

My fingers clutched the coral, and my legs shook violently, stealing more energy. A rustling of footsteps high above from the north tunnel echoed into the dome, and my attention shifted back up.

A high-pierced whistle screeched, then a venti swooped from the tunnel and dove crooked and lopsided for the president with one wing bent.

My heart stopped. Tawoli's alive?

A man with a blond bun clung to its feathers atop her back, directing the attack.

Isaac.

Alive.

Isaac was here.

My body jerked in shock. I lost my hold of the coral. Everything turned upside down as I fell. Fell. Fell. And splashed into the wicked cold.

26

KYRA

Isaac was on Tawoli.

Isaac was alive.

"Isaac!"

I splashed through the violent surface of the waves, gasping for air. Blue hair streaked to my right. How many sirens would I have to fight? One collided with my side and her sour fangs sliced into my shoulder. I howled out in pain. Claws dug into my stomach, just above my tattoo, and slit a vicious gash.

"Aaaah!"

"Kyra!" Isaac yelled and swooped Tawoli towards the treacherous waters.

His eyesight must have returned too because those gray eyes lasered into mine, promising safety. Or maybe he was a hallucination.

I grappled, twisted, and fought against the filthy sirens. Another latched onto my waist, dragging me under. I reached toward the dome ceiling and felt the air on my fingers.

Suddenly, a hand gripped my wrist, and I rose straight out of the water. Isaac!

We rose higher, and the grip on my wrist slipped an inch. I

thudded into the side of something solid. Tawoli. Water blurred my sight and leaked down my face.

"I've got ya, love." Isaac's lips were drawn tight as he heaved me between his torso and Tawoli's neck.

"Are you okay?" he whispered in my ear.

"You're alive!"

Tawoli flapped her fierce wings, circling thirty feet above the others. Scanning the area from high above gave me a clearer picture. Caspian, Jay, and the mystery man were all still unconscious, strapped vertically to steel tables.

"How are you alive? You drank the poison," I said.

"Apparently, wise Gemm didn't find it necessary to explain to us that the liquid wasn't lethal. Alaska thought we all knew what the potion was."

"Alaska? Is she okay?"

"Yes, she's the one who teleported me here. She said it was a drug to slow the heart for a few minutes. It lets the immune system triple its efficiency to heal injuries faster."

"Healing? But we have Jay to heal."

His breath warmed my ear. "That's what Gemm meant by *just in case*."

"Just in case...just in case we didn't have access to a healer anymore." I nodded, and a stabbing fear lodged in my chest at the thought of a world without Jay.

"But I couldn't feel you through the Link, Isaac. You had disappeared."

"Probably because of Moroka and the pearl." He kissed my temple. "Can you feel me now?"

In an instant, his mental wall dropped, and a potent rush of his love consumed me, stealing all breath. Raw Magik gushed through me, overflowing my veins with power. Flickers of fire sprang to life on my fingertips.

"Yes," I gasped. "Yes."

"Okay, then, problem solved. Now, let's go kill this bitch."

Tawoli lowered at Isaac's command, directly over President Stirk's hoverchair.

"Let them go!" I bellowed, aiming my hands straight at her.

"You're too late," Syvonne hissed. "It's almost done."

I clutched onto thick feathers with one hand and shot fire out the other. It burned a hole into the floor by the president's chair.

Syvonne *tsked* and shook a finger. "You've always been such an impulsive child."

"Shut up. You might be 'president'"—I let the sarcasm layer my words— "but you don't rule me, Syvonne Stirk."

"President Stirk is dead," she said simply.

I paused. "What? Then who are you?" I gritted my teeth. "Actually, it doesn't matter. I'll kill you anyway."

We shot forward, but an invisible wall blocked us.

"Typical. I expected nothing else from a hot head. You've always been a child who reacts instead of thinking things through. I was just like you, once upon a time, as were all the Golden Ones: my daughter and Brent here."

Her daughter?

And Brent?

Time stood still. My hands shook. A surreal terror seized my gut and coiled into a knot when she met my eyes.

"What are you talking about?" I gasped.

"You want to know who you are." President Stirk frowned. "You're my great-granddaughter, Kyra."

My entire body shuddered, rejecting the statement.

"It's not true. It's impossible. You're like thirty-six years old," I spat. "If you're Elana, you'd be ancient by now."

"I have my ways, child. And my plan is almost complete." With the flip of her wrist, the water surrounding us rose vertically up along the walls and came together at a point on the ceiling.

Droplets fell like rain onto my head. My heart hammered fast and hard. Shit!

"If she's Elana Elidi, isn't she supposed to have firepower?" Isaac's voice was in a trance.

What do we do, Isaac?

We fight back.

He gave me a little squeeze. Tawoli dipped low, and I aimed at Syvonne—Elana. Fire exploded from my hand, but it stopped in front of her face, turned to dirt, and then fell to the platform like ash. Elana tilted her chin. A rope of wind whipped us off Tawoli. Isaac and I both toppled from her back and fell. Fast. The ruby necklace slid off my neck and clattered to the platform. My side smacked hard upon landing.

Her wicked finger reached down and grabbed my necklace. "Thank you for this." Amusement lined Elana's voice, but she didn't so much as smirk.

"Give that back!"

If it was in the wrong hands, only disaster would follow. Sirens continually hissed and clawed at my boots. I scrambled up, summoning power to my fingertips.

"We have to keep Caspian and Jay safe," I said.

"And your father."

My chest tightened as I glanced at the mystery man with brown hair. Brent.

My father.

By my side, Isaac cast a blast of wind. Elana didn't even flinch. She blocked it swiftly with a gust of wind.

How? I concentrated on my Link with Isaac and merged our powers. His Magik slid into my veins, overwhelming me with the strength of his wind powers. Isaac's Magik was as natural to me as breathing.

Together, we held enormous energy. A thrust of fire and wind mixed into a tornado of death. Elana blocked it with a simple wave of her hand.

The terrifying gust ricocheted back to us, and we both flattened to our stomachs. A fireball crashed into the corralled wall behind us.

"Jay! Wake up," I yelled across the platform. If only I could touch him, we'd have more power.

"He won't wake unless I command it." Elana smiled for the first time, showing the sparkling teeth and wrinkle-free face of a borrowed body. Her lips moved like she was casting a silent spell.

An ear-splitting shriek echoed from the tunnel above, and massive tentacles reached out from the tunnel, slashing the air. They were over thirty feet long. The slimy tentacles wrapped around my body and pinned my arms behind my back. Yellow goo oozed off it and dripped down my neck.

Isaac was also bound by a wild tentacle. He wrestled against the hold. Electricity coursed through the veins of the magnificent monster, shocking me over and over. I commanded my Circle to obey, but no power came. Trapped again.

"Why are you doing this?" I screamed and fixated on Jay's unconscious form.

Elana moved her hoverchair closer and stared at me with venom in her eyes. "It's time to start fresh in this world. Thankfully, you did some of the hard parts for me and erased half the Ordull population." She chuckled. "Now, I just need the rest of the necklaces." Her hoverchair moved over to Caspian, and she yanked the pearl dangling from a long chain on his neck. "I got so much of what I wanted in one day." Elana slid the necklace into her pocket. "Forget about these men and help me."

Maybe if I acted like I was considering it, then she'd give me more information. "Why have you been capturing so many Mystiers as prisoners?"

"The weak Mystiers have been used in a project for your boyfriend to practice on. I can't stay in this handicapped body forever. I need to be stronger."

Guilt racked through me at the thought of what Jay had suffered under her command.

She continued, "For the rest, we run labs to find the strongest Mystiers to make more Golden Ones. The demon sisters gifted each tribe with one strong family. I've been searching for the strongest Vayuian, Cydian, and Draven male for a potential mate." Her eyes swiveled to Caspian. "But, apparently, this *boy* is my descendant, which eliminates the Cydian clan."

I shook my head, trying to process her words.

What does she mean, mate?

"So, that leaves me to mate with the strongest male in Vayu or Draven." Elana smiled. "We couldn't find any Vayu males with enhancements. My only option is Griffin." She patted Jay's thigh. "So, Kyra, you can help me by searching for any Vayu men we may have missed."

Rage boiled my blood, and my ears roared. "I'll never help you." I strained all my muscles against the tentacles.

"You're foolish to oppose me."

"Let. Him. Go."

Elana's jaw ticked. "I don't think so."

"Jay. Wake up!"

"Don't worry, I won't kill him. I need him to start fresh, a world run by future Golden Ones only, those with my blood. You see, I need a male Mystier powerful enough to make all my little Golden offspring."

"You're crazy!" I writhed against the cords. "He's *mine*."

She laughed. "I see that." She pointed to the jagged lines etched into Jadox's chest.

"You won't win."

"Of course, I will. I have over a hundred years of experience." Elana's grin was tinged with lunacy.

"How are you even alive?" Isaac finally spoke beside me, giving up his fight against the electricity that was zapping us.

Elana moved her hoverchair to him and pointed at his neck. Fire shot out and burned through the chain of his necklace, tearing into his skin. As Isaac hollered out in pain, the Vayu Crystal bounced off a tentacle and fell into her palm.

I sucked in a breath, desperate to do anything to help.

"Well, to stay alive…I borrow energy from other Golden Ones, my descendants," Elana said. "My precious daughter gave me so many extra years, and when she became too weak to continue, I took Brent when you were young."

I froze. "Took him?"

"Yes, I took him from you. One day, I'll take you too."

"To make sure Brent served me all these years, I generously gifted him with snippets of your life. I hired a man named Quamir to keep tabs on you. You might remember him, right, sweetie?"

I was speechless.

"Enough!" Isaac bellowed.

Elana clapped her hands together. "Right, it's time for the show! I've been waiting for this."

I growled, but most of my determination had been replaced with turmoil and an endless stream of questions.

"It's time for you to sever your Link with Griffin. I need him as my mate, so he can no longer be attached to you."

I paused. Severing the Link is what I had wanted before to free both Jay and Isaac from further suffering. But not like this.

"But you need him alive. Severing could kill him," I forced out through a clenched jaw.

"I doubt it. I killed my lover long ago; you shouldn't have a problem with it either."

"You mean my great-grandfather!" I yelled. "And you drained my grandmother's life! Now, you'll kill my father. When will you stop?"

"Not until I make an entire Golden fleet in my name. The three demon sisters will regret their choice to exclude me from tradition." Elana laid a pale hand on Brent's shoulder. "Awaken, grandson, and retrieve the Severing Spell."

Brent's eyes snapped open, and his gaze automatically met mine. They were full of sorrow.

I'm sorry for this. Forgive me.

"Stop wasting time!" Elana commanded. "Retrieve the Severing Spell. Kyra will have it buried deep within."

My father looked unwilling to dig into my mind. He mouthed, 'I'm sorry,' and focused on the man next to me. Isaac suddenly stiffened. He screamed so loudly that my knees buckled and slammed straight into the floor. The tentacles' grip loosened, for just a moment, before gathering me back up. My heart drummed wildly. Isaac's eyes squeezed shut and his back arched. Every tendon in his neck bulged. My blood was on fire with rage.

"Stop! What are you doing to him?!" I screamed.

"...Librarian?...severing spell..." Elana spoke between Isaac's agonizing screams. "...deep in his mind."

His screams froze time and silenced the siren's song, stopping my heart from beating.

Tears fell, and the skin on my shoulders rubbed red and raw from the constant writhing against the tentacles. Nothing was worse than watching someone you loved seize up in pain. Loved. I loved him.

"I found the spell," Brent whispered tiredly.

"Excellent, give it to me." After a moment, Elana's cheeks rose with a devious smirk.

Isaac's chin drooped to his chest, but it rose and fell softly, at least. "Love...this is it. They got the spell from me. It's time to say goodbye."

"What do you mean?" My gaze darted between Elana, Isaac, and Jay.

All at once, multiple things happened.

Elana smiled.

Isaac's gaze was full of torment as sweat slid from his temple.

Jay still lay unconscious.

"Good idea, time to say goodbye. Let's allow the love birds a final moment." Elana slapped Brent across the cheek. "Wake Griffin up."

Brent sighed deeply, and then Jay jerked awake. He flailed against his straps like he was mid-fight.

Jay's shirt tore and shredded with each frantic thrash. "Let me go! Kyra won't come. It's useless."

Elana cleared her throat. "You're wrong, boy. Kyra is right here."

His head whipped to me, and those dark brown eyes melted my insides into a pool of lava. "No, no, no. You weren't supposed to come," he groaned but stopped wrestling the straps that had dug welts into his skin. "Let her go. I'll do what you asked."

"Yes, that's true, you'll soon do anything for me. First, you'll say goodbye. I'm still the sentimental type. My great-granddaughter deserves some closure."

"Kyra," Jay winced. "You weren't supposed to come here."

At the sight of Jay's pained look, it felt like arrows were splicing open my chest, shooting through my entire body.

"Jay, I—"

"Time's up." Elana grinned. The voice oozing from her mouth sounded other-worldly.

I stared into Jay's terrified eyes. And then a sensation akin to a meteor colliding with my skull hit me, cracking my bones.

I raised both hands, collecting every ounce of energy at my disposal, and directed flames at Elana—a black promise. Heat exploded in pops of fireworks, igniting the octopus. The cacophony of disaster pierced my ears.

But Elana was stronger. "*Yelas secar*," she said the spell to sever our Link.

Pain stabbed me a thousand different ways and attacked from all angles, shredding me. I gasped and wheezed. Choked on torture. My limbs felt like they were being crushed to ashes.

Jay's essence faded. Further and further away. My body ceased to exist, and the world imploded. Nothing mattered anymore. The force was so strong that I clawed at my throat, begging for air.

The wind lifted me from the tentacle's hold, and I whipped through the air in a cyclone of power. My eyes squeezed shut as a dizzying fog catapulted against my mind. I didn't want to separate from Jay. I needed him. I needed our Link. Some toxic force struck between us, pulling him further away.

I fought against it. *Jay. Jay. Jay*. Stay.

A scream rose from deep in his soul and crushed my spirit. The fire crackled and burned our connection. Heat erupted. A sharpness severed our bond.

Jay! No. Anything but this. Please.

I screamed and screamed and screamed until my throat burned raw. I was ripped in two from the inside out. A guttural yell tore from his lips. Elana was stealing Jay away, and I couldn't do anything to stop it. Panic smothered me completely, and bile rose in my throat.

A final slashing feeling sliced through my very essence.

Finally, the torture stopped. Only stars speckled my vision until I puked chunks on the platform when the wind released me. My breath was sucked from my lungs from the sudden loss, ripping me to shreds. Jay's eyes dropped from mine, empty, defeated, and lost.

"Get up, child," Elana scolded.

On shaking arms, I slinked away from the savage voice coming from Elana's horrid mouth.

Chaos erupted behind me. Jay thrashed and, finally, tore loose from his straps. Above, some sea plant—a fuckin' tree– burst through the dome ceiling.

Another hurtled in. Tree after tree.

The dome cracked again and again. The rest of the dome splintered into a thousand pieces of raining glass. Water and sharp edges spurted on us in a massive attack. They sped through the air, bullet-fast. Ocean water started pouring through the hole into the room.

Shivering, weak, and sobbing, I slowly stood. Elana had stolen a part of my soul.

"Ky-ra." Isaac's voice was weak and faint behind me.

I turned and gasped. He lay on the ground, wincing in pain. Blood ran from his nose and lips.

No. Not again. A sudden icy cold chilled my bones. Even though I could no longer feel Jay's presence, Isaac's pain seared deep through me as his eyes widened in shock.

"Isaac?" I shook his shoulders. "What's wrong with him?"

"I think..." Jay laid a hand on Isaac's shoulder. "He's dying."

"No, no, no. I can't lose him again. I can't." My hands found Isaac's chest.

Jay dropped to my side, the castle crumbling around us. We had no time. There was no other plan. No backup. The answer whispered through the remaining bond like an ancient spell.

Maybe severing my Link with Isaac would put the balance back in order.

Locking on Isaac's eyes, I pleaded, "We have to break our Link too."

Jay grabbed my hand weakly. "No, Kyra, you won't survive doing *that* again."

"I have to! Isaac is connected to you, too. He was being split. What if this is the only way to save him?"

"Is this…what…you want?" Isaac croaked between gasps.

"Yes." I swallowed all hesitancy. "You have to live."

Isaac nodded, and sadness coated his sweet brown eyes. I prayed to the goddess below that we'd all survive this.

On the edge of my vision, Elana still fought to protect herself from the cascading glass raining down, and Brent shot his power at her, even though it was weak. The room's walls started caving in from the pressure of the water.

"On the count of three," Jay said while holding my hand.

"One," I choked out, terrified that I'd never see either man again.

I grabbed one of Isaac's hands. If the upcoming pain was as excruciating as the first sever had been, these might be my last moments alive.

"Two," Isaac croaked.

I clenched my eyes shut and whispered, "I love you," as the water surrounded us, closing in from every side.

Jay squeezed my hand as if asking who I said that to, but instead, he said, "Three."

"Yelas secar!" I yelled. "Yelas secar!"

My heart raced, and manic energy swarmed my entire body, preparing for pain. But none came. And just like that, one moment, I was connected to Isaac's spirit, and the next second, our Link snapped. That was it.

Over and done. Why was it different this time?

Thankfully, Isaac rolled over, clutching his chest. The blood stopped dripping from his nose, and his cheeks turned pink again.

Then the reality of the water corrupted any sense of success. If we didn't get out, we'd all drown. There was no more time. My heart hammered, threatening to rip a hole through my chest.

"Get to the surface!" Jay roared. "Now."

I reached into the center of my Magik. If Elana had some water power, I would possess it too. Energy swirled stronger than I'd ever experienced as if waiting, ready to welcome me. I was the Golden One, Linked or not. I knew it would work, not because it was our only option, but because the strength ran in my blood. Dozens of spells spilled into my mind, slipping through the cracks in history. One jumped out as the answer.

"Ines meocha. Ines meocha," I prayed with all my might.

Immediately, every siren swam to my side. Holding my breath, I pointed to Caspian sinking lower, strapped to his table. A siren dove after him swept him into her arms, and rocketed straight up to the surface. Every fiber of my being knew these creatures would listen to my command this time. Caspian was in good hands. Another siren grabbed Jay and bolted like a torpedo straight up. He'd make it. He'd be okay.

Where were Elana and Brent? I scanned the castle collapsing around us. A giant shadow swam up from the depths. The next siren swam straight toward us, but she wouldn't make it before the creature devoured us whole. Light glittered off a tentacle—the octopus was back. Fuck.

Right on time, Brynn appeared from behind the crashing castle walls and butted her head straight into the octopus' side. The siren met us, grabbed Isaac's and my wrists, and swam up. Faster than I could've imagined.

We flew through the water like dolphins. It felt like I had spent an eternity under the sea. My chest burned violently. I needed to break the surface. Needed to gulp in the oxygen. Needed to see Jay once more. A lightheaded, dizzy spell pushed heaviness into my muscles. This was it. The end. We were too far from the air.

I met Isaac's eyes one last time.

27
ISAAC

I rolled to my side and coughed up water onto the sand. A soft hand rubbed my back. Squinting up, a golden angel gazed down at me, silhouetted by the sunlight. My love.

"Are you okay?" Kyra asked.

"Fan-fuckin-tastic," I spat out.

The beach was so quiet that it almost seemed like the last few hours were only a nightmare. I must've passed out at some point.

She laughed. "My next vacation won't be anywhere near the beach."

After pushing myself up, I glanced around. At least I had my eyesight again. Ahead, Griffin paced by the seagrass, punching the buttons of his s-watch, which was most likely broken. Soaked, Caspian sat on a log with his forehead dropped in his hands and one finger tracing his scar.

In the distance, Alaska kicked at seashells. Hopefully, she'd agree to teleport me straight to Wes soon.

I rolled the hem of my pants down a bit. As I suspected, only one Möbius Circle remained. Our Link was officially severed. The original blueish-white tattoo I had received in my youth sat alone. My shaking fingertips rubbed it. There was no proof that I was ever Linked to this wonderful woman next to me.

"Isaac." Kyra searched my face. "How do you feel?"

"I'm here...I'm alive." A long pause fractured the space between us.

I couldn't feel her thoughts or emotions anymore. A part of me had been ripped away.

"It's a lot to process." I rubbed my stubble. "So, let me get this straight. Your great-grandmother, who should be over a hundred years old, lives in the stolen body of a thirty-something-year-old. And she wanted to Link with Griffin, so she can…have Golden babies with him?"

Kyra started chewing on the side of her nail. "That's what it sounded like."

"Okay, and Elana needed a severing spell to do it." I ran a hand through my wet, tangled hair. "Which, apparently, my brain had stored from all my reading, subconsciously, and Brent, your father, retrieved through mind control?"

"Yes, and when she forced my sever with Jay, you…you crashed, Isaac. I didn't have another choice." Kyra sounded so exhausted, so quiet.

"I saw the pain you and Griffin went through, but it didn't hurt that bad for us."

At my words, her eyes dropped. I wanted to wrap an arm around her waist and snuggle close to her. Instead, I only cleared my throat and stared at the wispy clouds above that floated by without any trace of the fierce storm.

I finally dared to reach for her hand. Tears glistened in her amber eyes. If only I could send her a witty message through our bond, but when I pushed with my Magik, there was no outlet. No option. No Kyra. Her feelings had vanished from my heart. Her thoughts had disappeared from my mind. Her memories were stolen from me. Our thread was gone.

I sighed and took her hand in mine. "It'll be okay."

One tear slid down her cheek. I wiped it away with my thumb, and she leaned into my touch slightly. But just after, she glanced across the beach with a torn and wrecked look. Kyra watched Griffin chuck his s-watch into the waves as he hollered in frustration.

"I'm sorry, Isaac."

"There's no need to apologize."

I could tell Kyra didn't believe me when she continued, "All three of us were connected. Once Jay and I were no longer Linked, the energy was uneven."

"Were you saving him or me?" I regretted the question the moment it hit the air.

"Does it matter?" Kyra mumbled.

"I'm not sure, eh…yes, I think it does…very much."

She shoved her thumbs into her temples. "I need to start over...with both of you. We had thought the Link forced romantic feelings. Now we know that's not fully true, but—"

"But a part of you wonders if it was still *partially* true?"

She nodded.

"As I said before, I'll always care for you." I forced a smile.

She pushed her toes deeper into the sand and stared at the tiny grains.

I needed her to be happy, whether with or without me. My job was to make her smile and lighten her life. "So, you made new siren friends. Are you going to start a sorority?"

Kyra pushed me gently, obviously thankful for the subject change, and rested her forehead on my shoulder. Maybe I didn't need the Link after all to read her mind.

A shiver jolted through her body. "Everything feels different now."

I used all my restraint not to reach out and tuck her wet golden hair behind her ear. "Tell me about it."

"I'm even stronger."

That wasn't what I had expected her to say at all. "Really?"

She nodded adorably. Divinity above, I'd miss our Link.

"After we all severed, more Magik arrived deep in my Circle. I can feel hints of water inside me, a part of me. The same with air and earth."

When Kyra started rolling her pants down a little, my breath hitched. I shook my head, trying to erase the promises I had kissed on her lips.

"Jay's second tattoo is gone," Kyra whispered. "But look. I still have all three."

Sure enough, below her belly button, the golden tattoo was still hooked with a greenish-brown Dravian tattoo and the Vayuian blueish-white swirl matching mine. And a faint outline of a bruise lingered in an arc by the others.

"Why do you think they're all still on you?"

Kyra tapped a quick beat on her thigh with one finger and scrunched her nose. "Elana made it sound like Golden Ones have access to all four elements, which I think is true."

"Now, you just need the aqua Cydon Circle."

She shook her head and frowned. "I can't put my brother at risk."

A pack of pelicans swooped into the water, grabbed fish, and soared back up. I relished the soft breeze that nipped my cheeks, reminding me of my strengths, powers, and purpose—to protect Wes and Vayu.

As if reading my mind, Kyra asked, "Isaac, Elana doesn't know about you and your enhancements. You need to avoid all of this, so she doesn't learn about you. She leaned back and looked away. "You're safe now to be happy with Wes and rebuild Vayu."

"So, that's it, love? You're picking Griffin?"

"I never said that." She stared at the waves. "I guess you'll have to read the next installment of my autobiography." Her joke fell flat, so she pressed on and pushed me again. "Oh, come on, Isaac, you're the Library Master. You know how stories work."

I knew exactly what she meant, but I just wanted to hear her talk longer, so I rested my chin on my hand. "Enlighten me."

"In my first book, I met and fell for a boy from Draven."

"Was I the villain?" I smirked.

"You're always the evil one up to no good. Now, let me finish." She poked my side. "In my second book, I spend all my time with the arrogant sweetheart with wind power who doesn't know when to shut up."

I leaned in. "He has a huge cock, right?"

"Oh, well...probably." She bit her lip, blushing.

"And he knows how to use it?"

"I bet he does." Her smile was the source of the sun itself.

"So, tell me what happens in this third installment of your life story." I studied her every move, wondering if she was about to tell me goodbye.

"No one knows the future, well, except for Gemm, I guess."

"Damn, I wish I was that old grandma."

Kyra's laugh sprinkled the air like gold dust.

Sighing, I turned her chin to me. "Are you gonna be okay, love?"

Her fingers traced circles on my wrist. "You're both alive. That's all I can ask for right now. But Isaac— I think you need to take a break from calling me that nickname...until...I figure everything out."

My heart dropped.

"I need to work through everything. Including my feelings. Give me a little time."

Griffin marched over, interrupting, and sat right next to Kyra. I didn't envy her for the conversation they needed to have. The three of us sat in silence. My eyes darted to where their forearms brushed against each other. The energy shifted, and I reeled in all my self-control not to break down. She obviously still loved him. Kyra kept her hand right next to Griffin's in the sand. One of his fingers slowly brushed over her knuckle. Tendrils of hurt wrapped around my throat.

She had Griffin, and I had Wes. With him, of course, I'd be happy.

Kyra called out, "Caspian, come over here."

Caspian trudged over, looking like death itself.

"We need to figure out a plan," Kyra said.

The ever-soldier took charge. With a stick, Griffin drew a map in the sand. "We're here, The Crooked Chateau is here, and Narelle is at the nearest safe house."

"We need to find a place to rest," Kyra said. "We don't know the extent of the destruction from the rebels' attack. I think we should contact that society, the one against Elana."

I nodded, willing to agree to whatever plan Kyra deemed best but knowing that my responsibilities were with Wes. It was looking possible that whatever uprising she was planning would have to be completed without me. How could I be in two places at once?

Griffin thumbed the emerald necklace looped over his shirt. "Elana has the Elidi Ruby and Vayu Crystal."

"And Moroka took my Cydon Pearl," Caspian choked out the words, his eyes back to normal again. "My entire castle is demolished."

"Well, actually, Jay did that with his swimming trees." Kyra snorted awkwardly, then rubbed her tired eyes.

"Listen, we don't even know if Elana survived down there," I said.

"She's alive. I'd know if she died," Kyra said.

"I agree. I'd feel it deep in here," Caspian pointed to his Circle. "If our father or evil granny were wiped out."

"So, are you two going to Link?" I looked between the siblings.

For the first time, I noticed similar features in their matching complexion and jaw, chin, and nose shape. The biggest difference was the color of their eyes. One set of amber orbs glowed like fire, and the other sparkled as blue as the sea. Even Kyra's eyebrows were the same color as Caspian's brown hair.

"No, I won't put my sister at risk now that I've heard how much it hurt to sever." Caspian shuffled his feet. "I don't care about some stupid prophecy anymore."

"I'll figure out a way to stop Elana." Kyra bounced up to her feet and started pacing the shoreline. "And I won't let her control Brent! *And* she is batshit crazy if she expects to make a new generation of Golden Ones." Her voice grew louder by the second. "*And* if that bitch expects to ever have babies with…with…." Her voice cracked, showing me where her heart belonged.

"Kyra…" Griffin said softly. "That won't ever happen. I promise."

Her honey eyes warmed and melted into the gaze of the man sitting across from me. I needed air. Lots of it. Buckets of air. I shot up, wincing from my injuries, and jogged in the opposite direction.

"Isaac!" Kyra yelled. "Where are you going?"

Underfoot, the sand squished between my toes as I walked further away from them. Why exactly was I barefoot? I wasn't even sure when or where I had lost my shoes. The trauma of the events under the sea would soon come crashing down on me in a wave of exhaustion, but for now, I sucked in the air. I held that oxygen deep in my lungs and let it fuel my tattoo. A tingle struck my Circle, and new power teased my fingertips. I cast a gust of wind straight ahead to the open horizon. But it wasn't wind—something unreal happened, shocking me back a step.

A stream of gas surged away, fast, into the sky. I froze as a bird dropped from mid-flight and crashed straight into the waves below.

Damn, sorry, bird.

"Isaac, wait!" Kyra called out.

I swiveled on my heels, checking if she had noticed that weird poisonous gas.

"Isaac, please, I need time." Her breath came ragged and tired as she gripped both my shoulders. "I need some time to get my shit together. I want a happily ever after, but if my heart is being pulled two different ways, I can't string you both along." Tears started falling. "But I'm afraid of losing you."

I couldn't look at her face. Instead, Wes's sweet smile flickered in hiccupped memories. I had never wanted to lose him, but I did. I had never wanted to lose his mother, Rajitha, but that happened too. And I had never expected to care about losing Zeph, but her death also hit me hard. Never in a million years did I want to lose Kyra, either. All those losses made me hold on tighter to those I loved. But that pattern had never worked for me in the past. It was time to let go, to release, and see what fate had in store.

"I love you, but I won't wait around as a backup plan forever. I'll give you until Wes's birthday to decide. I need an answer by then, though, Griffin or me."

It was a blemish of lies. I never wanted to live without her, even if she was a thorn in my side half the time. My heart rammed chaotically, unsure if I made the right choice—an ultimatum. For Wes's sake, I had to establish boundaries and a limit. Our little family of two couldn't live in limbo forever. I hoped with all my heart that

Kyra would choose to make it a family of three, but she needed time. If only I could give her all the time in the world. If only I was strong enough to share her with another man.

Griffin watched us from afar, arms crossed as he stood as still as a statue.

"When's his birthday?" she asked softly, worry lines inked into the creases of her face.

"After the full Teal Moon in one month."

"And what will you do until then?"

I blew out a long sigh. "I need to check on him and explain everything, but otherwise, I might stay with you until his birthday. It'll give me a chance to sway you to the dark side."

"You're not dark, Isaac." Her features finally softened. "Spending more time would be...it'd make me happy."

"I always want to be the one to make you happy, love."

Her smile was the center of the planet, spurting with volcanic energy.

I took her hand in mine. She made me feel more whole than I had ever imagined, Linked or not. But I refrained from saying my ambushing thoughts aloud—I wasn't the only one to make her happy.

"Are you happy, love?" I asked.

Her golden eyes glowed fiercely. "I'm happy enough...for now."

I'd fight for her—for us—for our future. I'd battle with every bit of Magik I possessed.

28

KYRA

Alaska transported us all to the safe house nearby. This was our only option until we could safely communicate with the Aurum Orbis Society. My mind and body didn't feel connected. I wished the Links would return, for only a moment, to better understand all the emotions.

Chocolate licked my fingers that hung leisurely by my side. I scratched her ears and crouched low to kiss her forehead.

"I'm glad you're okay, girl. I missed you."

Loud giggles echoed down the hall where Wes and Landon were having a pillow fight. Life continued, despite the chaos.

I surveyed our main room—a kitchen—with a slanted table and four rusty chairs. We'd have to make do with the cramped corridors until we formed a plan. Earlier, Narelle and Alaska situated mattresses in three separate rooms.

One held Jay, Alaska, and Gemm—all the Dravians together with Chocolate, of course.

The second held me, my brother, and Narelle.

And the third housed Isaac, Wes, and Landon. We couldn't split up the boys if we tried.

A faint breeze blew through the cracks in the wall. The harsh winter winds here in the north finally calmed into a mild temperature, preparing for spring again. We all needed new life and new hope, so the coming season promising rebirth couldn't arrive fast enough. The squeals of the boys in the next room inspired my goal. I had to fix what I had broken and return all the lost males, no matter the cost. But it wasn't the whole group's priority.

Alaska wanted immediate revenge on Moroka for murdering Paola—understandably. Narelle wanted to create a relief program for all the Cydian villagers who had to evacuate. Caspian wanted to save our father from Elana's clutches. Landon wanted a dog of his own. Wes kept asking to live with Landon and called him "cousin." Isaac wanted his Vayu Crystal back. And Jay…well, he was quiet during our group meeting, but I'm pretty sure Jay just wanted to keep us all safe for another day. One day at a time.

I sat in a crooked chair that teetered on one leg and munched on dry cereal, wondering which obstacles would be thrown at me next.

At least I had found some clarity and comfort with my own Magik. All my life, my inner demons convinced me that men needed to love me for me to be considered worthy, which only fanned my bitterness. Now that I knew Brent never wanted to leave our family but was stolen away, it eased that desperate need to attach to someone. My inner struggle wasn't complete, but I was healing.

It didn't matter if I was someone's daughter, lover, or sister. I was still me. My heart, my power, and my fire were enough. No matter what type of family, friends, or love surrounded me, I didn't need to be connected or linked to someone. I was Golden and would always be Golden.

Jay walked around the corner and plopped in the rickety chair next to mine, making it screech across the hardwood. His hands were cupped together, hiding something. When I met his brown eyes, he opened his palm to show a single red rose, blooming at hyper speed in front of my eyes. I tilted my head, staring at the petals growing and shifting.

"For you," he mumbled and tucked it in my hair.

"Thank you," I whispered and chomped another bite of cereal.

"We need to talk," he said.

I glanced behind him to the hallway.

"Don't worry. Isaac and Caspian just left to hunt for dinner."

I blew out a breath and leaned back in the chair, waiting for whatever he wanted to say.

"You've been avoiding me."

"Prove it."

"Come on, Kyra. It's time to talk about your little family *reunion*," he said.

I let a small smile creep up. At least he wasn't angry, but then what was he feeling?

"The president is your great-grandmother." It wasn't a question. "And she erased my memory."

I rolled my lips, waiting, letting him process it all aloud.

"Elana made me do awful things. Horrendous, unforgivable things."

"Jay—"

"And you fought to save me," he said with his brows knitted together. "But then, when you found me as the president's loyal soldier, you...you tried to show me the truth."

Tears welled, but I held them back. This conversation wasn't about me or my feelings. Jay needed to let this all out; my role was to listen and give him that outlet.

"...But when it became too hard to handle, you slept with Nilson," he said the last words as though they tasted like ash in his mouth.

"We never had sex, Jay. What you heard was the hammock swing and me having a nightmare." I wanted to drop my eyes to the floor, but I held his deep gaze. "But we did kiss."

He exhaled slowly. "You...kissed?"

An apology wouldn't be enough. But I also wasn't sure I was truly sorry. Because that kiss with Isaac meant something—it still meant something. I couldn't erase that, and I didn't want to erase that.

"Okay, okay, I can handle a kiss. I'm not mad, Kyra. My heart is a bit cracked. We can start fresh, without the Link, to see what's real."

My heartbeat finally slowed, and relief washed over me. He was still giving me a chance. But how could I tell him I wasn't sure if he was the one I'd choose in the end? It was selfish to ask them to wait.

"Petal..." Jay reached over and took my hand in his. The use of my nickname only made my heart cartwheel again. "You're chaotic. And stubborn. And impulsive. Like, the whole world will implode if you don't move or say exactly what's on your mind."

This time, I let a tear fall.

"And there's radiant strength sewn into your skin."

A little chuckle escaped my lips. "Weird metaphor, Jay."

"Okay, let me try again. You're filled with music. From your toes to your fingertips, rhythms, melodies, and beats flow through your blood. Sometimes it's hard and fast; other times, it's slow and dark, but I always hear it."

I held my breath. Maybe my drumming heart beat only for him. How was I to know for sure?

"And you always smell like toasted s'mores roasting on a campfire," Jay said.

Another smile rose on my cheeks. "I'm not sure if that's good or bad."

"Everyone loves s'mores, Kyra. That's why they want some more."

"Hmm, what if a s'more doesn't know yet who should devour it... her." My cheeks flushed.

"I'll wait as long as you need because I already know how I'll devour you."

I studied him thoroughly, holding the silence a bit longer. "You'll wait as long as I need?"

"Forever and a day, I promise."

Heat clustered in my center and spread through my body. We stared at each other like it was our last moment alive, and the clock on the wall ticked on, recording this moment in time.

"Severing with..." I glanced at the hallway.

"Kyra, you can mention Nilson." Jay shook his head. "We're all adults and are well aware of this dynamic. Plus, I have the memory burned into my brain of you screaming out his name. I think I can handle it if you talk about him."

I winced and swallowed the mound of rocks lodged in my throat, then continued, "Severing with Isaac didn't hurt, but with you, it was excruciating."

"I know. I was there." Pain layered his eyes.

"Does that mean...you and I are destined or something, like, we should have never broken our bond?"

He laid a big hand over mine. "Kyra, only you can choose who you spend your life with. There are no soul mates, no predestined person for any of us. You make a choice and make the best of it. Relationships are about picking someone and working hard to make it last, through the good and bad, the ups and downs."

"You truly believe that?"

"Yes. One of us might flow more naturally for you, but that doesn't matter. What matters is who you *want* to take the journey through life with, during both the fun and the hard times." He leaned over the table and took my hand in his. His lips kissed down my forearm. "It's your choice who you decide to grow with." He paused and studied my face. "But no matter who you choose, you will always be my roots, gnarled, twisted, and rough."

...My very source of life, I said silently to myself, sad that he couldn't hear me through our tether.

Chocolate barked in the other room as his lips left a phantom tingle on my skin. "I'm gonna go get Chocolate some food. Do you need anything?"

Shaking my head, I watched Jay leave, then pushed away the empty cereal bowl, and stared at the paint smudges on the wall.

Jay's words hit me deeply, and he was probably right, but that didn't make my decision any easier.

My sights landed on my reflection in the shiny refrigerator door, the metal distorting my features like I was in a circus funhouse. Maybe I still had more to learn about who I was to fill in the gaps and make my shape crystal clear. Silence flooded the halls for the first time since we arrived. Without the boys' laughter, the safe house felt less full of life. I knew what I had to do to make things right—and, hopefully, I'd have Jay or Isaac by my side along that journey.

Love was reciprocal, and I was running out of chances for their patience.

Suddenly, a heavy burn seared my tattoo, a different sensation than usual. I gasped and rolled down my waistband. A faint bruise covered my skin. Wait, no. I poked at my skin. It was a new, gray Circle— actively forming, looped to the Vayuian tattoo. A shiver crept up my spine. Gray? What did it mean?

The shadowy gray circle reminded me of a decaying scar. I quickly covered my skin and glanced around the empty room. No one else had seen it. I wouldn't tell anyone until I knew what it meant. And my tattoos weren't a priority, anyway. Other crucial plans came first, like saving my father, ridding Elana of her power, and returning the other males.

Gemm hobbled around the corner while clutching her cane.

"Morning, Gemm."

She hummed a tune under her breath and collapsed into the chair.

"Once, there was a story."

I rested my chin on my hand and leaned forward, intrigued as always when she spoke.

"Once, there was a three-way link." Her eyes were far away in another galaxy as her voice rose, and I wasn't so sure I wanted to hear it anymore. Prophecies involving me never turned out well.

"Uh, I need to go shower, Gemm."

She smacked her cane against my chest. "Once there were so many risks, the obstacles stacked higher than a pile of leaves."

I huffed a breath. "I don't know what that means, Gemm."

"After the Links severed, one of them became cursed and was slowly trudging towards death."

"Death?" My chest tightened. "What? No, I won't let him die."

"Only one. Which do you speak of child?" Her eyes finally met mine.

"Which one do I have to save? Which one, Jay or Isaac?"

"On the full Teal Moon, one man will lay down his life for love." Gemm grasped the edge of the table. "Oh, good morning, Kyra. Did Alaska burn the pie?"

"What?" I sniffed the air. "No, no, everything's fine. Gemm, do you remember what you just said?"

"When the ingredients are mixed, it's hard to determine why pies taste so good."

"Uh, okay, I'll be right back."

I scurried out of the kitchen and jogged around the corner. How could Jay or Isaac be cursed? Which was it? No! I wouldn't allow that to happen. I'd save them both, no matter what.

Down the hall, Jay and Isaac shook hands and glanced up at me at the same time.

Gray eyes. Brown eyes.

My breath hitched at the sight of their truce. I couldn't lose either. Which one possessed the curse? How could I find out?

They separated and walked to their respective doorways. Both Jay and Isaac leaned against their doors, watching me. The tattoos on my stomach swirled with heat and shot energy through my veins.

Isaac lifted a bottle of water to his lips. He winked and turned, walking into his room, leaving the door wide open as an invitation. Jay crossed his arms casually. His stare pinned me to the wall, kissing me through his intense gaze. My eyes darted back and forth between their two rooms. After gulping a deep breath, I took a step toward my future.

About Cassie Swindon

Cassie's next writing idea includes fairy-tale retellings. She's very interested in turning the tables to show stories with gender reversal from other perspectives. Of course, she finds the best place for brainstorming ends up being in the shower or while trying to fall asleep, which isn't convenient in the least for taking notes. In her spare time, she collects bookmarks, stickers, washi tape, and cats.

Sign up for my newsletter here:
https://cassieswindon.com/

facebook.com/cassie.swindon.3
twitter.com/CassieSwindon
instagram.com/cassie_swindon_author
bookbub.com/profile/cassie-swindon
amazon.com/stores/author/B091N72414
goodreads.com/cassieswindonauthor
tiktok.com/@cassieswindon

REVIEWS

It is significantly helpful to Indie authors like me if you could write an honest review on Goodreads or Amazon!

Check out free short stories as prequels to my upcoming works in progress at www.cassieswindon.com

And sign up for my newsletter to stay updated on new releases at www.cassieswindon.com

Follow me on Instagram at cassie_swindon_author for lots of book reviews and bookish content.

Cassie Swindon

Syvonne's Sting

Moonlight shone through the basement window and reflected off the silver lining of my hoverchair. Shadows crept up the dingy walls with purpose. I pinched my nose plug tighter and held back a gag from the smell still creeping in.

Near the aisle of caged prisoners, Brent glared at me. He was much more tolerable as a teetering toddler than a fifty-year-old. His amber eyes shot murderous daggers, but that didn't bother me. I was in power. I had all the control.

A soft whimper cried from the top row of cages. Beady brown eyes, crusted with grime, locked onto mine. That young girl would be next in line to be a test subject for daring to make a sound.

"Is she here yet?" I directed my hoverchair between the aisles of cages.

"No, Elana," Brent said calmly.

I slapped Brent hard across his stupid face, stinging my hand. "I told you to call me Syvonne in the presence of others."

He didn't even flinch but worked his jaw in the same way Kyra did last week. Whether I despised her choices or not, Kyra's Golden Circle contained the Magik that I wanted, just barely out of my reach.

"Elana—" Brent mumbled.

"You do not listen! Call me Syvonne or President Stirk, but not my given name, grandson."

Brent gestured to the filth surrounding us. "It doesn't matter what I call you down here. Your prisoners have no one to tell. Plus, if you wanted to keep your identity such a secret, maybe you shouldn't have told Kyra."

I leaned forward and tightened the electrical cords restraining Brent. "Do not challenge me."

"Oh, of course, Syvonne Stirk, Queen of Torture and President of Almighty Wrath," he groaned against the cords digging welts into his arms. "If the necklaces are so important, explain why you imprisoned the demons in the same place as the jewels?"

"You're asking the wrong question. You should be able to figure it out. The power of those jewels, together with the spell, was the only way I was able to imprison them at all. Only a willing soul could touch the necklace and free the demon. Caspian aided Moroka by taking the Cydon pearl. You rescued Oniskel from the crystal years ago, but I don't know where that Soul Sucker is hiding."

A small smirk flickered on Brent's face so fast that I wondered if I had imagined it.

"What do you know?" I asked.

"Hmm?"

"You're holding something back." I tugged his cords tighter.

"Who me?" A corner of his lip twitched mischievously, a look I despised. "Why would I ever keep a secret from you, ole' Granny?"

I glanced down at the three gems around my neck. "You're a bigger fool than I thought if you think your mind games can penetrate this protective shield."

"Can't blame me for trying." He smiled lazily, a look that mirrored his mother. It was too bad I had to suck her spirit dry too. Sometimes my daughter provided tolerant company. But Brent had only been a pain in my ass for the last twenty years. I wouldn't mourn him in the least.

"I want a bedtime story, Grams." Brent yawned. "If you're about to replace me, then at least finally tell me how you managed to steal all three necklaces from the other tribes so long ago. It must not have been easy."

Memories flashed from before The Fall. I had spent years planning, revenge always on the forefront of my mind. No one was any more worthy than me of receiving an enhancement, yet the demons singled me out as the only one not to receive a gift. I didn't receive mind control, teleportation, superior hearing, or anything else. Nothing. I was ignored and cast aside. Forgotten—despite being a descendant of the strongest lineage of fire Magik. Now, I'd finally be acknowledged.

"You won't get any answers from me." I pushed a finger against my temple, increasing the shooting pain of a splitting headache. "Even though you have less than one Lunar cycle left in your pitiful life, I won't spill my secrets. None of you deserve the truth, which is why I will start afresh. All the new Golden Ones will follow my orders this time."

Brent leaned back a bit, scraping the legs of the chair against the concrete floor. "Will your story start where you murdered your lover?"

My hand started shaking at his accusations, so I hid them behind my back. Memories of slicing a sharp point through skin and muscle crushed me like a boulder.

"No? Hmm, let me think," Brent continued, "How about when you captured so many Mystiers for genetic testing like a crazed scientist?" He tilted his head sarcastically. "No? Okay, I'll try again. Maybe your story would start when you used my powers to stay young?" Brent's eyes scanned my thirty-year-old body, and his tone remained frigid. "No? Then maybe your climatic chapter would be a grand monologue about killing the rest of the Ordulls?"

"You're not as entertaining as you think you are. I'm growing bored of your voice." I slammed a hand against one of the cage doors, making a young girl shriek in fear.

"Ooooh, I know, I know." Brent wiggled dramatically, ignoring me while shifting the tight electrical cords higher on his chest. "The huge turning point of your story is when you abduct your great-granddaughter's one true love and force him to reproduce with you…." He scrunched his nose. "Yup, that's soap opera shit. Great-granny banging the boyfriend and making babies. I admit, even I didn't see *that* one coming."

"Shut. Up."

Brent's laugh turned repulsive. "And you *truly* think my daughter will agree to work with you after you make Griffin a sex slave? Fuck, skip the book. This should be a big-screen epic movie. Bring on the extra-large popcorn!"

"If Kyra is as strong as they say, then maybe I'll just suck her energy out as your replacement instead of Caspian.

Brent silenced and sighed, staring at the clock ticking. Each second passed faster. Faster. Faster. I was running out of time.

"Where the Flames is she?" I screamed, my voice echoing down the empty tunnels.

"I'm here," a snakelike voice slithered from the dark hallway, and a silhouette emerged like a pleasant nightmare. "But my sister refuses your offer."

Surh-Sig glided closer, ghost-like, even captivating the attention of Brent. A cloak of spoiled skin hung off her skeleton figure like a cape. Sliced flesh draped over rotten skin that harbored chew marks, indented with holes only one type of fang could produce—a demon's canine.

I ground my teeth together and steered my hoverboard further from the Skin Scraper—just in case. This was a creature I'd never trust, especially since she and her sisters were the cause of all my problems.

"Moroka is on her way, but Oniskel does not like your offer," said Surh-Sig, in a monotone voice.

"Then Oniskel will pay," I hissed under my breath and clenched my fists into balls.

I wanted immortal powers and unlimited strengths beyond anyone's imagination instead of being confined in this deteriorating, handicapped body.

I'd continue on this path until I was so strong that no one would dare challenge me. With my wind to summon tornadoes, my water to create tsunamis, and my fire to erupt volcanoes, I'd be unstoppable.

Linking with Griffin would fix my problems. He was from the strongest Draven lineage. My only option. I only needed one more elemental necklace in my possession for everything to be complete. My fingers traced the chains hanging from my neck. The Elidi Ruby, Cydon Pearl, and Vayu Crystal all belonged to me. Now, I only needed to find the Draven Emerald.

With Brent's mind control, it was only a matter of time until I'd convince Oniskel to join my team too. Her level of resentment wouldn't win against her need to feed. The temptation of the task I offered her was too substantial—a thousand savory meals— every Ordull woman. Each one needed to die.

Our world would finally consist of Mystiers only. With me as the ruler and Jadox Griffin as my mate, I'd create an entire line of Golden Ones, my heirs to rule Lodesa under my order. No one would question my powers again.

"I need water, Elana. You must give me water." Brent's head sagged to his chest, suddenly heavy and defeated after his ramblings. "Please."

"No."

"If Surh-Sig…snaps out…of her trance…." Brent rasped between broken words. "She'll kill…us both."

Pathetic. His shaggy brown hair hung over his face. I rolled my eyes and unlocked the closest cage. The youngster within curled further into the back corner. Despicable. Disgusting. I reached in and grabbed her tattered clothes, soiled in urine.

"Come here, child!"

Tears spilled over her dirty cheeks as the girl cowered like a mouse.

Clutching her sleeve hard, I yanked the girl out of the cage and gagged on the stench soaked into her knotted hair. "Go get him water from my office. If you try to escape, you'll die."

On trembling hands, she crawled across the cement floor through puddles of goddess-knows-what. She dragged herself closer to my office doors at a snail's pace.

"Hurry up!"

Panting, the little girl dropped flat to her stomach between the column of filled cages. A little hand poked through metal bars and petted the girl's caked hair. Worthless. All of them.

Surh-Sig sped towards the girl, onyx eyes narrowed on her prey.

"Don't even think about it, demon. She's mine to do with as I wish."

Surh-Sig crouched over the small body. Before I had a chance to launch my hoverchair between her and the meal, Surh-Sig sank her fangs into the girl's throat. Blood spurted out and painted the demon's exposed bones crimson.

"Great, now I have to get water myself." I shook my head and flipped the button on my hoverchair, moving my vehicle forward. "Brent, order the Skin Scraper back to her cell when she's finished."

The only sound that responded was the munching and sucking of Surh-Sig's jaw, chomping down on the girl's flesh.

"Brent?" I changed direction and flew to where he was strapped to the chair. I poked his chest using the electric rod tucked into my belt loop. "Wake up."

Shit. His limp body was useless. If he didn't still have some control over Surh-Sig's mind, then I was royally fucked.

The disgusting slurping sounds behind me stopped. I whirled around and met Surh-Sig's hungry gaze. She was no longer hypnotized by my grandson.

"That was only an appetizer," she said.

"Shit." I punched the switch on my hoverchair fast and steered toward the exit. "Shit! Shit! Shit!"

A sharp claw reached up from the ground and hooked over the top of my chair. It lurched all movement to a stop, and I toppled over the front to the hard floor with a thud. A haunting hand emerged from below, skin pale, almost translucent, with inky black veins. Spindly arms followed, covered with sticky sea plants. Moroka's greasy, spaghetti hair hung from her wrinkled face. I cringed when I met her sharp red eyes. They leaked red, running rouge down her ghostly face. The blood tears were never-ending, dripping onto her crimson lips.

"You no longer have your toy to control, Elana," Moroka hissed. "The man is unconscious." Her hideous body flopped like a fish behind her, sliced in half, oozing a path of unending blood.

I held my breath, architecting an exit plan with each moment. Moroka's rough hand slowly ran over my outfit. I shuddered as she licked her lips, then started singing in a blood-curdling pitch:

No matter how hard or long you strive,
Your spirit broke an empty soul.
Useless to try, no Magik will thrive,
There's nothing left to make you whole.

My heart pounded. A desperate zap surged in my Möbius Circle, calling my Magik. The necklaces that were draped over my chest thrummed with raw power. Electric wires still surrounded the exterior of The Crooked Chateau to prevent any Mystier from attacking again, so even if I summoned my Magik, I'd be too weak against these immortals.

"Brent. Wake up!"

"You're a fool, Elana," Moroka sneered and grabbed my ankle. "And I'm hungry. How rude of you to not have refreshments for all your guests." The Blood Maiden's long tongue wagged in the air between us as her foul breath clouded my space. "You locked me under the wretched sea for eighty years. Your blood will be the sweetest of all."

I scrambled back, furious that I didn't have legs. No escape. Nowhere to run. There was no way I was dying tonight. My hoverchair floated high out of reach. Fluorescent lights flickered on the ceiling, casting two ominous shapes looming over me. I rubbed a thumb along the Elidi Ruby and commanded, *"Digati impetu, Digati impetu,"* to convince flames to attack.

The sisters cackled, and a slimy arm gripped my throat.

Suddenly, a back door slammed open, and footsteps thundered close.

"Release the president!" a female voice yelled, followed by a muffled gunshot.

An intoxicating scent flooded the room immediately. I leaned my head back against the wall and breathed in green gas. Both demons collapsed at my feet in a heap, their chests rising and falling slowly.

"Bind them with these." I reached for my neck, but my arm felt like jello. "The demons' greatest weakness is these gems."

My most loyal guard unclipped the necklaces hanging over my shirt. Staring at the demon's unconscious forms, I sucked in the dreamy aroma spiced with joyful childhood memories full of frolicking in an Elidi village with my friends. All dead by now. Once upon a time, we hopped between lava pools and played with magma and molten rock at the base of a volcano.

"Madame President, are you okay?" a soldier's voice fogged in and out of focus.

Memories flashed again, changing to a time when strong arms cocooned me and pillowy lips met mine. We had made a vow to Link in the coming year. A promise to stay together forever. Happiness was at my fingertips. But on the night of the Luna Festival, when they were supposed to grant me my enhancement gift, the sisters proclaimed me unworthy of a blessing. Apparently, I had a wicked soul. The entire village gasped in shock. They'd never respect me again because of these sisters.

"Madame President, focus on me." Fingers snapped in front of my face, and a hard surface rubbed under my stubs.

I shook my head and scanned the room. Some of my most trusted Ordull soldiers surrounded me while others cuffed the two demons sprawled on the floor. Only one of my guards had ever stepped inside this basement before, and I had intended to keep my secrets hidden.

"What is this place?" one whispered.

"Are those cages?"

"Why does it smell so bad?"

"Who is that?" With judgment layered deep in her eyes, another soldier stupidly gaped in the direction of Brent's hunched form strapped to the chair across the way. She'd pay for that later.

"Take the demons to their quarters and keep them locked up." I cleared my throat, raw and scratchy from the fumes.

Now that they had seen The Cavity, it was only a matter of time before my soldiers started to turn on me. When would they see through my disguise? I had to remain in control of the thousands following my every order...until I could destroy them all.

"Let's get you some fresh air." The leader, Two, adjusted the belt connecting me to the hoverchair and led me to the elevator.

Soldiers dragged the demons in the opposite direction while the others formed a square around me, armed and ready. The elevator doors opened and shone a blinding light. I squinted and blocked my eyes. I gulped, trying to shake the memories—images I hadn't experienced in eighty years—a past I wanted to forget.

As we slowly rose, a heavy feeling of loss enveloped me completely. The life I might have had vanished that fateful night when the sisters stole my future. Of course, my only option was revenge. It took me years to find the Unetlo Book, decipher one of the most ancient spells known to Mystiers, and cast a curse on the sisters. They turned into monstrous demons with a simple flick of my wrist. They deserved it. After that, Linking with a random Cydian man was just the icing on the cake. No, he wasn't my true love, but it didn't matter anymore.

Once protective shields around villages had dropped, I revealed the Mystiers to the Ordulls, resulting in The Fall. It was the perfect way to piss off every Elidian who had shunned me.

The elevator doors opened, and we entered the lobby of The Crooked Chateau. Tilted abstract paintings hung on the walls like an art gallery, depicting burning reds and scorching oranges swirling together into power. My paintings. My creations. I'd be the power to show everyone their mistakes from so long ago. Each Mystier would understand that the demon sisters were wrong. I was meant to have an enhancement, rule, live forever, and pass along my Golden Circle to my descendants.

If they listened to my orders, they'd live. If not, oh well.

"Madame President?"

I glanced up and met the blue eyes of my second-in-command as she leaned against the front double doors.

"Go ahead."

My entire army would be dead soon, Two included. I'd have no need for Ordulls. After giving me a faint smile, Two heaved it open, and the old wood creaked and groaned on its hinges. My hoverchair glided outside, and I sucked in a deep breath. Midnight claimed the estate's walls and the great stone stairway, which led through the shrubs up toward the tree line. An ugly electric fence towered around us with spiked metal sticking out every few inches.

"Madame President, are you feeling better?" Two's voice was flat, as always.

“My gaze shifted to the peaceful stars sparkling above.

“Do you have any orders?” Two asked.

“Have you found the whereabouts of Jadox Griffin?”

“Not yet, but our soldiers are hopeful that they’re in the northern sector.”

“They?” I huffed. “So, he still travels with Kyra?”

“We believe so, Madame President. As well as Isaac Nilson, the Vayuian.”

A tightness formed in my chest. I slid a hand through my long, silky hair, reminded of its stolen youth. But I wanted the youth to belong to me, not deteriorate and require me to change bodies and rely on others as an energy source.

“You have one week to find them,” I threatened.

She hesitated and gestured to a woman behind her, who automatically retreated into the building. I squinted at the side of the oldest warehouse building in Andersonville, where graffiti painted the side.

“Two, what does that say?” I asked.

Two’s stance stiffened. “It’s a political statement, Madame President.”

Rage boiled in my veins. “What. Does. It. Mean?”

“It’s a symbol written by the Aurum Orbis Society.” Her voice softened. “It means *a painful death for the president*.”

My heart rate quickened, and the fence closed in on me. No, I would never die.

“Triple the guards around the perimeter. Change the locks on each gate. Only you and I will know the codes. And *find* Griffin! You have three days.”

She stepped back. “Yes, ma’am.”

“And wake up Brent by any means necessary. Then bring him to me!”

She pivoted faster than a venti, disappearing into The Crooked Chateau.

I longed to use my Magik, but these damn fences controlled me as much as they protected me. A rustling sound down the dark street sent a shiver up my spine. I peered into the distance through the holes in the fence. A dark figure slowly approached. One step. Another. Closer. Quiet.

A slender, tall woman wearing all brown emerged from the shadows. Our hair was cut the same: thick and straight, and she brushed a silky strand behind her ear. The woman was striking, and I loved that her features were the opposite of mine. Where she was dark, I was light. Her raven hair complimented her darker skin. Obviously Dravian.

"Don't come any closer," I said, keeping my voice calm.

"My name is Alaska, and I offer my services."

I studied her from head to toe, checking for any signs of hidden weapons. "What exactly are your *services*?"

"I will give you all the information you need on the whereabouts of my brother, Jadox."

"Why would you do that?"

"I heard you have access to the Blood Maiden?" Anguish layered each syllable she spoke.

I nodded, wondering how she could possibly have gained that intel.

"I get to kill her," Alaska seethed. "Let me kill Moroka, and I will give you any information you want."

"Won't your dear brother be upset by this negotiation?"

She stepped forward, letting the streetlight illuminate the sharp edges of her jawline. "Jadox is the one who erased my girlfriend's memory years ago. We could've had that time together. His entitled ass stole the best thing in my life. He ripped us apart because he thought he knew what was best for me. Now, I'll never have that chance."

My hands formed a steeple under my chin. "Let me guess, Moroka killed your lover?"

"Yes." Hatred sparked dark in her eyes as she clicked a button on her s-watch.

A giant image of a beach scene was projected on the side of a building. Moroka slid in slow-motion to a woman. The demon chomped her fangs through the woman's body. Again and again. Blood poured out and flowed into the Blood Maiden's mouth. Alaska turned away from the image, and the video feed cut off.

I recognized the projected image to be a past soldier of mine. If she had been undercover, who else in my army could I not trust? "What was her name?"

"Paola. Paola Perez," Alaska whispered.

"She worked on my lab team." I eyed Alaska. "Is this a trick?"

"No games."

An owl hooted during her long pause, claiming the night. Curiosity bested me. Alaska was a Dravian, and the earth element was the only one left that I still needed to master. The graffiti taunted me behind Alaska's raven hair.

"I need more than intel first," I said. "I need to know you're good for your word. Does your brother have his memory back?"

She nodded.

Using Alaska would be beneficial. Griffin would fight to protect his sister. That much I was certain about that soldier. He'd lay his life down to save anyone he cared about, regardless of their actions toward him. It was his weakness. I could use Alaska to get Griffin here. He'd come to me willingly instead of wasting energy and resources to find him.

"I'd include one more piece before making this bargain," I said.

Alaska impatiently shifted on her feet and crossed her arms. "Am I not giving enough? My information? My brother?"

"I guess it depends on how much you want to kill Moroka."

"Fine," Alaska snarled. "What else is your price?"

"You must obtain the Draven Emerald necklace from a volcanic wasteland."

Her brows knit together. "But...my brother has it. I saw the emerald around his neck this morning."

A smile crept up my face, no matter how much I tried to contain it. "Lovely, then convince him to bring it along to his new home."

“I advise against this alliance, Madame President.” Two silently appeared behind us. “She is a witch and can’t be trusted.”

What Two and my army of soldiers didn’t know, was that I was the strongest Mystier to ever exist. I needed the Draven Emerald to finish what I had started. I needed Griffin to create a fleet of Golden Ones. I knew what I had to do.

GLOSSARY OF TERMS

(alphabetical)

Circle- the branding Möbius circle tattoo that a Mystier obtains when coming of age. There are four color shades of the tattoo depending on which tribe the Mystier originates from.

Elements- fire, earth, air, water.

Hybrid- this term has not been formalized since it is rare that a Mystier and Ordull mate and produce offspring. A hybrid would have Magik of some sort but may not fit within the typical rules.

Magik- sacred elemental powers that only Mystiers possess, not to be confused with witchcraft or the mythical sorcery found in Ordull fairytale books.

Mystier- a human who can harness Magik.

Ordull- a human not possessing Magik.

₾sμwi - cursed dark Magik where little information and history is known.

CHARACTERS

(alphabetical)

Alaska Griffin - Jadox's little sister. Enhancement- teleportation. From Draven.

Brent Elidi - Kyra's biological father. Enhancement- mind control/manipulation.

Brynn - hydraco creature based in Cydon.

Caspian Arno - Kyra's biological brother and Brent's son.
Enhancement- holding breath extra duration (AKA Caldo). From Cydon.

Chocolate - Jadox's brown lab based in Draven.

Elana Elidi – Kyra's great-grandmother. Only member in leadership tribe without an enhancement.

Gemm Griffin - Jadox's grandmother. Enhancement- prophecies. From Draven.

Hallie Kozelski - Kyra's step-sister. Ordull. From Andersonville.

Isaac Nilson - Librarian and leader of Vayu. Enhancement- eyesight and weather.

Jadox Griffin - Past soldier for the Ordull army. From Draven. Enhancement- smell and healing.

Kyra Kozelski/Kyra Elidi - the Golden One. Enhancement- hearing and knowing ancient spells.

Landon Kozelski - Hallie's son. Ordull.

Moroka - The Blood Maiden/water nymph. Harnessed by the pearl.

Narelle - Caspian's wife, from Cydon.

Paola Perez - Alaska's Ordull girlfriend/soldier in the army. From Andersonville.

Rajitha - Isaac's Ordull ex-girlfriend and Wes's mother.

Surh-Sig - The Skin Scraper/earth nymph. Harnessed by the emerald.

Syvonne Stirk - President of Lodesa (truly Elana Elidi).

Tawoli - venti creature based in Vayu.

Wes - Isaac (and Rajitha's) son - hybrid. From Vayu.

Zeph - Isaac's Mystier ex-girlfriend. From Vayu.

CREATURES

(alphabetical)

Gorula – (Goldie) A mammal with six long arms that end in sharp claws and fur that ranges from peach to gold, beige, brown, and tan. Five feet tall and 400 pounds of mostly muscle. Omnivore. Likes to dig in the dirt and swing from trees like a monkey. Usually lives in/near Draven. If a Mystier accepts a gift from a Dyad, there is/will be a price to pay.

Hydraco - (Brynn) Swimming creature that looks like a crocodile with a seahorse tail. Greenish in color with scales and all-white eyes. Estimated to be over 2,000 pounds each. Territorial- like to bite. Usually stays near Cydon's underwater castle unless pulling a chariot.

Venti/Ventus - (Tawoli) Flying creature. A mixture of an eagle and a horse. Beak mouth. Omnivore. Covered in feathers of white, beige, powder blue, or gray. Nine-hundred pounds. Twelve-foot wingspan on average. Gallops on four legs with hooves or flies. Usually lives in/near Vayu.

For drawings of the four fantastical beasts, check their images at www.cassieswindon.com

DEMONS

(alphabetical)

Moroka - An immortal demon called The Blood Maiden by legend. She is a mermaidesque figure without legs, whose lower half never healed. She was banished to the ocean by the pearl. The most ruthless of the sisters, she sucks the blood from her victims as her nourishment. Always cries never-ending crimson tears.

Oniskel - She is the Soul Sucker by legend. Tall and slender woman with red hair down to her ankles. Gold butterfly wings attached to her back, with the ability to float. She wears a transparent/golden silk toga. Honey drips out of her mouth, and spiders endlessly crawl out as she speaks. She sucks souls out of mortals for nourishment. Oniskel was banished to a mountaintop by the crystal.

Surh-Sig - An immortal demon called The Skin Scraper by legend. She is a skeleton-like figure who drapes herself with an assortment of others' skin. Surh-Sig has disfigured bones as hands with crooked fingers, obsidian eyes, sharp fangs, and a slimy, long tongue. She is known for also eating mortals' skin for her nourishment. She was banished to The Forbidden Caves by the emerald.

MYSTIER TRIBES

(alphabetical)

The locations of the village tribes are named after the most powerful ancestors in their tribe. Before The Fall, about 80 years ago, there were over 50 Mystier clans. Now only four remain.

Cydon - Cydians possess water power. With training, they control elements involving water, ponds, rivers, lakes, oceans, and waves. Their Circle tattoo is a blue/green/aqua swirl. The strongest family of this element, blessed with enhancements, is debatable.

Draven - This village is on the northeastern coast, full of dens and treehouses deep in the forest. Dravians possess earth power. With training, they control and manipulate elements such as soil, rocks, and plants. Their Circle tattoo is a green/brown swirl. The strongest family of this element, blessed with enhancements, are the Griffins.

Elidi - Elidians possess firepower and are wild at heart. With training, they control elements involving heat and flames. Their Circle tattoo is a red/orange swirl. Mystiers with this Magik are rumored to be rare and nomadic in nature.

Vayu - This Mystier city is on the Northwestern coast, with a population ten times that of the other villages. Vayu's skyscrapers look like they are floating when viewed from across the ravine that separates the city from the Ordull world. Vayuians possess air power. With training, they control elements involving wind and oxygen. Their Circle tattoo is a white/blue/gray swirl. The strongest family of this element, blessed with enhancements, are the Nilsons.

LOCATIONS

(alphabetical)

Andersonville - the capital city of Lodesa (where Kyra grew up).

Aurella Fortress - an ancient, crumbling castle on the edge of Vayu's border.

Crooked Chateau - originally an art museum and community center with a ballroom, which has a shifting purpose as the novels progress.

Forbidden Caves - on Draven's border, the setting for many legends.

Galudi Lighthouse - originally a port for Lodesa to trade with other countries, haunted by ghosts from The Fall.

Lodesa - the country.

Vuldow - The Shadow Land in the south is miles of a dystopian-like terrain, not due to a nuclear bombing that the Ordulls assume, but because of the massacre during The Fall eighty-two years ago that wiped out hundreds of cities.

See the full epic map at the beginning of this book or online at www.cassieswindon.com

NECKLACES

(alphabetical)

All four elemental necklaces have the power for enhanced protection and power when used.

Crystal - necklace from Vayu that bound Oniskel to the top of a mountain peak.

Emerald - necklace from Draven that bound Surh-Sig to the forbidden caves. Helps Alaska teleport more than one person at a time.

Pearl - necklace from Cydon that bound Moroka to the depths of the sea.

Ruby - necklace from Elidi that burns when touched by someone without a protective spell.

UNETLO BOOK

The strongest and oldest spell book belonging to the Mystier race, residing in the Vayuian Library from year 05G-present day. Spells are listed alphabetically.

Atuyasdodi promitto - I vow to Link to you

Aurum shiyo - ridding of a curse/dark Magik

Avanido muati - revert the demon beings back to their original nymph form

Ayasdi sospit- protect a loved one

Dehano huc - come

Digati impetu - attack

Hostia donadagohvi - let go

Ines meocha - obey

Memi anvadis - return one's memory

Monile volare - levitate

Opus amare – open love

Reditus atsutsa - return to me

Tenebris agvnig - summoning of darkness

Terra angakok – heal

Tohiyus elawe - leave

Uyetsgi waklo - wake/rise

Vand zalit - release

Venereae ostaguyelu - protection against pregnancy and STDs

Yelas secar - sever/cut

ENHANCEMENTS

(alphabetical)

Healing – Jadox.
Hearing – Kyra.
Holding breath – Caspian.
Mind control – Brent.
Prophecies – Gemm.
Scent – Jadox.
Sight – Isaac.
Spells – Kyra.
Teleportation – Alaska.
Weather – Isaac.

CASSIE SWINDON

SHATTERED

THE LINKED TRILOGY
BOOK THREE

GOLDEN CHAINS

Cassie Swindon

New Adult Romantic Suspense

FREE SHORT STORIES

www.ingramcontent.com/pod-product-compliance
Lightning Source LLC
Chambersburg PA
CBHW070836020826
48982CB00020B/1367/J

* 9 7 8 1 7 3 7 3 4 6 9 3 7 *